Ravyn stepped forward, the cell's iron bars like icicles beneath his hands. "I know you can hear me."

Laughter echoed in the dark. The figure in the cell sat up slowly and turned. It took all of Ravyn not to wince. Elspeth's black eyes were gone. In their place, catlike irises, vivid and yellow, lit by a man five hundred years dead.

The Shepherd King did not move but for his eyes. "You're alone, Captain," he said. It was still Elspeth's voice. Only now, it sounded slick, oily. *Wrong.* "Is that wise?"

Ravyn stiffened. "Would you hurt me?"

His answer was a twisted, jagged smile. "I'd be a liar if I said I hadn't played with the idea."

Praise for

One Dark Window

"*One Dark Window* is an evocative tale of romance, mystery, and alluring monsters, told in beautifully lush prose. Rachel Gillig has created a story that left me entranced."

—Lyndall Clipstone, author of *Lakesedge*

"An enchanting tale with sharp claws and teeth—Gillig's prose will pull you in and won't let you sleep. Pulse-pounding, darkly whimsical, and aglow with treacherous magic, *One Dark Window* is everything I love in fantasy and more."

—Allison Saft, author of *A Far Wilder Magic*

"A beautifully dark fairy tale of blood, rage, and bitter choice that whisked me away to mist-wreathed woods ripe with romance and menace."

—Davinia Evans, author of *Notorious Sorcerer*

"*One Dark Window* is a page-turner. Gillig's lush language is somewhat reminiscent of Alix E. Harrow's excellent portal fantasy, *The Ten Thousand Doors of January*, as well as Robin McKinley's redolent fairytale retellings such as *Spindle's End*, *Beauty*, and *Deerskin*.... A richly detailed and decadent world that at once feels familiar, distinctive, and wistful to the reader."

—*Chicago Review of Books*

"Readers will be enthralled with Elspeth's—and Nightmare's—riveting adventure."

—*Booklist*

"The steamy romance that emerges between Elspeth and Ravyn delights. Fans of Sarah J. Maas, Naomi Novik, and Hannah Whitten will want to check this out." —*Publishers Weekly*

"Elspeth's slow-burn romance with a mysterious highwayman adds depth to the story....A finely detailed magical system enriches Gillig's debut; fantasy readers will enjoy."

—*Library Journal*

"Spooky, lush....Gillig executes familiar fantasy romance tropes with flair." —*Paste*

By Rachel Gillig

The Shepherd King

One Dark Window

Two Twisted Crowns

TWO TWISTED CROWNS

Book Two of The Shepherd King

RACHEL GILLIG

orbitbooks.net

This book is a work of fiction. Names, characters, places, and incidents are the product of the author's imagination or are used fictitiously. Any resemblance to actual events, locales, or persons, living or dead, is coincidental.

Copyright © 2023 by Rachel Gillig
Excerpt from *Half a Soul* copyright © 2020 by Olivia Atwater
Excerpt from *Tonight, I Burn* copyright © 2023 by Katharine J. Adams

Cover design by Lisa Marie Pompilio
Cover images by Trevillion and Shutterstock
Cover copyright © 2023 by Hachette Book Group, Inc.
Author photograph by Rachel Gillig

Hachette Book Group supports the right to free expression and the value of copyright. The purpose of copyright is to encourage writers and artists to produce the creative works that enrich our culture.

The scanning, uploading, and distribution of this book without permission is a theft of the author's intellectual property. If you would like permission to use material from the book (other than for review purposes), please contact permissions@hbgusa.com. Thank you for your support of the author's rights.

Orbit
Hachette Book Group
1290 Avenue of the Americas
New York, NY 10104
orbitbooks.net

First Edition: October 2023
Simultaneously published in Great Britain by Orbit

Orbit is an imprint of Hachette Book Group.
The Orbit name and logo are trademarks of Little, Brown Book Group Limited.

The publisher is not responsible for websites (or their content) that are not owned by the publisher.

The Hachette Speakers Bureau provides a wide range of authors for speaking events. To find out more, go to hachettespeakersbureau.com or email HachetteSpeakers@hbgusa.com.

Orbit books may be purchased in bulk for business, educational, or promotional use. For information, please contact your local bookseller or the Hachette Book Group Special Markets Department at special.markets@hbgusa.com.

Library of Congress Cataloging-in-Publication Data
Names: Gillig, Rachel, author.
Title: Two twisted crowns / Rachel Gillig.
Description: First Edition. | New York, NY : Orbit, 2023. |
Series: The Shepherd King ; book two
Identifiers: LCCN 2023002308 | ISBN 9780316312714 (trade paperback) |
ISBN 9780316312882 (ebook)
Subjects: LCGFT: Gothic fiction. | Fantasy fiction. | Novels.
Classification: LCC PS3607.I44448 T96 2023 | DDC 813/.6—dc23/eng/20230210
LC record available at https://lccn.loc.gov/2023002308

ISBNs: 9780316312714 (trade paperback), 9780316312882 (ebook)

Printed in the United States of America

LSC-C

Printing 9, 2024

To anyone who's ever felt lost in a wood. There is a strange sort of finding in losing.

The Twin Alders is hidden in a place with no time. A place of great sorrow and bloodshed and crime. Betwixt ancient trees, where the mist cuts bone-deep, the last Card remains, waiting, asleep. The wood knows no road—no path through the snare. Only I can find the Twin Alders…

For it was I who left it there.

Prologue

Elspeth

The darkness bled into itself—no beginning, no end. I floated, buoyant on a tide of salt water. Above me, the night sky had blackened—moon and stars masked by heavy, water-laden clouds that never receded.

I jostled without pain, my muscles relaxed and my mind quiet. I did not know where my body ended and the water began. I merely yielded to the darkness, lost to the ebb and flow of the waves and the sound of water washing over me.

Time passed without mark. If there was a sun, it did not reach me at dawn. I passed minutes and hours and days afloat a tide of nothingness, my mind empty but for one thought.

Let me out.

More time passed. Still, the thought persisted. *Let me out.*

I was whole, swallowed by the water's comfort. No pain, no memory, no fear, no hope. I was the darkness and the darkness was me, and together we rolled with the tide, lulled toward a shore I could neither see nor hear. All was water—all was salt.

But the thought nagged on. *Let me out.*

I tested the words out loud. My voice sounded like tearing

paper. “Let me out.” I said it over and over, briny water filling my mouth. “Let me out.”

Minutes. Hours. Days. *Let. Me. Out.*

Then, out of nothingness, a long black beach appeared. Upon it, something moved. I blinked, my eyes clouded by a film of salt.

A man, clad in golden armor, stood on the dark shore just beyond the break in the tide, watching me.

The tide drew me in, closer and closer. The man was aged. He bore the weight of his armor without wavering, his strength deeply rooted—like an ancient tree.

I tried to call out to him, but I knew only the three words.

“Let me out!” I cried. I became aware of my wool dress, the heaviness of it. It pulled me down and I slipped beneath the surface, my words cutting off. “Let me—”

His hands were cold as he pulled me from the water.

He carried me onto black sand. When he tried to stand me up, my legs faltered like a newborn fawn’s.

I did not know his face. But he knew mine.

“Elspeth Spindle,” he said quietly, his eyes—so strange and yellow—ensnaring me. “I’ve been waiting for you.”

PART I
To Bleed

Chapter One
Ravyn

Ravyn's hands were bleeding.

He hadn't noticed until he'd seen the blood fall. With three taps on the velvet edge of the Mirror, the purple Providençe Card, Ravyn had erased himself. He was utterly invisible. His fingers, knuckles, the heels of his palms, dug at the hardened soil at the bottom of the ancient chamber at the edge of the meadow.

It hardly mattered. What was another cut, another scar? Ravyn's hands were but blunt tools. Not the instruments of a gentleman, but of a man-at-arms—Captain of the Destriers. Highwayman.

Traitor.

Mist seeped into the chamber through the window. It slipped through the cracks of the rotted-out ceiling, salt clawing at Ravyn's eyes. A warning, perhaps, that the thing he dug for at the base of the tall, broad stone did not wish to be found.

Ravyn paid the mist no mind. He, too, was of salt. Sweat, blood, and magic. Even so, his calloused hands were no match for the soil at the bottom of the chamber. It was unforgiving, hardened by time, ripping Ravyn's fingernails and tearing open the cracks in his hands. Still, he dug, enveloped in the Mirror Card's chill, the chamber he'd so often played in as a boy shifting before his eyes into something grotesque—a place of lore, of death.

Of monsters.

He'd woken hours ago, sleep punctuated by thrashing fits and the memory of a piercing yellow gaze, Elspeth Spindle's voice an echoing dissonance in his mind.

It was his castle—the one in ruins, she'd told him, her charcoal eyes wet with tears as she spoke of the Shepherd King, the voice in her head. *He's buried beneath the stone in the chamber at Castle Yew.*

Ravyn had torn himself out of bed and ridden from Stone like a specter on the wind to get to the chamber. He was restless—frantic—for the truth. Because none of it seemed real. The Shepherd King, with yellow eyes and a slick, sinister voice, trapped in the mind of a maiden. The Shepherd King, who promised to help them find the lost Twin Alders Card.

The Shepherd King, five hundred years dead.

Ravyn knew death—had been its exactor. He'd watched light go out of men's eyes. Heard final, gasping breaths. There was nothing but ghosts on the other side of the veil, no life after death. Not for any man, cutpurse, or highwayman—not even for the Shepherd King.

And yet.

Not all the soil at the base of the stone was hard. Some was loose, upturned. Someone had been there before him—recently. Elspeth, perhaps, looking for answers, just as he was. There, at the base of the stone, hidden a hand below the hardened topsoil, was a carving. A single word made indecipherable with time. A grave marker.

Ravyn kept digging. When his fingernail ripped and the raw

tip of his finger struck something sharp, he swore and reared back. His body was invisible, but not his blood. It trickled, crimson red, appearing the moment it left his hand and scattering over the hole he'd dug, the ground thirsty for it.

Something was hidden in the earth, waiting. When Ravyn touched it, it was sharper than stone—colder than soil.

Steel.

Heart in his throat, he dug until he'd unearthed a sword. It lay crooked, caked in dirt. But there was no mistaking its make—forged steel—with an intricately designed hilt, too ornate to be a soldier's blade.

He reached for it, the salt in the air piercing his lungs as he took short, fevered breaths. But before Ravyn could pry the sword free, he caught a glimpse at what was buried beneath it.

Resting perfectly, undisturbed for centuries. A pale, knobbed object. Human. Skeletal.

A spine.

Ravyn's muscles locked. His mouth went dry, and nausea rolled up from his stomach into his throat. Blood continued to drip from his hand. And with every drop he gave away, he earned a fragmented, biting clarity: Blunder was full of magic. Wonderful, terrible magic. This was the Shepherd King's body. He was truly dead.

But his soul carried on, buried deep in Elspeth Spindle, the only woman Ravyn had ever loved.

He tore from the chamber, taking the sword with him.

Bent over himself beneath the yew tree outside, Ravyn coughed, fighting the urge to be sick. The tree was old, its branches unkempt, its canopy vast enough to keep the morning rainfall off his brow. He stayed that way for some time, his heartbeat reluctant to steady.

"What business have you to dig, raven bird?"

Ravyn whirled, the ivory hilt of his dagger in hand. But he was alone. The meadow was empty but for dying grass, the slender path back to Castle Yew unmanned.

The voice called again, louder than before. "Did you hear me, bird?"

Perched in the yew tree above Ravyn's head, legs dangling over the edge of the aged branch, sat a girl. She was young—younger than his brother, Emory—a child no older than twelve, he guessed. Her hair fell in dark plaits over her shoulders, a few stray curls framing her face. Her cloak was undyed, gray wool with an intricately hemmed collar. Ravyn searched for a family insignia, but there was none.

He didn't recognize her. Surely he'd recall such a striking face—such a distinct nose. Such vivid, yellow eyes.

Yellow.

"Who are you?" Ravyn said, his voice scraping his throat.

She watched him with those yellow eyes, tilting her head to the side. "I'm Tilly."

"What are you doing here, Tilly?"

"What I've always done." For the briefest moment, she reminded him of Jespyr as a girl. "I'm waiting."

Rain fell in earnest, carried on a swift wind. Droplets pelted the side of Ravyn's face, and the wind caught his hood, pulling it off his brow. He raised a hand, shielding his eyes from the sting.

But the girl in the tree remained unmoving, though the branch beneath her trembled and the yew tree's leaves whistled in the wind. Her cloak did not shift, nor did a single strand of her hair. Water and wind seemed to pass entirely through her, as if she was made of mist, of smoke.

Of nothingness.

Only then did Ravyn recall he was still using the Mirror.

This had been his purpose—why he'd forsaken sleep and come to the chamber. He'd dug with blunt fingers, met bone with blood, and found the Shepherd King's body. But the Mirror Card held the answers he truly sought.

He'd used the Mirror a thousand times before to be invisible. But Ravyn had always been careful never to use it too long. He'd had no desire to incur the Card's negative effects—to see beyond the veil into a world of spirits. He'd never wanted to speak to a ghost.

Until now.

Ravyn cleared his throat. He knew nothing of spirits or their temperaments. Were they as they were in life? Or had the afterlife . . . remade them?

He raised his voice against the wind. "Who do you wait for, Tilly?"

The girl's eyes shifted to the sword in his hand, then back to the chamber.

"Do you know the man who is buried there?" Ravyn asked.

She laughed, her voice sharp. "As well as I know this glen, bird. As well as I know this tree, and all the faces that have tarried beneath it." She twisted her finger in the tail of her plait. "You've heard of him, I suppose." Her lips curled in a smile. "He's a strange man, my father. Wary. Clever. Good."

Ravyn's breath faltered. "The Shepherd King is your father?"

Her smile faded, her yellow eyes growing distant. "They did not give him a King's burial. Perhaps that is why he does not . . ." Her gaze returned to Ravyn. "You haven't seen him with your Mirror Card, have you? He promised he would find us when he passed through the veil. But he has not come."

"Us?"

The girl turned, her eyes tracing the woods on the other side of the meadow. "Mother is over there, somewhere. She does not come as often as she did. Ilyc and Afton linger near the statuary. Fenly and Lenor keep to your castle." Her brow furrowed. "Bennett is often somewhere else. He did not die here. Not like the rest of us."

Die. Ravyn's throat tightened. "They are... your family? The Shepherd King's family?"

"We're waiting," she said, crossing her arms over her chest. "For Father."

"Why does he not return?"

The girl did not answer. Her gaze fluttered across the meadow to the ruins. "I thought I heard his voice," she murmured. "Night had fallen. I was alone, here in my favorite tree." Her eyes flashed to Ravyn. "I saw you, raven bird. You came as you always do, in your black cloak, your gray eyes clever, your face practiced. Only this time, you were not alone. A woman came with you. A strange woman, with eyes that flashed yellow gold, like mine. Like Father's."

Ravyn's insides twisted.

"I watched you both leave, but the maiden returned." Tilly held out a finger, pointing to the chamber's window. "She went inside. That's when I heard it—the songs my father used to hum as he wrote his book. But when I entered, he was not there. It was the woman who hummed as she raked her hands through the soil above Father's grave."

"Elspeth," Ravyn whispered, the name stealing something from him. "Her name is Elspeth."

Tilly didn't seem to hear him. "Twice the maiden visited and dug at his headstone. She wandered through the meadow, the ruins." Her lips drew into a tight line. "But when dawn came, her yellow eyes shifted to a charcoal color. So I came back here, to his grave. To watch. To wait."

Ravyn said nothing, his mind searching for answers it did

not have. He remembered that night he'd brought Elspeth to the chamber. He could still smell her hair—feel her cheek against his palm. He'd kissed her deeply and she'd kissed him back. Every part of him had wanted every part of her.

But she'd torn herself away, her eyes wide, a tremble in her voice. She'd been afraid of something in the chamber. At the time, Ravyn had been certain it was him. But he knew now it was something else—something far greater than him—something she carried with her, always.

His eyes snapped back to the girl in the yew tree. "What happened to your father?"

Tilly did not answer.

Ravyn tried again: "How did he die?"

She looked away, her fingers dancing a silent rhythm on the yew branch. "I don't know. They caught me first." Her voice quieted. "I passed through the veil before my father and brothers."

It wasn't the Mirror's chill that was seeping into Ravyn. It was something else. A question that, in the dark corner of his mind, he already knew the answer to. "Who killed you?"

Those yellow eyes flared. They landed on Ravyn. "You know his name." Her voice went low, a deep, scraping whisper. "Rowan."

The King's insignia flashed in Ravyn's mind. His uncle's flag—the unyielding rowan tree. Red Scythe Card, green eyes. Hunters, brutes.

Family.

Ravyn's bleeding hands shook.

"We've waited a long time for Father," Tilly said, her gaze turning upward, as if she were speaking now to only the yew tree. Her voice grew firm, her fingers curling like talons in her lap. "We will keep waiting, until his task is done."

A chill clawed up Ravyn's neck. He thought of the creature

in Elspeth Spindle's body—of yellow eyes and twisting, silken words spoken in the dungeon. A promise to help find the lost Twin Alders Card.

But Ravyn knew better. No promise comes without payment. Blunder was a place of magic—barters and bargains. Nothing was free. "What does the Shepherd King want?" he asked the girl-spirit. "What is he after?"

"Balance," she answered, head tilting like a bird of prey. "To right terrible wrongs. To free Blunder from the Rowans." Her yellow eyes narrowed, wicked and absolute. "To collect his due."

Chapter Two

Elm

The Prince rode faster than the other two Destriers. When he dismounted at the old brick house, Elm Rowan was struck by how still the world seemed when he was not on horseback. It unnerved him.

A mourning dove cooed. Elm took off his gloves, dipping his hand into his tunic pocket, the feel of velvet at the edges of his Scythe Card a familiar comfort.

He came to the front door, wrapping his fingers in a fist. The door was aged, traces of lichen sheltering in the crags. The whole north side of the estate was covered in moss and ivy, as if the forest was dragging Hawthorn House deeper into its depths, vines thick as a man's arm wrapping around the chimney, serpentine.

No one was inside the house. The warning had come days ago. Still, Elm pressed his ear to the door and listened.

Nothing. No muffled shouts of children, no ring of iron pots from the kitchen. Not even a dog barking. The house was still, as if kept that way by the tendrils of greenery reaching in from the mist.

The Destriers arrived behind him and dropped from their horses. "Sire?" Wicker said.

Elm opened his eyes and exhaled. He had no mind to command them. But Ravyn had made himself scarce, and Jespyr had remained at Stone to keep an eye on Emory, leaving Elm—petulant to his bones—to do the King's bidding and look for Elspeth Spindle's missing kin.

"It's empty," he muttered through his teeth. "Opal Hawthorn is no fool. She and her children would not have come back to this place."

"Her husband seemed to think they'd be here," the second Destrier—Gorse—muttered.

Elm twisted the brass handle and pulled Hawthorn House's door open, the rusted hinges shrieking. "Tyrn Hawthorn would say anything to be free of the dungeon."

"He's got Cards," Wicker said pointedly. "To hear him boast, you'd think old Tyrn had collected the Deck himself."

"Then the least we can do is relieve him of his greatest treasures. Search the house." Elm cast an eye over his shoulder to the sky. "Quickly. I'd like to outride those clouds."

They took to the library first, emptying shelves, shaking old tomes until the house smelled of leather and dust. "I found a Prophet!" Gorse hollered through a row of mahogany shelves.

Elm drew his finger across the uneven mantel. The stones were cracked, but the mortar held firm—no hidden space to hide a Card. He stepped out of the library and started up the stairs. Oval niches held worn-down candles, every stone in the wall housing a shadow.

The first room off the stairwell was upturned, clothes and blankets and an odd sock strewn about. Two narrow beds, two wooden swords. The room of Elspeth's young cousins, Elm guessed.

The next room was markedly more feminine. Elm lingered at the threshold, drawing cold air into his nose—the scents of wool and lavender. A quilt lay on the bed, the linens unwrinkled, neatly tucked. A small table with chipped green paint held a candle, and next to it, an oval looking glass. Just below the looking glass sat a fine-toothed comb.

Trapped in the wooden teeth were several strands of long black hair.

"There is nothing left of her here," a voice called from behind Elm's shoulder. "Whatever Elspeth took from this place, she carries with her."

Elm jumped, his hand dropping to his belt. A ring of steel cut through the hallway and he pivoted, slicing his knife toward the voice.

He stopped the blade just before it grazed Ione Hawthorn's throat.

She stood before him, clad in white like a bride. Long and flowing, her dress fell to the floor. Her yellow hair caught the hallway draft, and when she stared at Elm, her pink lips pursed, forming a question she did not speak.

Her gaze dropped to his knife. "Prince Renelm."

His mind was racing, a rhythmic discord against the heaving of his chest. "What the hell are you doing here?"

"It's my home. Why shouldn't I be here?"

Elm's jaw seized. He jerked the knife away, slipping it back into place on his belt. "Trees, Hawthorn, I might have killed you."

Her voice held a fine point, like the tip of a needle. "I doubt that."

Elm dug at his pocket for the familiar comfort of his Scythe. He had not used his red Card in four days—not since that night at Spindle House.

After the Destriers had been called and Hauth, broken and bloody, carried away, Ravyn had put Erik Spindle and Tyrn Hawthorn in chains. Jespyr had ridden to Hawthorn House to warn Elspeth's aunt, Opal Hawthorn, that the Destriers were coming. And Elm—Elm had tapped his Scythe three times and compelled what remained of Elspeth's family to flee. Her stepmother, Nerium, her half sisters, Nya and Dimia—

And her cousin, Ione Hawthorn. They had all vanished into the night, not a trace of them remaining.

Until now.

Ione stood in front of Elm, looking up at him with sharp hazel eyes. She reminded him of fresh parchment. Unblemished, full of promise. The Maiden Card did that—made its beholder look unbearably *new.* It struck Elm as odd that she would still use the pink Card of beauty here, alone in Hawthorn House, so far from the scrutiny of Stone's court.

He leaned closer, his shadow swallowing her whole. "It's not safe for you to be here."

Ione's eyes widened. But before she could speak, footsteps sounded behind her.

Gorse stopped in his tracks at the top of the stairs, his gaze trained on Ione.

"If you're looking for my father, I'm afraid you'll be disappointed," she said, eyeing him with disinterest. "I'm alone. My family is elsewhere, without so much as a note."

Gorse's brow lowered. He turned to Elm. "Sire?"

More steps sounded on the stairwell. "Holy shit." Wicker stopped just behind Gorse, his fingers sliding to the hilt of his sword.

Ione's lips drew into a firm line. "I seem to be missing something. Why are you here?" Her gaze darkened. "Is Hauth with you?"

"The High Prince is at Stone, clinging to life," Gorse snapped. "Attacked, by your cousin. All because your family didn't have the stomach to burn her when they had the chance."

Ione glanced at Wicker's hand, which rested in a stranglehold over his hilt. "My cousin," she whispered, drawing the words out. The needle in her voice returned. "What did Hauth do to her?"

"Nothing more than she deserved," Gorse replied.

Ione's expressions were few. But her eyes held a tell. Elm might have studied her face more, had Wicker not been gripping his sword. "Stay your hand, Destrier," he said.

Gorse's hand dropped to his own sword. "The King will want her right away."

"Trees." Elm reached into his pocket once more for the Scythe. When his fingers snagged velvet, he tapped it. "Ignore her," he commanded the Destriers. "Keep looking for Cards."

Their hands went slack on their hilts. Gorse and Wicker blinked and looked away, a glassy sheen over their eyes.

Elm jerked forward, his hand closing around Ione's arm. "Not another word," he warned. He wrenched her forward, pushing past the Destriers and hurrying down the stairs.

The sound of Ione's bare feet slapping against stone floors echoed in the empty house. When they reached the parlor, she wrenched her arm free. "What's going on?"

Elm's throat caught, his voice rough. "Your cousin Elspeth—" *No, not Elspeth anymore.* He clenched his jaw. "She tore into Hauth at Spindle House. Broke his spine. He's hardly alive. My father is out for blood. His inquest—" His eyes swept over Ione, a chill crawling over him. "I have to bring you to Stone."

Ione did not flinch. She hardly even blinked. "So do it."

"You don't—" He took a steadying breath. "Clearly, you do not understand."

"But I do, Prince. Had you not come and offered yourself as an escort, I would have found my own way to Stone."

"I'm not your goddamn escort," Elm bit back. "I'm *arresting* you."

Ione turned to face him, but her expression remained unchanged—utterly blank. She should have been crying. Or screaming. It was what most people did when they faced an inquest. But she was just...calm. Eerily so.

Elm looked her up and down, an acrid taste in his mouth. "You've been using that Maiden Card too long, haven't you? Where is it?"

"Why? Would you like to borrow it, Prince?" Ione studied Elm's face. "It might help with those dark circles beneath your eyes."

She didn't wait for him to scrape together a reply. She opened the front door, the clamor of rainfall loud on Hawthorn House's thatched roof. Elm's exhale met the cold air, his patience for difficult weather—and difficult women—scant on the simplest of days.

"Forget the Maiden, then." He pushed past her, her white dress stirring in his wake. "Do you at least have your charm?"

Ione pulled a gold chain out from the neckline of her dress. On it was her charm, a horse tooth, by the looks of it. A token to keep her mind and body safe in the mist. She glanced back at Hawthorn House. "What's become of my family?"

"Your father's at Stone, along with Erik Spindle. Your mother and brothers are gone—disappeared. Nerium and her daughters, too." He looked away. "Your cousin is chained at the bottom of the dungeon."

Ione stepped outside. She plucked a wet leaf from a hawthorn tree and ran it through her fingers. Droplets cascaded down the branch onto the tip of her nose and down the crease of her lips. When she said her cousin's name, it came out a whisper—soft as a child's secret. "Elspeth."

She looked up at Elm. "She kept so many things hidden, even from me. I'd hear her footsteps in the hall at night, after we'd all gone to sleep. I listened to the songs she hummed. She spoke like she was carrying on a conversation, though she was so often alone. And her eyes," she murmured. "Black. Then, in a flash, yellow as dragon's gold."

The lie slipped out of Elm before he could think. "I know nothing of that."

"No?" Ione tucked her damp hair behind her ear. "I thought you might, seeing as you spent time with her at Castle Yew after Equinox. You, Jespyr, and of course, the Captain of Destriers."

A thousand worries stabbed at Elm. The King knew Elspeth Spindle could see Providence Cards. He did *not* know that was precisely why Ravyn had recruited her. That Ravyn and Jespyr and Elm, the King's chosen guard, had brought an infected woman into their company to steal Providence Cards. To unite the Deck. To lift the mist and heal the infection.

To save Ravyn's brother, Emory.

To commit treason.

Glass cut through his mind. The Scythe. He'd forgotten he was still compelling Gorse and Wicker. Elm reached into his tunic—tapped the velvet three times—and the pain ceased.

Ione watched his hand in his pocket.

Thunder rolled. Elm looked up at the sky and shivered. "It's going to storm." He led Ione to his horse. "It won't be an easy ride."

She said nothing. When Elm lifted her onto the horse, she pulled her dress over her knees and swung her leg astride. He climbed up behind her, his jaw flexing when she settled into the saddle, the curve of her backside pressing into him. Her hair smelled sweet.

He spurred his horse. Hawthorn House disappeared into the wood, its final resident taken from its threshold in a flurry of rainwater and mud.

Ione leaned against his chest, her eyes lost on the road. Elm glanced down at her, wondering if she understood the fate that awaited her at Stone. If she knew this was likely the last time she'd leave her family's home and travel the forest road. If she'd look back.

She didn't.

Chapter Three
Elspeth

Gold armor glistened and creaked as the man who had dragged me out of the water sat next to me on the black sand. Together, we watched the water roll up to our ankles before passing back down, the tide constant, the measureless flow of waves without variation.

"Taxus," he finally said, raising his voice above the sound of the waves.

Salt water dried on my lips. I licked them, my voice cracking. "What?"

"Aemmory Percyval Taxus." He dragged his gauntlets across the sand. "That's my name."

I blinked, sand in my eyelashes. "You... you are..."

When he looked my way, his yellow eyes tugged at my lost memory. "You'll remember soon enough." He glanced back at the dark horizon. "There is little else to do here but remember."

My name was Elspeth Spindle, and I knew it only because he, *Taxus*, called me by it. I tested it out loud. It came out a slithering hiss. "Elspeth Spindle."

Taxus was gone, though I hadn't seen him leave. I turned my head both ways, searching for him, but he had left no footprints in the sand.

I looked out onto the water—ran my hands through sand until my skin was raw. My long hair was stringy with brine. I pulled a strand from my scalp and wrapped it around my finger so tightly my fingertip turned purple. I didn't eat—didn't sleep.

Time didn't find me. Nothing did. And the nothingness was cavernous. When Taxus returned, looking down at me like he knew me, my brow twisted. "You're wrong. I don't remember who you are. I can't—" I looked back out onto the water. "I can't remember anything."

"Shall I tell you the story?"

"What story?"

"Ours, dear one."

I sat up straighter.

"There once was a girl," he said, his voice slick, "clever and good, who tarried in shadow in the depths of the wood. There also was a King—a shepherd by his crook, who reigned over magic and wrote the old book. The two were together, so the two were the same:

"The girl, the King, and the monster they became."

Chapter Four

Ravyn

The Mirror Card's chill no longer lingered on Ravyn's skin. He was back at Stone, but he was not warm. The cold of the dungeon clawed its way up dark, icy stairs, seeking purchase in his chest.

He held two skeleton keys in his hand. When he paused at the top of the stairs, peering down, his grip on the keys tightened. He didn't hear his sister approach. But what kind of Destrier would she be if he had?

"Ravyn."

He turned, hiding his startle behind a scowl. "Jes."

Jespyr leaned against the corridor wall, blended well enough into shadow to almost render a Mirror Card unnecessary. Her gaze lowered to the skeleton keys in Ravyn's clutch. "You'll need another pair of hands to open that door."

"I was going to find a guard."

Something shifted in her brown eyes. "I'm capable enough."

There was an accusation somewhere in the firm notes of Jespyr's voice. Ravyn ignored it. "The King wants to see Els—" He flinched. "He wants to know about the Twin Alders Card. In private."

Jespyr folded her hands in a net. "Is that wise?"

"Probably not."

The sound of the gong echoed through the castle. Its toll announced early afternoon. Midday, midnight—the hour meant little to Ravyn. All he knew of time was that he always seemed to be running out of it.

Jespyr dragged her boot over a wrinkle in the corridor rug. "Are you well enough to do this? You've hardly spoken about what happened. About Elspeth."

The muscles along Ravyn's jaw tightened. "I'm fine."

She shook her head. "I can always tell when you're lying. Your eyes get this vacant look."

"Maybe that's because they *are* vacant."

"You'd like everyone to think that, wouldn't you?" Jespyr approached—pulled the second key from his grip. "You can talk to me, you know. I'm always here, Ravyn." The corner of her lips quirked. "I'm always right behind you."

They made it to the bottom of the stairs without slipping on ice. In the antechamber, the dungeon door waited. It was twice as wide as Ravyn's wingspan. Forged of wood from rowan trees and fortified with iron, it took both skeleton keys to unlock.

Facing their respective locks on opposite sides of the door, Ravyn and Jespyr slid their keys into place. Ravyn made sure to turn his back, lest his sister see his trembling fingers.

The mechanisms embedded in the stone wall released the latches. Ravyn pressed his fingers in the holds and pushed the door open just wide enough to slip through, the weight of the ancient wood great.

"Leave it open," he said, taking both keys. "Destriers will be here soon enough to collect Erik Spindle and Tyrn Hawthorn for their inquest." He stepped through the door.

"Do you want me to come with you?"

"No. Get a Chalice Card from the armory. Meet me at the King's chamber."

"Are you sure you're all right to do this?" Jespyr asked again.

Ravyn had been a liar always out of necessity, never a fondness for the craft. It was one of the many masks he wore. And he'd worn it so long that, even when he should take it off, he didn't always know how.

He stole into darkness. "I'm fine."

The air grew thinner the farther north he trod. The dungeon walk sloped, falling deeper into the earth. Ravyn wrapped his arms in his cloak and kept his eyes forward, afraid if he looked too closely at the empty cells, the ghosts of all the infected children who had died there might emerge from shadow and claim him.

The walk was littered with blackened torches, this part of the dungeon rarely patrolled. Ravyn continued until he was at the end—the last cell.

The monster waited.

Flat on the floor, eyes on the ceiling—as if stargazing—what had once been Elspeth Spindle's body lay still. Air plumed out of her—now the Shepherd King's—mouth like dragon smoke. When Ravyn's footsteps stilled at the foot of the cell, the Shepherd King did not turn to look, the sound of his teeth clicking together the only greeting he tendered.

A knot in Ravyn's throat swelled. Before he could stop himself, his eyes traveled the length of Elspeth's body.

What had once been Elspeth's body.

"Are you awake?"

There was no answer.

Ravyn stepped forward, the cell's iron bars like icicles beneath his hands. "I know you can hear me."

Laughter echoed in the dark. The figure in the cell sat up slowly and turned. It took all of Ravyn not to wince. Elspeth's black eyes were gone. In their place, catlike irises, vivid and yellow, lit by a man five hundred years dead.

The Shepherd King did not move but for his eyes. "You're alone, Captain," he said. It was still Elspeth's voice. Only now, it sounded slick, oily. *Wrong.* "Is that wise?"

Ravyn stiffened. "Would you hurt me?"

His answer was a twisted, jagged smile. "I'd be a liar if I said I hadn't played with the idea."

There was no one there to overhear them. Still, Ravyn pulled his Nightmare Card from his pocket and tapped it three times.

Salt burned up his throat, into his nose. Closing his eyes, Ravyn let the salt swallow him, then pushed it outward, entering the Shepherd King's mind. He combed through darkness, searching for any hint of Elspeth.

He did not find her.

When Ravyn opened his eyes, the Shepherd King was watching him. A voice, masculine, slippery—poisonous—spoke into his mind. *What do you want, Ravyn Yew?*

Ravyn ran the back of his hand over his mouth, hiding his flinch. He was still looking at Elspeth's body. It was *her* skin—lips—hands. Her tangled hair, long and black, that spilled over her shoulder. Her chest that rose with the swell of her lungs.

But just like her voice, there was something undeniably *wrong* about Elspeth's body. Her fingers were rigid, curled like talons, and her posture was twisted—her shoulders too high, her back too curved.

"The King wishes to see you," Ravyn said. "But before I bring you to him, I want two things."

The Shepherd King unfolded himself from the ground and stood in the center of the cell. Then—too fast—he crept to the front of the cell. "I'm listening."

Ravyn's grip on the bars tightened. "I want the truth. No riddles, no games. Are you truly the Shepherd King?"

Yellow eyes roved over his hands—his broken fingernails, dirt still embedded in the dry cracks of Ravyn's skin. Elspeth's body bent, vulturelike. "They called me that name, once."

"What did *she* call you?"

For a moment, there was nothing. No movement. Not even air turned to steam from the Shepherd King's nostrils. Then, when he seemed to have frosted over entirely, his pale fingers began to trill, as if plucking the strings of an invisible harp. "She saw me for what I truly am." He drew the word out, whispering it into Ravyn's mind. *Nightmare.*

"And you know where the Twin Alders Card is, Nightmare?"

"I do."

"Will you take me to it?"

His voice was near and far. "I will."

"How far is the journey?"

The Nightmare lowered his head and smiled. "Not far. Yet it is farther than you've ever gone before."

Ravyn slammed his hand on the bars. "I said no goddamn games."

"You asked for the truth. Truth bends, Ravyn Yew. We must all bend along with it. If we do not, well..." His yellow eyes flared. "Then we will break."

He spoke with his own voice into Ravyn's mind once more. *Before your lifetime,* he said, *before the story of the girl, the King, and the monster, I told an older tale. One of magic, mist, and Providence Cards. Of infection and degeneration.* His smile fell away. *Of barters made.*

"I'm familiar with *The Old Book of Alders*."

"Good. For you're about to step into it."

Ravyn drew in a breath, the ice in the air nesting in his lungs.

"The Twin Alders is the only Card of its kind," the Nightmare continued. "It gives its user the power to speak to our deity, the Spirit of the Wood. And it is *she* who guards it. She will have a price for the last Card of the Deck. Nothing comes free."

"I'm prepared to pay whatever price she asks." Ravyn pressed against the bars, his voice lowering. "And when I do pay, Nightmare, the Twin Alders Card will be mine. Not the King's, not yours. *Mine*."

Something shifted in those yellow eyes. "What is the second thing you wish of me, Ravyn Yew?" the Nightmare murmured.

Even with frost all around them, Ravyn could smell blood on Elspeth's clothes. He took a step back, but it was too late. A light tremor had begun in his left hand. He knotted it into a fist. "When I bring you to the King's chamber, you are not to harm him. You are not to do anything that might jeopardize me taking you out of Stone in search of the Twin Alders Card."

"Rowan has agreed to my offer, then? To trade my life for young Emory's?"

"Not fully. Which is why you need to be on your best behavior."

The Nightmare laughed. The sound shifted through the dungeon, as if carried on dark wings. "My best behavior." His fingers curled at his side. "By all means. Take me to your Rowan King."

Along the dungeon wall were hooks with varying weapons and restraints. Ravyn retrieved a pair of iron cuffs fixed to a chain and opened the cell door. The Nightmare held out his wrists.

Pale, bruised skin peeked out from beneath tattered sleeves.

Ravyn bit down. "Pull your sleeves so the iron doesn't sit directly on your wrists. I don't want to give Elspeth any more bruises."

"She can't feel them now."

Muscles bunching in his jaw, Ravyn took care not to touch the Nightmare's skin when he locked the cuffs in place. "Let's go."

Even with chains, the Nightmare's movements were eerily quiet. It took all of Ravyn's control not to look over his shoulder. The only reason he was certain the monster was behind him at all was because he could *feel* him there, wraithlike, as the two of them crept out of Stone's frozen underbelly.

They climbed the stairs. Ravyn shook his hands, the dungeon's icy numbness shifting into prickles along his fingertips. He was still wielding the Nightmare Card—he used it to call for Elm. His cousin did not answer.

But another voice did.

She's dead, you fool, came a familiar, derisive tone from the depths of his mind. *Why cling to hope? Even if you unite the Deck and lift the mist and cure the infection, she will not come back. She died in her room at Spindle House four nights ago.* A low, rumbling laugh. *All because you were ten minutes late back from your patrol.*

Ravyn ripped the burgundy Card out of his pocket and tapped it three times, quelling the magic. His pulse roared in his ears. It hadn't been the Nightmare's voice, but another—one that mocked him, uttering his worst fears every time he used the Nightmare Card too long.

His own.

The clicking sound of teeth ricocheted off stone walls. "There was no need for your Nightmare Card, Ravyn Yew. I am the only one for a hundred cells." He paused. "Unless you were hoping to hear another voice when you reached into my mind."

Ravyn stopped in his tracks. "Were you there," he said, keeping his eyes forward, forcing ice into his thinning voice, "when Elspeth and I were alone together?"

"What's the matter, highwayman? All your rosy memories beginning to rot?"

Ravyn turned—pushed the Nightmare against the wall, his hand closing around the monster's pale throat.

But it felt too much like her throat. It *was* her throat.

He ripped his hand back. "Everything was a lie." He hadn't let himself think it until now. And now that he was thinking it—

He'd taken knife wounds that hurt less. "Every look. Every word. You lived eleven years in Elspeth's mind. There's no knowing where she ended and you began."

A smile snaked across the Nightmare's mouth. "No knowing at all."

Ravyn was going to be sick.

"If it is any consolation, her admiration for you was entirely one-sided. I find your stony facade excruciatingly tedious."

Eyes closed, Ravyn turned away. "And yet you were there. When we were together."

There was a long pause. Then, quieter than before, the Nightmare spoke. "There is a place in the darkness she and I share. Think of it as a secluded shore along dark waters. A place I forged to hide things I'd rather forget. I went there from time to time in our eleven years together. To give Elspeth reprieve. And, most recently," he added, tapping his fingernails on the wall, "to spare myself the particulars of her rather incomprehensible attachment to you."

Ravyn opened his eyes. "This place exists in your mind?"

Silence. Then, "For five hundred years, I fractured in the dark. A man, slowly twisting into something terrible. I saw no sun, no moon. All I could do was remember the terrible things that had happened. So I forged a place to put away the King who once lived—all his pain—all his memories. A place of rest."

Ravyn turned. When his eyes caught the Nightmare's yellow gaze, he knew. "That's where she is. It's why I can't hear her with the Nightmare Card. You have Elspeth hidden away." His throat burned. "Alone, in the dark."

The Nightmare cocked his head. "I am not a dragon hording gold. The moment Elspeth touched that Nightmare Card and I slipped into her mind, her days were marked. *I* was her degeneration."

No. Ravyn wouldn't accept it. "Tell me how to reach her."

"Why would I when it is such a delight, watching you unravel?"

Ravyn's hand fell to his belt and the ivory hilt upon it. "You will. When we leave this wretched castle, you will tell me how to reach Elspeth."

The Nightmare's smile was a thinly veiled threat. "I know what I know. My secrets are deep. But long have I kept them. And long will they keep."

King Rowan was not in his chamber.

Ravyn swore under his breath. "Wait here," he told the Nightmare. He left the monster, shackled and bloodstained, standing in the center of the King's pelted rugs, and headed down the royal corridor to Hauth's room. When he stepped inside, it took all his restraint—and sheer luck for the meagerness of his lunch—that he didn't vomit for the smell.

The High Prince's room was overwarm, amplifying the putrid odors of blood and sickly body odor. Filick Willow stood in a line of three other Physicians at Hauth's bedside. The King was there, too, standing next to Jespyr near the hearth. He was drunk. He'd *been* drunk at Hauth's bedside for three days now, tapping and untapping his own Nightmare Card, trying to reach his son's mind.

But wherever Hauth lingered, if he lingered at all, the King could not reach him. Nor could a Scythe command life into his unseeing green eyes. The skin that peeked out from bandages and blankets was cut and scabbed. And beneath the bandages—

Hauth had been destroyed. In a way Ravyn had not seen in twenty-six years of life. Not even wolves tore their meat like that. Animals rarely killed for sport. And this—what had been done to Hauth, ripping and breaking and sloughing—went beyond sport.

It suddenly felt a terrible idea, bringing the King to face the monster who had broken his son.

Jespyr caught Ravyn's gaze. Her jaw tensed, and she spoke into their uncle's ear. It took the King a moment to focus. When his eyes finally homed in on Ravyn, they were dark under a furrowed brow.

"Well?" he barked when they were in the corridor. "Is she here?"

Ravyn drew in a breath of fresh air. "In your chamber, sire."

The King's crude fist curled around the glass neck of a decanter. "A Chalice?"

"I have one here," Jespyr said, a sea-green Providence Card in her hand.

"Let's see the bitch try to lie about the Twin Alders now."

When the King wrenched his chamber door open, the Nightmare was perched like a gargoyle in an ornate high-back chair. They stared at one another, two Kings with murder behind their eyes. Rowan green, Nightmare yellow—and five hundred years of imbalance between them.

The Nightmare opened his clawlike hand in greeting. In the other, he held a silver goblet already filled with wine. "Well, then," he said. "Let the inquest begin."

Jespyr eyed the shackles around his wrist skeptically. She exhaled, then tapped the Chalice Card three times.

King Rowan kept the distance between him and the Nightmare's chair wide enough a carriage could drive through. He might have been drunk, but he wasn't stupid. He'd seen in horrid detail exactly what this monster was capable of doing when provoked. "Tell me, Elspeth Spindle, how is it you know where the Twin Alders Card is hidden?"

The Nightmare twisted a finger in the ends of Elspeth's black hair. Ravyn watched, scorched by memory. He'd had his own hands in that hair. Run his fingers through it—sighed into it.

He jerked his eyes to the wall.

"Simple," the Nightmare murmured. "I was there when the Card disappeared."

The King's gaze ripped to the Chalice in Jespyr's hands, then back to the Nightmare, as if he could not decide which—his eyes or his ears—to distrust more. "That's impossible."

The Nightmare merely grinned. "Is it? Magic is a strange, fickle thing."

"So it is magic that gives you this—this—" The King's tongue tripped over his words. "Old knowledge of the Twin Alders?"

The corners of the Nightmare's mouth tipped. "You could say that."

"Where exactly is the Card hidden?" Jespyr cut in, shoulders bunching.

The Nightmare gave her an indifferent glance. "Deep within a wood. A wood with no road. But to those who smell the salt—" A flash of teeth. "It beckons."

The King regained himself with a deep, unsteady breath. His gaze flickered to Ravyn. "Was my nephew aware of your infection?"

Ravyn went cold, a thousand alarm bells ringing in his ears.

The Nightmare's oily timbre cut through them. "Your Captain is not the all-seeing bird you imagine him to be. He knew nothing of my magic until it was too late."

It was the truth—only slightly twisted.

A furrow broke the stone mask of Ravyn's expression. The Nightmare noticed it and smiled, as if he knew what Ravyn had only just realized.

Providence Cards did not affect the Shepherd King. It was written in *The Old Book of Alders.*

For our price it was final, our bartering done. I created twelve Cards... but I cannot use one.

But they did affect Elspeth. Hauth had used a Chalice against her. Ravyn had spoken into her mind with the Nightmare Card.

And the monster in front of him was both Elspeth *and* the Shepherd King. The Nightmare could succumb to the Cards—and also void their magic.

It was not so different from Ravyn's own magic. He, who could use only the Mirror, the Nightmare, and presumably the Twin Alders Providence Cards. The other nine Cards, he could not use—but neither could they be used against him. He could deny the Scythe's compulsion, lie against the Chalice.

Just as the Nightmare was doing now.

"Who knew of your infection?" the King snapped when the silence drew out too long.

"My magic was always a secret."

"Even from your father?"

The Nightmare rolled his jaw. "That is a question for him. I do not own anything that Erik Spindle, with his callous indifference, has ever done."

"Can you truly see Providence Cards with your magic?"

"I can."

"And you will use it to find the final Card for me?"

The Nightmare's expression remained unreadable. "I will. So long as you honor your side of our bargain, Rowan. Have you released Emory Yew to his parents?"

The King's hands knotted at his sides. "Tell me where the Twin Alders is, and I will release him tonight."

The Nightmare perked a brow. "Very well." He drew air into his nose. "Listen closely. The journey to the twelfth Card will three barters take. The first comes at water—a dark, mirrored lake. The second begins at the neck of a wood, where you cannot turn back, though truly, you should."

The Nightmare's gaze shifted to Ravyn. His words came out sharp, as if to draw blood. "The last barter waits in a place with no time. A place of great sorrow and bloodshed and crime. No sword there can save you, no mask hide your face. You'll return with the Twin Alders…

"But you'll never leave that place."

Chapter Five

Elm

The forest road was dark, the wood swollen with water. When lightning cracked the sky, Elm pulled his hood over his head and narrowed his eyes against the sting of rainfall.

Ione had not donned a cloak. Or shoes. Her feet and ankles peeked out from beneath her white dress, the fine fabric speckled by mud. She must have been cold, but she didn't complain.

Her voice vibrated through her back, a delicate hum against Elm's chest. He couldn't make out her words over the noise of his horse. "What?"

"Is she all right?" Ione asked, louder this time. "Elspeth."

Even saying Elspeth Spindle was alive felt less than true. "I don't know." Elm gritted his teeth. "Does it bother you that she tore your betrothed limb from limb?"

Ione kept her eyes ahead. "As much as it bothers you, I imagine."

Hauth. Blood on the floor, blood on his clothes, blood all over his face. Yes, it bothered Elm. For all the wrong reasons. "Count yourself lucky you didn't have to see what was left of him when she was through."

They came to the crossroads, the forest road diverging. Elm veered the horse east, to the place he hated most in the world. Stone.

"When does the inquest begin?" Ione asked.

"Anxious for the Chalice, are we?"

"I'm not afraid of the truth."

Elm bent, putting his mouth near her ear. "You should be."

"Yes. I imagine I should."

He glanced down. He hadn't spoken much to Ione Hawthorn. Most of what he knew about her, Elm had gathered in glances—many of which had been stolen.

Her face had always been easy to read, even from across the great hall at Stone. Her expressions were genuine, her smiles so unrestrained that Elm had almost felt sorry for her. That kind of naked authenticity had no place in the King's court.

He'd always thought she was beautiful. But the Maiden—that useless pink Card—had curated her beauty until it reached unearthly perfection. Her hair and skin were without blemish. The gap in her front teeth was gone. Her nose was smaller. The Maiden hadn't made her taller, hadn't—thank the bloody trees—diminished any of her remarkable curves. But she was different than the yellow-haired maiden he'd watched smile at Stone. More controlled.

Colder.

His eyes raked over her. Had Elm not noticed the dip in her throat, the swell of her breasts as she breathed—the shape of her thighs beneath her dress—he might have kept his eyes on the road. Had he kept his eyes to the road—

He might have seen the highwaymen.

They wore cloaks and masks and stood in a line, blocking the road. Elm yanked the reins, pulling his horse to a stop. The animal whickered, then reared. Ione slammed into Elm's chest and he put an arm around her waist, holding her firmly against him.

The first highwayman bore a rapier and several knives on his aged leather belt. The next held a shortbow, the arrow aimed at Ione's head. The third, taller and broader than the other two, carried a sword.

"Hands in the air, Prince Renelm," called the man with the shortbow. "Reach for your Scythe and I'll shoot you both."

Elm's nostrils flared. Slowly, he slid his arm off Ione and raised his hands into the air. "Bold of you," he said, appraising them. "Three is a small number to take on a Prince and a party of Destriers."

"I see no party." The highwayman with the sword kept one hand on his hilt and stepped to Elm's horse, taking the animal firmly by the bridle. "You look alone to me, Prince."

Elm said a silent curse for leaving Gorse and Wicker behind at Hawthorn House.

Ione was silent, her spine pressed firmly against his chest. Elm tried to lean back, afraid she'd feel the pounding of his heart—but there was nowhere to go. Smooth as a snake, Ione's hand glided behind her, prying along the hem of his tunic near his belt.

Elm froze.

Ione tugged at the fabric, searching, icy fingers grazing over his lower abdomen, near the pocket along his hip.

The pocket where he kept his Scythe.

"Don't you *dare*, Hawthorn," he said into her hair.

The threat in his voice did nothing. In one smooth maneuver, Ione's fingers were in his pocket, grasping his Card.

Elm kept his eyes on the highwaymen and his hands in the air, his thoughts scrambled, an unwelcome vulnerability twisting in his stomach. He didn't want Ione Hawthorn to touch his Scythe. He didn't want *anyone* to touch his Scythe.

The highwaymen stalked forward.

"He's not entirely alone," the highwayman with the knives corrected, stepping closer. He let go of the hilt of his rapier and reached for Ione's leg, his hands rough as he pushed the hem of her dress up. "Not with this exceptional creature." He ran a finger down Ione's bare calf, his muddy glove leaving a mark upon her. "Trees, your skin is cold."

Ione's entire body went still, her leg tensing under the highwayman's touch. Elm's voice came from the back of his throat. "Get your fucking hand off of her."

"Then give us what we want, Prince."

"Which is?"

"Your Cards," said the man with the sword. He was looking at Ione's leg. "Give us your Scythe and Black Horse. If you throw in the Maiden Card—and the woman attached to it—we'll let you keep the horse."

Rage burned in Elm's mouth like bile, fingers curling to fists in the air.

"Keep those hands up, Prince," said the highwayman with the shortbow. "Move, and I'll send this arrow into the woman's heart."

Ione's voice seeped out of her mouth. "So kill me. If you can." Her hazel eyes lifted to the highwayman with the bow. She drew in a breath—then tapped the Scythe three times behind her back. "Let loose your arrow."

The highwayman looked as if he'd swallowed his tongue. His bow jerked, the tip of the arrow shifting directions. With a strangled cough, he shut his eyes and released his arrow.

Elm slammed Ione forward, flattening her against the horse. But no arrow whizzed overhead. He heard a sickening sound and looked up, face-to-face with the highwayman touching Ione's leg.

The tip of the arrowhead, crimson red, protruded from the man's throat. The highwayman choked, blood spilling out of his mouth and neck. His fingers grasped for purchase as he dropped to the ground. He caught Ione's dress, yanking her—and Elm—off the horse.

Elm hit the muddy road, his arms caged around Ione. She coughed, his Scythe locked in her fist, her entire body seizing as she tried to wrench herself free from the highwayman with the arrow in his throat.

Elm pushed to his feet and kicked the bastard away, and then he was running, closing the distance between himself and the second highwayman—the one with the sword. Elm wore no sword to match. Reluctant Destrier that he was, he'd left it at Stone. His only blades were two throwing knives he kept on his belt, mostly for show.

The first knife missed. The second nicked the highwayman along his inner thigh. Elm reached into his pocket. The Scythe was gone, but he carried another Card. A brutish one he almost never used, inherited when he took up the Destrier cloak.

The Black Horse.

Elm tapped it three times, harnessing an old weapon he always kept with him. He may have been less powerful without Ravyn and Jespyr—but he had enough rage for the three of them.

He dodged an arrow as it sang through the air, then the swipe of the sword. He closed the distance between himself and the highwayman, denying the blade its leverage, and sent his fist across the man's face.

He struck again and again, his knuckles colliding with the highwayman's cheeks and nose and jaw. The world around Elm crumbled, and suddenly he wasn't hitting a stranger in a mask anymore, but his own brother, his father—even Ravyn.

The highwayman fell backward onto the road and did not stir. Elm stood above him, his hands screaming out in pain. He turned to look for Ione—

And came face-to-face with the shortbow.

"Acquiesce," the highwayman said, his arrow aimed at Elm's chest. "I don't want to kill you. Just give me the Scythe." He trembled. "And I will let you go."

Elm raised his hands once more. Only this time, they were covered in blood. "Would that I could. But I don't have it."

Whatever boldness the highwayman possessed, it was hanging by a thread. His eyes were wild, his breath as panicked as a trapped animal's. "Yes, you do. You made me shoot him. You forced me!"

Elm had little talent for soothing. Still, he lowered his voice, forcing his fury back down his throat. "Put the bow down," he said. "There is no escape if you injure me. My family will hunt you. And when they find you..." He looked into the highwayman's eyes. "Get away while you can."

But the highwayman did not answer. He dropped the shortbow to the ground, holding only its arrow. Without blinking, he pressed the tip of the arrowhead into the soft skin below his palate.

His eyes were so empty he might as well have already been dead.

Ione came out from behind Elm's horse, her bare feet silent as they trod across the muddy road. She did not look like a bride any longer. Her white dress was stained with blood and soil. Pink lips pressed into a thin line, Elm's Scythe flipping between her fingers. Her hazel eyes narrowed on the highwayman.

"Go on, then," she said without feeling.

A chill crawled up Elm's back. He whirled on the highwayman. "Wait," he said. "Don't—"

The highwayman shoved the tip of the arrow into the flesh below his jaw. He made a terrible strangled sound and collapsed, his black mask absorbing, then letting his life's blood onto the forest road.

The salt was strong in the mist, as if the Spirit of the Wood, smelling blood, had come to watch the mayhem on the forest road. Elm checked that his horsehair charm was tight around his wrist and dragged the bodies into shrubbery. Two of the highwaymen were dead. The third—the one he'd beaten with his bare fists—was unconscious.

Elm searched their pockets, removed their masks. He did not recognize them. But he hated them—their arrogance. They'd wasted their lives for Providence Cards.

He stepped back onto the road and released himself from the Black Horse, returning it to the fold of his pocket. "Are you harmed?"

Ione stood next to his horse, her head downturned as she flipped something in her hand.

His Scythe Card.

"Hawthorn," Elm called above the rainfall. He came closer, careful not to step in blood.

"I've never held a Scythe before," she said, twisting the Card between lithe fingers. "Hauth never let me touch his."

"It's not a Card to toy with. The pain is excruciating if you use it too long. Hand it back before you get hurt."

Ione retreated a step. "Yet you take me to the King, who would surely see me injured, though I knew nothing of Elspeth's magic." A twitch lifted the corner of her mouth. "Or had any hand in Hauth's *unfortunate* circumstances."

"Your fate is not of my making." Elm took a rattling breath and wiped his bloody fingers on his tunic, the dark fabric quick to absorb the stain. "Give me the Scythe."

Ione held the red Card out. But as soon as Elm reached for it, she pulled it behind her back. "What will you give me for it?"

Elm glowered. He knew nothing of the Maiden's negative effects firsthand. What he did know he took from *The Old Book of Alders,* which stated that anyone who used the pink Card too long would suffer coldheartedness. He imagined callousness, disinterest, even disdain. But as he traced Ione Hawthorn's face, he saw none of those things in her expression.

He saw nothing at all. Her features were too well guarded. It worried him, not being able to read her—a woman who had sent an arrow into a man's neck without a second glance.

Elm spat into a broom shrub, phlegm and blood. "It's *my* Card. I don't owe you anything."

"I saved your life."

"I would have managed without your help." He gestured to the puddles of blood on the road. "All you did was make a mess."

"I could have let him shoot you. I might have fled with the Scythe. But I didn't."

"Out of the goodness of your heart." Elm took another step forward. "If only you had any."

"I saved your life," Ione said again, sharper this time. "Everything has a cost."

Elm was so close to her his body blotted out the rain. He could feel her breath on his face. "Give me the Scythe. Now."

"Don't come any closer. In fact, don't move at all."

The smell of salt stung Elm's eyes. Before he could reach out—twist Ione's arm and rip his Card out of her grasp—he felt his muscles strain. Sweat dampened his palms, then the back of his neck. He tried to reach forward, but he couldn't move. He was frozen, rooted to the ground.

"Hawthorn," he warned, his jaw straining. "Stop."

"Payment first."

Heat crept up Elm's neck. His muscles—his joints and bones—did not heed his command, no matter how ardently he told them to move. Such was the Scythe's power. Ione could make him jump on one leg until his ankle snapped. She could make him throw his charm to the ground and run, unbidden, through the mist. She could even make him take the knife off his belt and plunge it into his own heart.

An old panic buried deep within Elm stirred. It had been a long time since someone had used a Scythe on him. "What do you want?"

Ione's eyes trailed his body. "Your word," she said. "Your honor."

"To what end?"

"You must convince the King to give me free rein of the castle."

"That might not be possible."

Ione ran the edge of the Scythe across her bottom lip. "They say you're the clever Prince. I'm sure you'll think of something."

Elm still could not move. The panic was rising in his chest, wrapping itself around his lungs. If he wasn't free of the red Card soon, he was going to scream until his throat ripped open. "Trees—fine! Whatever you want. Just give me the goddamn Scythe."

Ione tapped his Card three times, releasing him. She slid her hand from behind her back and held it out. A single drop of blood fell from her nostril.

Elm ripped the Scythe from her hand. "Never," he seethed, bending until their faces were even, "do that again."

The blood beneath Ione's nose grew thin, diluted by rainwater. "Neither you nor your red Card mean a thing to me, Prince. I only want balance. I saved your life." Her hazel eyes burned into his. "Now it's your turn to save mine."

Chapter Six
Elspeth

I remembered irises in a parlor. A tree with red leaves growing in a courtyard beneath the shadow of a narrow, towering house. A wood. Wild yellow hair. Laughter in a garden. Hands with crepe wrinkles working a mortar and pestle.

A library. A touch of velvet.

White robes. Blood on the flagstone. Claw marks in the dirt. A voice, spun of silk, in the walls of my head. *Get up, Elspeth.*

I clutched my throat, digging into my own mind for the voice. It was not there. I felt its absence, the darkness of my thoughts hollowed out, like an unfilled grave. *Nightmare?*

Taxus stood above me. I didn't know how long he'd been there, watching me. "You are remembering," he said slowly. "I will leave you now. You will be safe here."

I cast my gaze to the dark water, the endless, listless shore. "Where is *here*?"

"A place to rest. To recover."

"I don't want to rest," I whispered. "I want you to let me out."

His yellow eyes softened. "Soon, my dear."

He walked away, leaving no footprints. I watched him go

until the gold of his armor disappeared into darkness, then stood on shaky legs and tried to follow. "Taxus—wait."

But he was gone.

In his absence, I tried to piece the shattered mirror of my memories back together. I remembered impressions—colors and smells and sounds. The names were harder to recount, like working an atrophied muscle.

Strained, they came. Opal. Nya. Dimia. Erik. Tyrn.

Aunt. Half sisters. Father. Uncle.

Then, on a day or a night without marker, I remembered a walk through the wood. A nameday. An old rhyme. *Yellow girl, soft and clean. Yellow girl, plain—unseen. Yellow girl, overlooked. Yellow girl, won't be Queen.*

Ione. I'd joined my cousin Ione in town. Followed her to my father's house. Left early…

And met two highwaymen on the forest road.

Chapter Seven

Elm

Stone stood steadfast against the storm. It jutted out of the mist, its towers orange with torchlight. By the time they reached the drawbridge, Elm was soaked through his jerkin.

Thunder rumbled above charcoal clouds, nightfall close on their heels. When the guard raised the gates, Elm steered his horse to the west side of the bailey.

Two grooms hurried forward, their gazes wide when they spotted Ione.

Elm dismounted and turned into the bailey. He walked ten paces before he realized Ione was still in the saddle. Her yellow hair was dark with water, clinging to her in long, heavy cords. Tremors traveled up her legs and into her spine, racking her entire frame. Her lips had gone blue, and her dress—stained with blood and soil—clung to her skin. She looked like a storybook mermaid, washed ashore after a storm.

"Trees," Elm muttered. He reached up a hand to help Ione off the horse, but her body was rigid and he was forced to wrap an arm around her waist and lift her off the animal.

When she leaned onto his shoulder, her breath blew like winter wind across his neck.

"Next time we ride," he gritted, setting her on bare feet, "wear a damn cloak."

She looked up at him through wet lashes. "I d-doubt there will be a n-next t-t-time, Prince."

When they got to Stone's fortified doors, the guards opened them without question. Elm stomped into the castle, dripping rainwater along wool carpets and stone floors. Behind him, he could hear Ione's teeth chattering, nagging at his last raw nerve.

He jerked his head toward the grand stairwell. "Five minutes to get you warm, Hawthorn." He glanced at her bare feet. "Unless you'd like to lose your toes in the dungeon."

They only managed ten steps up the stairs before a voice called from the landing above. "Renelm."

Elm swore under his breath and looked up. Tried to smile at the Destrier. "Linden. Getting better every day, aren't you?"

If Hauth was capable of genuine connection, Royce Linden was the closest thing he boasted to a friend. They carried themselves with the same menacing gusto, two bulls on the brink of a charge. Brown eyes shadowed under a crude brow, Linden wore the Destrier cloak like a threat.

But the cloak did nothing to hide his barely healed scars. Scars Elspeth Spindle had unwittingly carved into him weeks ago on Market Day.

Elm's eyes traced the jagged lesions that stretched from behind Linden's ear to the hollow of his throat. "You'll never be a looker," he said. "But that wasn't exactly in the Cards, now was it?"

Linden's mouth stayed a tight line. He stopped at the stair just above Elm, leveling their heights. "You've not come to see your brother."

Elm dropped his smile. It was exhausting, playing nice. "I've been busy."

Linden peered over his shoulder at Ione. "So we've finally caught one of the bitch's kin." His eyes narrowed. "Shouldn't she be on her way to the dungeon?"

Elm shifted, blocking Ione and her bloody dress from Linden's view. He reached back and caught her arm. "Soon enough." He took the stairs two at a time, pulling Ione behind him. "Give Hauth our best, should he stir."

The sting of Linden's gaze followed them up the stairwell. "Th-that was s-s-stupid," Ione said. "Y-you sh-should j-just t-take me to the d-dungeon. H-he'll think—"

"Royce Linden is the least of your worries."

On the fifth landing, Elm led them across the gallery to the velvet-draped wing where the royal family lived. Every few moments he would stop and listen, waiting for the deep timbre of Ravyn's voice to enter his mind.

But the only sounds that reached Elm were the sharp flurry of his own thoughts and the ruckus of Ione's chattering teeth. If Ravyn was in the castle—if he was using his Nightmare Card—Elm was left out of the conversation.

"Hurry," he said, throwing himself at the door with the fox carved into the mahogany frame. His swollen fingers were clumsy at the latch. When the door swung open, he ushered Ione in with a shove.

"What—"

"Quiet." He closed the door abruptly. "This hall is crawling with Physicians."

Ione rushed to the hearth, the fire well tended. A small moan escaped her throat as she hunched next to the flames, firelight dancing over her skin. She reached her hands as close to the heat as she dared. "Is he g-going to live?" she said. "Your b-brother?"

Elm couldn't lock the door. Ravyn kept the castle keys on

his belt, and Elm had lost his personal key ages ago. He pulled the hickory chair that had been in his room since boyhood and leaned it up against the door, its legs creaking a feeble complaint. "I haven't consulted a Prophet on the matter," he said, fumbling with his clothes.

His belt fell with a clang. Next off was his soaking cloak. His jerkin and tunic were harder to strip, but not as difficult as his undershirt, wet silk clinging to the lean lines of his stomach and back. When he was free, he wore only his wool pants.

He dropped his wet clothes in a heap on the floor and kicked off his boots, grabbing a flagon of wine from the table.

"Here," he said, crouching next to Ione at the fire. "It'll help with the cold. Drink."

Ione's gaze flashed across Elm's skin, over his shoulders and down his chest, finally landing on the flagon. Her blue lips drew into a line.

"Do you see any poison up my sleeve?" Elm demanded, gesturing at his bareness. "It's just wine."

When Ione still did not drink, Elm brought the flagon to his lips and swallowed deeply.

The wine slid down his throat, planting small fires on its way to his stomach. "See? Still breathing." He held the flagon out once more. "Now drink."

Ione took it, lifting it to her lips. Elm noted the slope of her neck—the way her bottom lip hugged the flagon's mouth.

He turned away and tossed another log on the fire.

Toes inching out from beneath her dress toward the flames, Ione said, "Something tells me it wouldn't be too great a hardship, poisoning me, if you wanted to. You seem the type who would resort to poisons."

Elm snatched the flagon back and took another pull. "You don't know a thing about me, Hawthorn."

Ione unfolded herself and stood. Her gaze lowered to her dress, the once-white fabric dark and stained. She reached behind her back, fumbling with the lacings. "I need your help, Prince. The knots have tightened with rainwater."

"And you mistook me for your maid?"

"Don't tell me you're uncomfortable undressing a woman."

Elm's insides yanked. He didn't move, glaring into Ione Hawthorn's unreadable eyes, unsure if it would anger her more if he helped or refused her. He wanted very much to make her angry. Wanted to see what the Maiden would let her feel.

When he stood to full height, he buried her in shadow.

Ione's eyes flickered over his bare chest. She turned, presenting the back of the dress, her shoulders rising and falling as she waited.

The lacing was intricate. And Elm's fingers were swollen and bruised. A blade would have to do. He retrieved one of his ceremonial knives from the heap on the floor, then came behind Ione. When he slipped his left hand beneath her wet hair, his knuckles dragged across the nape of her neck.

It was surprisingly heavy, her hair. Dense. Long enough to wrap around his fist and tug.

Elm pushed the thought away, moving the mass of yellow-gold hair over Ione's shoulder. With his right hand, he gripped the knife. "Don't move."

He tore the tip of the blade through the dress's lacing. When the skirt, then bodice, fell to the floor, Elm bit the inside of his cheek. "I hope it wasn't a favorite."

Ione stepped away. "Your father gave it to me on Equinox, after my engagement to Hauth was announced." She glanced at the dress with marked disinterest. "Now it's for the fire."

The hearth was the only light in the room. Still, it was not difficult to distinguish the outline of Ione's body, all her curves—her starts and stops—beneath her damp silk undergarment.

Elm forced his eyes back to the fire. "And the Maiden Card my father gave you? I assumed you had it tucked away in *that,*" he said, turning his nose at the ruined pile of fabric.

Ione twisted her hair, wringing out the last of the rainwater. "You might have searched me for it. Hauth would have."

Elm's mouth pressed into a hard line at his brother's name. "Our methodologies are *dissimilar,* his and mine." He stole a glance at Ione, only to whip his eyes back to the hearth. "There's a chest at the foot of my bed. Take anything you like."

The iron hinges creaked. Ione shuffled through his clothes, pausing every so often to run her hands over the material. "You wear a lot of black," she murmured. "For a Prince."

Elm said nothing. When he turned, Ione had pulled a dark wool tunic over her head. It fell past her knees, her frame lost under the excess fabric.

It was one of the garments he wore when he moonlit as a highwayman. "Here," Ione said, tossing a fresh shirt and a velvet doublet of the same bottomless black color at Elm. "It suits you."

Hair tousling, Elm slid the shirt over his head, dropping the Scythe in a side pocket. He shrugged on the doublet. But when he tried to tighten the lacing, the corded silk slipped through his swollen fingers.

He swore under his breath.

"My turn." Ione stepped forward, reached for the laces—then pulled her hands back. "That is, if you'd like my help."

Elm glared down his nose. "And to think, I didn't even have to kill anyone for you to owe me a favor."

The corners of Ione's lips twitched. She wove her fingers through the laces, threading the doublet with precision. Once woven into place, she took the tails of the strings and yanked, jerking Elm forward as she closed the doublet's seam.

"Gently does it," he grunted. "I'm delicate."

Ione's eyelashes grazed her cheeks as she lowered her eyes, looping the remaining string into a tight knot just above Elm's navel. She smelled of outside—of rain and fields. A heady, wistful smell. It made Elm feel hazy.

He pulled away. As he did, salt bit his nose, as if someone had splashed icy seawater in his face. It filled his ears—his eyes—his nostrils. He coughed, the sound of his cousin's voice filling the dark corners of his mind.

Elm, Ravyn called. *Where are you?*

He took a shaky breath and turned his back to Ione. *ME? What about you—you've been gone an age. I had bloody Destrier duty without you.*

I'll explain everything. Are you in your room?

Yes, but—wait, Ravyn, I'm—

He was already gone. Salt retreated from Elm's senses like an ebbing wave. When he turned back to Ione, she was watching him.

He lunged for the chest of clothes, digging through it. "Take these," he said, throwing a pair of wool socks toward her head. "It's cold where you're going."

Ione caught them just before they hit her face. She held them up to the light, brow furrowing. "These are sized for a man."

"Which I happen to be." Elm found a pair of dry boots under his bed and shoved his foot into one, the leather stiff from disuse. "When I said you didn't know a thing about me, Hawthorn, I assumed there was some level of comprehension—"

"I'm surprised, is all. There are no garments for women in your room."

"Why on earth would there be?"

"I saw several pairs of stockings tossed around Hauth's chamber when I visited it." Ione closed the lid to the chest and perched upon it, pointing her toes as she slid the socks on one at a time. "I assumed all Princes kept women."

Elm glowered at his boots, his swollen fingers too clumsy to lace them. "Would that I had the time." He stood, searching his messy floor. "You'll need a cloak."

"I'm fine as I am."

"You'll lose your toes, then your fingers. Maybe the tip of your nose. Or that wicked mouth."

"What's my mouth to you?"

"Nothing." Elm's exhale shot out of him, disturbing the hair above his brow. "But it might be difficult holding up my end of our bargain if you're in pieces."

Ione didn't seem to hear him. She turned her head, her back straightening, eyes on the door. Elm heard it, too—the sound of heavy footfall. But before he could speak—before he could move—the latch lifted.

The hickory chair fell with a bang and Elm's chamber door swung open.

When Ravyn stepped into the room, shoulders tight, his gaze froze on Ione. He took her in with sharp eyes that jumped from her wet hair to the black tunic she wore, then to the heap of her bloodstained dress upon the floor.

"Ione Hawthorn," he said, his gaze finally moving to Elm. "I'm surprised to find you here."

Chapter Eight
Ravyn

Ravyn's words tasted like ash in his mouth. He stared at Ione Hawthorn and she stared back, her hazel eyes masked by indifference. The knot in Ravyn's chest tightened. Elspeth's cousin. Her *favorite* cousin. Ione was meant to be far away from Stone. And now that she was here—

She would surely die.

He didn't know where to look. Ione Hawthorn—hair soaked, eyes cold, wearing one of Elm's tunics. Or his cousin, who looked half-drowned.

"She was at Hawthorn House," Elm said, already defensive. "Gorse and Wicker saw her. They'll be here soon. I had no choice but to bring her."

Ravyn's attention returned to the dress on the floor. Even in the dimly lit room, the bloodstains were unmistakable. His eyes flew back to Elm, then his right hand, the knuckles swollen and dark with bruises. "What happened?"

"Highwaymen attacked us on the forest road. Three of them."

When Ione spoke, her tone was hollow, fringing on bored. "Rest easy, Captain. The bloodstains aren't ours."

Ravyn kept his gaze on Elm. "You're all right, then?"

His cousin's face was drawn. "Never better. Where the hell have you been?"

"At Castle Yew."

"Why?"

"Digging under a particular stone."

Elm stiffened. "And?"

"It's true. All of it."

Ione was perfectly still, listening. For a reason he didn't fully understand, Ravyn wanted to shout at her. "The King has begun his inquest. He's just seen—" His throat closed on the name. "The prisoner. Now he'll have the others."

Elm's cheeks went bloodless.

"Captain," a voice called from the open doorway.

Royce Linden was a shadow in the hall, the light from Elm's hearth reaching only the edge of his browbone and nose. "The King has requested I wield the Chalice at his inquest."

Elm crossed his arms over his chest. "That's Jespyr's job."

"She's gone to the dungeon to put the bitch back in her cell."

Ravyn bit down. Hard.

Linden shifted under his gaze, eyes dropping to his boots. "I saw the Prince and Miss Hawthorn arrive some moments ago and volunteered to summon them. I did not know you had already come to do so, Captain."

Elm's voice went low. "Did the King summon Miss Hawthorn specifically? Or were you just feeling terribly eager?"

Linden opened his mouth, but Ravyn cut him off. "She's the kin of an infected." He pushed ice into his voice. "Miss Hawthorn will submit to the Chalice, same as her father and uncle."

He could feel Elm's gaze burning into his back. Ravyn ignored it. Elm wasn't the only one who got to be angry. Ione

Hawthorn was supposed to be gone—disappeared into the night alongside her mother and brothers and cousins.

But Ravyn was out of options. If he was going to convince the King to keep trusting him, despite his flagrant attachment to Elspeth Spindle, he needed to be beyond reproach. He would have to wear the mask of the Captain of the Destriers—the cold, unfeeling leader of Blunder's ruthless soldiers—just a little while longer.

"Lead the way," Ravyn said to Linden.

No one spoke, Stone's tall, shadowy corridors echoing with their footfall. The torches were lit, illuminating ancient tapestries that lined the castle walls.

Linden took the lead. Ione followed behind him, her steps silent beneath her wool socks. Ravyn wondered where her shoes had gone.

Elm walked beside him. When Ravyn tapped the Nightmare Card once more and called his cousin's name, Elm jumped.

What? he snapped.

Why didn't Ione Hawthorn disappear with the others?

I don't know. Elm kept his gaze forward. *She must not have been in Spindle House when I compelled the others to flee.*

Then why not use your Scythe on her today?

I couldn't with Gorse and Wicker there, could I?

Ravyn's left knee popped as they took the stairwell. *What happened on the road?*

I told you. Highwaymen.

Ravyn was four years older than his cousin, but the difference had always felt slight. Mostly because Elm had been taller than Ravyn since he'd turned seventeen. Like the fox carved above his chamber door, Elm was cunning, and slow to trust. With only a few glances, he could map body language—hear the shift of breath just before a lie—sense a person's energy without having to speak to them.

But Ravyn had ignored his cousin's talents, his warnings. Elm had all but begged him to keep his guard up against Elspeth Spindle. Ravyn hadn't listened. If he had, he might have sensed what Elm had all along, hidden behind two charcoal eyes that flashed yellow.

Danger.

Perhaps, had Ravyn heeded Elm's warnings, they might not be on their way to an inquest. Hauth might never have had the chance to get Elspeth alone.

And the Shepherd King might have been kept at bay.

Ione cast a backward glance. Elm shifted, his shoulders tensing, something strained and unspoken passing between them.

They reached the second landing. But before they could descend to the throne room, Ravyn caught his cousin's arm, holding him back.

What's going on, Elm?

She saved my bloody life, all right? Elm ripped his arm out of Ravyn's grasp. *I didn't have time to reach for my Scythe. She took it from my pocket.* He stared down the stairs and ran a hand through his tangled auburn hair. *The rest happened... swiftly.*

Ravyn stared at his cousin. *SHE killed them?*

"The King is waiting for us, Captain," Linden called from below, his fingers now wrapped around Ione's arm.

Ravyn held up a menacing finger to Linden and kept his gaze on Elm. "There's nothing you can do for her now," he said under his breath. "She made her bed when she said yes to Hauth."

Elm's expression went cold. "Do you really think she knew what she was saying yes to?"

"She knew Elspeth was infected. And I—" Ravyn dragged a hand over his jaw. "If I'm to leave for the Twin Alders Card, I can't afford any more of your father's distrust. I can't lie for Ione Hawthorn."

Something flashed in those brilliant green eyes. "Then I will."

Ravyn shook his head. "No, Elm."

"I owe her."

"She hasn't earned your kindness."

"It's not kindness," he bit back. "It's balance."

Ravyn took a deep, steadying breath. *She will never leave this place, Elm. Either by the dungeon's frost or the King's command, she will die.* He put a hand on his cousin's shoulder. *Don't be turned by her beauty. We've enough on our plate already.*

Elm's smile did not touch his eyes. He rolled his shoulder, and Ravyn's hand fell. *Because you've never been turned by a beautiful woman, have you, Captain?*

Chapter Nine

Elm

The great hall was full of light, drenched in the aroma of herbs and butter-glazed foods—perfumes and wine. Laughter bounced against its ancient walls, and music tangled in tapestries, pirouetting around pillars and knotting itself in skirts. But just a wall away, past great iron doors, another hall waited. One devoid of color, of smell, of sound, its only adornment a looming chair made from the hardy wood of rowan trees. Besides the dungeon, it was Elm's least favorite part of the castle.

The throne room.

"Open it," Ravyn said to the sentries guarding the door.

The hinges groaned like waking beasts. Elm kept his eyes forward, gritting his teeth, their steps echoing in the cavernous room.

There were twin hearths, one on each side of the throne room. Both were lit, roaring with smoldering logs, their flames casting long, jumping shadows across the stone floor. Between the hearths was a dais. Upon it, King Rowan sat on his throne, his face shadowed by a heavyset brow. He wore his crown—gold, forged to look like twisting rowan branches—and a matching gold cloak with fox fur at its collar. There were no seats beside the throne on the dais—no one equal to the King. King Rowan's only companions were three enormous hounds, whose dark, unblinking eyes traced the room.

The King watched them approach. In his right hand was a silver goblet. In his left, a Scythe.

Destriers lined the walls, lost in shadow. Wicker and Gorse were among them.

Ten paces from the dais, Linden let go of Ione's arm. She stood in the heart of the throne room, shoulders even, her hair catching fingers of firelight.

Ravyn and Elm stood behind her.

The King leaned into his throne. "Come," he growled, ushering Ravyn forward to his usual place on the left side of the throne. Ravyn stepped onto the dais, his arms folded tightly behind his back. The King watched through narrow eyes, then turned his gaze on Elm. "And you."

Elm blinked and didn't move. He wasn't the High Prince. His place had always been on the perimeter—lost in the shadow of the hearth with the rest of the Destriers. "What?"

"There is a vacancy at my side," the King said. "Fill it. Unless you, too, would like to submit to the Chalice."

Elm stumbled forward. He positioned himself on the right side of the throne and tried not to think of the hundreds of times Hauth's boots had scored the stones beneath his feet. He glanced over his father's head at Ravyn, who stood entirely still.

Elm straightened his shoulders and pressed his lips together in a firm line. But his tolerance for stillness was less evolved than Ravyn's. Even when he imagined himself perfectly still, his boot tapped. When he willed it to stop, his fingers twisted in his sleeve. When he bound them into fists, his head filled with the gnawing sound of his molars grinding together.

The King stared down at Ione. "I see Renelm did not put you in chains."

Ione's eyes flickered to Elm. "His methodology is *dissimilar* to your other son's, Majesty."

"Indeed." The King looked out over the Destriers. "Shackle her."

A Destrier next to Gorse stepped forward, a chain rattling in his hands. He took Ione's wrists, first one, then the other, roughly locking the cuffs in place. When he let go, the weight of her iron restraints rounded Ione's shoulders.

Elm's stomach constricted.

A guard brought forth a tray, a crystal goblet filled with wine upon it.

Linden took the goblet in one hand. With the other, he reached into his pocket and retrieved a Chalice Card.

"Bring them in," the King barked, making Elm jump.

The throne room door opened once more, the echoes of rattling chains abounding. Jespyr and three other Destriers stepped forward, bringing two men with them. One was tall with dark, graying hair and piercing blue eyes he refused to lower. The indefatigable Erik Spindle.

The other prisoner was shorter. His hair was thinning and his clothes ragged. There were bruises on his face and he walked with a limp. Tyrn Hawthorn did not look at his daughter, nor the King. His gaze remained low. Elm winced at the sight of him, Tyrn's defeat—his sorrow and shame—wafting, fetid, through the throne room.

The Destriers planted Erik and Tyrn on either side of Ione and stood in a line behind them. Jespyr looked up at Elm from behind Erik's back. Her face was drawn, her jaw strained. Still, she shot him a wink—a brief reassurance.

King Rowan's voice cut through the room. "Elspeth Spindle

is charged with high treason for carrying the infection." The throne groaned, the King's fingers white as he clung to the armrests. "Furthermore, she is charged with the slaying of Physician Orithe Willow and the attempted murder of my son, High Prince Hauth Rowan. Of these crimes, I have found her irrevocably guilty, and sentence her to death." He let out a slow, venomous breath. "It is my intention, through this inquest, to learn how much I should attribute these crimes to you, her kin."

Tyrn let out a low whimper, earning looks of disgust from the Destriers along the wall.

The King continued, his malice thinly veiled. "Tyrn Hawthorn, Erik Spindle, Ione Hawthorn. You have been summoned to Stone, charged with treason for aiding Elspeth Spindle. You committed this treason knowingly, and with full understanding of the law, which states that all infected children—for the safety of our kingdom—be reported to my Physicians." The King shifted on the throne, his voice lowering. "You shall submit to an inquest, the depths of your crimes measured by myself, my Captain, your Prince, and the Destriers. When your wives and children are discovered, they shall do the same." He tapped his Scythe three times. "Drink."

Linden brought the crystal goblet forward. Tyrn Hawthorn resisted the Scythe's magic, his hands shaking as he tried not to reach for the goblet. When he finally succumbed and drank, two Destriers had to shove his mouth shut to keep the wine from spilling out.

Linden flipped the sea-blue Chalice Card in his fingers, tapping it three times.

The goblet passed to Ione, who took its stem in both hands. She shut her eyes and raised it to her lips, strands of yellow hair falling from behind her ears, covering her face like a veil. She lowered the cup, a drop of wine lingering on her bottom lip. When she opened her eyes, her hazel gaze was sharp—focused.

And aimed directly at Elm.

There was no need for a Nightmare Card—Elm knew what she was thinking. *I saved your life. Now it's your turn to save mine.*

Erik stared straight ahead and drank from the goblet, his features stony.

The King tapped his Scythe thrice more and stowed it away in his pocket. "Let us begin." His green eyes shifted to Tyrn. "Have you always known of your niece's infection?"

A low, ugly sob escaped Tyrn's lips. "N-n-n..." He choked on the word, his tongue mangling on the lie. "N-n-n-n-n..."

The King nodded at a Destrier, who came forward and backhanded Tyrn across the face.

Tyrn groaned, blood sliding out the corners of his mouth. Still, he tried to best the Chalice and lie. "N-n-n-n-n..."

The Destrier slapped him again. When the truth seemed to strangle him entirely, Tyrn took a swelling breath, defeated. "Yes, Your Grace."

The King's gaze turned hateful when it landed on Erik. Of all the betrayals he'd endured thus far, it was clear he felt this one the keenest. His former Captain of the Destriers—hiding an infected daughter. "Did you know of her magic, Erik? This *ability* she has regarding Providence Cards?"

Erik stood like a soldier, shoulders square, legs firm. He did not try to lie. "No, sire."

The King's eyes jerked down the line. "And you, Miss Hawthorn? Did you know of her magic?"

Ione stared up at the throne. "No."

"No, *Your Majesty*," Linden echoed, sounding too much like Hauth.

"Asshole," Elm muttered, loud enough to earn him a sharp

look from Ravyn and a familiar murderous glare from his father.

The King returned his attention to Erik Spindle. "Hauth carried a Scythe and a Black Horse nearly everywhere he went. And Orithe Willow was no feeble-bodied fool. Did you train your daughter in combat?"

"No, sire."

"Then how—" A line of white spit formed along the King's bottom lip. "How was a girl of her stature able to best them?"

"Whatever skills Elspeth possessed," Erik said, "I was never witness to them. I saw little of her." He turned to the side, his blue eyes burning into Tyrn. "She lived with her uncle."

The King's wrath returned to Tyrn. "I understand your wife and sons were conveniently absent from both Spindle and Hawthorn House when my Destriers came to collect them. Where are they?"

Tyrn's shoulders began to shake. "I don't know, Your Grace."

The King leaned back into his throne. "You don't know," he repeated. "Perhaps I do not need them. After all, your daughter is here, within my clutches." He peered down at Ione. "You are terribly brazen, Miss Hawthorn, to continue to use the Maiden Card I gifted you."

Ione said nothing.

The King folded his hands over his lap. "Where are your mother and brothers—your aunt and cousins?"

Ione kept her eyes forward, unflinching. "I don't know, sire."

"But you knew Elspeth Spindle caught the fever. You knew it when my son pledged to marry you."

"Yes." Linden opened his mouth, but Ione cut him off. "Yes, *Majesty.*"

The King's eyes blazed. "You agreed to marry Hauth, knowing you'd be tethering him to a family that carried sickness? You disgust me."

"The disgust," Ione said, her tone idle, "is mutual."

Silence pierced the room. Even the hounds held still. Linden reached out, his hand an open palm, and slapped Ione across the face.

Elm went rigid, hands curled into fists so tight the fresh scabs along his knuckles split. Salt shot up his nose, into his mind. *Don't move,* Ravyn warned. *Stay right there.*

The King drained his goblet. "Try again, Miss Hawthorn."

Ione's cheek was red only a moment where Linden had struck her. Then, slowly, the red blanched away, her skin perfect once more. "I never lied to Hauth about Elspeth. He did not ask me about my family. He did not ask me much of anything."

The throne groaned under the King's shifting weight. "Were you there when she attacked him?"

"No."

"How did she come to be in a room alone with him?"

Someone shuddered down the line, drawing the King's gaze. Tyrn.

"Well?" the King barked.

Tyrn covered his eyes, wiping away tears. Or maybe he was simply trying to hide his face from Erik Spindle. "I—Prince Hauth, he wanted to speak—" He took a weak breath. "I brought Elspeth to the Prince, Majesty."

Up until that moment, Erik Spindle had been as good as glass—smooth, still. Now his entire body was directed at his brother-in-law, his blue eyes filling with fire.

Elm's pulse pounded in his ears. The hair on his arms prickled, the tension in the room so taut it might snap him. He dug his hand into his pocket, his fingers wrapping around the Scythe and its familiar velvet comfort.

But his debt gnawed at him. *I saved your life. Now it's your turn to save mine.*

It had to be now—now that she was under the Chalice—when the King would believe her. But Ione Hawthorn hadn't given him exact instructions, only that she wanted enough freedom to roam the castle uninhibited.

In Elm's vast experience, there was very little the Scythe could not make someone do. Despite the Chalice, he could make Ione tell a lie to save herself.

But there would be a cost. A lie was still a lie, and the Chalice repaid lying tenfold. It wasn't long ago that he'd watched Elspeth Spindle vomit blood thick as mud, trying to lie under a Chalice.

No, he couldn't make Ione lie; it was too risky. He would have to absolve her by proxy. The falsehood would have to come from someone else. Someone he could stomach sacrificing to the Chalice's poison.

You, he said to himself, his gaze falling to Tyrn Hawthorn, his face still hidden in his hands. He tapped the Scythe in his pocket three times. *You'll do nicely.*

When Elm felt the salt sting his nose, he pushed it outward, his green eyes narrowed, focused entirely on Tyrn Hawthorn. On what Tyrn *wanted*.

And Tyrn, so keen to hide his miserable face, kept the Scythe's glassy deadness hidden behind his hands. Tyrn *wanted* to keep his daughter safe. *Wanted* to absolve her.

Tyrn's voice was loud, even behind the muffle of his hands. "My loyalty is to you and your family, my King," he said. "Prince Hauth—I would never plot his injury."

He choked on his words a moment. Elm kept his focus tight. *Tell them what happened*, he murmured into the salt.

"I delivered Elspeth to him because Prince Hauth promised he would handle her infection swiftly, without family dishonor. He said it was the only way to save Ione's reputation."

Now for the tricky part. Not an outright lie, but a mixing of truths. Something to keep Ione away from the hangman. Something that would slip into the King's cracks and give him pause.

Lucky for Ione, Elm had years of practice learning the King's cracks.

Tyrn coughed. When he spoke the words Elm compelled him to say, his voice was tight. "Please, sire. If you harm my daughter, everyone will know. She is beautiful, she is beloved. My family is gone—people will gossip. But if you let my Ione remain here, she will placate your court. Stop tongues from wagging. Keep people from knowing the truth of what happened to Prince Hauth."

The King's voice was ice. "And why should I wish to hide what happened to my son?"

Tyrn dropped his hands, revealing blurry eyes. "Because it was your fault. It was you who forged the marriage contract with a family that carried the infection. *You* who valued a Nightmare Card above all else." His voice went eerily quiet. "You are just as much to blame for what happened to Hauth as my daughter is."

The air in the cavernous room stilled. The King's mouth was open, tiny red lines shooting across the whites of his eyes. On his other side, Ravyn was staring into Tyrn Hawthorn's face, searching it. The Destriers shifted as they cast sidelong glances, their shadows dancing on the floor.

Ione stared at her father, slack-jawed.

The telltale agony—the one Elm knew far too well—of using the Scythe too long began. A shooting pain, needle-thin, slid through his head, starting near his temple, prodding deeper with each passing second. He blinked away the pain, but there would be no hiding it if his nose began to bleed.

He prayed this was enough to keep Ione alive—that the King was fearful enough of rumor and dissent to stay his hand, at least until Elm could come up with a better plan. He tapped the Scythe three times and let out a long, ragged exhale.

Everyone was still focused on Tyrn. No one noticed Erik Spindle shift until the former Captain of the Destriers had shoved Linden and Ione aside and wrapped his chains around his brother-in-law's throat.

The visage of the indefatigable spindle tree shattered into a thousand splinters. "You did this?" Erik said, voice breaking. "You gave Elspeth up?"

Tyrn's face was turning red. "No more than you did."

Linden drew a dagger. "Get back, Spindle." When he stepped closer, Erik pivoted, far quicker than a man his age ought to be. He caught Linden's wrist—twisted—and ripped the dagger from his hand.

"Where is she?" he demanded, the tip of the blade aimed at Linden's throat. "Where is my daughter?"

There was a mad dash for the heart of the room. Elm launched himself off the dais the same second as Ravyn. Destriers swarmed, smothering the light from the hearths as they hurried past, plunging the throne room into shadow.

Jespyr got to Erik first. She dug her fists into his tunic, yanking him backward. Erik let loose a wordless cry and swung the dagger wildly through the air. Its blade found no purchase in a Destrier.

It caught Ione instead.

So sharp it made no sound, the dagger cut across Ione's hands, cleaving the flesh of her palms.

The King barked orders, but Elm did not hear them. He was shoving Destriers—bashing against the sea of black cloaks—forcing his way into the tumult.

The throne room floor was marked in red. Ione slipped, caught between Tyrn and the two Destriers fighting to keep him still. They were crushing her. Elm shouted her name, then again, louder, panic-tipped. “Hawthorn!”

When she looked up, her eyes crashed into Elm’s. She managed to push away from her father. When she reached out, her fingers fell from Elm’s grasp, slick with blood.

“Come on,” he shouted. His muscles strained—shoulders sang in pain—every fiber of his strength spent reaching, reaching—

He caught the chain tethering Ione’s wrists. It was cold, heavy. Elm wrapped his swollen fingers around it and pulled, squeezing Ione between Destriers, freeing her from the bedlam.

She crashed into his chest and pressed her head against his sternum. It rose and fell with Elm’s torrid breaths. When he reached for her hands, a hiss slipped through his teeth. Erik Spindle had cut his niece palm to palm, a long, ugly valley of red—of flesh and muscle.

Elm held her hands against his chest to stanch the bleeding, then reached into his pocket. The moment velvet touched his fingertips and salt pinched his nose, the world around him faded.

He imagined a crisp winter breeze, a frozen statuary. All was silent, all was still. The statuary was a perfect rendering of the throne room. Only, in his imagination, it, and everyone in it, was enveloped by ice—frozen.

The smell of salt grew stronger, biting at his mind. He ignored it, twirling the Scythe between his fingers. Ice. Stone. Stillness. Silence. “Be still,” he said to himself. “Be still.” He kept saying the words, willing the world around him to yield to his Scythe. *Be still, be still.*

BE STILL.

When he opened his eyes, the throne room was frozen in place. Erik—Tyrn—Ione—the Destriers—the King—all frozen, their eyes wide and glassy. Everyone but Ravyn, who turned to look at Elm. There was blood on his face.

The chaos had ceased. All was silent, all was still.

All but for the blood that slid from Elm's nose.

Chapter Ten

Elspeth

Water washed up my legs, the tide unrelenting, never high or low. I was not hungry or thirsty or tired. There was a new name that was giving me pause. Like all the others, it began as an image in my mind. But where Ione's had been a bright yellow flower and my father's a crimson-red leaf, this image was dark, difficult to discern. Almost as if it did not want to be seen.

A bird, black of wing. Dark, watchful, clever.

Something in my chest snapped, my lungs emptying of air.

New memories spilled into me. They were not like the others, softened by childhood or tethered by family. These were fresh—forged when I was a woman. A man, clad in a dark cloak, a mask obscuring all but his eyes. Purple and burgundy lights. Running in the mist. A hand, coarse with calluses, on my leg as I sat in a saddle. That same hand in my hair. A heartbeat in my ear—a false promise of forever.

His name slipped from my lips. "Ravyn."

A giggle sounded in my ear.

My eyes jutted open. When I looked to my side, a girl sat next to me in the sand. A child. Her hair was woven in two perfect plaits, as if a woman who loved her had taken time to braid them with care.

But more than her hair, more than the tilting of her head, it was her eyes I noticed. Her brilliant, yellow eyes.

"Who are you?"

A grin cracked over her little mouth. "You know who I am. I'm your Tilly."

My name unraveled itself from my mouth like a long piece of string. "I'm Elspeth Spindle."

She giggled, and the sound carried up and down the beach. "Can we swing in the yew tree like you promised?"

I looked out onto the vast emptiness. "I see no tree, Tilly."

Her smile faded. "All right." She picked up her skirt—heaved a sigh. "I'll wait in the meadow. In case you change your mind."

She walked away on tiptoe, but none of her footprints appeared in the sand. I watched her go, prickles dancing up the back of my neck.

More voices sounded in the darkness, soft as waves upon the shore.

I looked up. From the far side of the beach, children emerged. Boys, all with yellow eyes—save the tallest. His eyes were gray.

None of them left footsteps in the sand.

The boy with gray eyes bent to one knee. Peered into my face. Sighed. "You're with us, but you're never really here, are you, Father?"

Chapter Eleven

Ravyn

Stop fidgeting!" Filick Willow snapped, his fingertips cold as he pressed the skin above Ravyn's brow together. "I can't sew properly when you move like that."

Ravyn stopped tapping his foot and sat still on a stool in the King's chambers. The enormous hearth burned, fueled by pine kindling. Filick leaned over him with needle and stitching, meticulously repairing the split above Ravyn's left brow.

It was late. The Destriers were gone—sent to sleep. Dark shadows lingered beneath the King's eyes as he paced in front of the hearth, drinking deeply from a silver goblet. Every so often his voice would hitch, snagged on rage.

"Some Captain of the Destriers," he fumed. "Immune to Card magic. Unrivaled in combat." He glowered at Ravyn over his shoulder. "Knocked senseless by Erik Spindle, a man who's spent three days freezing in the dungeon."

Ravyn shook his head, a knot already forming where Erik's chains had collided with his temple. "It's nothing."

"What did I just say about holding still?" Filick said, yanking the needle and pulling seams of flesh together. "You'll look like a common cutpurse if this doesn't heal well."

Elm snorted from the hearth.

"And you," the King said, turning on his son. "A dead man could have wielded the Scythe sooner than you."

Elm picked dried blood from beneath his fingernails. "You have a red Card in your own pocket, do you not?"

The King's face mottled. "You stood at the right hand of the throne. The Scythe—and all the pain it brings—is your responsibility." His voice lowered. "Hauth understood that."

Elm's eyes narrowed at his brother's name. But before he could reply, the King's doors pushed open. Jespyr stood in the doorway, her face drawn—her wavy hair shooting in every direction, flecks of dried blood splattered across her cheeks.

"Well?" the King demanded.

"Spindle and Hawthorn have been returned to the dungeon, sire."

"In separate cells, I hope," Filick muttered.

The King exhaled. A moment later the entire tray of silver goblets clanged across the floor, wine spilling onto the stone at their feet. "Hauth does not stir. Orithe is dead. Erik, Tyrn—men in my closest circle—have spent over a decade in deceit, hiding Elspeth Spindle's infection. And yet, until the Twin Alders is safe in my hands, it seems I am the one who must yield." His gaze returned to Ravyn, his wide nostrils flaring. "This is all your fault."

Ravyn knew enough of his uncle's ire to keep a stern jaw and say nothing.

Elm had no such restraint. "How do you imagine that?"

The King began to shout. "Was she not staying at Castle Yew? Nested like a cuckoo under my Captain's bloody nose?"

"In his defense," Elm said, "it's a rather large nose."

The whites of the King's eyes turned red. For a moment, he looked as if he might wrap his brutish fingers around his son's throat. "I should purge all three of you from my guard for such abhorrent ineptitude."

After a stifling pause, Jespyr spoke. Her voice was calm. "Oversights were made, Uncle. We have been tireless in our patrols—keen to manage your kingdom well. We didn't see what was in front of us. Elspeth was such a quiet, gentle presence beneath our father's roof."

"A liar's ruse."

The blow to Ravyn's head had sent his mind wandering. He sat in the King's overwarm chamber—but a sick part of him would rather have been in the dungeon.

Ten minutes, he said to himself for the hundredth time in four days. *It all might have been different had I gotten to Spindle House ten minutes sooner.* His eyes lifted to the King. "It's not us who made a liar out of Elspeth Spindle. The moment the infection touched her blood, she was bound to be a liar. That's how things are, in Blunder."

The King's step caught. He turned, eyes burning into Ravyn. Silence stole the air in the room. Even Filick's hands stilled. Everyone was watching. Waiting.

"Get out," the King said. "Everyone. I'd like to speak to my nephew alone."

Ravyn felt Jespyr's eyes boring into him. He did not face them. He was locked into the King's stare. Filick tied the last stitch on his brow and pulled away, following Jespyr wordlessly out the door.

Elm lingered by the hearth.

"Go, Renelm," the King commanded.

Elm shot Ravyn a pointed glance and turned away, slamming the door behind him.

The King waited for the silence to settle. "Do you value your place here, nephew?"

Ravyn held the King's gaze. "I don't know what I value, Uncle."

"You do not wish to be my Captain?"

"It doesn't matter what I want."

The last container that hadn't been shattered or thrown upon the floor was a silver flagon. "Finally, something we agree on." The King pulled a long drink. When the flagon dropped from his lips, his eyes were unfocused. "I will let Ione Hawthorn remain in the castle. If only to dissuade rumors of Erik and Tyrn's treachery at court. Still, people will wonder at Hauth's absence. There will be gossip and unease. Blunder needs control, not violence and backhanded treachery."

He stared into the fire a moment longer, then crossed the chamber to his velvet-draped bed. The frame creaked beneath his weight. "Let Elspeth Spindle keep her word, then," he muttered. "Follow her out of the castle into the mist—let her find the Twin Alders Card for me. Then drag her back. If either of you tries your hand at anything clever, I will pluck Emory back from Castle Yew. He won't have a fine room and fire for comfort this time." The King yawned. "He'll have a cell."

Ravyn's fury was a swift wave. He felt it in every strained muscle, hot words of malice catching in his craw. But his face remained without expression.

"When you return, I will do as the *Old Book* says." The King closed his eyes. "I will spill Elspeth Spindle's infected blood come Solstice. Unite the Deck. After five hundred years, I will be the Rowan who finally lifts the mist." His voice began to drift. "That is what people will say, when they speak of my reign."

"As you say, Uncle. We'll leave immediately." Ravyn turned to leave.

"Elm stays here."

He froze at the door. "He's my right hand."

"And *my* second heir." The King sank into his bed. "I cannot risk him to the same danger that broke Hauth."

"The Ni—Elspeth—she wouldn't hurt him."

The King barked a laugh. "Even you don't believe that."

Ravyn combed his mind for a deception that would bend the King's will. But the words didn't come. His mind was brimming with fog, lost to exhaustion, so tired it hurt.

He pressed the heels of his palms into his eye sockets. "Elm won't like being left behind."

"He's a Prince of Blunder. What he likes is of no consequence."

Ravyn was not about to tread headfirst into the mist—into the unknown—alone with a five-hundred-year-old monster hell-bent on righting the wrongs of the past. He needed someone to watch his back.

Someone who had *always* watched his back.

"Jespyr," he said, unyielding. "I'll need my sister." It cost him, but Ravyn lowered his head. "Please."

The King was silent a moment. When he finally consented, it came as a low grunt. "Fine. Take another Destrier as well. Gorse."

Ravyn brooked no argument. He gave a curt nod and opened the door.

"You'll get your wish," the King called after him. "When this is all over, I'm stripping you of command." His words were coated in spite. "You've proven a wretched disappointment, Ravyn."

Ravyn lowered himself at the door, a final bow. "From you, Uncle, that is praise indeed."

Chapter Twelve

Elm

Elm caught Filick before the Physician got to the main stairwell. He had to hold the galley railing to keep himself upright, so tired his knees had begun to buckle.

Filick took a deep breath. "The King is in a foul mood."

"I've seen worse." Elm ran a hand over his face. "Do you know where they put Hawthorn? Don't tell me those idiots took her to the dungeon."

The Physician yawned. "She's on the servants' floor, I think."

"Did you send her a Physician?"

"What for?"

"Her hands. Erik tore them open."

Filick blinked, shook his head. "You're mistaken." When Elm's mouth dropped open, the Physician gave a stiff laugh. "I assure you, her hands were perfectly intact when I saw her."

"I assure *you*, there was a wound. A bad one."

"Likely someone else's blood." Filick put a hand on Elm's shoulder. "Get some sleep, Prince. I promise, Miss Hawthorn is safe and well."

Elm watched Filick disappear down the stairs into darkness, his thoughts straining against fatigue. He couldn't have imagined it—not the cold sting of Ione's iron chains, nor the curling dread he'd felt at the sight of her maimed palms.

The feeling of her hands, pressing into his chest.

Elm's eyes shot to his doublet. He half expected to see nothing. But when he looked down, they were there. Even in the black fabric, a stain remained.

Two bloody handprints.

The castle guards stationed on either side of the fifth door of the servants' wing made it easy to discern where the Destriers had stashed Ione. When Elm approached, the guards stepped into shadow and lowered their gazes.

He banged on the door, then swore for the bruises on his knuckles. "Open up, Hawthorn." When no one answered, he slapped the knotted pine. "Hawthorn!"

"She's locked in, sire," said the guard on his left, offering Elm a small brass key.

Elm weighed it in his palm. He'd always told Ravyn he looked like a jailer with his ring of keys. When actually it was Elm's—the second Prince's—duty to carry the castle keys. And Ravyn, like in so many other things he did, carried the iron ring so that Elm didn't have to.

"Off with you," he said to the guards. He waited for them to hurry away, then slid the key into the lock.

The door creaked open, the room lit by a single glass lantern. The smell of wool and fresh kindling filled Elm's nose. He shut the door, something shifting in his periphery.

"Trees," he said, whirling, "what are you—"

Ione Hawthorn stepped out of shadow, coming so close to Elm his spine crashed against the door. She held out a finger and poked it with impressive force into his chest, emphasizing each word. "What. Was. That?"

The intensity in her eyes startled Elm. She was no taller than his shoulder—his clavicle, really—but that didn't make her any less frightening. There was a quiet fury in Ione Hawthorn. The Maiden did a good job of masking it, or tempering it, but it was still there.

Perhaps there were some things not even magic could erase.

"Careful with that finger, Hawthorn. I told you, I'm delicate."

"What you are is a damn idiot." She stepped back. "My father—what he said during the inquest. That was you, wasn't it? You and your Scythe."

Hair fell into Elm's face. He blew it back with a hot breath. "Not my finest work, I'll admit," he said, a touch defensive. "Then again, I usually don't have to fight against a Chalice to get people to do what I want."

"And that was your best idea? Make my father *threaten* the King?"

Elm leaned against the door. "All I did was make him leverage the correct words." He frowned down at her. "You're welcome, by the way. The King won't kill you now. At least not right away, when he fears people will talk. He's always been afraid of that. *Talk.* He'll rue your every breath for what Elspeth did to his favorite son." He gestured to her room. "But I've spared you the dungeon. You'll be watched, but still welcome at court. I can arrange a guarded escort when you need range of the castle. And if the King changes his mind..." He bit the inside of his cheek. "I'll find a way for you to slip out of Stone unnoticed."

Ione said nothing, her nose twisting as if something wretched had died beneath it. Elm's shoulders stiffened. "That's what you wanted, isn't it? A life for a life?" He fixed her with a hard look. "We're even, Hawthorn."

"I didn't want to be paraded around court, fielding the gossip of what happened to your wretched brother. I *wanted* to get what I needed out of the castle and disappear. Trees, I thought you were clever enough to understand that."

Her words prodded into Elm's skin. Got under it. "You had your chance to disappear on the forest road," he said, matching her ire. "Yet you didn't." He pushed away from the door, his shadow looming over her. "What is it you need at Stone you couldn't leave behind?"

Ione said nothing. But her eyes were burning. Vibrant hazel, they were the color of a green field, punctuated by autumn leaves. Amber sap, slipping over moss. Heat and life and anger—so much anger they flared, even in the darkness of his shadow.

Still, she said nothing.

Elm moved so quickly the lantern's flame flickered behind its glass. He caught Ione's hand and lifted it, relishing in the surprise that crossed her face—the tilt of her brows, the little gasp that escaped her lips. "Show me your hand, Hawthorn," he said, his voice dangerously low.

Her fingers curled, not quite a fist, but enough to hide her palm. All Elm had to do was squeeze—apply the right pressure—and her fingers would splay for him.

He didn't. If she was injured, it would hurt like hell. And even if she wasn't—

"Please," he said, softer than before. "Will you show me?"

Ione didn't move. Her entire posture had gone rigid, those hazel eyes widening at his *please*. Almost as if she'd expected him to force her hand open.

Elm didn't like that. It made him feel dirty all over. He dropped her hand.

Ione noted his reddening cheeks. Slowly, she uncurled her fingers one at a time. When she offered him her upturned palm, Elm's breath caught.

The blood was gone, washed away. What remained was unblemished, finely lined skin. Not a single trace of injury.

He ran his thumb over her palm, pressing into the flesh, searching for what he could not find.

"You're not out of your mind," Ione murmured. "The cut was deep."

The urge to scrape his teeth across her palm—to press her skin like clay and test her fortitude—was overwhelming. "How?"

"Can't you guess?"

Elm recalled the feeling of Hawthorn House's aged wood door beneath his ear. Rain on his cheek. Frigid wind. Ione's yellow hair, damp and wild as they rode. The highwayman's hand on her leg. The ice in her voice, unrelenting and sure.

Kill me. If you can.

His vision snapped, everything coming into painful focus, the labyrinth beginning to unravel. His eyes traced her face—her unblemished visage. Her skin was too flawless, her face too symmetrical, her voice too even. He'd known from the start that this wasn't the real Ione Hawthorn. This was how the Maiden Card had remade her, masking her in unearthly beauty. Caging her. Protecting her.

Healing her.

"The Maiden." The words scraped out of him.

So small Elm almost missed it, the tip of Ione's brow lifted. "Seems you are clever. On occasion."

Elm stepped into the room, dizzy, elated, and a little sick to his stomach. "Trees, I need to sit down." He found the edge of the bed, plopped down, wincing at the thin mattress. "Five hundred years," he mumbled to himself. "For five hundred years, Maiden Cards haven't been used for anything but gifts for wealthy men's daughters."

“Five hundred years have been wasted on women, is that it, Prince?”

“That’s not—” He bit his lip. “Don’t twist my words. If the Maiden can heal, gross oversights have clearly been made.”

Ione sat next to him on the bed. She didn’t look tired, but her shoulders slumped, and her voice was dull. “Men have no use for the Maiden. What is beauty to real power? My father never let me touch his Providence Cards. But the Maiden—the Maiden I was gifted freely, like a horse a lump of sugar. Something sweet to distract me from the bit they shoved in my mouth.” She lowered her chin, hair spilling over her shoulder. “Is it any wonder, if women discovered the Maiden’s true potential, its healing power, that they kept it a secret?”

Elm was silent. But in his mind, he was shouting. Was his Rowan legacy that of idiots as well as brutes? Someone should have figured this out.

He pinched the bridge of his nose. “Where is it? Your Maiden Card?”

“Why should I tell you?”

“Still don’t trust me, Hawthorn?”

“You’re a Rowan.”

She said it softly. But an accusation hid in the melody of her voice—a quiet abhorrence. It sunk into Elm through all the sore, bruised pieces of him. “It’s here, isn’t it?” he said. “Your Maiden. That’s why you wanted to come back to Stone—to retrieve it.” He searched her face. “Where, Ione?”

But that face—that beautiful, unfeeling face—held nothing. Elm knew before she spoke that she wouldn’t answer his question. “Now that you know what the Maiden Card can do,” Ione said, tucking hair behind her ear, “are you going to use one to heal your brother?”

Elm hadn’t thought of that. He groaned and dragged his

hands over his eyes. "There are not enough curse words in all the languages," he muttered, "for me to answer that question."

"Because, if you do, he's going to—"

"The list of terrible things my brother will do if he wakes is longer than you know." Elm closed his eyes and heaved a long, aching breath. Days ago, when he'd stood in the icy dungeon with Ravyn and his father in front of Elspeth Spindle's cell, he couldn't imagine a situation more dire.

But it had become so, all because of Ione bloody Hawthorn and her Maiden Card. If he ever grew old enough to do so, he would tell this story to his children, with the firm lesson being don't *ever* strike bargains with beautiful women.

"It seems the best option is to keep the Maiden's magic a secret," he said. "For now."

When he opened his eyes, Ione was looking at him. Searching his face for something she couldn't seem to find. Her stare was like running unwashed wool over his bare skin. Elm felt itchy, too warm.

But with the discomfort came another feeling—something low in his stomach. A tumbling exhilaration, like clearing a fence on horseback. And though he was tired to the point of pain, maybe he'd remain awake just a little while longer to get that feeling to stay.

He stood, bracing himself a moment on the bedframe. "Come with me."

"Where?"

"The dungeon."

Ione went rigid. "What for?"

"Elspeth," Elm said, shoving his hands into his pockets. "I'm taking you to see Elspeth. Or what's left of her."

Chapter Thirteen

Elspeth

When they came back, the weight of my memories dragged me so far down I couldn't find a way out. Magic. My infection. Providence Cards. What Hauth Rowan had done to me that final night at Spindle House.

The monster who had saved me.

I screamed, calling out to the Nightmare who had taken my place. I ran the length of the beach, looking for a way out, only to come back to where I'd started. I swam in the water, only to remain ten paces from the shore. I screamed myself raw and cried until there were no more tears. "I remember, Nightmare," I shouted at the dark. "Let me out. *Let me out!*"

Silence was my only answer.

The children came and went as they pleased, never leaving marks upon the sand, nor ripples on the water. Slowly, I learned their names. Tilly, and her brothers Ilyc, Afton, Fenly, Lenor. The eldest—the one with gray eyes—was Bennett.

They didn't seem to notice each other, passing on the same

stretch of beach without ever lifting their gazes or trading words. I'd even witnessed two of the young boys pass *through* one another.

But they did speak to me.

"Will you come see what I've built?" Lenor said, reaching for my sleeve, his hand passing through my arm.

"I—I—"

His face dropped, and so did his yellow eyes. "Another time, then."

"I've trained every day for a fortnight," Fenly declared—the next moment or hours later, I didn't know. "Aunt Ayris said you might come see me compete in the tournament on Market Day." But even as he said it, I could tell he didn't believe it. Just like Lenor's, his eyes dropped. "But of course, you are busy."

"I'm not," I called after him, but he disappeared out over the water.

Ilyc and Afton, I realized, were twins. My stomach twisted at that. They reminded me of my half sisters. Only, unlike Nya and Dimia, they didn't speak that secret, knowing language of twins. They didn't speak to one another at all. Sometimes, their visages blended entirely together, two boys becoming one. "I want a Golden Egg Card," Ilyc—or was it Afton?—said. "You gave Bennett Providence Cards. I want one as well."

I held out my empty hands. "I have no Providence Cards to give you."

Their brows narrowed. When they spoke again, it was to shout at me. "You keep them all for yourself."

"I don't."

"I hate you."

I clasped my hands over my ears and shut my eyes. When I opened them again, the twins were gone.

Timelessness bled into despair. There was nothing to do on the long, empty shore but think—remember. And even my fondest memories became bitter in that place until, ravenous, my thoughts began to consume me. My family would surely die for hiding my infection. Not even my little cousins, Aldrich and Lyn, would be spared the King's wrath. Dead, all of them.

Because of me.

And the Yews—I had destroyed their hope of healing Emory. They'd needed Orithe Willow's blood to unite the Deck. And I'd *killed* him.

My thoughts festered until my mind turned septic.

But even then, a flicker of warmth lingered in the dead cold of my despair. A candle's worth of light—of hope. The softness of my aunt's hands as she combed my hair. Ione's arm in mine, our heels clacking on cobbled streets on Market Day.

Ravyn Yew, holding me in a hug tight enough to blot out all of Blunder.

My black wool dress sopped up water as I walked into the breaking waves. Bennett appeared out of the air and stood next to me. "The children miss you," he said, fidgeting with the two Providence Cards—Mirror and Nightmare. "Especially Tilly. Come to dinner. Just this once."

I knew by then he was not talking to me. None of the children had been talking to me. This beach—this dark-sanded oblivion—belonged to the Shepherd King.

I know what I know...

My secrets are deep...

But long have I kept them, and long will they keep.

Here. In the dark, on the shore. Where there was no sun,

no moon. Where the mourning dove did not call at dawn and no owl announced dusk. A place of desolation—emptiness and despair. This is where his secrets were kept.

And I was among them.

I looked into Bennett's gray eyes. "I cannot stay here with you and be forgotten," I said. "I'm going to get out."

I walked into the breaking waves. Swam with all my might. Screamed and swallowed brine. Kicked and clawed at the water until my muscles gave out.

I fell beneath the waves—

And sank deeper into darkness.

Chapter Fourteen

Ravyn

The guards who kept watch over Emory's door stepped into shadow. Ravyn unlocked his brother's chamber and lingered at the threshold. He slipped a hand into his pocket. Before he was aware of his own fingers, he'd tapped his Nightmare Card three times.

Salt pounded his senses. He pushed and pushed, looking for the familiar, comforting presence. Like leather and fire and the pages of a well-read book.

Jespyr.

Her voice was sharp with startle. *Ravyn?*

The Twin Alders, Jes. We're leaving at dawn.

There was a pause. Then, *What do you need from me?*

Ravyn's hand trembled on the latch to his brother's door. *Emory*, he whispered.

I'm on my way.

Salt fled his senses, Jespyr disappearing from his mind on the third tap. Ravyn heaved a breath, then opened the door.

Emory lay on his bench in the corner of the small chamber. Blanket tight under his chin, eyes shut, he almost looked asleep. But his shoulders were too tense, his thinned face too laden with furrows to be at rest. He shivered, his lips an awful gray.

Ravyn moved to his brother's wardrobe and flung it open, digging for the warmest cloak he could find.

Emory's voice was uneven, fraying at its edges. "What are you doing?"

"It's time, Em." Ravyn placed a wool cloak onto his brother's lap. "We're leaving. Now."

Emory tried to sit up. "Why?"

"Arrangements have been made."

"What arrangements?"

"Where are your boots?"

Emory flicked his hand toward the end of the bench.

Ravyn sat at the foot of the bench, hands deft as he pulled Emory's leather boots over thick socks. All the while, he could feel his brother's eyes on him.

"What arrangements?" the boy said again.

Ravyn tied the laces tight, though he was fairly certain his brother was no longer strong enough to walk without help. "I'm taking you home."

A rattling breath swept up Emory's fragile frame. "Did Uncle—"

"The King is aware," Ravyn said, harsher than he meant.. He heaved a sigh and finally looked up.

It hurt to gaze at his brother. More than Ravyn imagined it would.

Emory, who had once bloomed like a garden in spring, was wilted, frozen to his depth by chill and aggressive degeneration. A boy, who not long ago had stood tall, was now stooped, as if his spine—which protruded up his back in harsh knobs—weighed more than the rest of his body combined. His copper skin was wan, his cheeks gaunt, his fingertips blue. And his eyes—his brilliant gray eyes—were shadowed, dim, lit only by the deathly omen of what was to come.

He was degenerating. Faster than Ravyn had feared he would. And while Ravyn's degeneration made certain Cards impossible to use and Elspeth's had strengthened the monster in her mind, Emory's was simply…killing him.

Ravyn reached for his brother's shoulder. "Everything is going to get better for you, Em," he said. "I promise."

Emory's shirt slid, Ravyn's palm grazing his brother's skin. The moment it did, Emory's eyes glassed over. He shivered from deep within, his lips drawing into a pale thread. He reached up and gripped Ravyn's hand, his eyes rolling into his skull.

Ravyn recoiled, realizing what he'd done. His hand—he'd touched Emory. He tried to rip away from his brother's grasp, but Emory held him in a vise, nails digging into Ravyn's skin.

"The dark bird has three heads," Emory said, his voice strangled, an invisible rope around his neck. "Highwayman, Destrier, and another. One of age, of birthright. Tell me, Ravyn Yew, after your long walk in my wood—do you finally know your name?"

Ravyn ripped his hand out of his brother's grasp. The moment their hands separated, Emory's magic fled his senses. His eyes returned. Glassy. Filled with tears. "What happened?" he asked.

It took all of Ravyn's years of practice to keep his face even. "Nothing, Emory."

"Did I—did I say something?"

Emory's magic had never been a gift. To family, it was unnerving. To strangers, terrifying. A single touch, and the boy could read a person's deepest thoughts—their fears and desires—their shadow-laden secrets—their futures. It didn't matter how deeply it was buried, there was nothing Emory could not see.

It took the life out of him, using his magic. Whatever life that still remained.

Ravyn wrapped an arm under his brother's ribs and lifted him from the bench, careful not to graze his skin again. It took hardly any strength to lift him.

Emory's head slumped forward. His eyelids drooped, his words a raspy whisper. "I've forgotten... Where are we going?"

Ravyn clenched his jaw and kicked open the door to his brother's prison. Had the lantern on the table been lit, he would have smashed it onto the floor and cast the room into flame. "Home, Emory. I'm taking you home."

The boy weighed no more than a large saddle. But the stairs were long. By the time they met Jespyr in the east corridor, Ravyn was out of breath, a sheen of sweat upon his brow.

Emory was asleep. Jespyr gasped when she took him in her arms. "He's little more than a reed."

Ravyn turned away. If he looked too long at the tears in his sister's eyes, his own might fall. "Take him to Castle Yew. Go now. I'll be there shortly."

Jespyr did not linger. She turned west, slipping through a servants' door. Ravyn listened to her heavy steps until they were gone, then heaved a breath and straightened his cloak. He didn't look back at the stairs to Emory's room. It, nor any other part of the King's castle, had earned a single farewell from him.

Ravyn uttered one nonetheless. "Fuck you."

Chapter Fifteen

Elm

Shadows in the corridor loomed, only to scurry away. They seemed taller in the witching hour, dawn mere hours away. Elm rubbed his eyes and blinked. He needed sleep—badly. He opened his mouth to ask Ione if the Maiden kept her from feeling tired when footsteps sounded down the corridor.

Ione shoved him into a doorway. Elm's ribs collided with an iron doorknob, and he let out an abrupt breath. "That," he seethed, "hurt."

The echoing footsteps grew softer. Whoever it was, Physician or guard or servant, they were not coming their way. Ione stood rigid, waiting. Torchlight caught the bridge of her nose, the heart-shaped curve of her lips, the soft line of her throat and the shadow where it hollowed.

Elm looked away.

Only when the corridor was quiet again did Ione acknowledge him. "Sorry. I forgot. You're *delicate.*"

"Yes, I am. I should be abed, resting my delicate body." He waved his bruised knuckles in front of her face. "Not all of us have a Maiden Card to heal our mortal carcasses into perfection." He looked at her hands. "That cut. Did you feel pain?"

Every part of Ione's face was closed to him. "Yes. It takes a moment for the Maiden to heal me. When it does, it feels good, euphoric even, not to be in pain."

"Sounds nice."

"You could have a Maiden if you wanted." She slipped out of the doorway, her steps silent as she continued down the corridor. "You're a Rowan. Don't you take whatever you fancy?"

"Clearly not, when all I fancy is a proper night's sleep."

"It was your idea to go to the dungeon."

"And a brilliant one, considering Elspeth has the happy ability to see Providence Cards by color—even at a distance."

Ione skittered to a halt. "She does?"

"Indeed." Elm picked at his fingernail. "Rather handy. Especially for you."

"How so?'

He shot her a pointed look. "You asked for free rein of the castle, yet failed on numerous occasions to specify where in Stone your Maiden Card resides. Which has led me to one rather interesting conclusion." He cocked his head to the side. "You don't know where your Maiden is, do you, Hawthorn?"

Ione drew in a breath, then continued down the corridor. "How exhausting it must be, wanting everyone to know how clever you are, Prince."

Elm caught up with her in two strides. "But you're still using the Maiden's magic. If anyone else had touched it, your connection would be severed." He leaned over her, his voice tipped with satisfaction. "Which means *you're* the one who misplaced it."

A frown ghosted over Ione's brow. She didn't look at him. Not in the way she normally didn't look at him—too indifferent to bother. This time, she seemed intent not to meet his eye.

"What happened? Celebrate a little too hard on Equinox? Put your Maiden Card in a flowerpot and waltz away?"

"Something like that."

Elm chuckled to himself. "No shame in it. Spirit knows I haven't spent an Equinox sober in"—he counted on his fingers—"some years."

Ione kept her eyes forward. "Just get us to the dungeon. After that, you can go back to being the cantankerous, wayward Prince you were born to be. Trees know I'll be pleased to be rid of you."

Elm trailed her down the corridor to the stairs. He didn't have to tell her which turns to make. All they had to do was go down. "Is that what people call me? Wayward?"

"I've heard the word *prick* thrown around."

"Naturally."

Ione's shoulders rose, half the effort of a shrug. "It's said you like your freedom too well—that you're an unruly, rotten Prince. Unmatched with the Scythe, but a poor Destrier. That's what the men say, at least."

Rotten. Elm shoved the word down and schooled his features to a lazy smirk. "What do the women say about me?"

Ione kept her gaze decidedly upon the stairs. "Nothing of note."

"But with far less disappointment in their voices, I should think."

A faint blush rose up her neck into her cheeks. "Perhaps."

Elm's smirk budded to a smile. He traced Ione's blush with a curiosity he decided was purely scientific. It felt like a game of discovery, watching her face, seeing what sliver of emotion the Maiden would allow her to show—noting what had brought it on. Elm loved games. The playing, the cheating, the winning. Mostly, he loved the measuring of his opponent, the unearthing of their limitations.

Only now, he wasn't sure who his opponent was. Ione Hawthorn—or the Maiden Card.

He quickened his pace, matching Ione's step as they took the east stairs. "And what do you think of that, Hawthorn? My reputation with women?"

"I don't think of it."

He laughed, a low, rumbling timbre, and Ione turned at the sound. Her eyes narrowed. "You said you didn't have time for women."

"When?"

"In your chamber. When I was getting dressed."

He'd been paying attention to other things, in that moment. "I used to have time." Elm cleared his throat. "I've been busy of late."

Ione's voice hummed in her chest. "For a Prince who doesn't mind the King, and a piss-poor Destrier at that, one would think you had all the time in the world. Only, whenever I see you, you look as if you haven't stopped to catch your breath. Which raises the question—" Her eyes were dark in the dim light. "What, Prince Renelm, have you been doing with all your time?"

Moonlighting as a highwayman. Stealing Providence Cards to unite the Deck without the King knowing. Using the Scythe until it makes me bleed. Worrying about Emory. Arguing with Ravyn. Bickering with my brother's betrothed on our way to the dungeon to see a monster—

"You should know. You've taken up every moment of my time today." Elm leaned down, his mouth close to Ione's ear—testing to see if her blush would return. "And I can't say it hasn't been… interesting."

She pulled away, her expression a stone wall. "Don't."

There it was again. Even in the dim light of the stairwell—pink in her cheeks. "Don't what?"

"Pretend to flatter me."

"Who's pretending?"

Ione shook her head. A quick, dispassionate dismissal.

"Why, Ione Hawthorn." Elm scraped his teeth over his bottom lip. "Don't tell me it makes you *feel* something when I flatter you."

"It doesn't." Her face was unreadable. Unreachable. "I can't feel anything anymore."

The dungeon stairs had always been deadly. Now that it was autumn, frost already making its home across Blunder's fields, the steps were nigh unnavigable, slick with ice. Twice, Elm had to brace himself against the wall. When Ione slipped and crashed into him, her fingers flexed like cat claws, digging into the muscles along his abdomen. Elm wrapped an arm around her shoulders, steadying her.

"How far down does this go?" she said into his chest.

He gripped her tighter. "Far."

By the time they got to the bottom, Elm was stiff all over. Given the tension in her shoulders, the fine line of her mouth, Ione was no better. She released him with a breath, stepping into the antechamber. Only then did Elm realize, with a bitter curse, that he'd forgotten the dungeon keys.

It didn't matter. The door was already open.

A giant mouth of darkness greeted them, a bitter wind from deep within the dungeon snapping at their faces. "Where are my father and uncle kept?"

"On the south side. Your cousin is on the north."

Ione's back straightened, as if she was trying to force the shivers that racked up her spine into submission. She pushed into the dungeon on silent step, darkness swallowing her whole.

Elm groaned and hurried after her, catching her at the shoulder and spinning her toward the first of many passages north.

They walked in silence down rows of empty cells.

A chill sank into Elm. This wretched castle. He hated it to its last scrap of mortar, of stone, of wood and iron. He kept his eyes forward the way Ravyn always did, determined not to look into the cells, knowing they were empty—and had not always been so.

He didn't realize Ione had spoken until her hand grazed his arm.

He jumped. "Trees—what?"

"Anxious, are we?"

"Just cold."

"I might have thought you didn't mind the cold. What with you freezing us all into statues with your Scythe, back in the throne room."

"What's the matter, Hawthorn? Dis*heart*ened I cut the violence short?"

She ignored the quip. "Ending violence isn't exactly a Rowan thing to do, is it?"

Elm didn't bother masking his annoyance at being compared to his father and brother. "I try not to use the Scythe for violence."

"Why not?"

"To disappoint the hell out of them."

Ione, who often seemed to give her attention only by half, was watching him. She searched his face like she had in his chamber, still looking for something she couldn't seem to find.

A noise, like the snapping of teeth, echoed at the end of the corridor. Elm jerked to a halt, catching Ione's arm, stopping her. Ahead was the last cell. Elspeth Spindle's cell.

Or what used to be Elspeth Spindle.

"Listen," he said. "I should tell you—"

The noise echoed again, this time with the low, oily notes of a laugh. Elm swallowed. "Your cousin. She's not the same."

Ione said nothing. Her brows lowered. She pulled away from Elm, marching toward the cell. "Because of Hauth?"

"Not Hauth. Not this time."

When Ione reached the iron bars, Elm stepped behind her, close enough that he could pull her back. There was just enough light to see a shadow shift, and then the Shepherd King was there, fingers curling around the iron bars, his yellow eyes wide and his jaw clicking a chilling rhythm.

Click. Click. Click.

Elspeth. Shepherd King. *Nightmare.*

He did not shiver, seemingly untouched by the oppressive chill of his cell. His spine stooped, black hair falling like curtains over his face. He jerked his chin to the side and looked up, his gaze catching Ione.

For a moment, all was silent. Ione stared at what had once been her cousin. They looked like mirrors of each other—if one of the two had been dipped in ink.

Ione's voice drifted away from her. "Elspeth?"

"Sweet Ione."

Ione reached a hand through the bars. Elm tensed. "Don't," he warned.

She didn't listen. Her fingers grazed the skin along what had once been Elspeth's cheek, and she drew in a gasp.

A smile crept across the Shepherd King's face. "Do you finally see me, yellow girl?"

For the first time since he'd come upon her at Hawthorn House, Elm discerned unmistakable emotion on Ione's face. Her pallor turned gray. Her eyes widened, and her lips drew into a fine line. Her fingers trembled as they traced the Shepherd King's cheek. When she spoke, her voice was so thin it threatened to snap. "You're not Elspeth."

The Shepherd King's smile widened. "Nor am I a stranger. I was the shadow that moved just beyond the corner of your eye. I spoke in murmurs, hummed songs you did not know. The hounds brayed, warning you of the intruder in your midst. The horses shied away and the birds grew quiet. But your parents did not heed them. And you, yellow girl, were afraid to look too closely." His eyes dragged over her face. "But you're not afraid anymore, are you?"

Ione pressed against the bars. "You—Elspeth—she kept so many secrets from me."

The Shepherd King reached out, cupping her chin with a dirty, bloodstained hand. "She was wary. Clever. Good." He rubbed his thumb along Ione's cheek. "You and I are all that is left of her."

"Who are you?"

"Blunder's reckoning." The Shepherd King's grin was worse than any snarl. "I am the root *and* the tree. I am balance."

Ione reached out in a flash, her fingers wrapping around his wrist. "I want to speak to Elspeth."

"You cannot have her. She is with me. And I am letting her rest."

"I don't care. Give her back to me."

The Shepherd King's teeth scraped over his lip. For a moment, Elm thought he might tear into Ione's soft, unblemished cheek. But his grip on her face loosened, his brow easing. "She will be free. But not until my work is finished." His eyes flashed to Elm. "And old debts settled."

It was the first time he'd looked at Elm directly, those strange eyes so piercing, so monstrous, so *knowing.*

"Elm," the Shepherd King murmured. "A pleasure to see you again."

Elm. Not Renelm or Prince, like every other stranger called him. *Elm.* As if this man, this thing, already knew him.

And, of course, he did. For every conversation Elm had had with Elspeth Spindle—every treason she'd committed alongside him—every secret she'd heard—so, too, had the monster in her mind. Waiting, just behind her eyes. Listening. Learning.

Elm felt sick.

"You look pale, Princeling."

"It hasn't been easy, cleaning up after you."

"Yes. Your cousin intimated as much."

Ravyn hadn't said anything about going into the dungeon. He hadn't said anything of the Shepherd King at all, save digging up his grave. Elm brushed away the sting, his gaze flickering to Ione. "She's missing something. A Maiden Card. It's here—somewhere in the castle. Can you see it?"

Ione's eyes jumped between the two of them, and the Shepherd King stepped closer, his voice slithering between the bars. "Do you truly need it back, my dear?" he whispered. "Isn't it better this way, your body safe from harm? Your soft, sentimental heart, finally guarded?"

Ione's eyes narrowed. But the Shepherd King kept going. "Elspeth envied it—your heart. The ease of your laughter, the careless sincerity in everything you did. But I knew better. You were good, but never wary. It is why you hardly blinked when your father caged you like a canary on Equinox and left you in this cold, cavernous place." He stroked her hair with a listless finger. "The only reason you have not lost yourself to the despair of being shackled to *Rowans* is because the Maiden Card has kept you from feeling it."

Ione was quiet a long moment. "I may not feel despair," she finally said, "but I am still lost. I have disappeared into the Maiden, just as Elspeth has into you. And I want to be freed."

Her words wove through Elm's ribs, pressing into his chest.

The Shepherd King's smile faltered. "I cannot free you."

"But you can see Providence Cards by color," Elm cut in.

He cocked his head to the side, predatory. "One of my many gifts."

"My father keeps a Maiden Card in the vaults with the rest of his collection. Are there others in the castle?"

The Shepherd King shut his eyes—stayed silent a long moment—then laughed. A horrid, biting discord that echoed down the corridor. "Yes, dear boy. There are three Maiden Cards in Stone."

"Where are they?"

He stepped back into shadow. "That, I cannot say. The castle is vast, the pink Cards scattered. You and my yellow girl must find the Maidens yourselves."

Ione's hands balled into fists. "Tell me where to look. *Help* me."

But the monster was gone, retreated back into shadow.

Ione screamed against closed lips, then ripped away from the cell back down the corridor. Elm followed a pace behind.

"I look forward to when we meet again, Princeling," the Shepherd King called after him. "I have plans for you yet."

Elm turned, but he was gone, his farewell the same eerie knell as his greeting. *Click, click, click.*

The journey back to the antechamber felt even colder. When they reached it, Elm caught Ione by the arm. The ire she'd displayed at the Shepherd King's cell was gone now. There was nothing on her face.

"It's important to you?" Elm murmured. "Getting your Card back?"

She hardly seemed to hear him. "If you think this is about beauty—that I am opposed to what the Maiden has done—you are wrong. If I could still feel what it is to like something, I would tell you that I like being beautiful. I like being healed by magic and having no pain. I like who I was and how I looked before the Maiden Card as well. What I aim to get back, Prince, is my *choice*."

When all Elm could do is stare at her, she sighed. "Go to bed—back to whatever it is you do with your time. I don't want your help."

"But you'll need it, given that the castle is full of locks and I'm the one with the ring of keys." He ran a hand down the back of his neck. "Actually, Ravyn has the keys, but technically they're mine—"

"If this is about what happened on the forest road, our debt is settled."

"It's not."

"What, then?"

Elm bit the inside of his cheek. "I was a *prick* to Elspeth. Ravyn was falling in love with her, and I—" His eyes fell, his mouth turning with derision. "Let's just say I've never had anything like that. I was too concerned with losing him to note that Elspeth was losing herself until it was far too late."

He finally looked back at Ione. "I aim to be better. If you are disappearing like Elspeth did—and have little *choice* in the matter—I would like to help you."

The lines and muscles of her face gave nothing away. But she startled Elm, raising herself to her toes to meet his eye. She hooked his chin with her thumb, and though Ione Hawthorn was so cold in all her expressions, her touch warmed him. "Why?" she asked. "Why do you aim to be better?"

"Because I have to be," Elm said in one breath. "I care not what they say about me at court, even if it is that I'm a rotten Prince and a piss-poor Destrier." He leaned closer. "But I do want it said, loud enough so everyone hears, that I am *nothing* like Hauth."

Chapter Sixteen

Ravyn

Pressed up against the dungeon wall, cold in the clutch of his Mirror Card, Ravyn watched Elm and Ione disappear down the dungeon corridor. He didn't miss the strain in his cousin's shoulders, nor the way Elm shadowed Ione. Alert. Attentive.

It wasn't just balance. Elm was…entangled with her. Unguarded in the darkness of the dungeon, his face had been an open book. What Ravyn had suspected before the inquest hit him now like a blow. Elm. Ione.

Spirit and trees.

The Nightmare's laugh drifted like smoke up the stone walls. *You don't approve, Captain?*

It'll wreck him if the King decides to kill her.

I imagine he thinks the same thing about you and this body I currently occupy.

Ravyn tore the Mirror from his pocket and released himself. He wanted the Nightmare to see the hate in his eyes. *She has a name, parasite. Say it. Or don't speak of her at all.*

The Nightmare's yellow gaze met his wrath, measuring him. Ravyn took a step back. *As for Elm, you won't get your hands on him. He won't be coming with us.*

What makes you think I'd hurt him?

Ravyn scoffed. *He's a Rowan. Descendant of the man who stole your throne and killed your kin. You've had five hundred years to imagine your revenge.* His stomach turned as he looked at the old blood beneath the Nightmare's fingernails. *Surely you want him dead.*

I had plenty of time to hurt him. Only I didn't. The Princeling sensed me—saw my strange eyes—and recoiled. He understands, far better than you, Captain, that there are monsters in this world. He let out a long breath. *My claws would find no purchase in a Rowan who is already broken.*

When Ravyn's rigid jaw didn't ease, the Nightmare grinned. *Above rowan and yew, the elm tree stands tall. It waits along borders, a sentry at call. Quiet and guarded and windblown and marred, its bark whispers stories of a boy-Prince once scarred.*

His voice in Ravyn's mind went eerily soft. *And so, Ravyn Yew, your Elm I won't touch. His life strays beyond my ravenous clutch. For a kicked pup grows teeth, and teeth sink to bone. I will need him, one day, when I harvest the throne.*

Ravyn had sent three notes after his talk with the King. The first was to Gorse, the particularly harsh Destrier the King had chosen to accompany them on the journey for the Twin Alders. Given the swiftness of his uncle's choice, Ravyn was under no illusions that Gorse had been picked because he'd be particularly helpful. The Destrier was likely a spy—instructed to watch Ravyn carefully, and report on his actions the moment they returned to Stone.

Best of luck with that.

In the second note, addressed to Filick Willow, Ravyn had written—

The castle keys are in the cellar. See that Erik Spindle and Tyrn Hawthorn don't freeze to death.

And in the third, addressed to Elm, Ravyn had penned a single, wobbly line.

I'll see you soon.

Dawn was creeping upon them, the pressure behind Ravyn's eyes reminding him that he had been awake for far too long. It seemed like a cruel joke that only a day had passed since he'd dug up the Shepherd King's sword. It felt like a week ago.

He brought the Nightmare to the cellar off the stairs, with the stag carved above its door, and waited outside for the monster to change out of Elspeth's tattered dress. Somewhere above, the castle bell rang—five tolls.

When the Nightmare stepped out of the cellar, he was garbed head to toe in black—spare attire Jespyr had left behind. He looked as Elspeth had when they'd disguised her as a highwayman on their way to steal Wayland Pine's Iron Gate Card.

A knot choked up Ravyn's throat.

"Who will be joining us on our fair quest?" the Nightmare drawled.

"Jespyr and another Destrier—Gorse. But first, we go to Castle Yew. I need to know Emory is safe." He rolled his neck, joints popping. "I aim to ask the Ivy brothers to accompany us as well."

The knowing, mocking smile that so often snaked in the corners of the Nightmare's mouth slipped. "Good. We'll need at least one spare."

"What do you mean?"

He didn't answer. "This Destrier—Gorse. Can he be trusted?"

"No. The King bade me to bring him. The Spirit can eat him for all I care."

The word *King* held an acidic note. It was not lost on the

Nightmare. He pushed past Ravyn. "Careful, Captain. Your stony veneer is rubbing thin."

Ravyn caught his arm. The Nightmare had pulled his—Elspeth's—hair into a short plait. Ravyn blinked, tracing the plait once, twice, then a third time. "You *cut* her hair?"

The Nightmare jerked out of his grasp. "It was matted with blood."

Ravyn peered back through the cellar's open door. A pair of scissors sat upon the old wooden table. There were chunks of dark hair on the floor.

Whatever crossed his face stopped the Nightmare in his tracks. The monster peered through narrowed eyes, dropping his gaze to Ravyn's knotted hands. "It will grow back," he said slowly.

Ravyn pushed ahead without another word. When he passed a Black Horse tapestry, he ripped it off the wall with a violent yank, dusting his shoulders with mortar. He threw it to the ground, the iron rod striking stone with a loud clang. If he had known a way to rip the Shepherd King out of Elspeth and throw him on the floor, he'd have done that, too.

The Destriers waited for him near the castle doors, shifting like nervous horses at the sight of the Nightmare.

Gorse stood apart, arms crossed over his chest, looking less than thrilled to be selected for the journey.

"I'm off on the King's orders," Ravyn said, his voice echoing against the walls. He locked his hands behind his back, sure to look each Destrier in the eye. "Keep to your patrols—your training. Do as you would had I remained."

A Destrier in the back stepped forward. Oak. "Who shall we defer to in your absence, Captain?"

"Whichever Rowan—Elm or the King—sees fit to answer you."

The Destriers exchanged glances. Linden spoke, the scars on his neck stark in the early light. "You're not bringing Prince Renelm with you?"

"No." Ravyn heaved a breath. "I will return as soon as I can. Be wary, Destriers. Be clever."

"Be good," the Nightmare mocked from behind his back.

They left on horseback. The Nightmare chose a black palfrey from the stable. When he mounted, the horse's nostrils went wide, its skin rippling with noticeable distress. It reared, but the Nightmare kept his seat.

They tore through the bailey and over the drawbridge, first Gorse, then the Nightmare. Ravyn rode last. He allowed himself one final look at Stone.

There were few people in the bailey—no one watched them ride away. No one, save two tall men. One wore a golden cloak that caught the wind, and the other a plain black tunic. The King, and—

Ravyn's stomach plummeted into his boots. *Elm.*

The Nightmare slowed his pace. When he looked back at Elm, his voice drifted in the air, oil and honey and poison. "Neither Rowan nor Yew, but somewhere between. A pale tree in winter, neither red, gold, nor green. Black hides the bloodstain, forever his mark. Alone in the castle, Prince of the dark."

PART II
To Barter

Chapter Seventeen

Elspeth

In the water, neither awake nor asleep, I drifted through memories not my own.

I was a boy in richly woven clothes, standing in a wood. There were others with me. We turned through the trees with no path, our voices raised to the treetops, each person uttering their own beseech.

"Grant me health, Spirit."

"Bless me with good harvest."

"I will take Larch as my namesake for a blessing, great Spirit of the Wood."

Salt filled my nose, tickling it. I found a gnarled tree away from the crowd and put my hand on it. Pain touched my arms. When I looked down, my veins were black as ink.

I closed my eyes, magic all around me—in me. A hundred voices filled my ears. Not human voices, but another chorus. One of discord, yet harmony, that spoke almost always in rhyming words. It was my magic, my gift, to hear them. I'd been born with the fever.

I could always talk to the trees.

Your name-tree is cunning, they said, *its shadow unknown. It bends without breaking, though only half-grown. The Prince becomes King, and the King takes the throne. Will you come to the wood when Blunder's your own?*

"I will," I whispered.

What blessing do you ask, young Taxus?

"For the Spirit of the Wood to help me make Blunder a kingdom of abundance—of magic. That she might give me the tools I need to shepherd the land and its people."

The tree groaned beneath my hand, branches moving of their own accord until they all pointed west. The next tree did the same, and the one after it. On and on, they pointed me home.

When I reached the cusp of the meadow outside my father's castle, I waited. Then, near the seedling tree I'd planted on my seventh nameday, something materialized in front of me.

A stone, as tall and wide as a table. Upon it was a sword. It caught the midday light, shining like a beacon. Carved intricately upon the hilt was an image.

A shepherd's staff.

Chapter Eighteen

Elm

Elm watched the party ride away, Ravyn's note crumpling in his hand. *I'll see you soon.*

He pushed his hair out of his eyes and turned, keeping the gap between himself and his father wide. "Was this your doing?"

The King's gaze was fixed on the road ahead, his cloak billowing in the chill autumn air. "You're my son. You belong here."

"You never cared where I was or what I did before."

"I had little reason to until now." The King shot him a sidelong glance. "I'm told you sent the guards away from Ione Hawthorn's door last night. And that you spoke with her."

Elm clenched his jaw.

The King's timbre resembled the bark of one of his hounds. "Her family are vile, treasonous vultures."

"What Tyrn said at the inquest was true enough." Elm weighed his words. "Kill her, and people will talk. They'll find out about Hauth. And about who you put him in bed with for a Nightmare Card. Perhaps your court will take a harder look at you, Father. They'll see, for a man so wholly condemning of the infection, that you sure keep interesting company. Orithe Willow. Ravyn. Infected."

Displeasure deepened the lines in the King's face. "What," he said, wine on his bitter breath, "would you have me do?"

It began to rain. Elm winced against it, shrouding his voice in disinterest. "Keep Ione Hawthorn close. She can give your excuses for Hauth's absence. A symbol that all is as it ever was. For now."

In the distance, thunder rolled. The King's hand was ungloved, swollen and calloused, brutalized with age and years of swordplay. With it, he took the crown from his head. Examined it. "It rattles me to the bone, seeing your brother," he said in a low voice. "Even with his Black Horse and Scythe, he broke so easily—" He winced against the wind. "Life is fragile. The line of kings, fragile."

Elm had never spoken to his father like this, just the two of them, trading quiet words—not ever. It made his skin crawl. "Is that why Ravyn goes and I must remain? A pretense of strength?"

"Use your brain," the King snapped. "We may pretend at it, but nothing is as it was. Even should Hauth wake and face the kingdom once more, his spine is in tatters. He will never sire an heir—the Physicians are certain." He took Elm by the shoulder, his fingers prodding into weary, aching muscle. "I have Blunder to think of. Five hundred years of rule to think of."

Elm stared into his father's eyes, the words burning in his throat. "And so you reach deep into your pile of shit and pull the second Prince back into the light."

The King's grip tightened. "The throne of Blunder is Rowan. It is under our namesake tree that the Deck will be united. The mist will be lifted, the infection cured. When I die, I will be buried with my father and grandfather and their grandfathers in the rowan grove." His gaze dropped to the crown in his other hand. "And you, Renelm, will be the one to take my place."

Elm jerked out of his father's grasp. His body was screaming—denying. Bile churned, escaping up his throat into his mouth. "I don't want your throne. Hauth may yet—he may—"

"No. He will not." The King placed the crown back onto his head. He looked weathered, the wind and rain washing all pretense from him. He was just a drunk old man, grieving.

And somehow, that made it so much worse. Anger, Elm had come to expect. His father had always been a man of wrath and an abrupt, exacting temper. But this resignation—Elm did not know it. Could not stomach it.

He pulled away from the King.

"Where are you going?"

"To see Jespyr."

"She left with Emory this morning for Castle Yew."

Ravyn, Jespyr, now Emory, gone. Elm bit the inside of his cheek and kept going, hail pelting him as he crossed back into the bailey.

"I'll expect you at court tonight," his father called into the wind.

"I won't be there."

"You will, Renelm. You'll resign as Destrier. And you and Ione Hawthorn will pretend all is as it ever was, until I am ready to announce your succession. And her execution."

Elm slept the day away. He might have rolled over onto his stomach and slept through the night as well, but the echoing clamor of dinner in the great hall swept up the stairs. He woke with a start, heart pounding, sweat on his brow and chest, certain there was something he must do—something he'd forgotten.

Hawthorn. He ripped the blankets off. Ravyn and Jespyr and Emory might be gone, but Elm was far from aimless. He'd no desire to twiddle his thumbs and wait for his father to christen him heir—he had a promise to keep. A Maiden Card to find.

He stripped and scrubbed himself clean with cold water, wondering with a shiver what would happen if the King sought to kill Ione Hawthorn before they found her Maiden Card. Would she die? Or would the Maiden's magic heal her, even from a fatal blow?

His stomach knotted at the thought.

He left his chamber in a fresh black tunic and hurried down the corridor, gnashing his teeth against the raucous sound of court wafting through the castle. He knew what he would find in the great hall. Men, slipping Providence Cards between their fingers, talking too loudly of magic and money and Card trade. Mothers, ready to thrust their daughters onto his arm. His own father, grunting into his goblet, surveying his court, as if everything he held in his pitiless green eyes was owed to him.

"You look like you're about to hurl yourself down those stairs, Prince," a voice called from behind.

Elm's hand crashed into his pocket. He tapped velvet only twice before his brain caught up with his fingers. "Spirit and trees, Hawthorn, you have to stop doing that."

Ione stood half in shadow, half in light. "Sorry," she said, not sounding sorry at all. "I'd thought you'd heard me."

Her hair was fastened in a tight knot at the nape of her neck, and someone had given her a new dress. It was dark, grayish blue, the color of deep, icy water. It hugged her poorly, marring the shape of her curved body. The fabric bunched at her neck, secured by a gray ribbon just below her jaw, collar-like.

Two figures emerged out of shadow behind Ione. They

weren't the same sentries from her chamber door last night. They stood too tall—too broad—to be castle guards. And, unlike the castle guards, when they beheld Elm, they didn't cower.

Destriers. Allyn Moss and, to Elm's bottomless chagrin, Royce Linden.

"Gents," Elm said, offering them a mocking bow.

They lowered their heads in reply. Moss's eyes dropped. Linden's didn't.

"They've moved you to the royal wing, I see," Elm said to Ione. His gaze returned to the Destriers. "And you are—"

"Miss Hawthorn's guards," Linden replied.

"Not anymore. I'll see to that."

The Destriers exchanged a glance, and Linden's voice hardened. "The King wants a keen eye kept on her, lest she try to escape."

"I have two eyes, and they're keen enough." Elm pulled his Scythe out of his pocket, a quiet threat. "You're dismissed, Destriers. Enjoy your evening."

Moss hurried down the hall. Linden's pace was slower. He muttered something that sounded like *bloody git* as he passed, his eyes narrow as they darted between Elm and Ione.

Ione watched him go. Her face conveyed little, but Elm searched it anyway. When she caught him looking, he fixed his mouth with a lazy smile and offered her his arm. "I should warn you, I'm a horrid dinner companion."

Ione's hand pressed into his sleeve. The smell of her hair—floral, sweet—filled his nose. "That makes us a pair."

They walked in silence to the grand stairwell. The steward opened his mouth to announce them, but was quieted by a flick of Elm's wrist. Still, heads turned in their wake. Conversations went quiet as Elm and Ione—whom they all still assumed to be the future Queen—strode down the stairs. There were smiles, bows. Elm returned none of them.

Neither did Ione.

Elm peered down at her dark, shapeless dress. "Insulted the tailor, have we?"

"The tailor?"

"Your attire." His gaze swept down her body. "It's…it's a bit…"

Ione's voice went flat. "Please, continue. I live and breathe to hear your opinion of my gown, Prince Renelm."

"If you could even call it that." Elm plucked at the ribbon along her neck, his finger grazing the underside of her jaw. "It's the worst thing I've ever seen."

"All my dresses are back at Hawthorn House. Your father sent this one to my room."

"With his two dimmest Destriers in tow, I see."

Ahead, music swelled in the great hall, the climax of a jig. "Then your ploy during the inquest was a success."

"To a point." Elm leaned down, his voice in her ear. "My father wishes to keep everything under his thumb. Including you." He grimaced. "And, more effectively, me. We're to pretend nothing happened—speak nothing of your cousin or uncle or father—and certainly nothing of Hauth."

Ione raised her brows. "What excuse am I to give for my *betrothed's* absence?"

"Hauth is ill, but recovering."

The great hall was loud, the King's court well into their cups. Some remained seated while others gathered in groups, swaying to the music. Voices clamored against stone walls. Cheeks flushed and clothes shifted from dancing, the hall rife with forfeit sobriety.

The King's table was lifted on a dais similar to the one in the throne room. From it, green eyes watched. When Elm faced them, he noted the demand, expectancy, and annoyance stamped across his father's face. He knew what the King wanted. On his right side, in the seat that had only ever been Hauth's, there was a vacancy. An empty chair.

The High Prince's chair.

Elm pinned Ione's hand against his arm. There was no way in hell he was going up there alone.

She scowled down at his hand. "What are you—"

"One last stipulation, Hawthorn," he said through tight lips. He shot his father a void smile, pulling Ione with him to the dais. "If you want free rein of the castle, I am to be your chaperone."

Her exhale was a hiss. When they stood before the King, chins tilting in stiff reverence, Ione's eyes were so cold Elm felt a pinch of guilt for dragging her up there.

The King's displeasure was poorly masked. Still, he offered a curt nod, eyes flickering to his court, aware he was being watched. His gaze returned to Ione, bleary yet narrow, lingering a moment too long over her body—her poorly fitting dress. The corner of his lip twitched.

In that moment, he looked all the world like Hauth.

Elm slammed his hand into his pocket. Only this time, the Scythe's velvet edge did nothing to soothe him. But three taps—three taps and he could make his father roll his eyes so far back into his head he'd stop seeing straight. His finger twitched against the red Card's velvet edge, the idea headier than any wine.

Ione merely held the King's gaze, the frost in her eyes shifting to disinterest. She yawned.

"Sit," the King barked at them.

The only empty chair was Hauth's. On its right sat Aldys Beech, the King's treasurer, along with his wife and son.

Elm didn't bother to glance at them. "Shove over."

Beech's eyes, already too large for his head, bulged. "But, sire, the King has gifted us these seats—"

"I don't give a flying f—"

"What Prince Renelm means," Ione said, her voice easy, "is that, while he merely warms Prince Hauth's seat, *that* seat," she said, gesturing to the chair under Beech's narrow bottom, "belongs to me, your future Queen." She threw her gaze over her shoulder at Elm. "Unless you'd like to see me take my seat atop the Prince's lap."

Beech's eyes widened further—as did his wife's and son's. They attempted no further argument. Fleeing either her beauty or wrath, the Beech family vacated not only Ione's seat, but the dais altogether.

There was no getting comfortable. Elm half expected spikes to shoot out of Hauth's chair and impale him, the wood sensing his master's absence, conscious that the *spare* had taken his place.

What Ione had said about sitting in his lap hadn't helped him settle.

Elm ate quickly, waiting for his father to be distracted so that he and Ione might slip away from the wretched dais and continue their search for her Maiden Card.

But his father's focus was never long spent. King Rowan spoke to courtiers in grunts and nods, his gaze forward—but Elm was certain he was watching him. He was like a schoolmaster, waiting for his least-favorite pupil to step out of line.

When the gong chimed ten times, Elm let out a groan. "What a waste of time."

"You're in a mood," Ione said into her goblet, her heart-shaped mouth stained red along the inside of her lips.

"I'm always in a mood."

"A family trait, perhaps."

That set his teeth on edge. "You're not half as funny as you think you are, Hawthorn."

She took another drink. "I wouldn't know where to start, making a Rowan laugh."

Elm pressed the heels of his palms into his eyes. "I'm sorry. I'm being an ass." He flung a hand toward the great hall. "It comes easy, in this place."

"So your terrible mood has nothing to do with the party that left the castle this morning? The one with Elspeth and Ravyn Yew?"

Elm lifted his head from his hands, his eyes slow to focus. He ran his thumb along the rim of his goblet. "Who told you that?"

"The Destrier with marks on his face—Linden." She touched the high collar of her dress. "I think he thought it might hurt me, knowing my cousin was free of the castle and I wasn't."

"Did it?"

"It might have, once. I might have cried for the loneliness of it all." Her voice frosted over. "But I don't cry anymore."

The pinch of guilt Elm had felt for dragging her up to the dais wrenched. He looked out over the great hall. Most of the court was still seated at the long table, their goblets ever full, tended by servants who expertly wove through the hall. Those who stood came in a slow line to the dais, offering words of praise to his father and his council or asking after Hauth.

They should have been looking for Ione's Maiden Card, not wasting the evening on pageantry.

Once, he'd thought it necessary. He'd told Elspeth Spindle

as much on Market Day. *It's pageantry that keeps us looking like everyone else.*

Elm drained his goblet, then reached for Ione's, using the opportunity to speak into her ear. "I have another idea how we might find your Card." His breath stirred a loose strand of hair that framed her face. "But you may not care for it."

"I don't care for anything anymore, Prince. That's entirely the problem."

It was loud in the great hall. No one would find it strange that Elm might speak so near her ear. What *was* strange was Ione's quick intake of breath when he'd leaned close. The brush of pink in her cheeks. The gooseflesh along the nape of her neck.

Elm noted them all. It seemed, despite her many protestations, Ione Hawthorn could feel *some* things.

He hadn't heard the shuffling of feet. Shadows danced in Elm's periphery. He was still looking at Ione's neck when a feminine voice from below the dais said, "Good evening, Prince Renelm."

Elm pulled back—dragged his eyes forward. Wayland Pine, with his wife and their three daughters, stood before the King, the eldest slightly ahead of the rest. It was she who had spoken.

Elm couldn't for the life of him remember her name.

Like the Pines, the King was waiting for Elm to respond, wearing a glower that conveyed just how little effort it would take to reach over and throttle his son in front of them.

Pageantry.

Elm winked at his father, fixing his face with his custom brand of petulant, courtly charm. "The Pine family. How delightful." He turned to Wayland. "I was sorry to hear about your Iron Gate Card." His bruised hand flexed beneath the table. "Nasty things, highwaymen."

Wayland Pine, the poor bastard, looked close to tears at the mention of the Providence Card Ravyn had rid him of several weeks ago. "Thank you, my Prince." He bowed, his hand on his eldest daughter's back, pushing her slightly forward. "You remember Farrah, my eldest."

Elm hardly did. "Of course. Are you long at Stone, Miss Pine?"

Farrah's eyes flickered to the King. "For a week, Your Grace. For the feasts."

"For which we are most grateful to be invited," Wayland chimed, another bow.

The King raised a hand, acceptance and dismissal in a single gesture.

The Pines shuffled away, Farrah bidding Elm a backward glance. "What feasts?" he said to his father, watching the Pines disappear into the crowd.

The King leaned back in his chair. "Beginning tomorrow night, there will be six feasts. On the sixth, you will choose a wife."

It came quickly, Elm's rage. Like flames licking through a grate, he felt heat all over him. He tried to swallow it, but the pain of it was already there. His palms hurt. His eyes burned. His molars pressed so hard into each other they felt fused. For an instant, he considered flipping the table over.

If the King felt his fury, he made no note of it. "Your time under Ravyn's wing has ended. I should have married you off years ago."

With that, the King severed the discussion. He stood from his seat, everyone on the dais besides Elm and Ione standing in reverence as they watched the King and the two Destriers who shadowed him quit the great hall.

Elm felt reckless. He opened his mouth to call after his father, to unleash some of the venom pooling on his tongue, but a hand on his arm stopped him.

"You have the look of someone who's about to break something," Ione said in an even voice.

He wanted to. Elm didn't know what, but he vowed something would shatter.

Ione's grip on his arm tightened. So tight that when she stood, she pulled Elm with her. "Come, Prince. Let's get drunk."

Chapter Nineteen

Ravyn

The journey from Stone to Castle Yew was an hour's ride. They made it in nearly half the time. Better to ride fast and let the wind fill Ravyn's ears than suffer another word out of the Nightmare's mouth.

The Yews had always said their home was haunted. That the stone figures in the statuary wandered at night and the images threaded into Castle Yew's tapestries shifted one day to the next. That the torches flickered with no draft to shake them and the wood floors groaned out the name of whoever tread upon them.

The castle was eerie, though never terrifying. If anything, the spectral estate made Ravyn's family laugh. They joked that the ghosts had grown so bored by the house's current occupants that they'd been driven to restlessness.

But if there were ghosts in Castle Yew, they weren't starved for sport now. The house seemed to freeze, unearthly still, when the creature with yellow eyes stepped through the door.

The Nightmare strolled into the castle ahead of Ravyn and Gorse. He wove his fingers together, pressing them until the joints popped. His yellow eyes drifted toward the great hall, up wood panel walls, to the vaulted ceilings. Then, with an unimpressed sigh, he slipped down a corridor and disappeared.

Gorse grunted and retreated to the east wing, where the Destriers stayed when they came for training.

Ravyn's parents and their steward, Jon Thistle, hurried out of the great hall. His mother Morette's gaze was wide. "Was that—"

"Yes." Ravyn stripped off his gloves and threw them onto the floor. "The one and only Shepherd King. Save yourself the agony of speaking with him. He's remarkably vile."

"I might be, too, after living five hundred years," muttered Thistle.

Ravyn glanced to the dark stairwell. "Jes and Emory? They arrived safely?"

"They're resting upstairs."

"It's happening, then." His father, Fenir, had eyes that were like Jespyr's—warm, deep brown. They searched Ravyn's face. "The King has released Emory—for good? He'll be safe on Solstice?"

Ravyn gave a curt nod.

"Which means King Rowan has decided Elspeth's blood will unite the Deck."

Morette's voice was soft. But the weight of her words slammed into Ravyn so hard he found himself biting down. He turned away from his parents, back out Castle Yew's doors. "Emory *and* Elspeth will be safe on Solstice," he said—to them, to himself. "I'll see to it."

The short walk to the armory felt longer, quieter, without Elm at Ravyn's side.

He found Petyr and Wik Ivy—his trusted highwaymen—arguing over a whetstone. Their eyes lit when he told them he, Jespyr, Gorse, and the Shepherd King were leaving the next morning for the Twin Alders. Wik didn't wait to be asked; he volunteered straightaway to join. "Gotten fond of pinching ole Providence Cards," he said, a few gaps in his smile for teeth lost in brawls.

"It won't be like stalking the forest road and ambushing caravans," Ravyn warned. "The wood we travel into—no one's been there for centuries. I don't know what awaits us."

"Don't worry, Captain." Petyr patted Ravyn's back hard enough to make him cough. "We'll hold your hand when you get scared."

Ravyn spent the remainder of the day in Emory's room, reading to him, keeping the fire warmer than it needed to be just to see a flush in his brother's face. Only after dusk had fallen and Jespyr taken his place at their brother's bedside did Ravyn go looking for the Nightmare.

He was in the meadow, near the ruins tucked away behind Castle Yew's unkempt gardens, swathed in mist and sunset's usual grayness. He sat in grass beneath the shadow of a yew tree, his eyes distant.

He cradled something in his lap. "You've been digging," he murmured.

Ravyn glanced at the chamber at the edge of the meadow. "I found your sword." *And your bones.*

"So the thief becomes a grave robber." The Nightmare's gaze dropped to his lap. "You might have availed yourself of this, too. I imagine it has some value yet."

Ravyn stepped forward, his brow lowering. He realized the thing cradled with delicate care upon the Nightmare's lap—

Was a crown.

A golden crown that had long lost its sheen. Caked in soil, its markings were difficult to discern, though it seemed to have the same intricate, woven design as the hilt of the sword Ravyn had pried from the chamber's earthen floor.

As if reading his thoughts, the Nightmare looked up. "Where is it—my sword?"

"In my room."

"I'd like it back."

Ravyn returned to the castle. When he trudged back into the meadow, he threw the Shepherd King's sword onto the grass. "I'm not a bloody grave robber."

The Nightmare unfurled a single finger and traced the blade's hilt. Wind whispered through the yew trees, and Ravyn looked up. If he tapped his Mirror Card and waited, he was certain he'd see Tilly, watching them.

"I met your daughter. The one with braids in her hair and eyes like yours. Tilly."

The Nightmare's shoulders tightened. He kept his eyes on the sword. "You'd be wise not to use the Mirror Card so recklessly, Ravyn Yew. To see beyond the veil is a perilous thing."

"She told me you're seeking revenge for what the first Rowan King did to you."

A smile crept over his lips.

Ravyn hated the sight of it. "Your daughter's spirit has waited five hundred years in that tree for you. All your children wait."

When the Nightmare turned, his smile was gone. "I, too, have waited."

"To kill the Rowans?"

"My aim is vast. There are many truths to unveil in the wood. Circles that began centuries ago will finally loop." He let out a sigh. "Though I fear, with so many idiots around me, that I must do everything myself."

Ravyn's tongue tripped over a flood of curses. He took a steadying breath. "What is your plan for when we return with the Twin Alders Card?"

The Nightmare wrapped his fingers around the hilt of his sword. He cocked his head to the side, surveying Ravyn like a wolf might a sick, mewling fawn. "I told your uncle he would have my blood to unite the Deck on Solstice, did I not?"

"You did. But you are certainly a liar. Even under a Chalice, you lie."

"We have that in common."

"I'm nothing like you, parasite."

"But you are." The Nightmare's laugh echoed through the meadow. "More than you know." His gaze flickered over Ravyn's face. "Though undoubtably I am better rested. When was the last time you slept a night through?"

Ravyn braced himself with his arms, coating his words with spite. "When I was with Elspeth." He turned. "We meet here at dawn."

The Nightmare's voice held him back. "Bring the Maiden Card from your collection. We'll need it for the journey."

"The Maiden?"

"The pink Providence Card with a rose upon it. You know the one. Or maybe you don't. Your observational skills have proven abysmal—"

"I know which Card—" Ravyn pulled in a breath and counted to three. "Why the hell would we need a Maiden?"

The Nightmare tapped his fingernails over the crown in his lap. "Pray that we don't."

Ravyn's eyes lifted to the chamber. And because every conversation with the Shepherd King seemed to drag up the past, he said, "On the subject of Providence Cards—" He nodded at the dark window. "I found two in there when I was a boy.

I bled onto the stone, and it opened for me." He reached into his pocket and retrieved his Mirror and Nightmare Cards. "These were inside."

Those yellow eyes grew distant. "And?"

"Did you put them there?"

"No."

"Who did?" He paused. "Was it one of your children?"

The Nightmare did not speak. He had gone still. Unmoving, unblinking—staring into nothingness.

"Hello?"

No answer.

Ravyn drew a finger over his Nightmare Card. When the monster remained unfocused, he tapped the Card three times. There was a bite of salt, then Ravyn pushed the magic outward. Not to speak to the Nightmare—but to search the dark chamber of his mind.

Elspeth. Where are you?

The Nightmare's stillness broke, his gaze snapping into focus. He rose to his feet and, with impressive might, shoved Ravyn to the ground.

Salt fled Ravyn's senses as his head slammed onto grass. The cold, blunt tip of the Nightmare's sword scraped over his throat.

"I told you once before, stupid bird. You must come invited into her mind."

"And I told *you* I would find her when we were out of Stone." Ravyn's hands were fists in the grass. "It is injustice enough that the spirits of your children keep wait while you, monstrous, remain. But Elspeth is not a spirit you can ignore. She is not dead. Let. Her. Out."

Even in the darkening meadow, those yellow eyes flared. They were the only part of the Nightmare not consumed by the shadow of the yew tree, as if he were the tree itself—and the shadow. "Do you never think beyond your own selfish wants, Ravyn Yew?" he snarled. "If I called her out of darkness into my terrible mind, it would *pain* her. You cannot imagine the rage that comes with having no control over your own thoughts—your own body. You, traitorous thing, who have never truly ceded authority. Liar, thief—immune to the Chalice and Scythe—you know nothing of losing control." His lips twisted, snarl letting to a smile. "But you will. You will learn, just as I did, what it feels like to lose yourself in the wood."

Chapter Twenty

Elm

The first thing Ione did when they got to the yard was hand Elm the full flagon of wine she'd smuggled out of the great hall. The second was to rip her dress.

She used both hands, tearing the neckline down to her sternum, destroying the stifling collar. The fabric made a sharp sound, buttons flying, powerless against her impressive yank.

Elm stopped drinking. "I could have helped with that."

Ione gave her version of a smile, which was hardly a twitch of muscle in the corners of her mouth. Maybe it was all she was capable of. Or maybe she simply didn't want to give him the satisfaction of making her smile. She took the wine back. "Developed a taste for removing my clothes, have you, Prince?"

That shut him up. Elm looked away. He wanted to break things. And her, ripping her dress like that, only maddened the desire.

"Is this what you usually do," she asked, watching as he took a discarded javelin off the ground and shattered it against a nearby sparring post, "when you're drunk and angry?"

Elm snatched the flagon out of her hand. "Among other things."

"Such as?"

He met her gaze over the rim. "Can't you guess?"

If the Maiden allowed Ione a flush, it was too dark in the yard to note it. She sucked her teeth. "I hope you don't plan on talking to Farrah Pine the way you talk to me. She's sweet."

Elm handed her back the wine. "You don't care how I talk to Farrah Pine."

She sighed. "No, I don't."

Another javelin, shattered. "Just as well. I won't be speaking to any of the women on my father's list, her included."

"You had an easy enough time back at the great hall," Ione said. "For a moment, you almost sounded charming. If not a little—"

"Roguish? Utterly irresistible?"

She drank, a bead of red liquid lingering on her bottom lip. "Angry. Under it all, you sounded angry."

Elm stepped closer, suppressing the urge to run his finger over her lip and wipe the wine away. "I am angry. I think, if I'm honest, I've been angry all my life."

Ione's eyes were honed, searching the pages of him. When the silence between them sharpened to a point, she took a deep breath. "Then be angry, Prince." She handed the wine back to him. "It looks well on you."

"Careful." Elm brushed his thumb along the flagon's wet rim—where her mouth had been. "That sounded an awful lot like a compliment."

"I prefer to think of it as advice."

"I'm sure you do." He took a drink. "But you'll forgive me if I have a difficult time taking advice on how to *feel* from a woman who can't even muster a smile."

She gave half a shrug. "Give me something to smile about."

"I can think of a few."

He saw it in her eyes—the flash of surprise. The widening of her pupils. And while the Maiden shielded her expression, it didn't mask it entirely. There were still glints of something. Ione Hawthorn could feel *something*, of that Elm was certain.

She ignored his remark with a dismissive tilt of her chin. "I used to smile. I had little lines here." She ran a finger, a gentle brushstroke, from the crease in her nose to the corner of her mouth. "From laughing." She touched the outside of her eye. "Here as well. They're gone now, of course. But I used to smile. I used to laugh."

Elm's eyes remained on her face, the smoothed-out terrain of her skin. "I remember," he said quietly.

She scowled up at him and snatched the wine back, the dark liquid sloshing in the flagon. "No, you don't. I'd wager all my money you never once glanced at me before Equinox." She winced down a gulp. "If I had any money to wager."

Wagers, barters, games. That's what it boiled down to with Ione Hawthorn. Every look was a challenge, every question a test, a measurement. To what end, Elm wasn't certain. But it made him tighten, chest to groin, knowing he wanted to play her games. And maybe it was the wine, or the way those hazel eyes pinned him in place, but he wasn't ashamed to admit he'd do terrible, terrible things to win.

He fixed his mouth with a lazy smile. "Just as well you have no money. I'd take every last coin."

Ione watched him over the lip of the flagon. "You're full of shit, Prince."

Elm stepped closer to take the wine back. Only this time, his fingers folded over hers along the flagon's silver handle. He leaned in, his voice a low scrape. "You don't think I noticed you, Ione?"

A breath hastened through the slim part between her lips.

"Not before the Maiden. Men like you do not take pleasure in yellow flowers when there are roses in your garden."

"I don't take pleasure in either—horticulture's not exactly a strong suit." When she rolled her eyes, Elm tightened his hand over hers. "Wager something you do have, if you're so sure."

Their faces were close now. So close Elm could see the frayed threads along the collar where Ione had ripped her dress. They danced along her throat, her sternum, the swell of her breasts—moving with the rapid up-and-down tide of her breathing.

His eyes lifted to her face. She was watching him. And though her mouth bore no smile, there was a glimmer of satisfaction—of triumph—in her hazel gaze. "A kiss," she murmured. "If you can prove you remember me before Equinox, I'll kiss you. If you can't, I get five minutes with your Scythe."

When he found it, Elm's voice was rough. "No kiss is worth five minutes with a Scythe. Not even from you."

"One minute, then."

The urge to reach out and snag her face, to press the tips of his fingers into her cheeks and watch her lips part for him, took considerable effort to banish. Elm caught Ione's hand instead, slapping his palm against hers in a handshake. "Deal."

No one was there to see them slip out of the yard into a servants' passage. The long, winding corridors housed only shadows. For the time it took them to reach the cellar, Elm and Ione were utterly alone, as if the castle belonged only to them.

"Please don't be locked," Elm muttered when they reached the door.

The handle to the cellar turned.

The hearth hadn't been lit, and the dogs were elsewhere. Elm moved to the shelf, the space so familiar that, even half-drunk, he had no trouble finding a lantern and the fire striker.

The flame bloomed, too bright, then dimmer. Ione stood in the doorway. "What is this place?"

"Somewhere we won't be overheard." Elm headed back to the door. When he passed Ione, he made sure no part of his body touched hers. "Light a fire, will you? I prefer to be comfortable when I play games and win wagers." He turned toward the stairs.

"Where the hell are you going?" she called after him.

The indignation in her voice made the corner of Elm's mouth curl. "A Chalice, Miss Hawthorn. I'm going to fetch us a Chalice Card."

The fire was alive and breathing by the time Elm got back. Ione sat on her knees, stoker in hand, tending the flames. There was soot on her fingertips. "You took your time."

Elm's arms were full. A Chalice Card, a new flagon of wine, a silver cup, a loaf of olive bread stolen from the kitchens. The last item was from the library—an hourglass he and Ravyn used when they played chess. "I came prepared."

He hurried to the hearth, the castle's chill settling over him like a varnish. He sat cross-legged in front of the fire, opposite Ione, and opened his arms, the hourglass rolling onto the floor.

Ione picked it up. "What's this for?"

"Parameters." He set the flagon of wine, then the cup, between them. "It's dangerous to use a Chalice for too long. Even if you don't lie."

"You enjoyed my inquest so much you'd like a repeat?"

He narrowed his eyes at her. "We're looking for your Maiden, are we not? I thought we might go over Equinox night. Parse the memories you have of your Card. You were drunk, yes?"

Her voice was clipped. "Yes."

"And so your memories may not hold true. I'm hoping the Chalice will stop you, if you venture into a memory that might be false. If it proves unsuccessful, there are other Cards in my father's vault that may help us narrow our search."

"If it's my memories you want, why not use the bloody Nightmare Card my father gifted the King?"

Elm pulled the Chalice Card from his pocket. "This," he said, waving it in her face, "was in the armory, left over from yesterday. The Nightmare Card is currently being used in Hauth's chamber by the Physicians attempting to revive him. Would you like to go there and ask them for it?"

Her mouth drew into a fine line.

"Neither would I. And so, we begin with the damn Chalice."

Ione ran a finger over the curved shape of the hourglass, tilting it so that a few grains spilled into the second half. "It feels rather unfair, seeing as I've already endured an inquest, to be the only one put under the Chalice."

"You won't be. I'll be joining you." When the corners of Ione's mouth twitched, a smile slid over Elm's mouth. "How else am I to prove I remember you and win our little wager?"

"Then let us be equal. For every question I answer about Equinox, you must answer one of your own."

Elm was aware, somewhere in the back of his head, that this was a terrible idea. He had far too many secrets, and none of them pleasant. But the cellar was warm, and the wine he'd consumed in the yard had settled into him. He didn't want to break anything anymore. This terrible idea felt unreasonably good.

"All right."

"Any topics you wish me to avoid, Prince?"

Ravyn. Emory. The Shepherd King. His childhood. His brother.

His father. The impending doom of his life, should he be forced to marry a stranger, forced to become King—

Elm swallowed. "Nothing is off-limits."

Ione tapped her fingers on the stone floor. "And our wager? When do I get my minute with your Scythe?"

"That," Elm said, a low laugh humming in his throat, "we can save for last." He dipped the flagon, filling the cup with wine. "Think of it as a reward."

That seemed to please her—not that her face showed it. But she lifted her chin and stretched her arms over her head, loosening herself. Then she turned the hourglass over and placed it on the stone floor between them.

The sand began to fall. Elm took the turquoise Card into his palm and kept his eyes on Ione. "Ready?"

She nodded. He tapped the Chalice, watching Ione's throat as she tipped her head back and drank from the cup. When she winced down the wine, she passed it to him.

Elm hesitated only a moment, partially because the Chalice always turned the wine sour, partially because of the low, hot twinge in his gut that told him, after this, there was no going back. Once laid bare to Ione Hawthorn, he would forever be laid bare, just as Ravyn had laid himself bare to Elspeth.

And look where that had gotten him.

Elm winced at the thought. Then, before Ione could note his hesitation, he threw his head back and drained the cup. The wine coated his tongue, so bitter he coughed. He wiped his mouth with the back of his hand. "I hate that part."

"Under a Chalice often?"

"Mercifully, no. And *that*," he said, pointing a finger in her face, "was your first question. Now it's my turn." He leaned forward, elbows on his knees. "Where's your Maiden Card?"

Her sigh came out a low, irritated hiss. "You'll have to do better than that, Prince. I simply don't know."

Elm crossed his arms, feeling like a sullen boy under her withering stare. "How is that possible?"

"It's my turn." Eyes never leaving his, Ione pressed a finger into her bottom lip. Weighing. Measuring. "Why didn't you go with your cousin Ravyn and the others this morning?"

"Straight for the throat, then." Elm ran a hand over his face. "I wasn't invited to join them. Forbade, actually."

"Why—"

"My turn, Hawthorn." This time, he chose his words well. "What *can* you remember from Equinox?"

Ione's expression remained smooth, though her shoulders stiffened. "I remember sitting on the dais, just as I did tonight. Everyone was coming up to offer Hauth and me congratulations on the engagement. There was talk of my father's Nightmare Card. I was trying to speak to Hauth—trying to know him. But for every question I asked him, every bit of exuberance or enthusiasm I tendered, I gained a bit of his scorn."

Her voice quieted. "I saw it, plain on his face, that he didn't know how to talk to me, merely look at me—and only after I was using the Maiden Card. He said, like I'd surprised him in an unpleasant way, 'You are very animated, Miss Hawthorn.' "

"He's a bloody idiot."

Ione didn't seem to hear him. "I was nervous, and Hauth kept signaling servants to fill my goblet. I drank, and the rest of the night is fuzzy, measured only in glimpses. I remember I was cold—that there was cracked stone beneath my hand." Her voice softened. "Mostly, I remember the sharp feeling of salt in my nose."

Elm's gaze snapped to her face. "From the mist? Or something else?"

Ione lifted an idle finger to her torn collar, tracing the frayed edge. Just like in the corridor last night, when the subject of losing her Maiden Card on Equinox was broached, she didn't meet Elm's eye.

He'd assumed she'd misplaced it in a state of celebratory folly. But the salt, and this—this reluctance to look at him—

Something felt wrong. Very wrong. Like Elm had opened a door he shouldn't have. A door that kept dark, unspoken things tucked away.

He had a door of his own just like it.

"Hauth," he said, his voice dangerously low. "Hauth used his Scythe on you, didn't he?"

Slowly, Ione nodded. "He made sure I was drunk first." She refilled the cup and took a deep drink. "I woke the next morning in his room, still wearing my Equinox dress. And the Maiden your father gave me—I was still under its influence. But the Card itself"—she opened an empty palm—"was gone."

Elm's jaw ached with strain. "Did he—"

"He didn't touch me. He made a point to tell me he hadn't. Not to show restraint or respect—merely to let me know he could have, had he wanted to. And would, whenever he liked." Ione drew in a long, tired breath. "He wouldn't tell me where he'd made me hide my Maiden Card. I pleaded, but he didn't relent. He said it would be easier, being his betrothed, if I didn't *feel* things so keenly."

Her eyes returned to Elm. "Your brother seemed to understand, better than I'd realized, that he was cruel, and that I, his future wife, carried my heart upon my sleeve. He decided, without hesitation, that I should be the one to change and not him. That life would be infinitely better for the both of us if I simply felt nothing at all."

Every word came out a curse. "He's a brute," Elm said. "He

does whatever it takes to make a brute of everyone he comes across. That's what he *likes*." He thought about touching her but held back. He didn't think she'd want to be comforted by a Rowan.

He held her gaze instead, reaching into the ice behind her eyes. "I'm sorry he did that to you. I'm sorry no one stopped him. I'm sorry you didn't feel safe enough to say anything." His voice softened. "Trees, Hawthorn, I'm sorry."

Ione's eyes widened. She went completely still but for her thumb, which ran in slow circles along the rim of the cup. "Is that what happened to you?" she said, her voice hardly a whisper. "No one stopped him—no one was safe enough to tell?"

And there it was. The coal deep within Elm. The beginning of his inferno, his rage. Anger, a lifetime in the making. "You've heard the rumors, then."

She nodded.

He dragged a hand over his face and heaved a long, rattling breath. "Ravyn," he managed. "Eventually, I told Ravyn what Hauth was doing to me."

"And he took you away?"

Elm nodded, slipping his hand into his pocket, his fingers dragging against velvet. His eyes stung, anger licking up his throat. "When my mother died, I inherited her Scythe. Suddenly, I wasn't just a boy Hauth could beat and break and use his own Scythe on. I could protect myself. So I did. I became better with the red Card than he'd ever been." His smile was derisive. "And he hated me all the more for it."

Ione's thumb had stopped moving on the rim of the cup. Elm forced himself to look at her, daring her to feel sorry for him.

But there was no pity in her hazel eyes. She handed Elm the wine. "My girlish fancies of marrying a Prince were quick to die. Your brother's charm was skin-deep. The real Hauth beat and clawed his way through life." Each word was the prick of a pin. "Sooner or later, someone was going to claw him back. And my dearest cousin, or what is left of her, was merciless in the task."

"I'm not sorry he's broken—only that it was not me doing the breaking." Elm took a deep drink. "Does that make me wicked?"

"If it does, you and I are the same kind of wicked."

The tangled mess in Elm's chest eased. It surprised him to note that the hourglass was more than halfway empty—that he had held a candle to the darkest part of himself, and not once had he tried to lie about it.

Ione's brow furrowed. "Why did it take you so long to inherit a Scythe?"

"What do you mean?"

"You said you inherited your mother's Scythe. But there are four Scythe Cards. And the Rowans own them all."

"An old lie."

Her brows perked. "You don't own all four Scythes?"

Elm shook his head. "We only carry three. One for the King, one for my brother, and one for me. Wherever the fourth Scythe rests, it is not with us. We make like it's in the vault, but it isn't." He took a swill of wine. "I had a lot of catching up to do when I finally inherited the red Card."

"But you did catch up," Ione said, watching him intently. "Quickly."

Hair fell into Elm's eyes. He pushed it back. Cleared his throat. "I've forgotten whose turn it is to ask a question."

Ione grabbed the wine out of his hand. "Yours."

"If Hauth was hell-bent on keeping you under the Maiden's magic, he'd likely make you hide your Card somewhere no one else might touch it. Do you remember going anywhere secluded? Somewhere in the gardens—the vaults—away from the crowd?"

"It's no use, Prince. The only clear thing I remember is salt, and cracked stone beneath my hand." She paused, her tongue passing back and forth over her inner bottom lip. "I have a blurry memory of spinning torchlight. I was dancing in the garden with Hauth. There were other male voices nearby. When Hauth dropped my hand and I fell, they laughed. Grasped at me."

Venom pooled in Elm's mouth. Whatever Ione saw in his face, it was enough to make her pause. "I am unharmed, Prince. All in one piece. One icy, heartless piece."

"That isn't funny."

"Don't grit your teeth so hard. I didn't expect we'd discover my Card within the hour." Her eyes dipped to the hourglass. "There are a few moments left. Let's talk about something different. Something besides my Maiden."

Elm rubbed his palms on his knees. "Ask me anything."

"How old are you?"

"Twenty-two vexing years. And you?"

"The same. Though I imagine my years were easier earned than yours." Her gaze shifted over his black tunic, then back to his face.

Elm studied those hazel eyes. "The way you look at me from time to time—it's as if you're searching me. What exactly are you looking for?"

"Maybe I find you handsome."

His lips quirked. "But that's not the only reason you look at me."

Ione's expression was smooth, carved out of marble, giving nothing away. "And me, Prince? Do you find me beautiful?"

Elm's laugh chafed his throat. "There's not a person in this castle who doesn't."

"That's half an answer."

"So was yours."

Her eyes narrowed. Slowly, Ione said, "I've been looking for Hauth in your face. For temper or cruelty or indifference." She leaned forward. "But I can't find any. I see guile, tiredness, fear. Anger, without a trace of violence." She drew in a breath. "You are both Rowans—and less similar than I ever imagined."

Elm felt something deep within him stir. He leaned back, resting his weight on his arms, ready to steer the conversation as far away from his brother as it could go. "You said you can't feel anything anymore. Yet I've watched your cheeks go pink. You feel heat, cold. Pain. What else can you feel?"

The light in the cellar was dim—but not dim enough to mask the faint flush in Ione's cheeks. "I c-can't—" She snapped her mouth shut, tried again. "N-n-noth—"

The Chalice didn't let her lie. What intrigued Elm was that she'd tried to. "Don't fight it."

She sucked her bottom lip into her mouth and scowled. For a moment, she looked like she might waste her breath again on lying. But then she took another drink of wine and said, "Desire. I can still feel desire."

Elm sat up on an exhale. "And how, Miss Hawthorn, did you discover that?"

"It's *my* turn to ask."

He opened his hands, offering himself up.

"Do you know where my mother and brothers are?"

The right question. But the wrong choice of words. "No." Energy pooled in Elm's palms. He tapped his fingertips on the floor. Wine. He needed more wine. "What kind of desire?" He dragged the cup out of Ione's hands and refilled it, watching her over the rim as he drank. "Spare no detail."

He didn't miss the way her eyes flew to the hourglass. The sand was almost gone. She could wait it out—punish him with silence and not answer the question. He deserved it, of course, the subject of desire decidedly *un*Princely—

"My skin feels overwarm. Especially here," Ione said, running her thumb down the center of her mouth. "And here." Her fingers trailed over ripped fabric below her collarbone. "Here." She lowered her hand, pressing it into her dress, just below her navel. Her eyes lifted, crashing into Elm's. "Between my legs. A thrumming, unquiet ache. A cruel trick of the Maiden, I think. My body is the same as it ever was. I can feel all the physical sensations of attraction. But my heart remains... locked."

Elm's mouth went dry, the hazy edges of his vision hurtling into sharp focus. He'd watched her hand go down her body—felt his own body respond. Wherever that unquiet ache was, he wanted to find it. Touch it. Put his mouth on it.

He swallowed, his words so rough they scraped out of him. "Do you feel it now?"

When her eyes stayed on his, he knew the answer.

Elm dropped his gaze to the hourglass. Empty. He ran the tip of his tongue over his bottom lip. "It's time, Hawthorn. Our wager."

Ione folded her arms in front of her. "Where's your Scythe?"

Elm retrieved it from his pocket, twirling it between his middle and index fingers.

"All right then, Prince," she said, the needle returning to her voice. "Make your case. Prove you remember me before Equinox."

He smiled. "Let's see—which memory of Ione Hawthorn shall I pull from...?" He took a long sip of wine, savoring the moment like he did before crushing Ravyn in chess. "How about when you were a girl and rode your father's horse on the forest road without shoes, yellow hair in the wind, mud caked up to your ankles? Or perhaps a more recent time. Equinox, two years ago. No one asked you to dance, so you simply danced alone—rather well, I might add."

Elm set the wine down and leaned forward. Even seated, he towered over her. "The smile lines, I was fond of." His gaze traced the corners of her mouth, her eyes. "Your eyelashes were blonder. You had freckles and red patches of skin. A gap between your front teeth. Your eyes are the only thing the Maiden hasn't altered too much. Only, before Equinox, they were happy."

He dipped his chin. A sharp floral scent filled his nose. "You were the strangest girl I'd ever seen. Because no one at Stone is happy. They pretend at it, or drink, but the performance has its tells. But not you. You were... painfully real."

Ione was frozen. Elm pulled back and slid the Chalice Card off the floor, holding it up between them. He wouldn't gloat. But it would be very, very easy. "Game's over, Hawthorn. Any last words?"

It seemed to hit her at once. What he'd said. That she'd lost their wager. "Go to hell, Prince."

Elm laughed, deep and loud enough to shake the barbs in him. "You have a wonderful mouth." He tapped the Chalice three times, severing its hold. "And now, it's all mine."

He hooked Ione's chin between his thumb and index finger, the same way she'd held his in the dungeon, and leaned in, halting just before their lips grazed. When Elm whispered into her mouth, he made sure to touch her bottom lip with his thumb, where he knew she'd be warm. "You really thought I wouldn't remember you?"

She had. He could tell by the flare in her eyes.

"All that talk of pleasure and warmth and that terrible, unquiet ache between your legs," he murmured. "You painted such a pretty picture for me. And wouldn't it be fun, denying me a kiss, had I lost our bet? To take my Scythe and render me helpless?" His top lip brushed hers. "Tell me, Hawthorn—does it make you *feel* something, toying with me like this?"

Her breath came in sharp, quick inhales. Her lips parted, and Elm's thumb slipped over her wet inner lip. When she looked up at him, there was enough honesty in her eyes to render a Chalice useless. "Yes."

"Then do it," he whispered, gliding a hand up her spine. "Use me. Toy with me. Feel something, Ione."

She lost a breath, and Elm sucked it into his mouth. That hazel gaze hardened a moment, cold and distrusting, but whatever Ione saw in his face was enough to make them thaw. She closed her eyes and leaned forward, pressing her lips against Elm's in a hard, punishing kiss.

The cup clattered against stone. Elm reared forward, sweeping Ione onto the floor, her hair soaking up spilled wine. His mouth found her jaw. He dragged kisses across it, then down the column of her neck, breathing her in with unsteady gasps.

A hungry flutter of noise scraped up Ione's throat, her hands frenzied. They grabbed at Elm's face, his hair, the muscles along his arms. She caught his wrist on an inhale, paused a beat, then shoved his hand against her breast.

Elm moaned, his palm filled with her. He kneaded with unrestrained fingers, spurred by the quickening breaths that bloomed from Ione's parted lips. She clearly wanted him to be rough with her. And he could. It was what he was most familiar with.

But if he was rough, it wouldn't last. And for a reason he had no time to work out, Elm wanted it to last with Ione Hawthorn. He softened his grip and slowed his hands, trailing them down to the undersides of her breasts, feeling the weight of them.

Then, so quick all Ione could do was gasp, he pushed them upward, meeting the pearl-soft skin with a kiss.

Her nails scraped through his hair and she arched her back, impatient. Her scent filled Elm's nose, sharpest in the line between her breasts. He ran his mouth slowly over them, between them. She smelled of magnolia trees and fields during the first summer rain. Heady, sweet, wistful.

It undid him. For a moment, he lost focus, every thought bowing to Ione and her smell and her thrumming ache, which, sometime between collecting her at Hawthorn House and there, on the floor of the cellar, had become Elm's ache as well.

He tried to kiss more of her, but her dress—that stupid fucking dress—was in the way. He reached for her torn collar, gripping the fabric with both hands.

Their eyes met, bleary and wild.

Ione seemed to understand. "Tear it off," she said. "Now."

Elm brought her bottom lip into his mouth. Pressed it with the tips of his teeth. "Beg me to."

She inhaled, to kiss or curse him—

A noise in the room pulled Ione's focus, her eyes darting to the cellar door. Which was now open.

Filick Willow, with his hounds and books, stood, wide-eyed, arrested at the threshold.

Elm dragged his hands off Ione and shot the Physician a murderous glare. "Are we no longer knocking, Filick?"

"I—I did knock." Filick's gaze flew to Ione. "Apologies, Miss Hawthorn, I'll just—" He hurried out of the room, leaving his dogs behind. One of them settled into his bed of hay in the corner. The other came over, tail wagging, and licked Elm across the face.

He reached for Ione, but she was already off the floor and on her feet, wine in her hair. "He's not going to say anything," Elm said, adjusting himself in his pants.

She hurried toward the door. "Wait, Hawthorn," Elm called after her. "Ione. Wait."

She didn't.

Chapter Twenty-One

Elspeth

The past sank into me in that dark, bottomless water until I was a part of it.

I stood in a castle, opposite a young woman. She was shorter than me, with dark hair, copper skin, and piercing yellow eyes. She was the sun—I felt her warmth even in the cold corridor as we walked together.

Ayris. My younger sister.

Light came through arched windows, catching dust particles that fell onto green woolen carpets. "Oh no," Ayris said, looking up at me. "There's a bruise under your eye."

I shrugged. "Training."

"With Brutus, no doubt. Only a fool would mark up your face before coronation." Her eyes rose to my head. "How does it feel—wearing the crown?"

I reached into my hair and touched something cool, its weight firm. "Like providence."

When we got to the gilded door at the end of the corridor, the guards opened it. One of them was young, a boy my own age of seventeen. He had green eyes—and not one but two bruises upon his face. He winked at Ayris, then me. "Good luck, Taxus."

“Nitwit,” my sister muttered beneath her breath.

The doors opened to a cathedral. Stained glass caught the light, turning gray stones a brilliant spectrum of color. Violet, green, pink, red, burgundy, blue. The colors danced before my eyes, so bright and beautiful I wanted to catch them—put them in my pocket.

Lords and ladies stood around me as I took my seat in my late father’s chair. The one forged of old, bent trees. “Long live Taxus,” came my court’s jubilant call. “Long live the Shepherd King.”

Elspeth.

Elspeth.

Elspeth!

I opened my eyes to darkness. Someone called to me, an oily voice. The longer he called, the more desperate his tone became.

I tried to swim toward the sound of his voice, but the water—the net of memories—held me fast. I could not move, could not speak.

Could not get out.

Chapter Twenty-Two

Ravyn

The quest to reclaim the final Providence Card was afforded no clamorous send-off. There was no applause, no music—no rose petals or handkerchiefs thrown when Ravyn quit Castle Yew.

The morning was eerily quiet. A cold snap had passed over Blunder, leaving frost in its wake. No one was there to bid him goodbye at dawn, save his parents—who watched him now from Emory's window.

They'd hugged him, graciously accepting his loss for words like they always did. He'd managed the same meager farewell he'd tendered Elm.

"I'll see you soon."

When he entered the meadow, the others were already waiting by the chamber.

Jespyr and Gorse appeared to have claimed as little sleep as Ravyn. The Ivy brothers, too. They were all bleary-eyed in the dim morning light, bent under their travel satchels. Jespyr slung a bow and a quiver full of goose-fletched arrows over her shoulder and fought back a yawn.

Petyr tossed a copper coin between his hands. He elbowed Jespyr in the ribs. "Rise and shine, princess."

"I see the lucky coin's along for the trip." She poked a finger into Petyr's dark, curly hair. "You know luck is all in your head, don't you?"

"There's nothing in his head," Wik said, biting into a piece of dried venison.

Gorse's gaze shifted over the Ivy brothers. "Who the hell are you two?"

"Courtesans, here to make your journey a little sweeter," Petyr said, puckering his lips. "How about a morning kiss, Destrier?"

Ravyn rubbed his eyes. "I asked them to join. Best practice is to ignore them." His eyes traced the meadow. "Anyone seen our *friend*?"

"You mean Spindle?" Gorse jerked his head west. "She was in the armory."

Ravyn kept his face guarded behind a crumbling facade of indifference. "That's not Elspeth."

On silent step, the Nightmare emerged out of the mist. Eyes wide with intent, he was the only member of their party who seemed fully awake. Only, instead of its usual malicious grin, his mouth wore a grimace.

"Why the sour face?" Jespyr called.

The Nightmare said nothing. His sword was noticeably sharper and had been meticulously cleaned—and so had his crown. It shone, a vibrant gold against the gray morning light. Ravyn traced its design, noting that the crown was carved to depict twisting branches.

It was not so different from his uncle's crown. Only the branches hewn of gold were not rowan, but another. More gnarled—more bent and awry.

The Nightmare tightened his hand in a clawlike grip around the crown, saying nothing as he pushed through the party to the stone chamber. He slid like a shadow through its darkened window. When he returned, the crown was gone.

Ravyn's voice was clipped. "You don't want to wear it into the wood?"

Yellow eyes narrowed over him. "It's not for me to wear anymore."

Ravyn turned to the group, salt brushing his nose. "Everyone have their charms?"

Jespyr wore a small femur bone on a string around her neck. The Ivy brothers had identical hawk feathers fastened on their belts. Gorse, like most Destriers, kept a horsehair charm around his wrist.

"Guard them well." Ravyn patted the extra charm he kept in his pocket—the head of a viper. "We'll be in the mist some while."

Gorse shifted his weight. "How long?"

"As long as it takes to find the Twin Alders Card. If that does not suit you"—Ravyn gestured back toward the meadow—"return to Stone. Or does the King expect a full report on my actions?"

Gorse snapped his mouth shut and glowered.

Ravyn was used to being glared at by a Destrier. He had none of Hauth's or even Elm's Rowan charm—never knew how to motivate men with words. His coldness, and his infection, had always made him an exacting, albeit unpopular, Captain of the Destriers.

So be it. Ravyn didn't give a damn what esteem Gorse held him in, so long as it was coated in fear. He held the Destrier's gaze long enough for Gorse to drop his eyes, then turned to the Nightmare. "Lead the way."

A low hiss slid out of the monster's lips. He pushed off the yew tree and turned east. When they entered the mouth of the wood, the mist swallowed them whole.

There was no path. Even had there been one, Ravyn could tell by the Nightmare's erratic steps that he would not have taken it. Sword gripped in a vise, he weaved between trees, lithe and silent, stopping only on occasion to look up at the tangled canopy of branches. An hour they spent, chasing him in crooked lines through the wood.

All the while, the ire etched onto the Nightmare's face deepened.

"Do you even know where you're going?" Gorse hollered, bringing up the rear. "We've changed directions five times over."

The Nightmare stopped abruptly, bent to one knee beneath a gnarled yew tree, and pressed his bare fingers against the trunk. He closed his eyes, his mouth forming words Ravyn could not hear.

The sounds of rustling leaves stopped. Birdsongs and the lilt of the wind through branches died to nothingness. Ravyn's skin prickled, silence washing over him. It was as if the Nightmare had called out in the language of the wood.

And the wood had stopped to listen.

Jespyr came up from behind. "*The Old Book of Alders,*" she murmured, watching the Nightmare run his fingers over the yew trunk, "is about the barters the Shepherd King made for Providence Cards. But he was born with magic." Her stance was rigid. "What was it?"

The Nightmare closed his eyes and tapped his sword on the yew tree three times. *Click, click, click.* From his mouth, Ravyn distinguished a single word. "Taxus."

The answer to Jespyr's question came ripping through the earth. The whole wood shook—quaking from deep beneath its soil. The ground rolled, knocking Ravyn and Jespyr into each other. They fell in a heap next to Petyr and Wik and Gorse, who stared up from the ground, wide-eyed.

The forest was *moving*, yew trees rearranging themselves. Roots wrenched from the earth, clouding the air with dirt. Branches snapped and leaves whirled all around them, caught in the windstorm of shifting trees.

The Nightmare centered himself in the tumult, crouched on his haunches, untouched by root or branch. He tapped his sword once more—this time on the ground—the sound distinct in the ripping din. *Click, click, click.*

The yew trees stopped moving. At the Nightmare's feet, beneath the litter of upturned soil and leaves and broken branches, was a path through the wood.

Cold sweat pooled in Ravyn's palms. He'd read *The Old Book of Alders* his entire life.

But this was his first true glimpse at the man who'd written it.

The Nightmare stood to full height. He looked over his shoulder at the party where they lay in the dirt.

"What," Jespyr called, incredulous, "is a *Taxus*?"

"An old name, for an old, twisted tree." When he caught Ravyn's gaze lingering at his sword, he traced a pale finger over the hilt. "Surely you didn't think it was sheep I shepherded."

The furrows in the Nightmare's brow deepened as they walked through the wood.

Ravyn didn't ask what was bothering him, and the monster offered no explanation. He hadn't said a word since the trees had rearranged themselves, making a path through the previously impenetrable wood. That had been hours ago.

So be it. The furrow between dark brows—the cold, permanent snarl—was a face Ravyn had never seen Elspeth wear. It was easier to hold the Nightmare in his periphery and not, a thousand times over, think it was Elspeth next to him. It kept him grounded. Miserable, but grounded.

And aware enough to see the wolves.

The first watched from the tree line, a beast with black fur and unblinking silver eyes.

"Hurry up," Jespyr called to Gorse, her bow fitted with an arrow.

Gorse pointed the tip of his sword to the tree line. "There are two of them."

"Three," Wik corrected. "Poor little pony can't count."

"Don't teach much arithmetic in Destrier school, do they?" Petyr chimed.

Ravyn kept his gaze forward. There were *four* wolves, actually, stalking them down the darkening path. He quickened his step until his mouth was in the Nightmare's ear. "We need to find higher ground."

The Nightmare said nothing.

"Nightmare."

The monster kept his eyes forward.

Ravyn shoved his hand into his pocket and tapped his burgundy Card. Salt shot up his nose into his mouth. He pushed it outward on a fiery breath. *I'm talking to you, parasite.*

Before she'd disappeared, entering Elspeth's mind had felt like slipping into a storm. Chaotic, windblown. But the Nightmare's mind was smooth, controlled, silent but for that strange, oily voice.

Only now, that voice was screaming.

Where are you, Elspeth? WHY WON'T YOU ANSWER ME?

Ravyn lost a step and knocked into the Nightmare's shoulder.

The monster reeled, yellow eyes flashing. His hand came to Ravyn's throat, fingers flexing.

It had never made sense how Hauth and Linden had been maimed, their bodies cleaved. Elspeth never wielded a weapon. Fingers should not make the lacerations hers had made, claw-like the way they'd torn through flesh.

But now, with the Nightmare's fingertips pressed into his throat, Ravyn was beginning to understand. They might look like fingers. But under the surface, there was something distinctly jagged.

The Nightmare blinked, his gaze coming into sharp focus. His grip on Ravyn's throat eased, but he didn't drop his hand. *I'd thought you'd learned your lesson about poking through minds uninvited.* His mouth curled in a snarl. *But you're a stubborn, stupid bird, aren't you?*

Blood drained from Ravyn's face. "Elspeth. You—you can't find Elspeth?"

The Nightmare said nothing. But for a sliver of a moment, his ire shifted to an expression Ravyn had not yet seen on the monster's face.

Despair.

Panic reached its fingers into Ravyn's chest. *Don't play with me, Shepherd King. Let her out of the dark. Let me talk to her. NOW.*

Jespyr shoved them apart. "If you two idiots can't focus, I'll be happy to lead this party. There are *wolves* at our backs."

The Nightmare's eyes drifted over her shoulder. When they landed on the wolf with silver eyes, the ire in his face vanished behind a smile. "Good," he said. "We're close."

The journey to the Twin Alders will three barters take. The first comes at water—a dark, mirrored lake.

The lake did indeed look like a silver mirror. It reflected the sky, the trees—their faces—upon its smooth, indifferent surface. Gorse touched the water and pulled back with a shiver. Jespyr secured her bow over her shoulder. The Ivy brothers passed bread between themselves.

Ravyn watched the wolves, now seven in number, line up fifty yards behind them. "They stalked us here. Why?"

The Nightmare crouched next to him, dipping the tip of his sword into the lake. "Why risk their lives when the water would happily kill us for them?"

Ravyn's gaze whipped back to the lake. It didn't look deadly. "Poison?"

The Nightmare's laugh hummed in his throat. "Magic."

The lake stretched on for miles. It would take them hours to go around. "We must swim to the other side?" Ravyn asked.

A nod.

"What kind of magic?"

"The kind the Spirit likes so well. A barter." The Nightmare's hand tightened around the hilt of his sword. "A drop of blood. Then the water will make of us what it will. If we survive the crossing, she will grant us safe passage to the next barter."

Ravyn kept his gaze on the water. Like Castle Yew—like the wood—the lake seemed to go eerily still in the Nightmare's presence. As if it had been waiting for him.

They drew blood. Ravyn dragged the edge of his dagger across his thumb, then squeezed the calloused tip over the lake's surface. He watched one—two—three droplets fall, staining the water's surface a fleeting crimson.

Jespyr and Gorse and the Ivy brothers did the same, cutting thin lines along the insides of their hands and bleeding into the water. When the Nightmare held the edge of his sword to his open palm, Ravyn stopped him.

"Keep your cut shallow," he said. "Don't give her a scar."

There it was again—that pained expression that crossed the monster's face. The one that looked like despair. More than wolves or the lake, that look terrified Ravyn. He stepped closer, lowering his voice so only the Nightmare could hear. "Tell me what's happening." A lump rose in his throat. "You can't reach Elspeth?"

The Nightmare looked out over the water. So quick Ravyn hardly saw it happen, he dragged his thumb across the edge of his sword and shoved it into the water. "Swim fast, Ravyn Yew."

He dove headfirst into the lake, shattering the smooth visage of the mirror.

Ravyn and Jespyr exchanged a tight glance. Gorse looked back at the wolves, who'd snuck twenty yards closer. He swore under his breath and dove into the lake, leaving short, choppy waves. Wik followed. Petyr kissed his lucky coin and joined them.

Ravyn looked at his reflection in the water. And maybe he was scared—maybe he was imagining things. Because the man who looked back up at him was not him. Not fully. He wasn't wearing the same clothes—his head was covered by a hood, a cloth mask obscuring his face. He wasn't the Captain of the Destriers, but the other Ravyn. The one who stalked the forest road.

The highwayman.

"Are you with me, Jes?"

His sister's voice was close, just as it always was. "I'm right behind you."

Ravyn bent his knees. To the sound of howling wolves, he dove off the embankment.

In stories, sirens were beautiful women whose songs pulled men into the deep. They were not dressed in black cloaks with masks fastened to their faces. They were not highwaymen.

But the creature that reached from the depths of the lake and took Ravyn by the ankle was.

His fingers were icy, piercing through Ravyn's boot and into his skin. He spoke with Ravyn's voice—wore Ravyn's face, his gray eyes bright. "Swim no farther," he said. "The freedom you seek has always been here, behind the mask. Be who you like. Love the infected woman. Steal, betray. Flout the King's law. Stay."

It was a test, honed by his blood—a trick of the Spirit of the Wood. To fortify him—

Or to drown him.

Ravyn flailed in the water. Lungs burning, he aimed a kick at the highwayman's face and wrenched away.

The weight of his clothes, his blades, was enormous. But he was strong. He'd never had a choice but to be strong. Ravyn breached the lake's surface and took a deep, gasping breath, searching frantically for the others. He saw Wik ten strokes ahead, then Petyr, struggling to keep up. "There are fucking demons in the water," he screamed.

"Get off me!" Gorse shouted somewhere nearby, his voice clogged with water.

Jespyr came into view. She was swimming fast, sucking in frantic gulps of air. Ahead of all of them was the Nightmare. He'd almost reached the embankment at the other side of the lake. Whatever monster chased him beneath the water, the bastard was outswimming it.

Ravyn's voice boomed over the lake. "Black Horse, Jes!" Icy water slipped into his mouth. "*Swim.*"

She didn't need telling twice. Jespyr disappeared a second

under the water. When she reemerged, her pace quickened tenfold. Ahead, Gorse did the same. He tapped his Black Horse Card and then the two of them were identical streams—currents pushing through the silver water—kicking with unearthly speed toward the shore.

Ravyn and the Ivy brothers were still in the center of the lake. And the monsters beneath the surface were catching up.

Legs pounding, Ravyn broke his pace to pull a knife from his belt. This time, when a hand found his ankle, he was ready.

The highwayman beneath the water yanked him back. "Stay, Ravyn Yew," he said once more. "The man beneath the mask—that is who you are meant to be."

Ravyn took in a gulping breath and let himself be pulled beneath the water until he was eye to eye with the highwayman, then plunged his knife into the monster's shoulder. A shattering scream shook the water. The monster flailed and disappeared into the deep.

Ravyn returned to the surface just in time to see Petyr get dragged under.

He dove, following the stream of bubbles that fled Petyr's open mouth. The lake monster beneath them had Petyr's body and face, but it was cloaked as a Destrier, and its fingers were long—tipped by claws that latched into Petyr's leg. Even when Ravyn levied the monster with a kick, those claws held on.

Ravyn wrapped an arm around Petyr's middle and pulled with all his strength against the monster's might. When they breached the surface, water blinded him—choked him. All he could think to do was drag in the occasional breath—just enough to keep himself conscious as he pulled Petyr toward the shore. He couldn't see, couldn't breathe—

His legs tangled in mud. The water shallowed, and then Ravyn was flinging himself onto the shore, crawling over the embankment out of the lake, dragging Petyr—and the monster fastened to his leg—with him.

Voices shouted, feet squelched through the mud. Jespyr, then Wik, grabbed Ravyn and Petyr by their shoulders.

Petyr wailed, kicking. The monster at his leg opened its mouth, letting out a shriek that echoed over the lake. Its claws flexed, tearing into flesh and muscle.

A ring of steel—a flash of light. The Shepherd King's sword cleaved the air.

There was another wrenching scream. Ravyn watched as the monster with Petyr's face staggered back. Its eyes rolled and its head fell from its shoulders onto the lake's muddy lip.

Ravyn tried to pull himself up—

And saw the blood.

Petyr's left pant leg was in tatters. So was the skin beneath it. His calf was open in long, red seams where the monster's claws had found purchase. Even through a wince, Ravyn could see there was something wrong with the wound. It wasn't bleeding freely as it should have been. The blood was coagulating too fast, slow as sludge as it slid from Petyr.

The odor came next—putrid as an animal carcass left to rot.

"What the hell is that smell?" Gorse said, his pallor going a sickly green.

"It's his leg," Jespyr whispered, hand covering her nose as she leaned over Petyr.

Two boots squelched in the mud at Ravyn's side. The Nightmare lowered himself to a crouch, peered at the wound—the sludging, fetid blood. "How unfortunate," he said with a sigh. "There *is* poison in the water."

Chapter Twenty-Three

Elspeth

In the end, he reached me the way he'd reached me as a child, just as the trees had once reached him.

On a rhyme.

In the wood, the spindle is slight. A delicate tree against hail, wind, and might. But how the tree carries, and how the roots dig. She weathers all storms, no matter their bite.

I managed to move. A small but incontestable ripple in those dark waters. I opened my mouth—called out his true name. "Taxus."

A cold hand found my arm—wrenched me to the surface. I looked up into yellow eyes.

"There you are." He wrapped me in his arms, holding me against his armored chest like a father would a child. "One day, you will be nothing more than memory, Elspeth Spindle. But not yet." His yellow eyes rose to the blackened sky. "Don't leave me alone with these fools."

Voices rolled through the air like thunder. Far away at first, then closer. A man's voice. "No—*no*! Don't move, Petyr."

Coughs, shouts.

"Tie it off below his knee. Jes—light a fire. Wik—help me move him."

I knew that voice. Turbulent. Deep, like the lines of a calloused hand. Rich, smoke and wool and cloves. "Do something," the voice called. "Nightmare!"

Ravyn.

"If I take you away from this place, Elspeth," Taxus said, "you will see what I see. But you will have no control of what used to be your body. You will live in my mind as I once lived in yours." He looked down at me, the lines of his face drawn. "Only my mind is monstrous."

"Are you trying to frighten me?"

"No, dear one. Only warn you."

Ravyn's voice sounded from above once more, louder. "Damn it, *help us.*"

Taxus kept those strange yellow eyes on me, waiting for my answer.

I reached out for his hand. When I pulled in a breath, my first words on that darkened shore became my last. "Let. Me. Out."

Chapter Twenty-Four

Ravyn

Petyr's blood was everywhere. And that smell, the putrid odor that wafted from the wound—impossible to stomach.

Gorse staggered away and was sick in the lake. Jespyr put a hand to her nose and stacked the dry brush she'd scrounged at the edge of the forest. Her hand shook on the flint. When a spark lit to flame and the brush was alight, she pulled a knife from her belt and held it to the fire. "How does it look?"

Ravyn's stomach rolled as he peered down at Petyr's leg. His blood was frothing, the flesh around it turning a bloodless gray. "Hurry, Jes."

Wik's belt was fastened around Petyr's leg in a tourniquet above the lacerations. "That's not an ordinary wound," he said to Ravyn.

Petyr thrashed in the mud. "Just cut the damn thing off and be done with it!"

"We're not cutting your leg off," Ravyn snapped. He jerked his gaze to the Nightmare. "What do you know about this poison?"

The Nightmare said nothing—did nothing. He stood eerily still, eyes glazed over, his gaze lost somewhere out over the lake.

Ravyn smelled hot steel, and then Jespyr was crouching next to Petyr. Her knife was red—smoking. When she looked down at the wound, she blanched. "You sure this will work?"

"Poison or not," Wik said, putting an arm over his brother's chest, "we need to stop the bleeding."

Jespyr looked at Petyr. Tried to smile. "Don't knee me. I like my teeth."

The rot in the air went acrid as she pressed the molten blade over Petyr's leg. He screamed, flailed. The flesh blackened and the wound sealed shut. Jespyr pulled the blade away—

And the wound pried itself open, blood sludging out of Petyr's leg faster than before.

Ravyn slammed his hands against it. "Tighten that belt!" he barked at Wik.

But no matter how hard he pressed into the wound, no matter how tight Wik tugged, they couldn't stop the bleeding.

Petyr was screaming—shaking. His eyes rolled back and the muscles in his neck and jaw bulged. Wik clung to him, muttering something that sounded like a bitter plea, and the two of them shook.

Ravyn looked up at the Nightmare. "Do something," he said, his voice breaking. "Please."

But those yellow eyes were unfocused. The Nightmare seemed a hundred miles away.

A cry crawled out of Ravyn, vicious and desperate. "Damn it, *help us*."

Those words seemed to wrench the Nightmare back. He looked down, his gaze homing in on Petyr. "The Maiden Card," he murmured. "Give him the Maiden."

Ravyn fumbled in his pockets, throwing his Mirror and Nightmare Cards into the mud, digging until his fingertips snagged the third Card. He wrenched the Maiden free. "Now what?"

The Nightmare was mumbling to himself. "It's hardly my fault, dearest, that they are pathetic swimmers."

Petyr's skin had gone colorless—pale as the surface of the lake.

"Nightmare!"

His nostrils flared. He looked down at the Maiden Card in Ravyn's hand. "Make him use it."

Ravyn didn't question it. He shoved the Maiden Card into Petyr's hand, curling his fingers to tap it once—twice—three times.

Petyr's eyes widened and his mouth fell open. He took in a ragged gasp, then another.

The putrid blood stopped.

Beneath Jespyr's shaking hands, Ravyn could see Petyr's wound…closing. Petyr took another breath, and the color in his face returned. Another, and the tension in his body eased.

On the fifth breath, he opened his eyes and looked up at Wik, then Ravyn. "I—I can't feel the pain anymore."

Ravyn stared into Petyr's face. It had never been the sort of face artists might flock to. There was a scar from a knife fight that stretched from Petyr's left eyebrow to the corner of his nostril. Crumpled cartilage in his ears, crooked teeth. Only now, they were gone. Petyr's scars, his imperfections—gone. He was covered in his own blood and lake mud, but he'd never looked so well.

Wik gaped at his brother. "Goddamn trees."

Petyr pushed up, blinked, turning his injured leg left, then right. He tore more of his pant leg to get a better look. The claw marks were gone—healed. Not even a scar remained.

Ravyn's voice came out a strangle. "How do you feel?"

Petyr ran a hand over where the wound had been, testing the skin. His brown eyes went wide. "Like nothing happened."

He looked down at the Maiden Card in his other hand. "Did *this* heal me?"

Only then did the Nightmare come back into focus. He was still talking to himself, his sentences broken between purrs and hisses. "I *am* helping them, dear one," he said under his breath. "More than they know."

Ravyn cocked his head to the side.

"Who the hell are you talking to?" Jespyr snapped.

The Nightmare ignored her. His gaze drifted to the ground—to Ravyn's Providence Cards in the mud. Mirror and Nightmare.

Gorse, who'd been useless, trying to save Petyr, came forward. "Am I seeing things, or is that a Nightmare Ca—"

Ravyn dove. He snagged his burgundy Card out of the mud, yellow eyes flaring above him. Tapped it once—twice—thrice.

Ravyn! called a woman's voice.

Wind kicked out of his lungs. He fell into the mud. That voice. Her voice.

Can you hear me, Ravyn?

He closed his eyes. *Elspeth.*

She made a pained sound that ripped the heart out of him, and then a different voice called. Male and monstrous. *Give her time to adjust, Ravyn Yew. Put away your Nightmare Card.*

If she wants me gone, she will tell me so herself. It is her mind. YOU are the trespasser.

An invisible wall of salt slammed into Ravyn. He called out for Elspeth once more, but she was gone. The Nightmare had shut him out.

Ravyn released himself from his Nightmare Card, jolted up—

And lunged.

He wrapped his fists into the Nightmare's cloak, looked into those terrible yellow eyes, and slammed him into the mud.

More terrifying than snarl or hiss, the Nightmare laughed. "Your stone veneer is crumbling, Ravyn Yew. Who will be waiting on the other side when the mask slips away? Captain? Highwayman? Or beast yet unknown?"

Ravyn drew a breath, his voice deathly quiet. "If it would not hurt her, I would flay you alive."

A crooked, malevolent smile was his only answer.

They ate a mile from the water. Ravyn found a stream and cleaned the putrid blood from his hands, his clothes, noting just how sore his muscles were—how much strain it had taken to cross the lake.

The Nightmare shoved aspen bark into their hands to remedy whatever lake water they'd ingested. When Jespyr asked how he knew the bark would aid them, he muttered something about the idiocy of Yews before disappearing behind the tree line.

Ravyn watched him go, Elspeth's voice ringing through his mind.

Alive.

She was alive.

The relief was like stepping indoors after a winter night's watch—so warm, it hurt.

Wik built a fire and pulled rations from his satchel, handing them down the line. When Ravyn sat next to Gorse, the Destrier got up and took a seat on the other side of the fire. His eyes slid over Ravyn's hands—his pockets. Ravyn knew what he was hoping to glimpse.

The Nightmare Card.

Only two burgundy Nightmare Cards had been forged. Both

had been missing for decades. Tyrn Hawthorn had brought one forward—traded it to King Rowan at Equinox for a marriage contract between Ione and Hauth. It was no doubt still being used at Stone by the Physicians attempting to revive Hauth.

Gorse wasn't the smartest Destrier. But the distrust coloring his face meant he had come to one of two conclusions. Either Ravyn had taken the King's Nightmare Card—

Or he, Captain of the Destriers, possessed the second one. Along with a Mirror Card he'd conveniently failed to mention.

Jespyr's mouth was full of food. "If there's something you want to say," she managed, watching Gorse as she heated dried venison over the flames, "now's a perfect time."

Gorse's lips welded to a fine line. His eyes dropped back to Ravyn's pocket. "That's a rare handful of Cards you've got there, Captain."

Ravyn leaned into the log at his back. "And?"

"Does the King know about them?"

"Why wouldn't he?"

A shrug. "Hauth liked to say the Yews have sticky fingers."

Not smart at all. Ravyn tapped his Nightmare Card three times, pushing its magic out like a cloud of hungry black smoke. *Is that what you think, Destrier? That I am a thief?*

Gorse blanched, his eyes widening in the firelight. "Stop."

Stop what?

"I'm sorry—I—I don't think you stole it. Just—get out of my head."

Jespyr's eyes bounced from Ravyn to Gorse, a smile curling the corners of her mouth. Wik chuckled into his food, and Petyr held up the Maiden Card. "Speaking of Cards," he said, "this was a damn interesting surprise."

"You sure it wasn't your lucky coin that saved you?" Jespyr said with a wink.

Ravyn released Gorse from the Nightmare's magic, his gaze dropping to Petyr's leg, its wound distinctly missing. Petyr had stopped using the Maiden Card twenty minutes ago. And while his face had returned to its familiar roguish expression, the scar upon it had not. He was healed. Completely.

"*He* seemed to know the Maiden would heal you," Wik said, jerking his head to the wood where the Nightmare had retreated.

Ravyn glanced over his shoulder to the trees. "I imagine there are many things he knows about Providence Cards."

Jespyr chuckled. "Too bad he's wholly unwilling to share them."

They went in separate directions, relieving themselves and changing into clean clothes in the underbrush. Ten minutes later, Ravyn and Jespyr regrouped at the fire. The Ivy brothers joined them. The Nightmare, slow in his steps, came last.

Jespyr kicked dirt over the dying fire. "Where's Gorse?"

"He fled five minutes ago," the Nightmare said with unsettling calmness. "Off to report Captain Yew's Nightmare Card to the King, no doubt." His lips peeling back, offering Ravyn a sneer. "I suppose he felt rather uninspired, following a liar into the wood."

Jespyr muttered into her glove, then disguised it as a cough. "He's not the only one."

Ravyn turned—searched the trees. The Black Horse could aid Gorse only so long. He didn't doubt that he could catch the Destrier, silence him with threats. Or worse. But the feeling that he was running out of time was an ever-ticking clock in Ravyn's mind—and it was getting louder. He would deal with Gorse, and the King, when he got back to Stone. For now—

"We keep going."

Forward. Always forward.

Chapter Twenty-Five

Elm

"You'll have to forgive an old man."

Midday light flickered through the library. Elm sat sideways in a satin chair, his legs thrown over its cushioned arm, a sketchbook splayed in his lap. Next to him was a stack of unread tomes. He drank broth from a cup and ran the tip of his stylus over blank pages, listless and irritated.

He was drawing a horse, mid-run—and was deeply dissatisfied with it. "I don't have to forgive a thing," he said to Filick Willow, ripping the paper from the binding and balling it into his fist. "I live off of my grudges."

The paper hit the Physician square in the jaw. Filick's gray whiskers twitched, hiding his smile. "I'll knock louder next time." He levied a pointed glance. "And that, in no way, should be taken as encouragement."

Elm started a new drawing. "You disapprove, old man?"

"There are many beautiful women in the castle these days. Your father has seen to that."

"And?"

Filick returned his gaze to his book of plants, as if he were lecturing one of them, and not the Prince of Blunder. "Why not choose a woman less... less..."

Elm kept his wrist light as he swung his stylus over the paper. "Less like Ione Hawthorn?"

"She's betrothed to your brother."

The smooth line of the horse's midsection wobbled. "I'm aware."

Filick forfeited with a grunt, sipping his tea. "I suppose, if your brother never wakes, the matter will resolve itself."

Elm paused. "Will he wake?"

"I don't know." Filick's blue eyes lifted. "Have you gone to see him?"

"You know I haven't."

"You should. If only for appearances."

Appearances. Elm ripped the paper, balled it, and threw it to the ground. He stared at the next blank sheet. His drawing began with a shape, two sweeping arches. "When do you think they'll get back?" he said quietly. "Ravyn and Jespyr and... *him.*"

Filick leaned back in his chair. "It's difficult to say. I don't think either Ravyn or your father expects a long absence. Though the Shepherd King may have different plans." His voice softened. "I'm sure Ravyn will do everything in his power to unite the Deck and cure Emory by Solstice."

Elm's throat tightened at Emory's name. "What of the Shepherd King?" He added to his sketch, drawing a large shadowed circle between the arches. "Do you think he will honor his bargain and give his blood to unite the Deck?"

"It's not his blood to give," Filick said, hard enough to make Elm look up. "It's Miss Spindle's, isn't it?"

Elspeth. If the Shepherd King was telling the truth—and that was a big *if*—the blood that would unite the Deck would be Elspeth's.

Elm sighed. "Ravyn must be in hell."

There was nothing to say after that, because saying the truth would hurt too much. Ravyn was in love with Elspeth Spindle. And by Solstice, she, if she wasn't already, would surely be dead.

Filick pored over his book and Elm his sketchbook, the afternoon slipping away. Elm's drawing became more detailed. The arches became an eye. Next to it he drew a contoured nose, then another eye. A face. A mouth. Shadows and highlights.

Deep within the castle, the gong sounded five times.

"It'll be dinner soon." Filick peered over his spectacles at Elm's black tunic. "I believe the traditional Rowan color is gold."

"So it is," Elm said to his sketchbook. "But I'm not going to dinner."

"Another drunken appointment in the cellar?"

His stylus stilled. He'd been tipsy, not drunk. Certainly not drunk enough to forget a single moment of last night. His skin—his fingers and mouth—had kept the score of it. When he'd woken that morning, hard and sore and so bloody *bothered*, it had taken ten minutes in a frigid bath just to make use of his own limbs. And still, he could not forget.

He'd wanted to go straight to Ione's room and finish what they'd started, to obey her command and rip her out of her dress. But pride had stopped him. He'd laid his darkest truths before her in the cellar—practically pleaded with her to toy with him.

And now—now Elm had no idea what to do. She'd run off without a backward glance, leaving him reeling. So he'd spent the day in the library, the only place in Stone he didn't hate. The only place he'd be free of reminders of Ione Hawthorn.

But that wasn't exactly true. Because, when Elm looked down at his sketchbook, he realized the face he's spent half an hour drawing was hers.

His fingers flexed along his stylus. It wasn't a true likeness. She looked too much at ease on paper, not frozen by the Maiden like she was in real life. But her eyes, he'd gotten right. Clear and unreadable. Cold, and just a little wicked.

He ripped her portrait out of the sketchbook, balling it in his fist. "My father is a fool if he thinks dangling Blunder's daughters under my nose will entice me to choose a wife. Taking Hauth's place is wretched enough without adding a strange woman to my everyday existence."

When Elm had told Filick that the King had thrust the throne upon him, the Physician had sighed in the way those who'd lived a great many years sighed at those who'd clocked only a few. "I know you well enough to keep my opinions to myself, Elm."

"A small mercy."

"But, if you'd humor an old man just once more," he said, "you'd let me tell you what a fine King you'd make—what a blessing you'd be to those of us who still hope to see a better future for this cold, unfeeling place."

Elm's chest tugged. He looked back at his sketchbook. "You're getting soft, Physician."

Filick's laugh was a low, steady rumble. "I am. And that changes nothing of what I've said."

A quarter of an hour later, when Elm was alone and staring at nothing, Filick's words stayed with him. And the irony, the bitter truth of it all, came crashing down. Ione. The Maiden Card. Hauth. The throne.

He could free himself from marrying—from becoming heir. Ione had all but handed him the means. All it would take was a Maiden Card and Hauth would be healed. The line of succession would return to normal. Elm could get his life back.

But that freedom had a cost. A terrible, violent cost. And

Hauth's wrath, should he be healed, was a darkness rivaled only by the five-hundred-year-old monster who had maimed him in the first place.

Elm couldn't risk waking his brother. Which left only one loathsome alternative. He, Prince Renelm Rowan, would marry and become the next King of Blunder.

The sound of rustling fabric and a small cough pulled him from his thoughts. His eyes shot up. Maribeth Larch, daughter of Ode Larch, whose estate yielded most of Blunder's grain supply, stood in front of Elm's chair, fingers inching along a nearby shelf. "Beg your pardon, Highness," she said. "I didn't intend to disturb you."

Elm snapped his sketchbook shut and fixed his mouth with an unfeeling smile. To disturb him was exactly what she'd intended. He could tell by the plant of her feet—the expectant look in her eyes—that she'd been standing there some time.

He didn't stand, didn't bow or offer her his hand. Which was rude and the opposite of what the future King should do. But he was comfortable, deep in his chair, and she'd intruded upon a rare moment of gentle solitude. "Miss Larch," he said. "Have you lost your way?"

She hadn't. The small smile fixed across her painted lips made that perfectly clear. "A Prince of many talents," she said, not answering his question, her eyes flickering to the sketchbook in his lap. "What are you drawing?"

"Nothing." Elm had seen Maribeth at court. He knew her father—her brothers. She was pretty, tall, with a warm presence and thick brown hair she often wore in a coronet. But now her hair was down, swept over her shoulder. "I'm waiting for inspiration."

Maribeth bent to peer at a low shelf, the rounded tops of her breasts swelling over her neckline. "Do you draw from reference or memory?"

The smell of wine. Heat from the hearth. The shape of Ione's mouth when she parted her lips—her eyes, clear and sharp and homed entirely on him.

"Memory," Elm said in a low voice, running his thumb along the balled-up portrait in his hand. "Why? Are you offering to pose for me, Miss Larch?"

She smiled, tucking a loose strand of hair behind her ear as she stepped forward. But the blush of red in her cheeks—the way her eyes flickered from his to the floor—gave her away. She was nervous. She took the chair Willow had occupied and lowered herself into it. Without meeting Elm's eyes, she inched her dress up her leg until it was almost at her knee, revealing smooth, olive skin.

She wasn't wearing leggings. "If you'd like to draw me, Prince Renelm, I'd be more than happy to oblige."

Elm sat deeper into his chair. He knew enough of life at court to know when he was being propositioned. It felt familiar, like a book he'd read many times. Which was why he'd been taking the contraceptive tonic since he was seventeen. They were alone, and unlikely to be interrupted. There didn't have to be a bed, but if she wanted one, there were plenty of empty guest rooms—so long as it wasn't his bed. If she wasn't already wet, he would get her there before he'd let her touch him. And even when he did let her touch him, he wouldn't let her take his clothes off. He'd do that himself. Or he'd leave them on, loosening only his belt and trousers. He felt safer that way.

He'd put his mouth against her ear and ask what she liked. She'd be reticent to say—or maybe not—but she wouldn't look him in the eye. He'd please her with his fingers or mouth. Maybe he'd give all of himself, working on her until she met her release, finding his own somewhere along the way or not at all, all the while knowing, behind the swell of his desire—the tight, rising exhilaration—an empty feeling waited. An aloneness.

After, despite the emptiness, Elm would help her dress. Cheeks red, mouth swollen from kissing, she'd finally meet his gaze. When he was younger, he fancied that's when women saw him. Not the Prince, not Renelm—but Elm. Elm, who wanted to be liked, to be seen. Petulant, reticent Elm.

But he knew better now. And it humiliated him that he'd ever thought the women he'd bedded had seen the real him. They hadn't. Mostly because he hadn't let them. He'd reached into women to find himself, when all he really wanted was for someone to look at him. To admit they knew what had happened to him as a boy and still hold him, unflinching, in their gaze.

The way Ione had last night.

His grip tightened on the crumpled portrait in his hand. "You don't have to do this, Miss Larch." He rested his face against his palm, keeping his eyes on Maribeth's face, away from her bare leg. "It'll come to no good."

Her smile faded.

Elm might have dismissed her outright, but the nervousness stamped across her face made him wonder if this had even been her idea. Perhaps she had a meddling mother. Or a grasping father, like Tyrn Hawthorn. "You're very beautiful." He forced lightness into his voice. "But you should know, these feasts are the King's doing. Not mine."

Maribeth's grip loosened on her dress, the fabric slipping back over her leg. She tried once more to smile. "And if I merely wanted my picture drawn?"

Elm offered his own smile. "Did you?"

"No, I suppose not." She cleared her throat. "A folly on

several accounts, for I imagine the King has picked someone out for you already, just as he chose Miss Hawthorn for the High Prince." She gave a rushed bow, then quit the library. "Good afternoon, Highness."

The stylus slipped through Elm's fingers. He sat up too quickly, his sketchbook spilling onto the floor. He didn't remember his father choosing Ione for Hauth—because the King *hadn't* chosen her. There'd been an agreement with Tyrn. A Nightmare Card for a marriage contract.

A barter.

Elm rose from his chair, tucking Ione's portrait into his pocket, and headed for the stairs.

He found the man he was looking for on the first landing, announcing families on their way to the great hall for dinner. "Baldwyn."

The King's steward jumped, his rounded spectacles falling askew. Baldwyn Viburnum had always reminded Elm of a kitchen rat, with his coarse, thinning black hair. His nose was short and narrow, and the spectacles that sat on its bridge were often smudged. Snide, without a whit of humor, Baldwyn was as pleasant to speak to as the inside of a chamber pot. He'd always been cruel to Emory.

Elm despised him.

Baldwyn straightened his spectacles and ran a hand over his hair. "Prince Renelm. Are you going down to dinner? It's the first feast in your honor."

"No, listen—"

Behind them, families waited to be announced. Which was utter nonsense. These fools had attended dozens of dinners together. If they didn't know each other's names by now, another screech from Baldwyn wasn't going to do the trick.

But it was tradition. And Elm was fairly certain Baldwyn would rather throw himself down the stairs than offend tradition. "Announcing," he boomed, "Lord and Lady Juniper and their daughter, Miss Isla Juniper."

The Junipers bowed to Elm, the daughter taking an extended glance, and went down the stairs.

"I need to look at the King's contracts," he said to Baldwyn, keeping his voice low. "His marriage contracts in the last month."

"Any particular reason, sire?"

Elm fixed his mouth with a false smile. "If I'm expected to wed, I'd like to understand the business end of things."

Baldwyn began to respond, but another family came up behind Elm. "Announcing Sir Chestnut and his son, Harold."

The Chestnuts bowed. Elm greeted them with a flick of his wrist and kept his eyes on Baldwyn. "Well, little man? Where can I find the contracts?"

"I keep them in the record chamber off the library, sire."

"Brilliant." Elm turned to leave—

"It's locked, Prince Renelm."

Elm heaved a sigh. "As to that. What did Ravyn do with the keys when he left?"

"You mean *your* keys, Highness?"

"Yes. My bloody keys."

Baldwyn cleared his throat as another family came up. "Announcing—"

Elm put a finger in his face. "The keys."

Baldwyn blinked down at his finger, momentarily cross-eyed. "I—the Captain left them with Physician Willow. But that's not a Physician's job, and Captain Yew had no business—"

"You're testing me, steward."

Baldwyn reached for his belt, brass clanging. Elm held out his hand, clamping his fingers around the iron ring that housed dozens of keys. "Much obliged."

He pushed through the families crowding the landing, never minding that they were all watching him. But the glee of embarrassing Baldwyn dissipated the moment Elm got to the record chamber. He hadn't thought to ask *which* key opened it.

Ten minutes later, he was still locked out. "Clever indeed," he muttered through his teeth. Ravyn would have known which key was right. *Well, bloody good for Ravyn. Must be nice, having all that control, never shouldering a father's disappointment, never making a complete ass of yourself with a woman in the cellar—*

A small brass key slid into place, and the lock clicked open. Elm kissed the key and immediately regretted it, remembering too late the ring had been fastened to Baldwyn's belt.

He crept into the chamber. There were cabinets—stacks of drawers—filled with parchment bearing the King's seal. He discovered property deeds and knighthoods. Detailed histories of Providence Cards and who owned them.

Then, finally, marriage contracts. Something Elm hadn't spent five minutes of his entire life considering.

There were so many of them. Hundreds. Which shouldn't have been a surprise. People got married all the time. But a Prince—a High Prince—wasn't *people.*

And neither was Hauth. It took Elm all of two minutes to spot the King's seal in the pile. He dug with hurried fingers, the smell of parchment filling his nose. He pulled the contract free, his eyes stilling on a name. *Ione Hawthorn.*

He read the contract, his gaze running over repeated words. *Providence Card, Hawthorn, marriage, heir.*

He froze and read it again. Then again. For every time he read it, the corners of Elm's mouth lifted until a smile unfurled.

He didn't put the contract back with the others. He slipped it under his tunic and left the room, keys jingling. And because he was a rotten Prince, and a piss-poor Destrier at that, Elm didn't lock the door behind him.

Chapter Twenty-Six

Elspeth

You vile, traitorous SNAKE.

Tether yourself, dear one, the Nightmare said, unaffected. *It's only hair.*

I was in a new darkness. Not the long, empty shore, but a room—trapped inside it. I couldn't feel my body, my hands and legs somewhere far away, numb to me. I was but a presence, my voice the only thing it seemed I could control.

Much like the chamber at the edge of the meadow, my room had no door, only a window—a hole in the darkness. But it was enough. I could see what the Nightmare saw now.

And what he saw was Ravyn.

He was walking with Jespyr ahead of the Nightmare, following a deer path through a wide glen. Light caught his black hair, lightening it like the sheen on a wing. His posture was tight but not entirely rigid. He kept one hand on the hilt of his sword while the other, ungloved, ghosted over the glen, brushing over foxtails and barley grass.

He was alive. Beautiful and alive.

And I could not touch him.

The Nightmare had not let Ravyn back into our shared mind

since yesterday, upon that muddy lakeshore. It was midday now, and the party walked at a languid pace. The sun hid behind the oppressive gray of the mist. But to me, against the desolation of that lone, dark beach, the world seemed full of color. Even the mist, pale and unfriendly, glistened anew, the wood welcoming me back with greens and blues and yellows and reds.

So this is what it was like for you, I said to the Nightmare, half marvel, half horror. *Trapped. Forced to see and hear everything I showed you.*

He made a low hum. Ravyn turned at the noise, shooting the Nightmare a look that could freeze a hot spring. I couldn't see the face the Nightmare made in response, but I felt the satisfaction that stole over his thoughts. He liked to stoke Ravyn's ire. Of that I had no doubt.

When Ravyn's eyes dropped a moment to my hair, his eyes went colder still.

I'd had the misfortune of catching my reflection in a stream we'd crossed that morning—and had yet to recover. Beyond cutting my hair, the Nightmare had done nothing to tend to my appearance. There was dirt caked into the lines of my face. Old blood beneath my fingernails. My lips were chapped and peeling.

Only, none of those things were mine anymore—not wholly. Like my mind, I didn't know what to call my body. *Mine, his,* or *ours.* For now, it seemed the lesser of evils to call it *his.* That way, I wouldn't have to own anything he did at its helm.

You could at least have washed my—your—hands. I groaned. *I can't even imagine what you smell like.*

It's better this way. The Nightmare examined blood-encrusted nail beds. *The less I look like Elspeth, the less Ravyn Yew startles every time he glances my way. It's fraying my nerves, listening to him sigh.*

No one cares about your nerves.

He laughed, and the sound turned the darkness I occupied warm, den-like.

"I hate it when he laughs," Wik said from behind. "Sends creepers up my back."

"Ignore him," Ravyn snapped.

Jespyr poked his shoulder. "Because you do such a fine job at that."

"Do as I say, Jes, not as I do."

Jespyr jabbed her brother in the ribs. Ravyn absorbed the blow, then pinched the tip of his sister's ear until she squealed. The moment was easy between the siblings.

Naturally, the Nightmare sought to ruin it. "Elspeth worries you no longer find her beautiful," he called out to them.

That's not what I bloody said.

"Apparently you aren't the only one, Captain, who loathes what I've done to her hair."

Ravyn stopped in his tracks. A moment later his hand was in his pocket, salt tipping the air in my dark, listless chamber.

An invisible wall clamped down around me. The salt dissipated, and then the Nightmare was laughing, holding out a finger to Ravyn. "You do not learn."

I want to speak with him, I seethed.

The Nightmare ignored me. If only, perhaps, to watch the rage in Ravyn's eyes swell.

But Ravyn's gaze was clever—honed. "She saw me look at her hair." He stood straighter. "She can see me now."

Ha! Call him what you like. But never mark him as a fool.

The Nightmare exhaled. *But he is a fool, dear one. Terribly, incessantly stupid.*

Take that back.

He cleared his throat. "She says you're stupid, Ravyn Yew."

Nightmare!

Ravyn's eyes narrowed. He was looking into the Nightmare's yellow eyes. Looking for me. And I was not above pleading so that he might find what was left of me. I had eleven years' practice, begging the Nightmare to be tolerable.

Please. Let me speak to him. Just for a moment.

He tilted his head to the side. *Being apart from you has its merits. It will motivate him to do whatever it takes to retrieve the Twin Alders Card.*

I am not part of whatever game you're playing with him. I matched the silk in his voice with iron. *What he and I share has nothing to do with you. Let me SPEAK to him.*

"What's he saying?" Jespyr said, peering over her brother's shoulder.

Ravyn's jaw twitched. "He's deciding whether or not to let me in."

I felt the Nightmare prickle under Ravyn's stare. He wanted to deny him. But when I said his name again—*Nightmare!*—he clicked his jaw three times and sighed. *A brief moment, my dear.*

The salt returned, washing over me. I yielded to it—desperate for it. *Ravyn?*

He was still there. He'd been waiting. How many times, when I was alone on that dark shore, had he been there waiting?

Elspeth.

His voice was a caress—so different from the way he spoke to the Nightmare. I bent to it, basking in the soft depths of his tone. *I'm sorry.*

He flinched, his entire face caught up in the act. *No. This isn't your fault, Elspeth.*

I reached for him—reached with no arms, no hands.

Once I'd looked at the Captain of the Destriers and thought, every time I beheld him, I was seeing a different man. Sometimes with a mask, other times without. But I'd never seen him like this—hands shaking, weathered to the bone, a sheen over his gray eyes. *Ten minutes.* Ravyn's voice wavered. *Ten minutes, and I'd have been up those stairs. And Hauth—you—* He glanced away. *I'm the one who's sorry.*

Look at me, Ravyn.

When his gaze met mine, I pressed against the window in my dark room. *You're not allowed to blame yourself for a second of those ten minutes. It was magic that made me... disappear. Terrible, inevitable degeneration. It wasn't anyone's fault. But I'm still sorry it happened. I would have liked—* My voice quieted. *I would have liked a little more time. With you.*

The lines in Ravyn's face strained, his voice deepening with insistence. *We'll get that time. I swear it, Elspeth.* He blinked too fast, then dropped my gaze. Because it wasn't my eyes he was looking into—not anymore. There wasn't a dark, endless shore between Ravyn Yew and me any longer.

Just a King, five hundred years dead.

The Nightmare's slippery tone entered our reverie. *That's enough for now. Put away your Nightmare Card, Captain.*

No. Ravyn's voice was hard once more. *I need her.*

Let him stay, I said. *Please.*

A flash of teeth. *No.*

Why?

I didn't hear his answer. A loud fluttering sound blotted it out.

All of our heads snapped up. "Arrows!" Jespyr shouted, pushing Ravyn off the path into the grass.

Ravyn landed in a crouch, three arrows buried in the ground where he'd stood, each tipped by a small glass vial that shattered upon impact.

A sweet-smelling smoke filled the air, shooting up the Nightmare's nose and deep into his lungs. He coughed, a vicious snarl emptying out of his mouth. My vision blurred and then the world tilted.

The Nightmare fell into the grass. I couldn't see Ravyn and Jespyr anymore. But I did see the Ivy brothers.

Petyr was in the grass, eyes rolling shut. Wik was next to him, unmoving—

An arrow lodged in his skull.

I screamed.

This, my dear, the Nightmare hissed, *is the sort of thing we might have seen coming, had Ravyn Yew not been poking about in our mind.*

The last things I saw before the Nightmare lost consciousness were two pairs of leather boots, stepping toward us through the grass.

"Well, well," came a voice from above. "Two more Destriers."

Chapter Twenty-Seven

Elm

The King was five cups deep and fuming.

"I told Filick where I'd be, and when I'd return." Elm leaned back in Hauth's chair, tensing as the wood groaned. He kept his face even, his fingers trailing the Scythe's velvet edge in his pocket. "You weren't *worried* about me, were you?"

He knew better than to poke the bear—most of the time. Only now, the bear was too drunk to poke him back. "You missed the first feast," the King said, his voice a low rumble.

Elm looked out over the great hall. There wasn't a single thing in the wide, echoing room he regretted missing.

The scene was as it always was. Tables heaping with food, servants carrying trays stacked with silver and crystal goblets, decanters full of wine. Courtiers, laughing and swaying to a string ensemble, jaws slack with laughter. Branches and stems, leaves and seed clusters, tucked into their clothes and hair—

Elm's gaze narrowed. He dragged it over the great hall once more. "Why on earth is everyone wearing *greenery*?"

The King muttered into his cup. "Baldwyn's notion."

"Don't tell me these feasts are in costume." Elm put a hand to his brow and groaned. "What's the theme? Shrubs?"

"They're wearing sprigs from their house trees, you imbecile." The King—who wore no adornment save a permanent scowl—pulled another deep drink. "You would know that had you attended last night's feast and not scurried away to Castle Yew."

"You've stripped me of my Destrier duties. I was bored."

"Then pick a bloody wife," the King spat. When heads turned, he pressed his lips together and lowered his voice. "What do the Yews have to say?"

Elm took a drink. "Not much."

"Emory?"

"Better now that he's at home where he should be."

The King kept his eyes forward on the great hall. Elm had long ago stopped expecting remorse from his father for what he had planned to do with Emory's blood. That clever, innocent boy. A boy Elm had watched grow up. Get sicker. Slowly die in Stone.

Elm had never caught the infection. But he knew all too well what it felt like to wither away at Stone. So when he had gone to Castle Yew last night, and there had been a thimble's worth of warmth in Emory's cheeks, he had all but kissed the boy.

Even without Ravyn and Jespyr present, Castle Yew was Elm's true home. The bed where he slept best. Where all his favorite books were kept. He spoke freely there, without pretense.

His aunt had wrapped him in her strong arms, and so had his uncle. They hadn't hugged him that tightly since he was a boy. "It's all right," he'd said. "I'm managing."

He'd told them everything. About what had happened on the forest road. The inquest. Ione and the Maiden Card and the King's feasts.

About becoming heir.

He'd reached into his satchel and pulled out the marriage contract with the King's seal. "I need you to put this in a safe place."

Fenir's eyes had widened. "This is—"

"Yes."

Morette had run her gaze over the parchment. Twice. Elm knew she'd seen what he had. "Well, nephew," she'd said, the corner of her mouth curling as she looked up at him. "I hope you know what you're doing."

"So do I."

The sharpness in the King's green eyes was beginning to blur. Perfect. Better he was pliable, because Elm was going to do something he had never done before.

Barter with the King.

"You're wearing black," his father barked out of nowhere in a voice that might have belonged to one of his hounds. "Don't you have any gold?"

"I like black." Elm kept his eyes on the crowd, watching for the one person who was not yet there. "It suits me."

The King finished his cup, raising a crude hand to the server, who came rushing back to refill it. Elm folded his hands on the table. "I've thought about what you said on the drawbridge. About being heir." He took a sip of wine. "I'd like it in writing. With your seal."

"It's already been drafted. Find Baldwyn to sign."

"Hold on. I have a price."

The King coughed. "Trees, Renelm."

"This issue of these ridiculous feasts. Of a wife."

"No," the King said. "I will not bend. The heir will marry."

"I didn't say I wouldn't marry," Elm bit back. "But I'd like your word that you will honor any contract I strike."

"Did you have someone in mind?"

"No one to whom you have not already given your seal of approval."

The King searched the great hall, as if he were looking for a loophole. But everyone in attendance had come by his invitation—selected for their property and wealth and all the things a sovereign might want for his heir.

The King ran a gnarled hand over his brow. "Very well."

Elm hid his smile in his wine cup. "You look relieved. I imagine you expected I'd give you more trouble."

"You always have."

Elm opened his mouth, a drop of venom on his tongue, but the gong rang, and he snapped it shut. Nine tolls. Nine—and still no Ione. It dawned on him that maybe she would not come. He should have told her he'd be absent at Castle Yew—that he hadn't resigned their search for her Maiden Card just because she'd left him panting in the cellar.

He stood, his bow to the King barely a nod, and was out of the great hall in less than a minute. He took the stairs two at a time. When he got to the fourth landing, he heard a man's voice, echoing from above. It almost sounded like Hauth's.

Linden.

He quickened his pace and reached the fifth landing—the royal corridor. Royce Linden had Ione's arm in his fist and was pulling her down the hallway. Ione said something Elm could not hear, and Linden's shoulders went taut. He reached over and gripped her cheeks, fingers digging into her skin—shouted into her face. "Traitor."

Elm's finger was on his Scythe in less than a breath. "Stand still, Destrier."

Linden went rigid. When he saw Elm coming, a flinch crossed his face.

It made Elm feel powerful, watching the brute cower. It made him feel like Ravyn.

"She should not be wandering the castle without a guard," Linden gritted out. "Had I not caught her creeping toward the gardens, she might have easily gone outside and disappeared into the mist." His jaw was rigid. "Though I suppose it is no wonder, with you as her watchman, that she was able to slip away."

"Take your hand off of her."

Linden's fingers on Ione's face went white with strain. Play strength—the worst kind of pageantry—for there was no disobeying a Scythe. His hand went limp, and Ione pulled away, her gaze unreadable.

Flames licked up Elm's middle. But his voice remained calm. "You're not to go near her again."

"I take my orders from—"

"One more word, Destrier, and I'll finish what began on Market Day and rip your face so far open not even the Spirit will recognize you. If you touch Miss Hawthorn again, by the fucking trees, I'll end you." He ran his gaze over Linden's scars. "Do you understand?"

Hate boiled behind Linden's eyes. It greeted Elm like a brother. "Yes," he said through tight lips.

"Yes, *Highness*."

"Yes, Highness."

Elm's anger wasn't spent. Not by a fraction. But, with a lazy wave of his hand, he released the Scythe. Linden stepped away, quickly disappearing down the stairs.

Only then did Elm dare to glance at Ione. "Hey, Hawthorn."

She was watching him, her face without expression. "That was excessive."

"Sorry." He rocked back on his heels, feeling wide open beneath her stare. "Why were you headed for the garden?"

"Why do you think, *clever* Prince?"

The pinprick of her voice found Elm's chest. She was angry, though the Maiden masked it well. It felt strange to Elm, liking that she was angry at him. Anger was better than nothing at all. "I'm sorry I haven't helped you search. I was away. Heir business."

As quickly as it came, the prick in Ione's voice was gone, her tone flattening. "I assumed you were avoiding me."

"Not at all. I spent the night at Castle Yew."

"And that had nothing to do with me?"

To say no would be a lie. It *had* been about her. Just not for the reason she thought. "You think very highly of yourself, Hawthorn, if you imagine all my comings and goings concern you."

A noise hummed in her throat. "Maybe not your goings."

Elm smiled—ran his tongue along the inside of his cheek. "That wicked mouth is going to get you into trouble."

Ione turned away, her gray dress spilling behind her as she headed down the corridor. "If you say so."

Elm followed her to a door with a hare carved into the frame. "I'm not inviting you in," she said at the threshold.

"I didn't expect you to. I merely wished to note," he said, tapping a finger over the hare, "what door to knock on in the morning."

"What for?"

"We keep up the search." Their eyes caught. Elm shoved his hands into his pockets, strangling the desire to touch her. "The Chalice didn't work. But there are other Cards that may help us find your Maiden."

Chapter Twenty-Eight

Elspeth

The moment the Nightmare lost consciousness to the sweet smell of smoke, I was propelled deeper into his mind, his memories swaddling me once more.

I sat in the meadow beneath a starry sky, listening to the trees whisper.

Your people come to the wood. They ask for blessings. The Spirit is pleased, young King.

My hands were busy. I'd pulled nimble branches from a nearby willow tree and woven them into a small circle—and was now adorning it with mayweed and tansy. A flower crown for my sister, Ayris. "But the blessings the Spirit gives," I said to the trees, "the gifts that come with the fever—they always carry a price."

Nothing is free, the trees replied.

"The magic she offers is degenerative. Some grow addled with it—or sick." My fingers paused on the flower crown. "Surely there is another way for the people of Blunder to know her magic. A safer way."

Nothing is free. Nothing is safe.

"Trees," I said, my voice firmer. "The sword the Spirit gave me has been my crook. I have moved forests to make a bountiful kingdom—shepherded the land. Now it's time for me to shepherd Blunder's people. You are the Spirit's eyes—her ears and mouth. You know her mind. Tell me, what must I do to make magic safer?"

The trees surrounding the meadow groaned. *Go to the stone she left for you,* they whispered. *Drop blood.*

I set the flower crown on the grass and hurried to the stone near the yew trees. I dragged my finger over the edge of my sword, wincing. When blood beaded to the surface, I held it over the stone, crimson droplets falling—once, twice, thrice.

A chasm opened in the stone, and the voices of trees echoed louder in my mind.

To bleed is the first step—drop your blood on the stone.

The next is to barter—match her price with your own.

The last is to bend—for magic does twist. You'll lose your old self, like getting lost in a mist. The Spirit will guide you, but she keeps a long score. She'll grant what you ask...

But you'll always want more.

I swallowed. "I want a way to keep magic from degenerating. To heal the fever."

The trees swayed. *There will be a way. But there are many barters to make before that day comes.*

I paused. "Then I want to be strong. Give me great strength."

The wind picked up, smelling of salt. *Bring a black horse from your stable, young Taxus.*

My vision winked. It was another night. I was not in the meadow, but in a wood. I clutched my sword, the shepherd's crook imprinting into my palms. My eyes had always been quick to adjust to darkness—I homed them on the wood, searching for movement.

When a shadow shifted beneath a juniper tree, a smile snaked over my mouth. The shadow grew to a plume of darkness.

And then I was upon him.

The clash of our swords echoed through the trees. Owls took to the sky, screeching in complaint. I paid them no mind and kept my focus on my combatant.

His steps were sure. With each blow, my teeth rattled. We parried through the wood, matching blow for blow. His sword hit my golden breastplate, and I sent my elbow into his jaw. He flinched, and it was all the time I needed. My foot swept his ankle. He fell with a curse, dropping his sword.

I stood above him, my smile widening. "Do you acquiesce?"

It was difficult to discern his features beneath the plume of darkness. But when he reached into his pocket, retrieving the source of the plume—a Black Horse Providence Card—and tapped it three times, I finally saw his face.

Young, handsome, with an angular brow. Even in the dark, I could see the green of his eyes. "You were right," he said, studying the Black Horse in his hand. "This Card lends incredible strength. I might have snuck up on you and won—if you weren't such an accomplished cheat and could see it by color."

"Magic against magic." I pulled him to his feet. "What's unfair about that?"

We walked out of the wood together. When we reached my castle, he offered me back the Black Horse. "Thank you for another eventful training."

"Keep the Card," I said. "There are more. And I will make others that offer different magic. As providence would have it, I have a knack for bartering with the Spirit of the Wood."

"And you'd give one of your precious Cards to a lowly guard?"

"No. But I would to the Captain of *my* Guard."

His green eyes widened.

My laugh sounded into the night. "Magic isn't just for those to whom the Spirit lends her favor." I crossed my arms over my chest. "Besides, you'll need something to your name if you're going to continue batting your eyes at my sister."

He had the grace to look embarrassed. "Ayris told you about us, then?" he said, rubbing his jaw.

"No. But I can read her well enough." I tilted my head to the side, hawklike. "Perhaps one day I'll make a Card to read your mind, too, Brutus Rowan."

Memories wove together, stringing me through time.

There were more Providence Cards. More colors—gold and white and gray—in my pocket. For each, I bled into the stone, and bartered with the Spirit of the Wood.

Then, there was a woman. With a kind face and gray eyes. Petra.

We stood together beneath the same stained-glass windows where I'd become King and embraced in front of Blunder's lords and ladies. Ayris and Brutus stood from their seats, hands clasped, echoing a cheer of jubilation.

Wife. Queen. Petra looked up at me and I kissed her mouth. The softness of her lips reminded me of velvet.

Nine months later, Petra looked up at me once more. She was on a bed in a vast chamber, men with willow trees woven into their white robes tending to her. A newborn boy rested in her arms. He had her gray eyes.

"Bennett," she murmured, her brow damp from labor. "I'd like to call him Bennett."

She held the babe out to me, and I rocked him. But even as I did, my hands itched to hold something else. When I passed Bennett back to Petra, I slipped my fingers into my pocket for the Providence Cards I kept there. Only then did I smile.

I took Bennett to the wood. Asked the Spirit to bless him with her magic. A day later, his infant veins were dark as ink. His magic was the antithesis of mine, the trees told me. My heir, my counterweight.

But that was our secret, his and mine. Our fond, silent riddle.

More children were born. Boys—all yellow of eye like me. Lenor. Fenly. A pair of twins, Afton and Ilyc, so alike I could hardly tell them apart even when I took the time to try. I visited their nurseries, their rooms and tutor sessions, but often I was in another chamber, one I had built around the stone in the meadow.

I brought my sons to the wood—asked the Spirit to bless them with magic. But for all four, she kept her gifts to herself.

Then, a little girl was born. Tilly. Full of whim and a deviousness that reminded me of Ayris. Only, unlike my sister, the Spirit christened Tilly with the fever, and she was granted strange, wonderful magic.

She could heal. With a single touch of her little hand, Tilly could wipe away any wound—and often did so without intention. The cuts I'd dealt myself, bartering for Providence Cards, vanished whenever Tilly reached for me. It hurt, feeling her touch. But when the pain was gone, I was left with nary a scar.

But it cost her, little Tilly, to heal. Every time she did, her own body grew more frail. And so, for my next Providence Card, I asked the trees, the Spirit, for magic that healed. Magic that made its user as beautiful and unblemished as a pink rose—Tilly's favorite flower.

Petra passed through the veil before Tilly's fourth nameday. I buried her on the west side of the meadow, near the willow tree, not knowing I would dig her up soon enough to forge the Mirror.

But before that, I made a different Card. One that would make others bend their wills to me, just as I bent to the Spirit of the Wood.

Brutus Rowan came with me. He kept a hand on the pommel of his sword as I staggered into the chamber. "What was her price this time?"

"My sleep."

His green eyes narrowed. "Do you ever wonder if the Spirit asks too much for these Cards of yours, Taxus?"

Upon the edge of my sword, I split a seam in my palm. Droplets of red fell over the stone. "Providence Cards are a gift, Brutus. Their magic is measured. Neither they, nor those who wield them, risk degeneration."

"Gifts are free, Taxus."

My words came out a hiss. "Nothing is free."

The stone opened to a chasm. My blood fell into it. I reached into my pocket—tapped the Maiden Card. By the time the cut in my palm began to knit, four Providence Cards rested within the stone, red as the blood I'd dropped. A scythe was fixed upon them.

I winked at Brutus and handed him one.

He stared down at it. "What would you have me do with this?"

"Keep my kingdom in order. My time is better spent here," I said gesturing to the chamber. "Only be wary, Brutus. To command this Card is to command pain."

Brutus turned the Scythe through lithe fingers. "It is you who should be wary, my clever friend. With Cards such as these, people will come to you, not the Spirit of the Wood, for magic. She will not thank you for it."

"You sound like Ayris."

"She's rubbed off on me. Despite my best intentions."

I shot him the same practiced smile I tendered my children. Only lately, I wore it when the subject of Providence Cards came up with my sister. "It is the Spirit who gave me the means to forge Providence Cards." I patted the stone. "She knows I use them for good."

"Even so, be wary, Taxus. Be wary, clever, *and* good."

"So says a Rowan, who is none of the three."

Brutus shot me a grin. "Which is precisely why your sister married me."

We traded false punches. When the chamber faded, it was to the sound of our laughter.

On a brisk autumn day, grass brown and dying, I walked through the wood I so often tarried in as a boy with Blunder's reverent—where we had asked the Spirit of the Wood for her blessings. The wood was empty now. No prayers echoed, the air stagnant, bereft of salt, as if starved.

Behind me, I could hear the castle bells. My children were being called to dinner, where they'd sit at the table in my hall, waiting for me.

But I was not hungry for food or company, only for velvet. For *more.*

I crept into the chamber. Spoke to the trees. Asked for an eleventh Providence Card.

What power do you ask this time, Shepherd King?

I ran a hand over my face. "I am not a stately ruler. It is a thorn in my side, sitting at court—listening to woe or flattery. I would rather know the truth of someone's thoughts outright and save myself aggravation. Grant me a Card for entering a person's mind." I cleared my throat. "Besides. My Captain has been distant of late. I would like to know his thoughts."

Have you considered asking Brutus Rowan what draws him away from you?

"I am his King. He is not as blunt with me, nor as nettlesome, as you, trees."

The wind stirred their branches. *To enter a mind is a treacherous walk. There are doors that are meant to remain behind lock. If you wish for that nightmare, give yourself to her, whole. For an eleventh Providence Card—*

The Spirit demands your soul.

I left the chamber, two burgundy Cards nestled in my palm, my fingers curling like claws around them. The castle bells were quieter—muffled. When I looked up, evening light was smothered behind grayness. It cloistered around the chamber like a wool blanket, seeping into the meadow, reeking of salt.

Mist.

Chapter Twenty-Nine

Ravyn

Ravyn's pulse was a barbarous rhythm, each beat hammering inside his head like a pike.

He'd had hangovers and head injuries. Twice, before his magic had made him immune to it, he'd been poisoned trying to lie against a Chalice Card. But this—coming out from the fog of the sweet, sudden smoke that had rendered him unconscious—was worse than all three.

He'd lost consciousness near midday. And now the light in the sky was new, the dawn pale. They'd lost half a day—and an entire night.

Wincing, Ravyn took in his surroundings. He was in a dirt courtyard. Around it was a crude wall of earth and wood that stood twenty hands high. When he tried to turn and see how far the wall went, his body didn't heed him. Pain cut into his wrists, and he felt a stiff surface press into his back.

He realized he was tethered to a wide wooden post. Arms, torso, legs—all bound.

Panic flooded Ravyn's throat like bile. He'd never been restrained. It was always he who had done the restraining. He called his sister's name and immediately regretted it, his headache responding with a punch.

A low groan sounded somewhere behind him. "I'm here," came Jespyr's voice.

She was tied to the post next to him. Ravyn couldn't see her, but his left wrist was tethered to her right. On his other side, the Nightmare was talking to himself in slow, slippery whispers.

Ravyn pressed his eyes shut and slowed his breathing. "Everyone all right?"

"I'm tied to a post with a grating headache and the dimmest Yews in five centuries," the Nightmare muttered. "Never been better."

The next voice was Petyr's. It was lifeless. "Wik's dead."

Ravyn's stomach dropped. He shut his eyes—let out a shaking breath—searched his mind for the right thing to say. Came up with nothing.

Jespyr said it for him, her voice coated with pain. "I'm so sorry, Petyr."

They remained quiet a long time.

"Elspeth," Ravyn finally managed. "Is she well?"

The Nightmare made a familiar clicking sound with his teeth. "Yes. But the more she *talks*," he said pointedly, "the less I can focus. Which is exactly how we got into this mess in the first place."

Elspeth's voice, that sharp, feminine timbre, untouched by the Nightmare's oil or spite—Ravyn had wanted to drown in it. She'd sounded so real. Real enough to make him think they might be together again after they dragged themselves out of hell.

But first, he had to discern where *hell* was, and who had tethered them there.

"I thought you said we'd have safe passage to the next barter if we made it across that bloody lake," Jespyr gritted out.

"The Spirit of the Wood has no need for crude walls or rope restraints, you little twit. Our captors are decidedly human."

Ravyn craned his neck, scanning as much of the courtyard as he could glimpse. "Did anyone get a look at them?"

"All I saw were their boots," Jespyr answered. "Two pairs, worn laces and soles. Hunting boots."

"Women," said the Nightmare. "They were women."

It hurt to think. But Ravyn knew for certain they were miles from Blunder. And those miles had been hard-earned. A stronghold this far from town would be of little use to the King. And as Captain, he knew Blunder's strongholds like the back of his hand.

So who the hell had built this one?

"I can see our weapons," Petyr said from the other side of the post. "They're in a heap against the wall." He shifted. Laughed. "They missed the knife in my boot." Then, as if it had injured him to laugh without his brother, the temper of his voice leached away. "I can't get to it."

"Someone is coming," the Nightmare hissed. "Bright with color." He clicked his teeth. "They've availed themselves of your Cards, Captain."

A figure appeared out of nothingness, Ravyn's Mirror Card held in a dirty hand. "Finally awake," came a woman's voice.

She was tall, adorned in clothes similar to what Ravyn might wear guised as a highwayman. Leather and wool and trousers that tucked into tall, worn-in boots. Her cloak was the color of peat moss. She wore the hood up, covering her hair save a few brown plaits that dangled near her ears.

Her face was obscured entirely by a mask. Not a highwayman's mask, but one of bone. A ram's skull.

"You have some quality Cards, Destriers," she said, twirling the Mirror between her fingers. "This one, plus the Black Horse and Nightmare, will come in handy. Though I doubt we'll have much use for a Maiden out here." Her head tilted as she surveyed Ravyn through the ram's empty eye sockets. "How's your head? I hear the smoke causes a brutal headache."

"She knows it does," came another female voice, somewhere near Jespyr. "Which is why she delights in making it. Too strong a dose this time, sister—they've been out for ages." A pause. "You're a Destrier?"

Jespyr's voice was even. "Don't I look like one?"

"Not really. Your face is missing that boorish, murderous quality."

"Come closer. You'll see it."

When the second woman came into view, Ravyn noted the same make of clothes. Her mask was bone as well—a wolf skull. She was just as tall as the other woman, just as broad in the shoulders.

"Who are you?"

The one in the ram mask opened her arms wide, a false welcoming. "Blunder's blight. Her vile outcasts. Her *infected.* Welcome to our hold, Destriers. It won't be a long stay. But I can promise your last hours on this earth will be full of wonder."

It wasn't a well-guarded fort. There were no sentries, and though dozens of men, women, and children passed through the courtyard, none of them bore weapons save a few bows and hunting knives. All were civilians, save the two women in charge. The one in the ram mask was called Otho, and her sister, with the wolf skull, Hesis.

The sisters moved around the post in tight, predatory circles. They didn't, for a single moment, believe that Ravyn, too, carried the infection.

"I know who you are," Hesis said. "Nephew to our vile King. You want me to believe that a *Rowan* would appoint an infected man as Captain of his Destriers?"

"It doesn't matter what you believe," Jespyr seethed. "It's true."

"And yet we found a charm on him. A viper's head in his tunic pocket."

Ravyn twisted against the ropes. "That's a spare."

Hesis laughed. She hit Ravyn across the face with a closed fist. The back of his head slammed against the pole—his headache so fierce his vision winked.

The Nightmare let out a low hiss.

"Say we suspend all disbelief," Otho hedged. "If you're infected, what's your magic?"

An easy question. And a long, complicated answer. "I can't use Providence Cards," Ravyn ground out.

"Yet you travel with a veritable arsenal."

"I can't use *all* the Cards."

Hesis sucked her teeth. "Sounds like another lie, Destrier." She hit him again.

"And your magic?" Jespyr demanded. "So we might know the merit of our kidnappers?"

Hesis disappeared out of Ravyn's view, her voice close to Jespyr's. "I can see through the eyes of crows," she said. "They speak to me, whispers and notions. It's how we found you lot. You made quite a lot of noise in the wood. Nests were upturned. I saw a hunting party in black cloaks cross Murmur Lake, coming our way." Her voice went slick with amusement. "My sister is an alchemist. That smoke that knocked you out? That pretty little headache, pounding in your skull? She made it. With magic."

"You're giving me a headache just fine on your own," Jespyr muttered.

A thud sounded on the pole. Jespyr groaned—then two more thuds as Hesis struck her.

Petyr swore, thrashing against the ropes. Ravyn bit down—hard.

The Nightmare's warning was but a whisper. "Careful."

The women turned, their focus finally landing on the Nightmare. "Who the hell are you?" Hesis said. "That's no Destrier sword we pulled from your hands."

A smile crept into his voice. "I was born with the fever, my blood dark as night. Perhaps you've heard of me."

"You must know of another stronghold," Ravyn offered. After so many years of lying, the truth was fragile upon his tongue. "Deep in the Black Forest, near the dried-out creek bed that runs northeast. A place children are brought when the Destriers and Physicians come sniffing too close."

The women's spines stiffened. Hesis let out a sharp exhale. "The children are brought there by highwaymen, not Destriers."

"All you know is that they wear masks."

Otho's laugh came out a bark. "You expect me to believe it was *you* who saved infected children all these years?"

"And I." Petyr's voice snagged. "My brother Wik as well. And you—you shot him. A man who lived outside the law for people like you."

Otho paused, watching Ravyn through the holes of her mask. "Yet your Captain still does the King's bidding. Still arrests infected folk and their kin. Still does unspeakable things to them."

Jespyr exhaled. "He doesn't—"

Hesis hit Ravyn square on the nose. He heard a *snap* all the way in the back of his head. Twin streams of blood fell from his nostrils over his mouth.

The Nightmare clicked his jaw. Once. Twice. Thrice.

"The Twin Alders Card," Ravyn managed, his words thick with blood, "that's why we're in the wood. We seek to unite the Deck—to heal the infection. We won't breathe a word of this place." His voice quickened, his control slipping. "After Solstice, when the mist is lifted, come to Castle Yew. We'll heal your degenerating—cure anyone who wishes to be cured. But you must let us go."

When they said nothing, utterly still, Jespyr's voice sounded from the other side of the post. "Our brother is infected. He's degenerating—dying. Please. *Let us go.*"

A ring of steel, then Otho and her ram's skull were an inch from Ravyn's face, a cold knife pressed against his throat. "Even if what you say is true," she seethed, "there are people here who have lost loved ones to Destriers. Parents, children. Our own mother's charm was destroyed, and a Rowan Scythe sent her to her death in the mist. There is payment due to the people of this fort. And a *Destrier* will pay it." She stepped back, nodding at her sister. "It's time."

Hesis disappeared into the fort. Clamoring voices sounded, growing louder. Doors banged open and the fort emptied itself, a crowd forming. Everyone wore skull masks—save one. A man, led by a rope. His face was bloody, his eyes wide, teeth flashing. He was tethered, but still he thrashed, fought.

Just as Ravyn had trained him to.

Gorse.

"We will have our payment, Captain," Otho said. "Now."

The Nightmare remained tied to the post next to Petyr, fingers curling like claws.

The Destriers—Ravyn and Jespyr and Gorse—were unleashed

in the dirt courtyard, rough instruments shoved into their hands. A club with rusted nails driven into it for Jespyr, a riding crop with rocks tied to its tassels for Gorse.

And for Ravyn, the dull, rusted blade of a scythe.

"For the kin of a Rowan," Hesis said behind her mask. She pushed him toward the others, and the crowd closed in around them.

It was clear what was meant to happen. The three of them hemmed into a circle, armed with poor weaponry—this was a blood sport. The kind without winners.

A man wearing an ewe skull called out to the crowd. "Are we ready to smell Destrier blood?"

A roar clashed against the walls of the courtyard. It rose up over the jagged fence into the forest, a long, devastating cry. Bile crawled up Ravyn's throat. He forced it back down.

Gorse shook and Jespyr's copper skin went the color of ash. At the post, Petyr tugged against his restraints.

The Nightmare stood eerily still.

The crowd went quiet as Otho came forward. Her arms were bare, her veins black as ink. She stepped to Ravyn, held a closed fist to her mouth—

And blew smoke into his face.

Salt cut across Ravyn's senses. He coughed, eyes rolling back a moment. The smoke burned down his throat—not sweet like the smoke that had rendered him unconscious, but hot and cold and acidic all at once.

Otho did the same to Jespyr—blowing smoke in her face. When she came to Gorse, he swung his whip at her.

Otho dodged it—dispelling her smoke a final time.

Gorse made a retching sound, his eyes rolling. "What the hell is that?"

Otho stepped back to the rim of the crowd next to her sister, her voice cutting through the courtyard. "Magic, alchemized by two things. Rage, and hate. Bones of the enraged infected—and your cloak, hateful Destrier. They make a wretched pairing, do they not?"

Ravyn felt his entire body go hot, his well-honed restraint snapping. He ran the back of his hand over his mouth—wiping away blood from his nose. He turned to the Nightmare. "Is this what it was like, when Hauth beat Elspeth's head in? Did you sit by then, just as you do now, enjoying the show?"

He hadn't meant to say it. The words had pried themselves out of him, acrid on his tongue. Only, no one seemed shocked to hear them. The crowd was expectant, as if they'd been waiting for him to say something vile. Some even cheered.

It was the smoke, he realized. Otho's smoke—her magic—had washed his mind clean, leaving but two things. *Rage,* and *hate.*

Ravyn shifted the rusty scythe between calloused fingers, his headache replaced by bloodlust. "You said you cared for Elspeth. That you protected her. And you did—just as well as you protected your own children, it seems."

The Nightmare's yellow eyes burned, his voice sharpened by malice. "You are, without a doubt, the greatest disappointment in five hundred years, Ravyn Yew. Every time I glance your way, I find myself wishing I'd spent another century in the dark—that I'd spared myself the agony of your stony, witless incompetency."

"Another century would have been too soon," Ravyn bit back. "At least then I might have had more than a single moment with the woman you stole from me."

Across the circle from him, Gorse sneered.

Jespyr turned on him, knuckles flexing around the club in her hand. "Something to say, coward?"

Gorse's bloody face went redder still. "What did you call me?"

"Ugly *and* stupid." Jespyr raised her voice. "I called you a coward, runaway Destrier."

Gorse's crop whipped through the air, the rocks at the ends so close to Jespyr's face they stirred her hair. "Better a coward than a thief and a liar," he spat, turning the crop toward Ravyn. "Our two-faced Captain stole the King's Nightmare Card. Worse, he's been fucking an infected woman—"

Jespyr's club slammed into Gorse's shoulder.

The crowd erupted in a hollering jeer. "And with that," Hesis called, "we begin."

Jespyr looked at her bat, then at Gorse, her gaze wide—like she hadn't meant to hit him. A moment later, her eyes narrowed. "You don't deserve to wear the Destrier's cloak." She turned to Ravyn. "Neither do you."

Vitriol poured out of him. "You think you could be a better Captain, Jes? Take it from me. Hell, I'll even waive the challenge. Because you couldn't beat me, not without your Black Horse—your precious little crutch." Ravyn's voice went dangerously low. "Go on, take my place. Be Uncle's puppet. Bow and scrape and swallow the bit he shoves in your mouth. You've always been better at those things than me."

Jespyr lunged.

Ravyn pivoted, but not before the nails in his sister's club took a bite out of his cloak.

"You want to talk about crutches, brother?" she seethed. "Let's talk about yours."

Ravyn held his arms open wide. "Do your worst."

Jespyr pushed left and the circle shifted. She, Ravyn, and Gorse moved in a slow rotation, never taking their eyes off of each other.

"You tell yourself the Destriers hate you because you're

infected. They don't—not all of them." Jespyr spat the words. "They hate you because you think you're better than them."

"I am better than them."

Gorse opened his mouth but Jespyr cut him off. "Big, strong Ravyn Yew. The Captain who never smiled, never fell, never flinched—who lies to his King, his men, and most of all, to himself." Her eyes went cold. "You're not better than anyone, brother. And you're not stronger than me. You just pretend that you are."

"You want to know what I've been pretending at all these years? I'll tell you." Ravyn went still, breaking the circle's rotation. "I pretend that I don't spend every moment of every day *hating* myself for being Captain of the Destriers."

"You're a traitor," Gorse spat. "And you'll bleed for it."

"Likely." Ravyn fixed his stance—aimed with both eyes open. "But not yet."

The scythe flew. Without his Black Horse, Gorse's reflexes were slow. The scythe caught him along the shoulder, the dull edge finding purchase over his breastbone.

Deep. But not, with such an aged, rusted blade, deep enough to kill.

The crowd roared. Ravyn was across the yard in a breath. Vision limned in red, he knocked Gorse to the ground, hand on the Destrier's throat. Gorse looked up at him with wide, bloodshot eyes. He'd dropped his whip. But his fists met Ravyn's ribs over and over again.

Air shot out of Ravyn's lungs. He kept his hand on Gorse's throat and thought about blood and whips and the smell of smoke, clawing its way up the dungeon stairs. Of terrible things he'd had to watch, had to do, as Captain of the Destriers.

Ravyn leaned close to Gorse's mottling face. "Be wary, Destrier," he ground out. "Be clever. Be good." Then, with a final, brutal push—

He crushed Gorse's windpipe.

A slow, hungry cheer raked over the courtyard. They'd wanted Destrier blood. And Gorse, taken by the great, final sleep, was a crimson canvas. Red spilled from the scythe wound, trickling into the dirt, feeding the soil, burrowing its way into the cracks in Ravyn's hands.

The smoke's magic slipped away, taking *rage* and *hate* with it.

Ravyn stared down at Gorse, hands shaking. This time, the bile refused to be forced down. Ravyn leaned over and was sick in the dirt, his ribs screaming pain as he heaved.

The courtyard went eerily quiet.

Ravyn looked up. Someone had breached the circle and was standing between him and Jespyr. An unmasked woman, shadowed by two young boys. She wore a green dress and a cloak of the same color with a white tree embroidered near the collar. Her graying gold hair was loose, her hazel eyes wide. Wide, familiar—

And trained on the Nightmare.

Opal Hawthorn put a hand to her mouth. "Elspeth," she said, tears in her eyes. "You're alive."

With a few booming commands from Otho, the courtyard cleared—spectators filing into the fort, the dark sockets of their bone masks trained on Ravyn as they went. They dragged Gorse's body with them, a bloody trail the Destrier's last mark upon the kingdom he'd served.

Ravyn locked his hands into fists. Even then, they shook.

Opal stood at the post opposite the Nightmare, staring at what used to be her niece, tears in her eyes. Ravyn knew her pain by heart. She'd seen a maiden with black hair and thought it was Elspeth—only to be met by terrifying yellow eyes.

Just as Ione had in the dungeon, Opal placed a hand on the Nightmare's cheek and lost the color in her own. "What's happened to you?" she whispered. "You're—different."

The Nightmare's expression was smooth. "I am."

"You're—you're not Elspeth."

The Nightmare said nothing. Opal's hand fell. She stepped back from the post and began to weep. Her boys stood next to her, their young eyes wide as they stared at the Nightmare. But when Ravyn moved to approach—to explain—Hesis pulled a rapier from her belt. "Stay back."

"I don't understand," Opal said, scrubbing tears from her cheeks. "Why have they been imprisoned?" Her eyes moved to Jespyr. "She's the one who warned me the Destriers were coming."

Otho's posture stiffened.

Jespyr reached for Opal's hand. Spoke in a gentle voice. "How did you and your boys end up here?"

"I brought her," Hesis said through her mask of bone. "The stronghold your Captain spoke of is full. But we have plenty of room here, far beyond the King's reach. Or so we thought."

Jespyr explained to Opal, Otho and Hesis leaning in to listen, what had happened to Elspeth that night at Spindle House. That Tyrn and Erik and Ione were at Stone. Why they had journeyed into the wood.

Ravyn withdrew to the post.

"All right, lad?" Petyr grunted.

Ravyn could still feel the pillar of Gorse's hitching throat in the center of his palm. "Fine."

Petyr lowered his voice. "The knife they overlooked is in my left boot."

When the hollows of Otho's and Hesis's masks were turned on Jespyr and Opal, Ravyn planted his foot next to Petyr's—made like he was tying his laces—and slipped his hand into Petyr's boot. When he withdrew it, his fingers were wrapped around a slender leather sheath.

The blade was small, its hilt a hook. Ravyn stood—rounded the post until he was near the Nightmare. "Don't move."

But when he pressed the blade against the rope, his hand shook so hard the rope quivered. He paused. Tried again.

Had they been soldiers under his command, Ravyn would have dismissed Otho and Hesis for their ineptitude—he was making a boar's ass of cutting a simple tether. But their focus was so tight on Jespyr, lost to her story of the Shepherd King, that they didn't notice the rope shake for a full minute before it finally cleaved.

The Nightmare held Ravyn in his yellow gaze the entire time. "Messy business, killing." The corner of his lip twitched. "Elspeth says you look terrible."

Ravyn's gaze shot up. "She didn't say that."

"No. She didn't." He cleared his throat. "It seems I owe you an apology."

"You mean Elspeth wants you to apologize."

"Annoyingly, yes." His mouth grew strained. "Witless though you are, you are not a disappointment."

Had it been a different day or week or month, Ravyn might have laughed, watching the monster squirm. But he was far too tired for that now. "Does it cost you—showing a fraction of remorse, Shepherd King?"

"Yes. And I require recompense." Those yellow eyes turned hard. "It's taking me centuries of restraint not to rip your head from your body after that outburst about Elspeth." A flash of teeth. "About my children."

"I didn't mean to say it. That smoke—that magic—"

"Rage and hate. Two things I know well enough."

Ravyn bit down. "I don't know what happened to your children. But I know you would not want to see Elspeth harmed. It is perhaps the only thing I understand about you."

Neither of them had apologized—not really. But an airing of truths, after so much malice, was the best they could do.

The Nightmare's gaze drifted up the fort walls. "I've had enough of this wretched place. Give me the knife."

"No. I don't want blood on Elspeth's hands."

The Nightmare's gaze lingered over Ravyn's nose. It had begun to ache, his nose—a hot, constant agony ever since Hesis had struck it. Broken, he guessed.

When the Nightmare spoke again, the smoothness in his voice was gone. "The knife. Now."

Ravyn faced those terrible yellow eyes. Looked for Elspeth. Could not see her. "Don't kill anyone," he growled.

When Hesis approached, Ravyn's hands were at his sides. Shaking, but empty.

"Opal Hawthorn is a good woman. Though her wits may have abandoned her, because she's insisting you and your sister possess *honor*." Hesis heaved a sigh, alternating her rapier between her hands. "Even if that were true—we cannot let you leave. You would inevitably return to Stone. I hear the King is fond of his inquests. Sooner or later, the truth of what happened and who you saw on your journey to the Twin Alders Card will out. I cannot allow—"

There was a tearing sound, a flash of movement in Ravyn's periphery. Hesis had but a moment to shift her blade from Ravyn to the Nightmare.

It wasn't enough.

The Nightmare sprang off the post. He struck the snout of Hesis's mask with the heel of his palm, an ugly *crack* echoing in the yard. She screamed, dropped her rapier.

Otho bolted toward her sister, but Ravyn surged forward—caught her with a broad arm—slammed her onto the dirt. When she tried to reach for her blade, Jespyr pressed a boot onto her arm.

"Pocket," Ravyn gritted out. "Our Cards. Hurry."

Jespyr reached into Otho's jerkin. She pulled out their Cards—Nightmare and Mirror and Maiden, then two Black Horses. Hers, and Gorse's.

Otho glared up at them through the empty sockets of her mask. "If the King uses a Chalice on you, it will be the death of every soul in this place. Their blood will be on *your* hands."

"It won't come to that," the Nightmare called, he and Petyr aiming toward their pile of weapons. "I have plans for the Rowans."

Petyr handed Ravyn his belt of knives—his satchel and sword.

Opal Hawthorn had retreated to the courtyard doors, wide-eyed, with her sons. "Castle Yew," Ravyn said as he approached. "If this place ever proves unsafe, go to Castle Yew. My family will protect you."

Opal nodded, but her gaze was lost over his shoulder. There were tears in her eyes once more. "And Elspeth?"

Ravyn's voice was ragged. "I'm going to get her back. No matter the cost."

The fort door groaned, and Petyr and Jespyr hurried through. Ravyn offered Opal his hand. He didn't think her the sort of woman who would mind that his fingers were trembling.

She shook his hand. Squeezed it tightly. "Good luck."

When Ravyn cast his eyes back into the courtyard, Otho was hurrying toward her sister. Hesis lay in the dirt, unmoving. Her mask was broken, shards of bone scattered around her. Blood trickled down her face.

"Nightmare," he said through his teeth.

The monster laughed as he slipped out of the fort. "She'll live. All I did was pay her back for breaking your nose."

"I didn't ask you to do that."

"No. But Elspeth did."

Chapter Thirty

Elm

Elm had not visited the catacombs beneath the castle since boyhood. Knuckles white, he held a torch in one hand and his ring of keys in the other, every bend along their journey begging him to flinch.

Not like Ione. Nothing seemed to frighten her—an interesting testament to the Maiden's effects. No shadow was large enough, no room cold enough to shift her unsmiling expression.

Her latest dress must have been another loan. It was pale gray, with sleeves that billowed down to her wrists and a collar that choked just below her jaw. Shapeless vile drapery. Twice, she caught Elm looking at it. Twice, she reprimanded him with a scowl.

The third time she caught him, they were near the King's private vaults. "Trees." Her voice echoed against stone walls. "*What?*"

Elm cleared his throat. "Nothing."

Ione's eyes dropped to the bust of her dress. "Go on. Tell me how much you hate it. I know you're dying to."

He ran a hand over the back of his neck and pinned his gaze on the path ahead. "You look good."

"Good?"

"Good, Hawthorn." He bit at a fingernail. "You always look good."

A pause. Then a sharp "What's the matter with you?"

Elm's eyes shot to her face. He thought he'd been hiding it well—all the discomfort of being in that cold, awful castle. The places Hauth had led him at the edge of a Scythe to toughen him as a boy. But before he could say anything, Ione added, "You're being strangely nice."

Ahead, Elm could see the yellow torches. The fortified doors. They were almost at the vaults. "I imagine there is an Ione," he said, "buried somewhere in there, who might appreciate a little niceness from a Rowan."

"Niceness." She said the word slowly, as if to taste it. "If only I could feel it."

"What did you use to feel? Before the Maiden."

"Everything. In terrible, wonderful excess. Joy, anger, compassion, revulsion—" Her voice chilled on the word. "Love. I knew them all so well. When the Maiden began to dull them, it frightened me—but it was also a reprieve. After a lifetime of feeling things so keenly, the numbness felt good." She heaved a sigh. "But even that went away. And nothing felt good, or bad, anymore."

She looked out onto the path ahead. "But I think about who I was before the Maiden. I try to make the same choices I used to make. I need to be able to live with myself when this facade"—she gestured to her face—"comes crashing down."

"What about killing those highwaymen? I doubt that's a choice the old Ione would make."

A muscle feathered in her jaw. "If you believe that you understand who I was before the Maiden, just because you once saw me ride through the wood with mud on my ankles, then you are not as clever as you think you are."

Elm lowered his voice. "And what happened the other night in the cellar? Is that something you'll be able to live with?"

Ione's chest swelled, a beautiful breath—an up-and-down sweep not even that horrid dress could confound. "That depends on you, Prince. Are you truly nothing like your brother? Or are you simply a gifted liar?"

He frowned. "I haven't lied to you."

"No?" She glanced up at him. "Then answer again. Did you know Elspeth was infected before she was arrested?"

The lie slammed into Elm's teeth. *I knew nothing of that.* Only this time, he swallowed it. He looked into those brilliant hazel eyes and did not flinch. "I've known since Equinox."

Ione stilled. "You didn't turn her in."

Elm gave a sweeping bow. "As you've noted, Miss Hawthorn—I'm a rotten Prince and a piss-poor Destrier. Must have slipped my mind."

They walked in silence the rest of the way to the vault. Two guards stood watch, stiffening at their posts, heads dipping in rushed deference. Elm flicked his wrist at the door. "Open it."

The door groaned, ancient, heavy. Elm's father kept many things in Stone's vaults. The histories of Rowan Kings. Gold.

Providence Cards.

The Shepherd King had said there were three Maiden Cards in the castle. One of which, Elm was certain, was here, in his father's collection.

Like all the dark, cold places of Stone, the vaults felt dead to Elm. Shadows dogged him, memories and echoes. A shiver ran up his back, the old bruises on his knuckles stinging with new life. "My father's collection should be near," he said, the yawning space throwing his voice back at him—a thin, distorted echo.

The floor was cluttered and ill lit. Ione's foot caught against a wooden chest. She swore, stumbling. When Elm offered her his hand, she glared down at it a moment. It was too dark to tell if there was a flush in her cheeks. But when Elm pulled her toward him, lacing their fingers together, he felt one in his own.

The King kept his Cards in a box as old as the castle itself. Cold, iron-forged—locked. Only three keys existed. His father had one. Aldys Beech, the treasurer, had another. And Elm, the second heir, a reluctant keeper of keys, had the third.

He handed Ione the torch and fumbled through the ring of keys. When he found the correct one, he slid it into the box. The latch ground to a slow, steady open.

Providence Cards waited inside, so seemingly innocent, as if men had not coveted and fought and stolen for them. They weren't all there. The Scythes were with the Rowans. Hauth's Scythe was in his chamber, along with the Nightmare Card. The Destriers had the Black Horses.

And of course, the Deck would always be incomplete without the Twin Alders Card.

"If Hauth was smart about hiding your Maiden, he'd have forced you to put it somewhere you could not access alone. Does any of this look familiar?"

Ione cast her gaze around the vaults. "No."

"I'm going to pull out the Prophet." Elm glanced down at the box full of Cards. "There is a Maiden Card in there, too. If it is yours, and I reach in and touch it—"

"The magic will stop."

"Is that what you want?"

Ione said nothing. She reached into the box. When she pulled out a pink Maiden Card, Elm heard her suck in a breath. It did something distressing to his chest, watching her shut her eyes as if she were bracing herself for something terrible. Once, twice, thrice, she tapped the Card. Everything went silent.

And Ione Hawthorn looked as she ever did. Unbearably beautiful. Unreachable.

It was the wrong Maiden Card.

Elm's stomach dropped. Ione said nothing. If she felt disappointment, it didn't show on her face. She simply handed the Maiden to him and watched, impassive, as he placed it back into the box.

Elm retrieved the Prophet, then the Mirror, and shoved them into his pocket. "It was a long shot."

She didn't seem to hear him. "Your hands are shaking."

"I'm cold," he ground out, slamming the box shut and locking it. "And I hate it down here."

"Is there any place in Stone you don't hate?"

"No." Then, "The library, maybe."

This time, Ione offered her hand. "Let me guess," Elm said. "When you're free of the Maiden, and all the *feelings* come back, you worry you won't be able to live with yourself if you didn't take pity on the trembling, rotten Prince."

"Trees, you're annoying." She gripped his hand tight enough to still Elm's tremors. "Now tell me how to get to the library."

Ione's eyes went wide when they stepped through the double arched doors. Her chin tilted up, her hazel gaze lifting to the towering library shelves and limestone pillars and that high, arched ceiling. It struck Elm with a feeling he hadn't yet worked out, that she'd brought him there to make *him* feel better.

She shouldn't be trying to make him feel anything—not with her affections locked away. But what Elm had suspected before, he was growing more certain of.

There were some things not even magic could erase.

The library wasn't empty. But the long mahogany table in front of the fireplace was. Elm's stylus and sketchbook were still splayed on the floor from two days ago. He collected them and slid into a chair with his back to the flames. Ione took the seat next to him.

Elm opened his sketchbook. He had nothing to draw. But he needed to keep busy, at least until the tight, oppressive buzzing in his hands—his chest and feet—became more tolerable.

He ran the stylus in long, sweeping strokes over the paper, pressing too hard, indenting several pages. "I'm sorry. I get like this, sometimes," he said, frowning at his hands. "At Stone."

Ione's silhouette was a soft specter in his periphery. She swept her hand over his sketchbook, a finger trailing the frayed ends of all the pages he'd ripped out. "It must be difficult, being here without your cousins. Being forced to take your brother's place as heir."

Elm's eyes shot to her face. "How do you know about that?"

"You stood in Hauth's place in the throne room. Sat in his chair in the great hall. I should think it obvious."

"The King hasn't announced it yet." Elm pushed hair from his eyes. "He's waiting."

"For what?"

For me to choose a wife.

When he didn't answer, Ione lifted her shoulders—an impartial shrug. "I figured he'd name you. I even considered asking you about it in the cellar, but…"

But things had gone unplanned, in the cellar.

Elm rolled his jaw. The anxiety from the vaults was slipping away, replaced by a new disquiet. He leaned over the table, resting his cheek in his hand. "About that, Hawthorn. If I was—If you didn't enjoy yourself—" He cleared his throat. "If you'd rather pretend it never happened, I'll understand."

"What makes you think I didn't enjoy myself?"

Elm's laugh held an edge. "To say you left in a hurry would hardly do it justice. You fled."

Ione lowered her gaze to the sketchbook. She took Elm's stylus, then ran it with delicate abandon over the paper. A lock of yellow hair fell from behind her ear. "Would it shock you, Prince, if I said had we not been interrupted, I'd have stayed?"

"To what end?"

The stylus stilled on the paper. And Elm was rewarded by a nigh-invisible flush. A pink hue, that climbed from beneath the awful frilly collar of her dress into Ione's jaw, settling in her face—making her mouth even pinker. It did wonderful, horrible things to his imagination. He wondered where else she was that shade of pink.

"You'd like me to tell you all the things we might have done?" she asked.

"Yes."

"In sordid detail?"

"Absolutely."

Ione ran the stem of the stylus down the center of her lips—looked him in the eye. "Beg me to."

Elm's hand flexed. He hauled in a sharp breath—

The corners of Ione's mouth twitched. She was toying with him—and he had only himself to blame. He'd told her to do so. And now she, like him, had made a science, a wicked game, of measuring his reactions to her.

A curse slipped from Elm's lips. He ran a hand through his unkempt hair. "You are so lucky we aren't alone right now."

As if summoned by his words, footsteps sounded. Someone cleared their throat, and then a chair on the opposite side of the table was being pulled out. When Elm turned, he was face-to-face with Baldwyn.

The King's steward carried an enormous ledger, which he dropped on the table with an unceremonious thud. He surveyed Elm over his spectacles. "Prince Renelm." His beady brown eyes flickered to Ione. "Miss Hawthorn."

Elm's teeth set on edge. "What do you want, Baldwyn?"

The steward undid the leather clasp from his ledger. "Your father had some vital papers drawn up, Your Highness." He took out ink and a quill. "I require your time and your signature."

"What for?"

"The business side of things, as you called it," Baldwyn said, dipping into the ink.

Elm glanced down at the ledger—the stack of parchment held within its bindings. Even upside down, he could read it.

Renelm Rowan. His Second Royalty. Keeper of Laws. Heir to Blunder.

Elm put a hand over his face. "That was quick."

"Actually, sire, the papers were ready yesterday. But I was told you were away, gallivanting at Castle Yew."

"The Gallivanting Heir—I like it. Add it to the title."

Baldwyn glanced up. "Humor," he said, his voice dried out by condescension. "How different you are from your brother."

The chair next to Elm slid back, and Ione pushed to her feet. "I'll leave you two—"

Elm wrapped his fingers in her skirt and held tight. "Not so fast, Hawthorn."

Ione looked down at him, eyes narrowing. "I'll only be in the way."

"Right where I like you. We need a witness, do we not, Baldwyn?"

"Just so. I have already asked—"

"Perfect. I volunteer Miss Hawthorn." Elm gave Ione's dress a hard tug. She dropped back into her chair with a plunk, hazel eyes flaring, only to go cold a second later.

Baldwyn flipped through the parchment, then turned the ledger around so that it faced Elm and Ione. He glanced over his shoulder to a scribe waiting in the wing of the library. "No need, Hamish," he called. "We have acquired a new witness."

The scribe nodded and stepped away. When he did, he had to force his way through a party of four women, none of them moving to make room. They spoke to one another in hushed voices behind gloved fingers, all of their eyes trained on Elm.

"Trees," he muttered, itchy beneath their scrutiny. But before he turned away, one of the four women caught his gaze. He couldn't remember her name. Yvette Laburnum—was that it? Her father was a busybody, but his estate brought more wine into Blunder than the rest combined, so he was tolerated.

Yvette had brown curly hair and wore a vibrant blue dress. But it was not the sharp cerulean hue of her attire that had snagged Elm's eye.

It was the inhuman, ethereal quality of her face. She was too perfect—her glowing skin without flaw, her face so symmetrical it almost looked uncanny. So much beauty, it hardly seemed real.

Because it wasn't.

Next to him, Ione leaned forward. She, too, was watching Yvette. Elm reached under the table, brushing his knuckles against Ione's leg, an unspoken acknowledgment of the thing—the magic—that had joined them in the library.

Another Maiden Card.

The Shepherd King had said there were three in the castle. One Maiden was stowed deep in his father's vaults. Another, it seemed, belonged to Yvette Laburnum.

Two down. One more to go.

The afternoon slipped away, tending to the King's paperwork. Elm's fingertips were ink stained for all the times he had signed his name, each *Renelm* less formal than the one before it.

Ione sat through it all, eyes vacant. Elm reached under the table more than once, pinched her leg, tugged her skirt—searched for a sign of life. Her eyes would flare a moment and the corners of her mouth twitch, but beyond that, nothing.

When the title was finally finished and Elm named heir to the throne of Blunder, the only observance was the snapping shut of Baldwyn's ledger. He bowed. "I shall see you at the feast in an hour, sire."

Ione and Elm lingered at the table. "How does it feel, knowing you will wear the crown?"

"Like falling off a horse." Elm reached into his pocket and pulled out the three Providence Cards he'd taken from the vaults, anxious to be rid of the subject of kingship. He put the Cards on the table—Scythe, Mirror, Prophet.

Ione glanced down at them. "Why did you take the Mirror?"

"If the Prophet Card does nothing to help us find your Maiden, combing your mind with a Nightmare Card is the next obvious choice." He shifted in his seat. "And I have no intention of waltzing into Hauth's room and asking for it."

"You'd steal it?"

Elm's eyes dropped to her mouth. He imagined whispering all sorts of things into it—telling Ione Hawthorn that it put him more at ease to be a highwayman than a Rowan Prince. "I think I can manage it." He slid the Prophet Card in front of her. "Have you used one of these before?"

She nodded, tracing the image upon the Card—an old man obscured by a gray hood. "My mother has one."

Had, Elm thought, a pinch in his gut. "They are not always literal, the visions of the future."

"I'm aware." Ione tapped the Prophet three times and shut her eyes.

She held still but for the rise and fall of her chest. A moment later Ione's eyes snapped open, her fingers rigid as she tapped the Prophet, freeing herself from its magic. Had Elm not become a student of her face, he might have missed the faint line that drew between her brows. "Did you see your Maiden?"

"I don't know. I—" She pulled her bottom lip into her mouth. "I don't know *what* I saw."

"Tell me."

"I was in a meadow. There was snow on the ground outside a small stone chamber. The Yew family was there, carrying a frail boy in their arms." Her voice quieted. "You were there, too, Prince. As were my father and Uncle Erik."

Elm went cold. "Was the boy Emory?"

"Yes. A tall man I've never seen before guarded me with a sword. He had yellow eyes, just as Elspeth does now. He took my hand, unfurled my fingers. There were three Cards, nestled in my palm. The Maiden, the Scythe—"

Her hazel eyes lifted. "And the Twin Alders."

Chapter Thirty-One

Ravyn

They hurried through the wood, dusk on their heels. Above, crows cawed, their wings darkening the gaps between trees. Ravyn recalled what Hesis had said about her magic. *I can see through the eyes of crows.*

Jespyr glanced skyward. "Wolves, now crows. Just once, I'd like not to be stalked through these wretched woods."

The Nightmare led them. He broke his pace to tap his sword thrice upon the earth, then placed a hand upon a gnarled aspen tree. He shut his eyes. Whispered.

Eyes shut like that, it could have so easily been Elspeth. Ravyn's insides wrenched. "What are you doing?"

"Asking for the way."

A great stillness came over the wood. No breeze touched them, no leaves crunched beneath their boots. The mist held them in its arms, salt and sting and a chill that went so deep, it reminded Ravyn of the dungeon at Stone.

Then, one by one, the aspen branches began to turn. Crooked, they bent, but never snapped.

All of them pointed east.

When the Nightmare opened his yellow eyes, they were bleary. "We're almost there."

The mist thickened, and the sky became dark. The Nightmare's sword gleamed in the dim light as he led them through bramble and dense underbrush. There was no path. But his gait was fast, sure.

A pulsing pain cut across Ravyn's face, radiating from his nose, which had begun to bleed again. When blood dripped into his mouth, he coughed—spat it out.

The Nightmare turned.

"I'm fine," Ravyn snapped. "Keep going."

The ground began to slope downward into a shallow valley, the mist so dense and the sky so dark Ravyn could hardly see an arm's length ahead. A thud sounded behind him, followed by a flurry of curses. Ravyn found Petyr caught in a dogwood—freed him with a firm wrench to his collar.

"We need to stop," Petyr said. "We'll snap our ankles wading through bramble like this." He made a face. "Your nose is a mess, lad."

"This whole journey is a mess," Jespyr muttered. One glance at Ravyn's face made her stop short. "He's right. We should break for the night."

"Here," came the Nightmare's slippery voice from ahead. When they met him at the bottom of the valley, he was standing stone-still at the edge of a new wood.

The trees in front of him did not merely stand close to one another. They were a *wall.* Just like the lake, the wood stretched farther than the horizon. There were hundreds—thousands—of trees, all woven together.

Ravyn's pulse quickened. He stepped forward, putting a calloused hand on a crooked trunk. "They're alder trees."

The Nightmare's voice slipped between his teeth. "The

second begins at the neck of a wood, where you cannot turn back, though truly, you should. Those here that enter are neither wary, clever, nor good. You know nothing of hell—

"Till you've crossed the alderwood."

Wind whispered through the trees and on it, the biting scent of salt.

"The Twin Alders Card," Jespyr said, her eyes cast skeptically down the endless row of trees. "It's inside?"

"Yes."

"How do we get in?"

"That is for tomorrow. For now—" The Nightmare turned, facing back the way they'd come. "Aspen," he murmured.

The aspen trees began to move into the valley. Dirt upturned, and the ground rolled. Petyr lost his balance and fell, and Jespyr braced herself on Ravyn before she, too, caught a mouthful of dirt.

The Nightmare swung his sword in low, circular patterns, and the aspens followed in accordance. When the trees were finished rearranging themselves, they stood in a circle around the party.

The Nightmare clicked his blade thrice more, and the trees went still, so close together a child couldn't slip through the gaps in their trunks.

"We should be safe from any manner of beast in here," the Nightmare said. He turned—aimed the tip of his sword at Ravyn's face. "Sit down, Ravyn Yew. I'm going to fix your broken beak."

Ravyn's broad back pressed against an aspen trunk. He didn't like it. It felt too much like the pole he'd been tethered to in that fort, where he'd forfeited all his composure.

Where he'd killed Gorse.

Petyr lowered himself next to him with a grunt. "Wik—" He exhaled, voice uneven. "He broke my nose when we were kids. Hurt like hell."

"I'm fine."

The Nightmare's chuckle sounded from a few paces away. He poured water from Petyr's canteen over his hands, washing away grime.

Jespyr crouched on the farthest side of the aspen circle, all of them looking away while she relieved herself behind a shrub. When she finished she stood—ran a hand over her cheek. Winced. "I'm not sure those bitches didn't break something in my face, too."

It was too dark to see much of her. The moon was but a pale smudge in the night sky, swathed in mist. Still, the swell of Jespyr's left cheek was unmistakable.

Ravyn hadn't noticed it during their fight in the courtyard. Otho's magic—that terrible smoke—had limned his vision in red. He hadn't known anything but rage and hate.

Guilt clutched him by the throat. He dug in his pocket—squinting in the dim light to discern which Card was pink. "Here," he said, holding out the Maiden Card to the Nightmare. "Hand this to her."

The Nightmare's nostrils flared, his gaze passing over the Maiden. "I can't touch it."

Ravyn raised his brows.

"Believe me, I wish I could. I'd have saved myself the aggravation of traveling with you were I capable of taking back the Twin Alders myself. But this is still Elspeth's body. Any Card I touch—she will absorb the object I paid to forge it."

Jespyr rounded on him, plucking the Maiden out of Ravyn's hands. "What did you pay for this one, Shepherd King?"

"His hair, shorn off with a blade," Petyr answered. There was a pause. "What? It's not like I haven't read *The Old Book*."

Ravyn touched his nose. Winced. "Didn't know you could read at all."

Petyr's elbow met his bruised ribs. "Laugh while you can. We all know that pretty pink Card won't do a thing to heal *you*."

Jespyr tapped the Maiden. Closed her eyes. Let out a long breath. "Trees," she said, her voice reverent. "It feels so good not to be in pain." She pressed a hand to her healed cheek, then tapped the Maiden thrice more. "Say Elspeth touched this Card instead of the Nightmare all those years ago. She would have absorbed...your hair?"

"Yes," the Nightmare replied. "I had long hair. Dark." His eyes raised over Ravyn's head. "Like yours. Perhaps it would have clogged her throat. Strung itself around her heart. Made a nest in her lungs."

Jespyr took her seat next to Ravyn. "Just when I think you're getting tolerable, you go and open your mouth."

The Nightmare approached on silent step. He loomed above them. Clicked his teeth—then gripped Ravyn's nose.

There was a terrible grinding sound, pain biting over the mask of Ravyn's face. "*Fucking trees.*"

"As I suspected," the Nightmare said, indifferent. "Decidedly broken."

Ravyn jerked his head back. "You're hardly a Physician."

"No. But I've mended my share of noses—my own in particular."

"I hope whoever broke it enjoyed the feeling."

"I'm sure he did." His voice caught in the mist. "He had an exacting hand, Brutus Rowan, when it came to pain."

They all went still.

Slowly, Jespyr leaned forward. "Did you know him well? The first Rowan King?"

"Piss on that," Petyr said. "Tell us what everyone's spent five hundred years guessing. Was he the one who killed you?"

The Nightmare didn't answer. His mouth was a tight line, and his eyes were on the trees. He had that faraway look he got when he was talking to Elspeth.

Ravyn rolled his jaw. "Well?"

Yellow eyes snapped onto him. "Yes. I knew him well." He leaned over Ravyn. "This is going to hurt. You may wish to distract yourself."

"How do you propose I do that?"

"Reach into your pocket."

Ravyn's brow knit, and the Nightmare blew out a breath. "Not stupid indeed," he muttered. "The Nightmare Card, Ravyn Yew. That's as good an invitation to enter my mind as you'll ever get."

Seams groaning, Ravyn shoved his hand into his pocket—wrenched out the Mirror, then Gorse's Black Horse.

His stomach turned. When he pulled out the Nightmare Card, his hands were shaking.

Three taps. Salt. Then—*Ravyn.*

He shut his eyes. *Elspeth.*

Are you—A sharp, angry sound fluttered through Ravyn's mind. *I keep trying to reach for your hand.*

A knot corded in Ravyn's throat. *I wish you could.*

They're shaking. Your hands.

I know. They've been shaking since—

The Nightmare reached forward. Gripped Ravyn's nose between both hands. There was another terrible grinding sound, cartilage and bone, and then Ravyn was reeling. Petyr and Jespyr pressed his arms down on both sides.

"Stay still, you bucking horse," Jespyr grunted.

Hold still, Ravyn.

Pain painted him. His face twisted, and he screwed his eyes shut tighter still, trying to hide it. But he couldn't—not this time. *Don't look at me, Elspeth.*

Ravyn.

He jerked his head—spoke to Elspeth—to himself—in a ragged voice. "I don't want anyone to see me like this."

Jespyr caught his left hand, then Petyr his right. And Elspeth—her voice was everywhere. A thousand rose petals falling over him. *You are in no danger of losing me—your sister—your friends. There is no weakness in pain, Ravyn.*

Pressure built behind his eyes. "What I did in that courtyard—what I said—"

Jespyr held his arm, bracing it against tremors. "I know. It was terrible. What I said was terrible, too. I'm sorry."

There was one more flash of white-hot pain, and then the Nightmare let go of Ravyn's nose. "Keep it elevated."

Ravyn pressed the back of his head against the aspen tree. The Nightmare bent over him. "Don't you understand?" he whispered. "There can be no stony facade—no pretending—after this. Death demands to be felt. It wasn't just Gorse who died in that courtyard today." His yellow gaze reached into the darkest parts of Ravyn. "But the Captain of the Destriers as well."

It was late. Ravyn and Jespyr and the Nightmare were still awake—barely. Petyr was snoring, curled around himself.

Ravyn's nose hurt a speck less. He kept it elevated, his eyes cast up the long trunks of the aspen trees, all of them reaching toward the sky like swaying arms, grasping at the moon.

Jespyr had the Nightmare Card. She was speaking to Elspeth—her face more relaxed than Ravyn had seen it in days. When she was done, she ran a listless finger over the Card's edge. Handed it back to Ravyn.

He tapped it.

You're tired, Elspeth whispered, her voice covering his mind like a blanket. *I'll be here when you wake up. Rest now.*

I don't want rest, Elspeth. His eyelids drooped. *I just want you.*

I know. She paused. *It's still very striking, your nose. Undoubtably your best feature.*

Muscles feathered in the corners of Ravyn's mouth. *You think so?*

Good night, Ravyn.

Good night, Miss Spindle.

He tapped the Nightmare Card and put it in his pocket.

"There it is," Jespyr said through a yawn. "A hint of that elusive grin."

"I don't know what you're talking about."

She poked his shoulder. "Stubborn till the end."

"Someone has to defuse your optimism."

"That's what Elm's for. But you—you're not a pessimist at all, brother." She smiled. "And it kills you."

The Nightmare's gaze shifted between them. Silken and slow, he said, "I had a sister as well, not two years younger than me. My father used to say we were as branches of our namesake tree. Twisted, and intrepid, Ayris and I."

He pulled away before Ravyn could ask more, retreating to the far side of the aspen circle.

"He frightens me," Jespyr said, settling close. "I spend most of the time hoping he doesn't look at me with those yellow eyes. He seems so sinister, so inhuman, but then—"

"He reminds us who he was," Ravyn murmured. "Before he became the monster."

They pressed their backs together, their gazes lifting to the sky. They'd sat like that as children—as Destriers on patrol—as highwaymen in the wood.

"I can't see any stars," Jespyr said.

"Too much mist." Ravyn's eyelids fell. "I don't know what's on the other side of those alder trees, Jes. When we find a way in, stay close."

When he drifted off to sleep, his sister's voice was in his ear. "I always do."

Chapter Thirty-Two

Elm

It was only the third feast, and Elm's courtly charm was wearing thin. But his father was on the dais, drowning himself in sullenness and wine, and Elm would rather dance until his feet bled than sit in Hauth's chair another moment.

The theme of the night was Providence Cards. Rather uninspired of Baldwyn, Elm thought, to make a theme out of something that already constituted so much of the idle chatter at court.

The costumes were...predictable. Gauche.

Most of the women wore pink gowns and roses in their hair—evoking the Maiden. Others were clad in violet for the Mirror Card, small silver looking glasses in their hands. Men wore turquoise for the Chalice—handy, for they all were drinking heavily from their cups.

There were a few white tunics adorned with feathered collars for the White Eagle, the Card of courage. One brave soul had fastened wires to the back of his doublet and strewn ivy around them to represent the Iron Gate. Another had stuffed his gold tunic with excess fabric, giving his midsection a rotund, oval shape. The Golden Egg.

Only the King wore red for the Scythe, and no one was festooned in black for the Black Horse. That right was reserved for the Destriers.

Elm wore it anyway.

The orchestra was larger by three violins, and played louder now that the dinner hour had ended and dancing begun. Wine flowed until it wore itself on everyone's face, staining cheeks and lips and teeth.

It paid to be tall, and despite the swell of the crowd, Elm could easily eye every corner of the hall, searching for that telltale yellow hair. Ione was not partnered with any of the dancers, nor was she seated at any of the tables. Elm was about to drop his dance partner's hands and go search the garden when he spotted a circle of women, standing along the farthest wall.

They were playing some sort of game with a Well Card. Of the six of them, four wore pink Maiden Card costumes, one violet for the Mirror. The final woman, yellow hair tied in a knot at the nape of her neck, had her back to Elm. She was clad in a deep burgundy gown, the color of wine. Her fingers were painted black to the knuckle, meant to convey claws.

The only Nightmare Card costume in the room.

The dance ended, and Elm realized he hadn't heard a word his partner had said. He gave her a bow and moved on quick step through the crowd. When the circle of women saw him coming, their Well Card was forgotten, their gazes homed entirely on him—save Ione's. She took her time turning around. When she finally deigned to, Elm saw that her lids were painted yellow—the same color as the eyes of the monster upon the Nightmare Card.

"Prince." Her gaze, her face, mouth—all of them were unreadable. "I'm surprised you're not wearing Scythe red."

"As am I to find you in something other than pretty, pretty pink."

"There is nothing wrong with pink." She dragged her painted eyes over Elm's black tunic and silk doublet. "You, terrible snob, look like a rich highwayman."

"I believe he's wearing black for the Black Horse, Ione," one of the women whispered behind her.

Elm and Ione replied at the same time. "He's not—"

"—I'm not."

The corners of Ione's lips twitched. Elm rubbed the back of his neck—grinned. "What about you?" He waved a hand at her costume. "That's quite the monstrous getup."

Ione's eyes dropped to her burgundy dress. "Your father gave it to me. He ordered my hands and face painted, too."

Elm's smile faltered. Like the others she'd been given since arriving at Stone, the gown fit Ione poorly, her body lost to excess fabric. The only part that fit her tightly were the frills beneath her jaw. He was starting to think it wasn't an accident, that all of her necklines resembled a collar.

It was one thing if Ione had chosen the costume herself. Knowing his father had orchestrated it to punish her—

Heat torched his throat.

"I imagine the King wanted to remind me that the only reason I'm here is because of the Nightmare Card my father paid him." Ione held up her hand, curling her painted fingers as if they were indeed claws. "Or perhaps he merely wished to call me a monster."

The women behind Ione leaned forward. "Not at all, Ione. King Rowan paid you special care, seeing to your costume."

"Truly," said another. "The Rowans have been most attentive."

"How difficult it must be, Ione," a third chimed, "for you to see things in a gentle light, what with Prince Hauth abed with illness."

Ione didn't even blink. "Difficult indeed." She turned to Elm. "I believe games have begun in the garden, Prince. Would you care to escort me there?"

Their eyes met. "Of course." Never dropping her gaze, Elm brought Ione's hand to his chest—pressed it into the soft fabric of his doublet. Adding the slightest pressure, he ran her fingers down his abdomen, wiping the black paint off her skin. He did the same with her other hand, his clothes absorbing her stain. "I'll take you wherever you want to go, Miss Hawthorn."

They left the circle of women, hands still entwined. When they reached the garden's gilded doors, Elm said, rougher than he meant to, "You're not a monster."

"I'm not anything until I have my Maiden Card back."

Night air touched Elm's overwarm brow. "Speaking of that," he said, looking out into the labyrinthine gardens. "What part of the garden were you trying to search before Linden stopped you?"

"The rose maze. There are statues there with old, cracked stone."

They followed the path, past courtiers playing games with White Eagle and Well and Chalice Cards. Past lovers sneaking behind hedges and beneath trees. Past bramble into dark greenery, until it was just Elm, Ione, the garden, and the mist.

"Do you have your charm?" Ione asked.

Elm flicked his wrist, his horsehair bracelet rubbing against his skin. "You?"

She stretched fabric and pulled the horse tooth on its chain from beneath the neckline of her dress.

Elm took a torch from its stand and led them into a maze crafted of carefully pruned rosebushes that had all lost their blooms. They searched every statue—every crack in them.

Nothing.

Ione stayed silent, the only sound between them the distant echo of courtiers and the castle gong, ringing through the garden—nine tolls. For each statue that held no Maiden Card in its cracks, Elm lost a whit of forbearance. By the time the gong struck ten, he was buzzing with disquiet. "Are you angry with me?"

Ione's gaze lifted slowly to his face. "No. Why would you think that?"

"We haven't found your Card."

"That's not your fault. *You* didn't hide it."

"No, but…you just seem—" He swallowed. "I don't do well with long silences. I tend to overthink."

"Is it Stone that bothers you, Prince? Or me?"

"You don't bother me, Hawthorn." He chewed the inside of his cheek. "At least not in the same way the castle does."

It was difficult to look at her. Beneath the ache that existed between them was a thin, fragile thread. One Ione had slipped through the eye of a needle and plunged into Elm's chest, past all his bricks and barbs, though she didn't yet realize it. It was uncomfortable, pretending she was not sewn into him—that it had not become vital to him, helping her find her Maiden Card. That he was not in some kind of pain every moment he was with her. It was all so terribly, wonderfully uncomfortable.

So Elm did what he always did when he was uncomfortable. He dropped his hand into his pocket and retrieved his Scythe. "What did you want this for?" he said. "When we played our little game with the Chalice and you were delusional enough to think I wouldn't remember you?"

Ione felt along the cracks of a nearby statue. "I wanted to see if I could compel myself to remember where I hid my Maiden."

"I could try. I can't guarantee it'll work—"

"No. I don't want anyone to use a Scythe on me. Not even you, Prince."

It took Elm a moment. He winced. *Fucking Hauth.* He placed his Card into Ione's hand. "You do it, then."

She cocked her head to the side, fingers closing around the Scythe. "You had some choice words for me the last time I held this Card in my hand."

Elm tugged a strand of her hair that had fallen from its knot. "That's because, wicked one, you stole it out of my damn pocket."

"So I did." Ione turned the Scythe in her fingers. "It almost felt...good, making the highwaymen do what I wanted."

"And the pain of using it too long? How was that?"

The Scythe stilled. "Terrible. I don't know how you bear it."

"I'm used to it." Elm kicked a rock down the path. "I had an extensive education in pain."

Ione took a step back. Narrowed her eyes over him. "You shouldn't be so cavalier about what happened to you, Prince."

"What would you have me do? Burn the castle down with everyone in it?"

"That would be a start."

A laugh rose up Elm's throat. "Trees, Hawthorn. What a Queen you'd make."

He hadn't meant to say it. And, graciously, Ione didn't reply. Her gaze merely flared a moment, then returned to the Scythe in her hand. She sucked in a breath, tapped it three times, and closed her eyes.

Elm stood very still. When those hazel eyes opened again,

they were unfeeling. "No," she said, handing him back his Card. "I just remember the same thing. Cracked stone."

They moved out of the rose maze to the rowan grove. The mist was everywhere, a salty bite across Elm's senses. It hovered densely over a small pond at the cusp of the grove. In the center of the pond was a tiny island, and upon it a statue. The stone was old, cracked. But there was no mistaking the man carved into marble.

Brutus Rowan. The first Rowan King.

Elm had thrown rocks at the statue as a boy. He didn't like Brutus's face. It was handsome, a smile carved onto its lips. But beneath the smile, a cold menace lingered. Brutus's chest was broad—puffed out in dominance. His brows were lowered, his vision fixed on something only he could see, a hunter watching its prey. It reminded Elm too much of his father—of Hauth.

He eyed the pond. "Do you remember swimming on Equinox?"

"No. But my dress was ruined enough that I might have."

"If I wanted to put a Maiden Card out of reach," Elm said, gesturing at the statue, "I might compel someone to take a little swim to hide it."

Her brows perked. "There?"

Elm was already taking off his boots. "No stone left unturned, Hawthorn." He shrugged out of his doublet and lifted his tunic and silk undershirt over his head. When he caught Ione tracing the bare skin along his back, he smiled. "Sorry." He nodded at his discarded clothes. "I should have asked if you wanted to help with that."

He dove into the pond. The water was cold and slippery with algae. Elm kept his eyes shut and kicked, reaching the island in ten strokes.

There was no room to stand, the island hardly larger than

the base of the statue. Elm braced himself on Brutus Rowan's marble arm and hauled himself out of the water, mist lingering all around him.

"Well?" Ione called.

He searched the statue's cracks. Some were fine, others jagged. There was a fissure in Brutus Rowan's chest, deep and wide enough for Elm to slip a finger into. But there was nothing in the gap—just cold stone. Not a single hint of a Providence Card's velvet edge. "Nothing."

He pulled his finger out, closed his fist, and hit Brutus Rowan over his stupid marble chest.

The statue groaned. The fissure in Brutus's chest widened, spreading down his legs until one large crack became hundreds.

"Shit."

Brutus Rowan's marble legs snapped at the ankles and the statue toppled into the pond, taking Elm with it. He hit the water, pushed under by the weight of the marble, held his breath, and swam. When his back collided with the grassy embankment, he flung himself upon it, hauled in a breath—

Mist rushed into him.

It tasted of brine and rot. It filled Elm's lungs, his body, his mind. He went rigid on the ground, his eyes wide as he fumbled for his wrist, for the familiar feel of horsehair—

His charm was gone. Lost, somewhere in the pond.

"Prince?"

Elm coughed. When he tried to speak, his voice was drowned out by another. It came in the mist, sounding near and far, like a storm. *Elm,* it called. *Rotten, ruined Elm. Neglected, now chosen. I see you, heir of Kings. I've always seen you.*

Ione was in the grass next to him, her hands on his shoulders. "What's wrong?"

A compulsion as strong as any Scythe's was digging into Elm, telling him to get up—to run deeper into the mist. He gnashed his teeth against it, his mouth dried out by salt. "Charm," he managed.

Ione ripped the chain off her neck in a single tug. Elm's hand was a claw in the grass. Ione pulled it toward her and slapped her own hand against it, her charm fixed between their palms.

The next breath Elm dragged in was bereft of mist. On the next, the rot and brine fled his body. His muscles loosened, and he looked up at Ione.

Yellow hair spilled from its knot, swaying with the rapid pull of her breaths. She studied Elm's face. "Prince Renelm. It would be terribly *un*clever to die searching for my Maiden Card."

Elm tightened his grip on her hand. "Don't call me that," he said, shaking. "It's Elm. Just Elm."

"Is that the privilege I get after twice saving your life?"

He pushed out of the grass, leaning close enough to see where the freckles on her nose should have been. "Thank you." His eyes dropped to her mouth. "I owe you."

Ione's breath quickened. "You're helping me find my Card. Call it balance."

He didn't. He wanted to call it something else entirely.

They held hands, Ione's charm pressed between them, until they were out of the mist and back through the garden's gilded doors. Elm had a spare horsehair charm in his room, and he needed new clothes before they continued to search. He was lacing a fresh doublet when his chamber door banged open.

Filick Willow stood at his threshold, eyes wide.

"Oh for the love of—Filick. I thought we talked about *knocking*."

There was blood on his white Physician's tunic. "Highness."

His gaze moved to Ione, seated on Elm's bed. "Miss Hawthorn. You should both come."

Elm's back stiffened. "What's happened?"

"High Prince Hauth." Dread. There was so much dread in the Physician's eyes. "He's awake."

Chapter Thirty-Three

Elspeth

The Nightmare watched Ravyn and Jespyr as they drifted to sleep.

Will they be safe in there? I asked. *In the alderwood?*

No.

Then you must keep them safe.

He lowered himself to a crouch, then slowly onto the ground. He hauled his sword onto his lap. *I have not done well, guarding those I cherish.*

When he slept, I waded through the darkness of his mind, his memories quick to find me.

I sat on the stone in the chamber I had built and looked up. The ceiling I had crafted as a younger man was weathered. Outside, the yew trees swayed, stirred by a chill autumn breeze. No dappled sunlight streamed between their branches.

There was only gray mist.

"Father?"

My gaze wrenched to the window. Ayris was there, standing

hand in hand with Tilly. My sister's usual warmth was guarded, her yellow eyes hard. But when she spoke to my daughter, her voice was gentle. "Go on, Tilly. Ask him."

Tilly curled a finger at the end of one of her dark plaits. Smiled sheepishly. "Can we swing in the yew tree like you promised?"

I looked at her, indifferent. It was easier, now I had fashioned the Nightmare Card—my soul lost to velvet—telling the children *no.* "Not now, my darling girl," I said in a voice smooth as silk. "I have work yet to do."

Her smile faded. "All right." She let go of Ayris's hand, picked up her skirt—heaved a sigh. "I'll wait in the meadow. In case you change your mind."

When she looked at me, Ayris, my sunshine sister, was full of frost. "Your work," she said, "has made a stranger of you."

She hurried after Tilly.

A moment later, the chorus of tree voices rattled through my mind.

Eleven Cards the Spirit has given you, Taxus. Do you still ask for more?

"This mist," I said, the word a hiss on my tongue. "It makes my people lose their way. Draws them into the wood. Its magic is not a blessing, but a curse."

That is the way of magic, the trees whispered.

"I want another Card. One that will lift the mist."

The Spirit will not give you a Card to undo the very thing she has created to lure people back into her woods.

"Then I want a way to heal the fever and the infection it brings. You told me, after barters were made, a day would come when I could heal it."

That day has not yet arrived, Shepherd King.

I ground my molars together. "I grow weary of your riddles,

trees. If I cannot get answers from you"—my gaze narrowed—"then I would speak to the Spirit herself. Give me a Card to do so."

Their pause was deafening. *Very well,* they whispered. *But of price, she will not say.*

"I don't care. I'll pay anything."

Anything?

"Anything."

Salt filled the chamber, stronger than I'd ever smelled it. My vision buckled and I fell. My head hit the earth with a brutal thud, eleven Providence Cards falling from my pocket and scattering around me.

When I woke, a twelfth Card was atop the stone. Forest green, with two trees depicted upon it—one pale, the other dark. In script above them was writ *The Twin Alders.*

I tapped it three times. Waited. Nothing. A curse formed on my lips. I tapped the Maiden Card to heal my head—

But the Card did not work.

My throat tightened. I tapped the Mirror—tried to go invisible. Nothing.

The Well showed me no enemies—the Iron Gate gave no serenity. I screamed myself raw and tapped the Cards until my fingers ached. Still, I could not wield them.

I crumpled to the foot of the stone, surrounded by the Cards' colorful lights. I'd found a way to speak to the Spirit of the Wood. I'd bled, bartered, and bent for twelve Providence Cards.

And I could not use a single one.

The pages of memory turned faster.

A town crier read a royal decree, warning all of Blunder to stay out of the mist.

Then, a woman, screaming in pain, veins the color of ink. She'd made it past castle guards into my throne room, begging for an audience with my Physicians. My Captain of the Guard, Brutus Rowan, tapped his Scythe three times, forcing her out.

"Blunder is in grave danger," he said to me in the privacy of my library. "This mist is a blight. And it spreads."

I was seated at a wide desk surrounded by stacks of inky parchment. I leaned over a notebook, scribbling madly. With my other hand, I twirled the Twin Alders Card between my fingers. "I've told you a hundred times already," I said, not bothering to look up, "I will find a way to lift the mist."

"People have lost their way in it. Trade routes have been disrupted. People are not asking for the fever any longer—the Spirit is *forcing* it upon them." He paused. "I've seen mere children with magic powerful enough to give my men pause."

"And that frightens you, Brutus? Unfettered magic?"

He said nothing.

"My orders go unchanged. Stay your hand. Neither you, nor your ponies, are to arrest or harm anyone who catches the fever in the mist."

"Destriers, not ponies," Brutus said, his voice hard as iron. "You named them so yourself."

I flipped through my notebook, landing on a page somewhere in the middle. "*The King's Guard wears no seal. The Black Horse is their emblem, their duty, their creed. With it, they uphold Blunder's laws. They are the shadows in the room—the eyes on your back—the footsteps upon your streets. The King's Guard wears no seal.*" I snapped the notebook shut. "Not a single mention of a Destrier." My eyes lifted to Brutus. "I believe it was you, Captain, not I, who *saddled* them with that ridiculous name."

A muscle along Brutus's jaw flexed. "I'm in no mood to laugh, Taxus."

"Just as well. I've forgotten the sound."

"There was nothing to laugh at when the mist arrived. Nothing to laugh at when you bartered away every part of yourself for the Cards."

I glanced at the red light coming from his tunic pocket. "You have benefitted from my barters, have you not? You have made a ruthless name for yourself at the edge of my Scythe."

He paled.

"Yes, Brutus. I know what you have been doing behind my back. I may not be able to trespass into your mind with a Nightmare Card any longer, but I hear plenty. Apparently, you have a fondness for using the red Card on criminals. Finding new ways to punish them. You've even sent them into the very mist you claim so loudly to abhor."

"Perhaps if you spent as much time ruling as you do scribbling about magic in that damn book," he bit back, "there would be no criminals for me to punish. Besides—you gave me a free hand to protect the kingdom."

When my voice slipped out of my lips, it was smoother than before. "And when you become red-stained, too familiar with pain—too reliant on the Scythe to put it down? I wonder then, Brutus, who will protect Blunder from you?" My hand dropped to the hilt of my sword upon my belt. "I care not that you are my sister's husband. Kill another soul with my Scythe, and I will not merely take it back. I will pry it from your lifeless hands. Now get out."

Red limned his green eyes. With a curt bow, he quit the library.

When the door slammed, I heaved a sigh. "There's no use hiding, Bennett. I can see your Cards."

A boy stepped out of thin air, twirling a Mirror Card between his fingers. He was young, no older than thirteen. His skin was a warm brown, his hair dark and unkempt. When he tilted his head to the side, birdlike in his movements, light caught his gray eyes and the high planes of his face.

"I know a part of you agrees with Brutus, Father. The mist is dangerous." Bennett dragged a thumb over the Mirror Card's edge. "Why not make peace with him?"

I set to scribbling once more. "And give your aunt Ayris the satisfaction of bridging the gap between us? I think not."

"Everyone is frightened of catching fever. Of degenerating."

"Not all who catch it degenerate. I never have." I raised my gaze. "You certainly haven't."

Bennett smiled. "Haven't I? There are Cards I can no longer use." He pulled a second Providence Card from his pocket, the Nightmare, violet and burgundy blurring between his fingers. "Someday, I won't be able to use these either."

"And yet you have incredible magic. You could undo my life's work, if you were feeling particularly spiteful."

"Which I commonly am." He paused. "The children miss you, especially Tilly. Come to dinner. Just this once."

I waved an impatient hand, dismissing him.

Bennett stepped to the desk. Peered into my face. Sighed. "You're with us, but you're never really here, are you, Father?"

The memory fell away.

In the next, I was hurrying out of the castle, tucking a few small provisions—bread and cheese—into a satchel.

I stepped into the meadow, passed the stone chamber—aimed toward the woods.

"Going somewhere, brother?"

My hand flew to the hilt of my sword, my mouth drawing into a fine line. "Ayris."

"You're easier to follow without your Mirror Card," she said, smiling at me. "Where are you going?"

I might have lied, once. But it took too much effort, fooling my sister. I needed to preserve my strength for whatever barter lay ahead of me. "To speak to the Spirit of the Wood. To learn about the mist—to ask her to withdraw it."

Ayris's smile slipped. "Alone?"

"It is better that way."

She rolled her eyes, then her shoulders, and stepped closer. "I know you're tired. Forlorn. I see it on your face. Let me walk with you into the wood."

"Brutus will be angry."

She ignored mention of her husband and looked up at me, her yellow eyes weary. "What was it Father used to call us? When we disappeared into the trees as children?"

"Twisted," I said, the corners of my mouth lifting. "Intrepid."

"It has not been like that for many years. There are twelve versions of you, brother, each more distant than the last."

I heard the sadness in her voice, but it hardly touched me. With my soul lost to the Nightmare Card, I felt as I once did when, by folly, I used a Maiden too long. Cold, unaware of the beating heart in my chest. Shut off.

And yet Ayris was still the sun to me. Even in the wood, cold and gray with mist, her presence was a light, a warmth. I wanted her near me, for there are some things not even magic can erase. "Very well," I told her. "So long as you mind the mist."

She smiled.

The memory faded.

When it returned, Ayris and I stood side by side. We stared up at a wall of alder trees.

Voices echoed all around me.

The wood that awaits you is a place of no time. A place of new barters, a hill you must climb. Betwixt ancient trees, where the mist cuts bone-deep, the Spirit safeguards, like a dragon its keep. The wood knows no road, no path through the snare. Step into the mist—it will guide your way there.

Ayris and I stepped into the alderwood, and the mist homed in on my sister. It shot into her nose, her mouth. She gasped—breathed it in—

And the warmth of the sun snuffed out.

Chapter Thirty-Four

Elm

The urge to vomit was oppressive.

Elm clamped his jaw so tightly he worried for his teeth. He dropped his hand into his pocket and ran a finger along his Scythe, begging the violent churnings in his stomach to settle. He pictured riding horseback through a meadow, free and at ease. *Calm,* he told himself. *Calm. Steady. Easy.*

Filick led them to the door with a rearing stallion carved into its frame. No one spoke a word. Filick entered the room, but Elm stalled at the threshold. He hadn't been inside Hauth's room since he was a boy.

Ione shifted behind him. Her voice was frostbite cold. "I don't want to see him."

Elm shut his eyes a moment. "You needn't go in."

"What about you?"

He didn't have an answer. He wanted to lock his fist in her skirt and keep her with him like he had in the library. Everything was out of focus, dark around the edges. He heaved a rattling sigh, his voice strange in his ears. "I'll be fine."

He stepped inside.

Hauth's bedchamber was overwarm, lit by dozens of candles,

the fireplace roaring. Not even the smell of the Physician's herbs and balms could mask the foul odor of unhealed wounds. Of blood.

Elm put a hand over his mouth and pushed past two other Physicians, planting himself against the wall where the most shadow remained. Filick moved to the center of the room, where Royce Linden and two other Physicians were gathered around a large canopied bed.

The body on the bed groaned.

No ease, no steadiness. Zero fucking calm. Hauth was awake.

"Any improvements?" Filick asked, rolling up his blood-stained sleeves.

"A little less blood in his saliva," another Physician replied.

Linden's voice was sharp. "That's good, right?"

Filick gave a stiff nod. "Has he said anything?"

"Nothing yet."

A tremendous bang shook the chamber. Several candles snuffed out and then the King was stomping into the room, eyes red and wide, mouth agape and smelling of wine. "Son," he barked, "how's my son?"

Drunk. The King was very drunk. Elm squeezed deeper into shadow.

"Alive and stirring, sire," Filick said. "He hasn't opened his eyes."

The King stalked forward, pushing to get to the bed. When he passed Elm, he held out a brutish hand. A test of obedience. "Come, Renelm."

Elm's vision went foggy. For a blissful second, he considered disobeying. He'd walk out the door and down the stairs and just keep walking. He'd done it once with Ravyn.

A stone dropped into Elm's stomach at the thought of his cousin. Trees, what he wouldn't give to see Ravyn walk through that door, all angles and blades, and simply lay waste to anyone who so much as looked at him wrong. Everyone was afraid of Ravyn. Even, though he'd never admit it, the King.

And Elm—no one was afraid of him. His Scythe, maybe, but not him. He was a rotted-out tree, and Ravyn the impenetrable, untouchable vines that held the pieces of him together.

The King came back into shaky focus. So did the candlelit room beyond him. The body on the bed. Elm sucked in a breath, dragged a foot forward—

Ione stepped into the chamber. She traced her cold eyes over the room, the Physicians, the King. When she found Elm, her gaze softened a fraction. Her body was rigid. But her shoulders rose in the smallest shrug. She'd come. Into Hauth's room.

For him.

The fragments of Elm's rotted-out heart rearranged themselves. He stepped forward, surer. Broader. So tall that, when he reached the bed in the heart of the room, he looked down even upon his father.

Ione came up next to him. Their knuckles brushed.

They stood at the foot of the bed, facing it together. Hauth's lips were a pale gray, pressed so tightly that they looked hemmed shut. His cheeks and neck were parceled by long, ugly claw marks, similar to the ones he'd gotten the night Wayland Pine's Iron Gate Card had been stolen. Only worse—deeper. His eyelids were split, purple with bruises, his skull wrapped in thick, bloodstained linen.

The King leaned next to the bed, coarse hands gripping the quilt. "What of my Nightmare Card?" he gritted out. "Have you been able to reach him with it?"

Filick shook his head.

"We should try again," Linden said. "Where's the Card?"

"There, sire," a Physician offered, pointing to a long mahogany chest at the foot of the bed.

All eyes turned to Ione, who stood near its latch.

"Get it," came the King's barking command.

Ione's eyes remained untouched. She pushed open the heavy lid of the chest. The smell of leather and copper filled Elm's nose, calling back the nausea from before. He clenched his jaw and peered into the chest, watching as Ione pushed past bandages and tonics, searching.

She moved a belt aside, and there it was—the Nightmare Card. The one her father had traded on Equinox to earn her a place on the dais. The Card that had tied her to Hauth.

Ione stared down at it. The room was overwarm. But there was nothing but coldness in her face.

"Are you daft, woman?" Linden said. "The Nightmare Card. Now."

"She's getting it, asshole."

Linden's gaze shifted to Elm. "She should not be in here. It was *her* cousin who did this. There are plenty of empty cells in the dungeon, yet she wanders the castle like a harlot, twisting her betrothed's brother around her finger—"

"No one asked for your opinion, Destrier." Elm's Scythe was already out. Already accessed. "Shut your mouth."

Linden's mouth snapped shut, a low, strangled noise coming from his throat.

Ione closed the chest, pinching the Nightmare's Card's velvet edge like it were a dead thing, and held it out.

The King wrenched it from her grasp. Tapped it three times.

Everything was so silent Elm could hear his insides scream. The King gnashed his teeth and tapped the Nightmare three more times and threw it on the floor. Defeat.

Elm let out a sharp exhale. Wherever Hauth was, his father was either too drunk or too unfocused to reach him.

Hauth's eyelids fluttered. When they opened, his eyes were bloodshot.

The King's voice broke. He reached for Hauth's arm. "Son?"

Linden leaned forward. He tried to speak but couldn't, shooting Elm a poisonous glare.

"Prince Hauth," Filick called. "Can you hear us?"

Hauth said nothing. A vein in his bruised forehead pulsed and his nostrils flared. His breath grew louder, labored. Bloody saliva dripped from the corner of his mouth. Filick wiped it away and pushed a poultice over his brow.

Hauth thrashed a moment, then stilled. He looked like he might close those horrid red-green eyes again, but they jerked wide, suddenly focused on something at his bedside.

Ione.

No one spoke. Then, as if it took all his strength to do so, Hauth dragged his eyes off of Ione. They rolled, disappearing under bruised eyelids.

He didn't open them again.

"You've signed it, then? My testament, naming you heir?"

Elm and the King stood alone in the hallway outside of Hauth's door. The Physicians and Linden remained inside. Ione hurried down the hall so fast Elm didn't even have the chance to call after her.

The King's voice came out harder. "I asked if you'd signed my testament."

Elm's hand drifted into his pocket. He tapped the Scythe three times, releasing Linden from its control. As he did, his knuckles grazed the second Card in his pocket—the one he'd snagged off Hauth's floor when no one was looking.

"Yes. Baldwyn has it stowed in his rooms."

The King let out a low breath. His shoulders released. "Good." His hands were shaking. From drink, but also—

Elm looked away. "Your son," he managed, bile in the back of this throat. "It's worse than I thought. The damage to his body."

"*My son.*" The King's green, bleary gaze found Elm's face. "Even on his deathbed, you will not call him a brother?"

"He never played the part well enough."

The King shook his head. Pressed the heel of his palm into his eye. "Your rancor is a mark upon you, Renelm. Wash it off."

"If there are marks upon me, it is because *your son* put them there." He turned to leave, but the King's voice held him back.

"Have you chosen a wife?"

Elm went still. "There is a contract."

"With whom?"

"You'll learn soon enough."

The King's eyes narrowed. "Who, Renelm?"

When Elm kept his mouth sealed, the King's hands flexed. He reached into his pocket—retrieved his Scythe—

But Elm was faster. On the third tap of his own Scythe, he said, "You won't use that Card on me. You won't make a puppet out of me the way he did."

The King's hand froze in his pocket. It felt good, watching surprise, then fear, flicker across his aged face. "You think you're special—that the hurt Hauth dealt you was personal. It wasn't." His words were ragged. "What happened to you has happened to Rowan Princes for centuries. It takes an understanding of *pain* to wield the Scythe. When you have a son, he will learn as well."

"That will never happen." Elm turned away, releasing his father from the red Card. "You will have my marriage contract before the last feast."

He heard his father shout, but he was halfway down the stairs, already a mile ahead. Elm quit the castle and went to the stables. The grooms were gone, so he found his horse and mounted without a saddle, hurtling out of the bailey at a full gallop. Three taps of his Scythe and the castle guards lowered the drawbridge—then he was free of Stone, the night air wrapping him in frosty arms. He hardly felt the cold. He was riding, fast and free and harder than he had in an age.

And all that rage, walled up deep inside him—Elm let it out. He yelled into the night and the night answered, his echo reaching over treetops and into valleys, a war cry. He yelled for that boy, small and brutalized, who'd needed saving. He yelled for his helplessness—the rope he'd corded around his own neck, tethering himself to the Scythe, to Ravyn. Tears fell from his eyes, and he let the wind strike them away. He yelled himself raw—until a sky full of stars danced before his eyes.

And something tore loose.

Elm didn't believe the Spirit of the Wood took note of the fleeting lives of men. But if she did, he swore she'd mapped his future in the twisted rings of the trees. That she'd designed his every failure, his every fear, to get to this moment. He'd needed Ravyn to leave him behind. Needed to face the throne, his father, the Rowan in him, alone.

His shout eased to a boyish whoop, and he laughed and cursed and roared into the night, the world emptying of monsters. All that remained was him and the night and the forest road. It welcomed him, ribboning him in darkness, leading him to the ivy-laden house with darkened windows, its scent now as familiar to him as his own name.

Blossoms and magnolia trees. Grass fields during the first summer rain. Heady, sweet, wistful. Hawthorn House.

Ione's house.

Hours later, when he was back at Stone, just before dawn, Elm's arms were full.

He didn't need to knock. He had a key now. But he did just the same.

Ione was in her nightdress, her yellow hair tangled from sleep. Her gaze widened as she took him in—his full arms and windblown face. But before she could open her mouth, Elm handed her the heap in his arms.

Ione peered down at it. "Dresses?"

"Come with me to the next feast," Elm said, the words rushing out of him. "I have the Nightmare Card. We'll find your Maiden. After that, I'll take you anywhere you want to go." His throat caught. "Please. Come with me to the feast."

Her indecipherable eyes measured him, her answer hardly a whisper. "All right."

Elm smiled, unconstrained. "Good." He glanced at the dresses. "Those are yours from Hawthorn House. You needn't wear another one of the abominations my father sends. Maybe this way, you can feel a bit more like yourself."

He didn't let himself stay. He stepped back down the hall. "A bit more like the real Ione."

Chapter Thirty-Five

Ravyn

Ravyn and Jespyr were still pressed back-to-back when a shadow moved over them. Ravyn's eyes snapped open, bleary in the dim light of dawn. "What's the matter?"

The Nightmare looked down at them, his face unreadable. "It's time."

Three clicks of his sword upon an aspen trunk, and the trees were moving. Ravyn yanked Jespyr away from rolling roots, and Petyr awoke with a cry, stumbling out of the way as the circle of aspens the Nightmare had drawn the night before was dispelled. When they were suitably scattered across the valley floor, the Nightmare tapped his blade thrice more upon the earth, stilling them.

The party turned. Faced the alderwood.

The wood breathed no sound. No birds flew from its treetops, and no wind stirred its branches. Its silence was ancient, and it loomed over them. Watching. Waiting.

They managed a scant breakfast and water, saying little, enveloped in apprehension. The unwelcome tremor in Ravyn's hands begged to quake. When he'd finished eating, he hauled himself up and stood at the edge of the alderwood.

The others joined him.

"The trees are too close together," Petyr said. "How do we get in?"

Jespyr glanced at the Nightmare. "Can't you move them with your sword?"

"Not these trees. This is the Spirit's wood. They obey only her." He lifted his sword—drew a pale finger over the edge of his blade, splitting a seam of skin. The finger went red, and the Nightmare pressed it into the bark of the nearest alder tree.

A wind began—a biting chill that chased salt up Ravyn's nose and into his eyes. He blinked it away, then blinked again.

The smear of blood was gone from the alder tree. In its place was a hole. Not a squirrel's burrow or a hollowed-out knot, but a deep, jagged hole. As if someone had reached into the tree with claws and torn out a chunk.

The hole stared at him, waiting.

Ravyn stepped forward and peered into it. He saw nothing at first—only darkness. The corrosive smell of salt was everywhere. Behind it, another odor lingered. It was foul. Fetid, like rot. Then, out from the darkness within the alderwood—

A flash of silver eyes.

Ravyn lurched back, knocking into Jespyr. "What the hell was that?"

"I told you," the Nightmare whispered. "This wood belongs to the Spirit." He nodded at the hole in the tree. "She will not grant us entry unless we pay her."

The Nightmare had always been pale. *Elspeth* was pale. But there had been an ever-present warmth that lingered in her cheeks—her mouth—the tip of her nose. Only now, it was gone. The Nightmare had gone a sickly gray. Unflinching, five hundred years old—

Fear, painted all over his face.

The hairs on the back of Ravyn's neck prickled. "What's the payment?"

"The alderwood is changeable, fickle, violent—just like the infection. It will have shifted a thousand times over since I was last here. We need a guide to cross it." He turned, his yellow eyes homing in on Petyr and Jespyr. "The payment is a charm."

Air fled Ravyn's lungs, punching its way across his bruised ribs. He reached into his tunic, tearing the spare charm—the viper head—out of his pocket. "Give it this."

The Nightmare didn't look at it. "We need a *guide*." He spoke now only to Jespyr, his voice eerily gentle. "You remember some weeks ago, when you dropped your charm in the Black Forest? When the mist twisted your mind? What were you running toward?"

Jespyr's pallor had gone sallow. Her hand was knotted in a fist, a small thread peeking out. Ravyn knew what she was holding. A dog tooth on a string. Her charm. "I can hardly remember," she managed. "All I know was that there was a voice in the mist. Like a storm, calling out my name."

"That was the Spirit of the Wood, beckoning you to this place," the Nightmare whispered. "This is where people come, when they are lost to the mist." He drew air into his nose. "Can't you smell them?"

As if stirred by his words, the wind picked up. Salt—

And rot.

Bile rose into Ravyn's mouth. "No. If Jespyr or Petyr give up their charms, the mist will infect them. Or *kill* them."

The Nightmare nodded slowly, unblinking.

"No," Ravyn said again. "There has to be another way."

"There is not."

"But you've entered this wood before!"

"I have."

Ravyn's mind went dark. He remembered standing near the cellar at Stone the morning their journey began. He hadn't known what the monster meant then, but now, it was so horribly clear.

We'll need at least one spare.

His skin went cold, then burning hot. "You knew this would happen."

The Nightmare's silence was confirmation enough.

"Nothing to say? No clever little rhyme?" Ravyn shoved the Nightmare against the trees, hands knotting in the collar of his cloak. "You're the goddamn Shepherd King! Think of another way."

The Nightmare could have killed him with a single flex of his fingers. For a moment, lips peeling back in a snarl, he looked like he wanted to. "There *was* another way. The Destrier. He might have been the one to give up his charm. But he is dead. The mist has no sway over you or me." He pushed Ravyn back with incredible strength, turning his gaze once more to Jespyr and Petyr. "It must be one of them."

Petyr's brown eyes were wide, color leaching from his face. "And if we don't?"

"Then we cannot retrieve the Twin Alders Card. The Deck will not unite on Solstice. And young Emory Yew will surely die."

Jespyr flinched at her brother's name. She looked down at her charm. "I'll do it."

"Like hell." Ravyn didn't know if he was whispering or shouting. "There has to be another—"

"Saying there must be another way does not make it so," the Nightmare hissed.

Petyr turned to Jespyr. Swallowed laboriously. "I—it should be me, princess. You're too important."

"I'm not any more important than you." Strain pulled at

Jespyr's face. "We'll toss your lucky coin. That is balance. That is fair."

With a shaking hand, Petyr drew his coin from his pocket. He handed it to Ravyn. Gave him a pointed look. "Heads."

"Tails," Jespyr murmured.

The coin was small in Ravyn's hand. He stared down at it, the edifice of his life crumbling around him. It was only a scrap of copper.

But it might cost a life.

" 'I'm prepared to pay whatever price she asks,' " the Nightmare murmured in his ear. "That is what you said when I spoke to you of retrieving the Twin Alders Card."

"If you think I meant my own sister—"

"I said it once, too. That I'd pay the Spirit anything she wanted for the Twin Alders. And I did. Once in the chamber, when she robbed me of my ability to use the very Cards I'd lost pieces of myself to forge—and again, here, at the edge of her wood. I paid. We all must."

Petyr planted his feet. Shut his eyes. "Go on, lad. Toss the coin."

Ravyn remained statue-still.

"Toss it, Ravyn," Jespyr said through her teeth.

He didn't budge. "Jes—"

"Toss. The. Coin." She looked into his eyes. "For Emory."

Ravyn's throat closed. He flicked his wrist—let loose the coin. It caught gray light as it spun in the air.

No one blinked. No one breathed. When the coin dropped back into Ravyn's palm, it felt heavier. He glanced down, caging his fingers around it before the others could see. "Heads."

Petyr let out a shaking breath, and so did the Nightmare.

Jespyr didn't move. Her gaze narrowed, trained on Ravyn's eyes. "You're lying."

"I'm not."

"You are. I can always tell." Conviction hardened the lines of her face. She marched toward the wall of trees. "Just this once, I wish you hadn't. You're not the only one who would do anything for Emory." She took her charm, and before Ravyn could reach out and stop her—

Shoved it into the hole in the alder tree.

The wood groaned in response. The wind rose in a torrent, mist gusting through branches. Then the trees began to move, a narrow path opening in the impenetrable line of alders.

Opening for Jespyr.

The mist was so dense that Ravyn could hardly see her. Jespyr sucked in a breath, and mist slipped into her mouth. She coughed on it—looked back at him. "Are you with me, brother?"

Something inside of Ravyn shattered. "I'm right behind you."

The light in her brown eyes faded. Jespyr turned to the narrow path between the trees—

And ran into the alderwood.

Chapter Thirty-Six

Elm

Elm kept his hand high on Farrah Pine's back. It was his fifth dance of the evening. Five dances, and Ione had still not arrived in the great hall.

The theme of the night was seasons, and the court was parceled by costumes of Equinoxes and Solstices—summers and winters, springs and autumns. The columns of the great hall were decorated with sprigs of holly, woven with garlands. Blood-red rowan berries hung from every archway. Sconces and chandeliers dripped candle wax. Decorative bells were stripped from the walls by drunken courtiers, their notes clanging through the room, fighting in discord with singing voices and the instrumentations of the King's orchestra.

It was pageantry Elm might never have endured had he not been waiting for Ione. He'd knocked on her door, but she hadn't been there. He'd searched for her in the great hall, only to be caught in the tide of courtiers.

When the dance finally ended in a sweeping crescendo, the gong struck nine. Elm dropped Farrah's hand, thanked her with a bow, then pushed into the crowd.

Hands caught his black doublet, stopping him.

Alyx Laburnum, and the two younger Laburnum brothers Elm hardly knew, shoved a goblet into his hands. They were all wearing autumn leaves in their hair. "Highness," Alyx said, his face easy with drunkenness. "Always a pleasure to see you."

Spending time with a Laburnum was the furthest thing from pleasure Elm could fathom. "Alyx," he muttered into his cup. "Enjoying yourself?"

"Not as much as my sister." Alyx took a deep swill from his own cup. "You and Yvette make a handsome couple on the dance floor."

Elm's smile did not touch his eyes. He hadn't said one word to Yvette Laburnum during their dance. He rolled his shoulder, Alyx's hand dropping off his back.

"She hasn't shut up about you since we arrived," one of the idiot younger brothers said. "Not that she shuts up much at all—"

Sentence half-finished, the boy's eyes drifted over Elm's shoulder. His brothers did the same, their jaws slackening. When Elm turned, Ione was standing under the archway, framed by candlelight and silk and sweeping garlands. She looked like spring—an Equinox goddess.

Her hair was parted to the side, a few strands tucked behind her ears. The rest was loosely spun behind her head, fastened by a pearl-studded pin. Sheer, delicate sleeves caressed the soft lines of her arms. And the neckline of her gown plummeted in a deep, ruinous V, revealing the long, beckoning line between her breasts. The bodice held her like a glove, kissing over her waist and down to her hips, where it was met with a flowing, lavender-pink skirt.

Ione cast her gaze over the crowd, passing Elm, then hurtling back. The muscles in the corner of her mouth twitched. She took her hands in her skirt and lowered to a curtsy, exposing even more of that heart-stopping neckline.

Elm ran a hand down the back of his neck, shoved the goblet back at Alyx, and headed straight for her.

She waited for him between the columns. When Elm offered his hand, she took it, and that thing between them—the thread, the unquiet ache—began to pulse.

"You're late," he said, his finger toying with the cuff of her sleeve.

"I know. I was in the dungeon."

Elm's gaze shot up. "Why?"

"To see my father." She looked away. "He's alive. Frostbitten like Uncle Erik, but alive. I asked him if he'd seen me on Equinox with Hauth—if he knew where my Maiden Card might be. He didn't. But he had seen Hauth and me dancing that night. He'd known I was too drunk to be alone with a man—and done nothing." Her eyes glazed over, unfocused. "I shouldn't be surprised, now that I know what he did to Elspeth, that his fear of offending a Rowan was greater than his desire to keep his own daughter safe."

Elm raised her hand to his mouth. Whispered over her knuckles. "I'm sorry, Hawthorn."

Her gaze came back into focus. "People are watching us."

So they were. When Elm glanced over his shoulder, half of the faces in the great hall wore the practiced look of watching but not watching—listening but not listening.

He didn't bother to mollify them with a smile. He was tired of all the pageantry. "Let them look," he said, lowering Ione's hand to his chest. "Dance with me, Hawthorn."

"Aren't you meant to be wooing Blunder's daughters?"

"I intend to. One, in particular." Elm's voice grew quiet. "Please, will you dance with me?"

Her eyes were guarded. "All right."

The song was an easy pace. When they entered the line of

dancers, Elm's other hand slipped across Ione's hip and over the small of her back, guiding her to the sway of the music.

"Reach into my tunic pocket," he whispered in her ear. "Left side."

A ghost of a flush kissed her cheeks. She dipped her hand into his tunic. When she pulled out the Nightmare Card, a hum sounded in her throat. "Thief."

"More than you know."

Her skirt brushed against Elm's leg when he turned her. "Won't they be missing it in Hauth's room?"

"Probably. Though I doubt anyone will bang on my door, asking for it. I'm the *heir.* The list of people who might reprimand me grows short."

Ione pinched the Nightmare Card between her thumb and forefinger. "Those yellow eyes…" She pressed the Card to Elm's chest. "Use it. Go into my head. See if you can find the Maiden Card."

He spun her, dipped her. "What, here?"

"Why not?"

"It takes focus to use a Nightmare Card. And you, in that dress—"

"How would you know what it takes if your father never had a Nightmare until Equinox?"

A coy smile lifted the corners of Elm's mouth. He spun the Card between deft fingers, then—prestidigitation—disappeared it into his sleeve. "There are two Nightmare Cards, are there not?"

For a fleeting moment, a flicker of something—not quite warmth, but nearly—touched Ione's scrutinous gaze. "The more time I spend with you, Prince, the less I seem to know you."

"That's not what I want." Elm twirled her away, then pulled her back into his chest. "I want you to know me very well, Ione

Hawthorn. Which is"—he dipped her again, bowing over her and speaking against her throat—"a rather horrifying feeling, if I'm perfectly honest."

The apples of Ione's cheeks rounded. Elm thought she might truly smile. He held his breath, waiting for it. But then she blinked, and her face was without expression, perfect and stone-smooth. Unreadable—unreachable.

He was so sick of the Maiden Card.

The song ended on a flurry, and then Elm was leading them away, back to the other side of the columns, away from the crowd. He looked left and right, but Stone was crawling with courtiers. Even the gardens, even the stairwell.

He could take her to his room, or the cellar again. Somewhere private. But for a reason he wasn't ready to tell her, Elm wanted them to be seen together—for people to get used to the heir of Blunder, leaning a whit too close to Ione Hawthorn's face.

He dug through his pocket, retrieving his Scythe. He tapped the red Card three times, focusing on the orchestra. *Louder.*

The music swelled, instruments sounding with new fervor. "So that no one will hear us."

Ione leaned against the column, autumn air flittering in through the garden door, catching in her skirt. "Will it hurt," she said, her gaze dropping to the Nightmare Card, "when you enter my mind?"

"No. I wouldn't have brought it if it did."

She closed her eyes. "Go on, then."

Elm tapped the Nightmare Card three times and fell beneath its salt tide. He'd used Ravyn's Card only a handful of times, but it was enough like the Scythe to know how to urge the magic outward—into a person. He had no trouble fixating on Ione.

He pushed the salt over her. When he spoke, it was with a closed mouth. *Hawthorn.*

She jumped. "Should—" Her lips snapped shut. *Should I think about Equinox?*

Yes.

Ione drew in a breath. Let it out. And then Elm was not seeing her anymore, but her mind. Her memories.

He was Ione, and Ione was in the throne room, looking up at the dais. The King sat in his throne. On his right, tall and broad and unbroken, was Hauth.

"You have done your kingdom a great service, Tyrn," the King said, an empty goblet in his left hand and the Nightmare Card in his right. "This Card has been lost for many years. Name your price and it shall be yours."

A hand gripped Ione's arm. She looked up at her father, but his gaze was on the King, wide with anticipation. He led her closer to the dais. "This is my daughter, Ione. She is amiable." Tyrn pulled her in front of him and pushed her a step forward. "And unwed."

Hauth's posture went rigid. He glanced down at his father. But the King was caressing the Nightmare Card in such a way it was clear what his answer would be. Hauth scowled. "Not very pretty, is she?"

Ione's entire body tensed.

"There are ways of dealing with that," the King muttered. He looked up and spoke to Tyrn as if Ione was not there. "I'll draw the contract myself."

Ione's memories jutted forward in a blur. Lights burst before her eyes, her ears buzzing with the sound of thunderous applause. She was looking out at the great hall, and everyone was on their feet, clapping. "Sit," Hauth said in her ear. "Let them all get a good look at their future Queen."

Elm could feel Ione's heart racing. The apples of her cheeks rounded with a smile. "Should I say something?"

"No."

"I'd like to."

Hauth's green eyes stalled on her face. He seemed confused, his expression caught somewhere between attraction and revulsion. His hand pressed into Ione's shoulder, and he forced her to sit. "You needn't say anything at all."

Wine was poured. Ione drank and greeted well-wishers as they filed up to the dais. For every person she spoke to—every smile or laugh or hum in her throat—the attraction in Hauth's gaze dissipated.

It was strange for Elm to look through the eyes of a drunk person while entirely sober. Ione's goblet was filled for the eighth time, her vision beginning to tunnel. She was staring into the great hall, swaying in her seat—gazing at a figure seated along the table.

Elm. She was looking at Elm.

He was talking to Jespyr, a remarkably sour look haunting his face.

"Your brother wears a lot of black," Ione said, her voice too loud. "For a Prince."

"An old habit of Renelm's," Hauth muttered into his goblet.

"For what purpose?"

Hauth looked into her eyes. Smirked. "To hide the blood I dealt him."

Ione's mouth dropped open.

Hauth laughed. "Trees. He's well enough." His smirk cut away to a sneer. "You should know—you've been gazing at him all night. Wipe that dazed look off your face." He shoved the wine under her nose. "I can't stand it."

Ione's vision buckled, and then she was in the garden,

dancing with Hauth. His grip was too loose, the indifference on his face distinct. He let go of her on a twirl, and Ione fell. "Drunk thing," Hauth said, laughing as she crashed into a circle of men.

They picked her up, too many hands eagerly reaching for her body. Ione jerked away, only to land back in Hauth's arms. He said something in her ear that was little more than a muffle in Ione's memory. She tried to back away from him, but his grip tightened, and then he was pulling her through the crowd.

Everything went dark, cold. Ione's vision was blurry, spinning so fast Elm's stomach curled. Salt pinched her senses and she coughed—the telltale sensation of a Scythe.

"Put it there," came Hauth's echoing voice.

Ione's hands scraped over a wall—the cracked surface of a long, pale stone dusted with ash—

Go back, Elm whispered into her mind. *Show me that again.*

The blurry tunnel of Ione's vision shifted. Once more, fingertips dragging through ash, her hand pressed over a pale, cracked stone.

Twisted by drunkenness, Ione thought she was touching a wall. But the ash was undoubtedly from a hearth. And the pale stone with the wide, jagged crack—

Elm sucked in a breath. *I know where your Maiden Card is.* He lifted a finger to tap the Nightmare Card, but Ione's voice stopped him.

Wait, she said into his mind. *I want to show you the rest.*

The next memory was stark, bereft of drunkenness. She stood in Hauth's room, morning light streaming through the window.

She was crying.

"Please. I don't feel like myself. I need the Maiden back."

Hauth ignored her.

Ione's vision flashed again, and she was in the yard at Castle Yew. Elspeth was next to her, and so was Elm, all three of them watching as Ravyn and Hauth sparred in front of the Destriers. When Ravyn stomped on Hauth's hand and the High Prince screamed, Ione smiled. But the effort was taxing.

After, she spoke to Hauth. "I don't see why you are so determined to lock my feelings away. It's not as if we are destined to spend much time together." She clenched her jaw. "If I promise to use the Maiden when we are together at court, will you tell me where it is?"

Hauth's skin was pale for pain. "No."

"Then I ask you to release me from this engagement."

He barked a laugh. "And subject my father to courtly gossip? He'd whip the both of us."

Ione turned to leave, lingering at the door. Her voice had grown so flat from when she'd spoken on Equinox. "So this is what you would have? A Queen with no heart?"

Hauth's green eyes held nothing but spite. He tapped his Scythe. "Go away."

The room bled away to another. One with dark walls and wind that whistled in through the windows.

Spindle House.

There was blood on Hauth's shoes from where he'd stepped in Elspeth's dark vomit, left over from the game with the Chalice. He paced the room, the veins in his neck bulging, two empty flagons rolling on the floor. "Your cousin," he shouted. "She's *infected*, isn't she?"

Ione's voice was cold. "No."

He hit her across the face with an open palm—took her yellow hair in his fist. "Tell me the truth, Ione."

She stayed unmoving, unflinching. "Elspeth isn't infected."

His face grew redder. "It's disgrace enough that my own

cousins carry that blight. But now my future wife's—it is too much."

He dragged Ione by her hair to the casement window, slammed it open. "You'll have your wish, my dear," he said, hauling her over the sill. "I release you from our engagement."

Ione clawed at him. Screamed. But with one brutal shove—

She was falling.

Elm's entire body seized, and he fell with Ione down Spindle House's reaching tower. He heard the sickly crunch of her skull, cracking against brick. When Ione peered down at her body, jagged, red-tipped bones had torn through her clothes.

Blood pulsed in Elm's ears. He struggled to tap the Nightmare Card. When he opened his eyes, Ione was watching him. He caught her cheek, pressed his forehead over hers. His voice shook. "Did no one help you?"

"It was late. No one saw me fall. And it hurt too much to scream—to even whisper. I simply lay there. Waiting to die."

She said it with so little affect. Like it bored her, the near-end of her life. "I watched the moon worry across the sky. My blood eased and my bones straightened, snapping back into place. The pain in my head faded, and then...I felt nothing. No despair, no fear. Only then did I truly understand what the Maiden had done to me.

"I left Spindle House and stayed the night in an alley in town. I thought about running away. To go deep in the mist and simply disappear." She sighed. "But I couldn't go without my Card. So I walked to Hawthorn House, washed the blood out of my hair, waited for my family. I didn't want to go back to Stone and face Hauth alone. They never came." She brushed a loose strand of auburn hair from Elm's brow. "But you, Prince Renelm, did."

Pain hit Elm's temples. He felt something warm slide from his nostril.

Ione's eyes tightened. She dragged her hand under his nose. When she pulled it back, there was blood.

Elm hadn't remembered, the music loud in his ears, that he was still using his Scythe.

Ione reached into his pocket. When her finger grazed his Card, Elm's connection shattered. The pain stopped.

"Sometimes," she muttered, wiping his blood on her skirt, "I think things would be infinitely better if there were simply no Providence Cards at all."

Elm gave a shaky exhale. "You'd make such a perfect Queen."

She laughed at that. Not a real laugh, but a cold, unfeeling one. "Just not a perfect Rowan Queen."

"What does that mean?"

"Elspeth," she said plainly. "I could never wear the crown that would see Elspeth, or anyone infected, killed. Not even now, when I feel nothing. It's why I wanted to be Queen in the first place. To have real power. To *change* things." Again, that derisive laugh. "I was a fool."

Elm blinked. And it became so painfully clear what he needed to do. He took Ione's hand, lacing their fingers together, and led her down the hall, away from the music that drifted through the columns. For the first time since he'd stood on that drawbridge and watched Ravyn ride away, Elm felt light. Like someone had punched a hole in Stone's ancient walls and let in the day.

When they got to the tall, fortified doors of the throne room, he nodded at the sentries.

The doors opened with an ominous rumble. Elm pulled Ione inside. "Don't let anyone in," he told the sentries.

The hearths were not lit. The room was dark. They were alone in that cold, heartless place. Alone, just her, him—

And the throne.

Ione's voice drifted past Elm's ears. "What are we doing here, Prince?"

He looked at the chair. That ancient monster, forged of rowan trees. "Elm," he reminded her. "Call me Elm."

"What are we doing here, Elm?"

Christening. Reclaiming. Fashioning a new King. Maybe a new Queen as well.

"Changing things."

Ash. A wide, jagged crack in pale stone.

Elm and Ione stood on the east side of the throne room, staring into the open mouth of the unlit hearth. "Look inside," Elm said, the shadow of terrible things hanging low. "There is a pale stone that lifts."

Ione dropped to a crouch. When ash brushed between her fingers, she drew in a breath. The muscles between her shoulders bunched, and a scraping sound filled the throne room. She pulled the pale stone away, revealing a dark, carved-out hole. In it were two things: a cluster of weapons—a chain and whip and a short, blunt club—

And a Maiden Card.

Ione pushed the weapons aside. The iron links of the chain clanged, and Elm's hands balled into fists. She took the Maiden Card and slid it into the bodice of her dress, then shoved the stone back.

When she turned, her expression revealed nothing—no joy that the thing she had so long sought was back in her possession. "What are the weapons for?"

"An education in pain."

Her gaze shot to Elm's face, then dropped to his hands, locked in fists. She caught one, brought it to her mouth—pressed her lips over it. "Thank you."

His voice was rough. "Don't thank me yet. There's still one last thing for us to do here."

Elm led her to the throne. His fingers ghosted over the armrest. Slowly, he lowered himself down into the dark seat.

Ione watched him. "Preparing for the future?"

"More than you know." He leaned forward—clasped his hands together. "I have a proposition for you, Miss Hawthorn. A final barter between us."

"So formal." She propped a shoulder against the throne. "What are we bartering, Elm?"

He liked hearing his name on her lips far too well. "This terrible chair. And you in it with me."

Ione's brows drew together, her gaze jumping between him and the throne.

"You can still be Queen of Blunder, Hawthorn. If you want to."

Her voice was needle-sharp. "What are you talking about?"

"Marriage contracts," Elm said, itching to touch her. "A Kingly duty my brutish father has never tended well. The last one he penned himself—poorly, might I add—was signed on Equinox. A Nightmare Card, for a marriage."

"To Hauth. A contract that bound me to Hauth."

Elm smiled. "To the *heir.*"

He'd known the moment he'd read it that his father had not taken pains to see the contract well worded. The King's handwriting had been difficult to read. It was the first time Elm had thanked the Spirit his father was a drunk. He'd gotten the keys from Baldwyn and fetched the contract—read it three times over. *Bound by this contract to wed the heir to the throne of Blunder,* followed by Ione's name and the King's signature.

And there was nothing to erase it, now that it was hidden safely at Castle Yew. Which meant Ione Hawthorn, if she wished, could still be Queen—still marry a Rowan. Only now, it wasn't the brutal Prince.

But the rotten one.

"Queen," Elm said. "We'll find your mother and brothers—release your uncle and father, if you wish it. You can be the ruler you were supposed to be. Wanted to be."

Ione's face was unreadable. "The King will never allow a wedding. My kin are traitors. *Infected.*"

"So are his," Elm bit back. "My father has always kept the infection close, so long as it served him. Ravyn, Emory—his own nephews, infected." Elm sucked his teeth. "There are many things the King does not want made public. Should he wish them to remain quiet, he will not challenge me on this."

Ione rounded the throne. Elm parted his legs, and she stood between them. "And if I hadn't saved your life?" she whispered, gazing down upon him. "Are you so honorable that you would marry me, a stranger who's been nothing but cold to you, just because your father skipped a few words in a marriage contract?"

His eyes glided over her mouth. "Charitable of you to think me honorable."

"You are."

"And you're hardly a stranger."

"You don't know the real me."

Elm softened his voice. "I know there is a warmth in you not even the Maiden can confine. No one who feels *nothing* would work so tirelessly to get their feelings back. I also know you love Elspeth—and not despite her infection. You simply love her."

He ran his thumb over Ione's bottom lip. "I think, behind the Maiden, you love a great many things, Ione Hawthorn. Even this wretched kingdom."

When she let out a breath, Elm leaned forward, traced his nose over her jawline—whispered into her ear. "I'd like to know the real you. Whenever you're ready."

Ione went still and didn't speak. The silence settled into Elm, shaking his resolve. "I'll make no demands of you," he managed. "When you release yourself from the Maiden and find you still do not care for me, we need never—"

"You think I don't care for you?"

His breath stole away from him. He looked into her eyes. "Do you?"

There was no reading her face. But in that moment, Elm was certain Ione was warring with something. Maybe it was the Maiden's chill. Or maybe—just maybe—it was the same thing he was warring with.

Hope. Delicate and thread-thin.

Ione lowered her head, brushed her mouth over his. "I'd like to try."

Tightness fisted Elm's chest. "I'd be your King, but always your servant. Never your keeper." He arched up, dragging his knuckles down her chin, making her lips part for him. "Think about it, Hawthorn."

When she spoke, her voice was full of air. "I don't want to think right now, Elm."

He reached into her hair and pulled the pin out. Yellow-gold waves fell down her back. Elm wrapped it around his fist like a bandage. "Then don't."

He kissed her, without pageantry. Ione sighed into his mouth, and Elm hauled her onto his lap, marveling once more how she utterly filled his hands. Her knees pinned his sides, and when she thrust her hips forward, her soft against his hard, she pushed Elm deeper into the throne.

"You look good in this chair." She glanced down through her lashes at him, the corner of her mouth twitching. "Under me."

Elm tugged her hair, baring her throat to him. He dragged his bottom lip up the warm column—took in a full breath of her. "That's the idea," he murmured into her skin.

Ione pressed harder into him. Rolled her pelvis over his lap.

Muscles spasmed everywhere. *"Ione."*

"Is this what you want?" Both of them were breathing hard. "Me? Here?"

It took all of Elm's fraying self-restraint to pull back. His body was pleading to the point of pain to be inside her. But he couldn't. Not with the part of her he wanted most still locked away. He shook his head. "When I bed you, Ione, I want you to *feel* it."

A flush blossomed from the torturous neckline of her dress, floating up her throat into her face. But her expression was blank.

"I'd like to know the real you," Elm said again. He kissed her slowly, intently. "I've wanted to know you since I saw you all those years ago, riding in the wood, mud on your ankles."

Ione withdrew. Whatever she saw on Elm's face made her eyes widen. She sat up, finding his hand, lacing their fingers. "Come with me."

She led the way out of the throne room. The King's court was still in the great hall, drinking and dancing, unaware that their new High Prince, moments ago, might have gladly debased himself atop the throne.

Ione led him up the stairs. When they got to her room, she shut the door and latched it, pushing Elm up against the wood. She kissed him once, hard, then pulled back.

"It's going to hurt," she said, "when the Maiden lets me go. When all the feelings I haven't felt come rushing in. Are you sure you want to see that?"

The moment held Elm in place. Even his breath had gone shallow. Ione dipped her hand into her bodice. When she pulled it back, the Maiden was between her fingers. "Do you?"

He managed only one word. "Please."

Never breaking their gaze, Ione held a finger up to her Maiden Card. With three taps, she released herself from its magic.

Chapter Thirty-Seven

Elspeth

The moment Petyr sought to enter the alderwood, the trees barred his way. It seemed the Spirit of the Wood would not let anyone who was not already infected into her lair.

He tried nonetheless. "I'll wait for you—" he called.

The trees slammed shut, locking him out and Ravyn, Jespyr—the Nightmare and me—*in*.

Ahead, Jespyr's laughter cut through the mist. "This way."

The Nightmare had known all along that, to enter the alderwood, someone needed to get lost in the mist. His own sister had done it. He'd known this was coming—

And said nothing. I didn't have claws or jagged teeth, but I had enough anger to turn the dark chamber we shared into a battering cacophony of fury. I screamed until I earned a flinch, then screamed again.

Enough, Elspeth! he snarled, hurtling after Jespyr through a bramble of thorns so sharp they cut through the sleeves of his cloak. He shielded his face with his arms, and the thorns bit into them, scoring his skin red.

I felt neither pain nor pity for the marks upon him, screaming all the louder. *Ravyn is moving heaven and earth to find the*

Twin Alders Card—to save Emory. If he loses a sister in the process, it will break him.

Yews do not break, came the Nightmare's menacing rebuttal. *They bend.*

I looked out my window into the alderwood. The hour was distinctly day. But the wood was so dense, the mist so oppressive, it felt like the blackest part of night.

The wood was alive—and voracious. Trees and roots skittered forward at terrifying speeds, grasping at Ravyn and the Nightmare. They snagged at hair and skin and clothes, as if they wanted a taste of the trespassers who had breached their terrifying haunt.

Worse, the alderwood spoke, and not into just the Nightmare's mind. From the way he jumped, gray eyes going wide, I could tell Ravyn could hear the trees, too.

Their voices were like a swarm of wasps.

Be wary the green, be wary the trees. Be wary the song of the wood on your sleeves. You'll step off the path—to blessing and wrath. Be wary the song of the wood on your sleeves.

Ahead, Jespyr's gait quickened to a sprint. She ripped through branches and brambles and vines thick as her forearm. Her laughter swam in the dense air, unnatural—both calm and frantic. "Can you hear the Spirit? She's calling my name. Calling me home."

Ravyn tripped, then bent over himself, gasping for air. "Keep going," the Nightmare hissed, wrenching him up by his hood. "If we lose her, we too will be lost."

They ran without respite, hunted by the alderwood.

Brush rustled from behind. The Nightmare whipped his gaze back—huffed air out his nostrils. It seemed the trees were not the only ones who wanted a pound of flesh. Animals with sharp shoulder blades and silver eyes stalked forward. Wolves, wildcats. Above, birds of prey darted between trees, far away and then—too close.

A falcon dove, screeching as it swiped razor talons at the Nightmare.

His sword flashed through the air. There was another terrible screech, then feathers and blood rained.

Nearby, a tree with thin branches and crimson leaves whipped Ravyn across the face. A thousand dissonant voices ricocheted in the salt-riddled air. *Mind the mist, it does not lift. The Spirit doth hunt, ever adrift. Stay out of the wood, be wary, be good. The Spirit doth hunt, ever adrift.*

Ravyn reeled, wiping blood from his cheek. He ducked, barely avoiding an errant branch as it swung for his neck—but not the next. Jagged, the branch caught his hand, tearing the skin at his knuckles.

There is no escape from the salt, the alderwood called. *Magic is everywhere—ageless. To the Spirit of the Wood, the exactor of balance, our lives are but of a butterfly—fleeting.*

Ahead, Jespyr's voice grew more frenzied. "The voices of the trees are clever. Isn't that right, Shepherd King? It is they who spoke the words you penned in your precious book. They who warned you against magic. They whom you did not heed."

The Nightmare's vision went wide—then instantly narrow. Time fell away, his memory knotting around me like a noose until it wasn't Jespyr I was trailing in the alderwood—

But Ayris.

"Come, brother," she laughed, her voice horrible and wrong. Lines of inky darkness chased up her arms. "The Spirit of the Wood awaits. New beginnings—new ends!" She turned, her yellow eyes cold, as if she no longer knew me. "But nothing comes free."

An animal snarl shattered the memory.

On your left! I shouted.

Fangs and hot, rancid breath. The Nightmare swore, veering as a wolf sprang at us. He cut the animal down with his blade. But a second was waiting on his other side, so close I could see the white of saliva strung between its jaws. It lunged, and would have caught the Nightmare's arm and ripped it open—

Had an ivory-hilted dagger not sung through the air, hitting the beast in its wide silver eye.

The wolf fell, and Ravyn was at our side, ripping his dagger free. He afforded the Nightmare a brief, disgusted glance, then hurried back onto the path Jespyr's erratic steps had cleaved.

The apology you owe him, I seethed, *is beyond measure. He just saved your life. OUR life.*

A humiliation neither of us should attempt to recover from.

Jespyr's laughter had grown distant. It sounded from not only ahead, but also below. A moment later, I knew why. Not ten paces away, the forest floor opened into a deep, jagged valley.

Dirt flew as Ravyn skittered to an abrupt halt. He teetered a moment at the valley's lip. The Nightmare, trailing too close, slammed into his back. "You bloody imbecile."

They stumbled, staggered—fell.

The Nightmare's vision winked, limbs tangling with Ravyn's as the two of them rolled over root and rock into the valley. They met the bottom with a flurry of curses, smashing through something brittle.

Brittle—and white. The Nightmare stiffened. When he pushed up onto his hands and looked around, I stifled a scream.

Coated in mist, the valley floor was a field of bodies.

Some were skeletons. Others only partially decomposed. Earth, flesh, bone. The smell broke through the salt in the air. It wafted across the Nightmare's sinuses, putrid—rot and decay. Death.

Every soul who'd gotten lost in the mist had come here to die. To rot.

Ravyn choked back a cry, a skull shattering beneath his knee as he scrambled to his feet. His eyes went wide, then he heaved his meager breakfast onto the ground.

Bleary, the Nightmare's gaze was hard to see through. Still, I could discern what awaited us on the other side of the valley. A looming hill. Jespyr was on it—climbing on all fours like a spider, her words garbled, her cries guttural.

Don't lose her, I urged him.

He didn't move, flashes of Ayris passing through his mind.

Nightmare. I drew in a breath. Spoke the words he had so often tendered me, when it felt impossible to drag myself forward. *Get up. You must get up.*

He let out a breath of fire and unfolded himself from the ground, facing the ominous hill. "Eyes forward, Yew," he murmured. "We're nearly there."

The incline of the hill was treacherously steep. The Nightmare let Ravyn go ahead of him, though I could tell by the gnashing of his teeth that their pace was not fast enough for his liking. Still, he kept his arms strained the entire way, as if he was preparing himself to catch Ravyn, should he fall.

He didn't. Calloused fingers found purchase in the earth, and Ravyn hauled himself up, foot by foot, up that tall, monstrous hill. When the incline crested to a flat crown, he fell onto grass. His hands were tattered, slick with blood. Welting bruises decorated every bit of skin I could see. His breaths were gasps. It seemed to take all of his remaining strength just to lie there and breathe.

My voice came out in broken pieces. *Help him.*

The Nightmare paused, looming over Ravyn like a shadow. Slowly, he knelt. "Look at me."

Ravyn's gaze seemed far and near. It crashed into my window.

"A King's reign is wrought with burden. Weighty decisions ripple through centuries. Still, decisions must be made." The Nightmare's whisper was like wind in the trees. "You are strong, Ravyn Yew. I have known that since the moment I clapped eyes on you. And you must keep being strong—" He turned and faced the hilltop. "For what comes next."

The hill's crown was mist and rock. In its center were two trees, their roots woven together like serpents. Tall with long, reaching branches, one tree was pale—white as bone. The other was black, as if charred.

I recognized them as if they'd been scrawled over my skin. The same image lived on the cover of *The Old Book of Alders.* Two trees, woven together at the roots. One light, the other dark.

The twin alders.

Jespyr lay supine beneath them. Her eyes were closed.

Ravyn ripped himself off the ground and ran to her, crouching at his sister's side, tearing the fabric along her sleeve. Long fingers of inky darkness swept up Jespyr's arm. A tributary of magic, settling into its new host.

The infection.

Ravyn swore, clawing at himself for his spare charm. He placed the viper head in Jespyr's hand and closed her fingers around it. He held his breath, waiting.

She did not stir.

His voice broke. "The Maiden?"

The Nightmare came up behind him. "Not for this. No Card can stop the infection, nor heal degeneration."

Yet, came a harsh, rattling voice from above.

The hill shook, knocking Ravyn off-balance. He fell, and the alders wrapped their roots around him, catching him at the wrists—the ankles—tethering him to the ground.

What are they doing to him? I shouted into the Nightmare's mind.

He didn't answer. His eyes were on Jespyr's unmoving form.

The trees bent over Ravyn. They had no eyes—no mouths—no faces. But they spoke. *Who is it?* called the rattling voice of the dark alder.

Higher, more dissonant, the pale alder answered. *Taste his blood.*

The roots around Ravyn's wrists tightened. When blood dripped from the cuts in his hands, the hilltop shuddered. *Yew,* the trees said together.

The pale alder shifted closer to Ravyn. *The yew tree is cunning, its shadow unknown. It bends without breaking, its secrets its own.*

Look past twisting branches, the dark alder called, *dig deep to its bones. Is it the Twin Alders you seek—or is it the throne?*

The Nightmare's hands were rigid, clawlike, at his sides. "Answer them," he told Ravyn.

Ravyn pulled in ragged breaths. "I seek the Twin Alders Card to unite the Deck."

To lift the mist, said the dark alder.

To heal the infection, said the other.

Ravyn nodded.

Then you must ask the Spirit herself for it.

The roots around Ravyn's wrists loosened, and another thunderous roll shuddered through the hill. The alder trees twitched. Slowly, they began to move farther apart, dragging their roots with them. When they were at a distance from one another, they stopped.

I stared at the space between them. Blinked—then blinked again. I was not looking through the trees at the other end of the hilltop. I was looking through a *doorway.* An opening to another place, between the alders.

A long, pale shore.

Ravyn pulled himself to his feet. "Is that where the Twin Alders Card is?"

It is where the Spirit of the Wood will speak to you.

Ravyn knelt—tugged on Jespyr's arm.

The alder tree's roots jutted over her, caging her to the ground. *She stays with us. If she does not feed us with her rot, we will feed her with our magic.*

Ravyn's voice trembled with loathing. "That is why people flock here when the Spirit snares them in the mist? To *feed* you?"

The dark alder extended a branch. *To feed. And to fuel. What we consume, we pour back into the mist. What you call an infection, we declare a gift.* The branch traced Ravyn's brow. *I would think you, of all people, would understand that.*

Ravyn recoiled. "My magic is not a gift. It's hardly anything at all."

The tree pulled back. And while it had no eyes, I was certain it had turned its glare to the Nightmare. *Seems you have much to learn yet. Now go. The Spirit will not wait forever.*

Ravyn looked between the trees at that pale shore. Roots no longer held him in place, but his legs did not move.

Forward, always forward, the pale alder mocked. *Isn't that your creed, Ravyn Yew?*

A frown drew across Ravyn's brows. He looked down at his sister, then back at the Nightmare—at me. "I'm not going anywhere without them."

Then your journey was for naught.

The Nightmare hissed. His thoughts swaddled me in darkness. Five hundred years became nothing, Jespyr shifting to a visage of Ayris, lying unmoving between the twin alders.

And I understood, better than I ever had, how he had become a monster.

His life had been a never-ending barter. He had given his

time, his focus, his love, for magic. He'd wielded it with great authority. But it was *magic* that had taken his kingdom, his family, his body, his soul.

It was balance, but it was not fair. And now he was full of agony, whittled down to something jagged—a tooth, a claw.

I know what you're thinking, I told him.

Do you?

It's the same thing you've thought for centuries, isn't it? That this pain might never have occurred if you had simply played in the wood with Ayris as a child and never asked the Spirit for her blessings. You'd have never gotten the sword. Never bled onto the stone. You might have held your children as dearly as you did your Cards.

I softened my voice. *For if you had, there would have never been any Cards at all. And none of this would have happened.*

He laughed, a bitter sound. *And now you know that every terrible thing that happened in Blunder took place long before I handed Brutus Rowan a Scythe. It happened because, five hundred years ago, a boy wore a crown—had every abundance in the world—but always asked for MORE.*

Ahead, the alder trees stirred. They shifted toward each other. The doorway between them to the pale shore—to the Twin Alders Card—was beginning to close.

Ravyn's voice was taut. "Please. I will speak to the Spirit, meet any price." He grasped Jespyr's arm, trying to pry her from her cage of roots. "But not my sister."

The trees didn't heed him, the gap between them closing further still.

There's a reason you are here a second time, I said to the Nightmare, my voice urgent. *You may have lost a sister to magic, but you must not resign Ravyn to the same fate. You are the Shepherd King—the author of everything I have ever known. You wrote Blunder's history, Aemmory Percyval Taxus. Now rewrite it.*

The alders were closing, the pale shore disappearing, our one shot at the Twin Alders Card—disappearing.

Ravyn wrenched at roots with bloody hands. But he couldn't get Jespyr out. He turned to the Nightmare. Shouted a broken plea: "Help me."

Our shared vision snapped forward. And though I had no control over my body, I'd swear it was me who tightened the Nightmare's grip on his sword.

He drew his blade over his hand, cut a thin slice in his palm, and stalked toward the twin alders. When he slapped a bloody handprint onto the pale alder, the hill did not merely shudder. It quaked.

The trees spoke as one, their voices a dissonant, wretched harmony. *Taxus.*

The Nightmare fixed the alders in his gaze—addressed them with a malice so ancient it coated my mind in brimstone. "There are many circles that draw through time," he said. "Many mirrored events, many woods that inevitably lead us to the same place. Much of what happened five hundred years ago has happened again." His eyes narrowed. "But not this. You will not make a monster out of him as you did me, forcing him to give up a sister. Let go of Jespyr Yew. Or I will cleave your roots from this earth."

The alders went rigid, their slithering roots and twisting branches halting to an eerie stillness. Then, so abruptly I'd no time to scream, they seized Ravyn, ripping him away from Jespyr. He shouted, thrashed, but was tossed with abandon through the doorway onto the pale shore. The trees turned their vicious branches on the Nightmare.

But his sword found them first.

He took to the roots, cutting Jespyr free with furious precision. The hill trembled, the opening between the alders as narrow as my bedroom door at Spindle House.

Keep going, I urged him.

He pried Jespyr's limp body off the earth and slung her over his shoulders. The two of them were struck over and over by flailing branches. Ravyn reached out, the space between the alders now so narrow he could not get back out. "Take my hand!"

The Nightmare took it. When Ravyn yanked him forward, the doorway between the twin alders slammed shut. The trees and the hilltop were gone. All that remained now was a pale shore, accompanied by the sound of waves.

And the oppressive smell of salt.

Chapter Thirty-Eight

Elm

By the third tap of the pink Card, the flawless—unearthly and unreachable—Ione Hawthorn was gone. The *real* Ione was there in her stead.

Freckles. The first things Elm saw were her freckles. They were concentrated along the bridge of her nose, then sparse over her cheeks and brow and chin, a final few resting in the bowl of her Cupid's bow. There was a vertical crease in the center of her bottom lip—lines in the corners of her mouth and eyes.

Smile lines, he remembered. *This Ione smiles.*

There was textured skin, some of it irritated, around her nose. Half-moon shadows beneath her eyes. Eyelashes were partially blond again, and the small gap between her two front teeth had returned. The hair along her brow didn't fall with such unnatural elegance as before. There were tangles—rogue curls. Disarray and imperfection. She looked so... human, like the girl he'd seen riding through the woods.

There were not enough pages in all the books Elm had read, in all the libraries he'd wandered, in all the notebooks he'd scrawled, that could measure—denote or describe—just how beautiful she was.

"There you are."

The frost and indifference in Ione's hazel eyes had vanished, vibrant colors of earth and fire and forest entirely unrestrained.

A small, fractured noise came out of her. She moved toward him but didn't make it two steps before her knees buckled, and then Elm was catching her, holding her as they sank onto the floor.

Body shaking, eyes screwed shut, Ione opened her mouth against his chest. Her scream was silent at first, then so loud it filled Elm's ears. Tears fell down her face and her breaths came in labored gasps, her lungs begging for air, denied again and again by her unending wail.

She'd endured a bartered marriage to Hauth, a brute, who'd gotten her drunk and used his Scythe on her—locked away her heart with three indifferent taps. He'd dragged her to the precipice of that window at Spindle House and pushed her to her death. She'd lain there in her own blood, staring up at the moon, thinking it would be the last time she'd see the night sky.

It tore at Elm, thinking she'd endured it all alone. That his stalwart opponent, the Maiden Card, had healed her so well she'd been spared feeling a single part of what had happened to her.

Until now.

Elm pressed his face into her shoulder, whispering the only consolation he could think to offer. "I'm sorry. I'm so sorry."

Her fingers dug into his tunic. Then she was pushing—forcing him away from her. When Ione looked up into his face, there was so much hurt in those hazel eyes Elm thought he might die.

She pulled farther back. "Give me a moment."

"Ione."

She folded over herself—hugged her arms over her chest. "Go, Prince."

Prince. Like his brother. Elm scraped a hand over his eyes, said, "I'm sorry, Ione," and left.

He trailed his thumb over the Nightmare Card. When he got to Hauth's room, he didn't bother knocking.

It was late. There was only one Physician on duty, standing near the corner of the room, sorting tinctures and vials. He jumped when Elm entered. But the other figure—seated at Hauth's bedside, did not startle so easily.

Linden watched Elm enter, his brow knit by a deep grimace. "What the hell do you want?"

Elm didn't look at Hauth. There was no use breaking things that were already broken. But an old, familiar rage had crawled up his throat for every second he'd lived in Ione's memories. He didn't want to merely break things.

He wanted what the Shepherd King had gotten. The privilege of holding Hauth Rowan's life in his hands and finding it forfeit.

Elm wrenched open the chest at the end of the bed—threw the Nightmare Card back into it. "He's not worth it," he said—to Linden, to himself, he didn't know. "He's not worth another moment of your time."

He returned to Ione's door—slid down the face of it and sat in a heap, listening to the sound of her cries through the wood. He made himself listen. Made himself feel it.

His hand slipped into his tunic pocket, searching for comfort along velvet trim. Elm pulled the Scythe out and examined it, flipping it through his fingers. Red—the Rowan Card. His savior. His crutch. Did he even know who he was without it? Did his father? Had Hauth?

Ione's sobs carried through the door. Elm closed his eyes

and leaned his head against the wood, his shoulders shaking as tears fell down his face.

The door opened and Elm fell backward, hitting his head on the floor.

Ione looked down at him. With surprising strength she pulled him to his feet, then closed the door behind them and brought him to the bed.

Elm lay on his side and faced the wall, hollowed out. The mattress shifted and two hands wrapped around him. Ione pressed her body against his back, melding around him. Elm closed his eyes, tears he thought had all been spent stinging him once more. "Do you hate me, Hawthorn?"

Her arms tightened around him. "No, Elm. I don't hate you at all."

They slept. When Elm woke hours later, pale daylight shining in the window, Ione was still holding him. He memorized the map of her arms over his chest, perfect lines, she the stylus and he the paper.

Her voice fluttered past his ear. "Are you awake?"

He turned. Morning light kissed her hair, her ear, the high points of her face. Her eyes were swollen from crying.

Elm ran his hand across her cheek. "Ione."

She pulled him until they were pressed together, her mouth tucked against the hollow of his throat. For a long while they did nothing but breathe, so close to one another their inhales and exhales matched, a slow, steady rhythm. "When did you see me riding?" she said, her voice a gentle hum against his skin. "With mud on my ankles?"

Elm ran his fingers through her hair in long, tender strokes.

"I was sixteen, maybe seventeen, patrolling the forest road with Jespyr. We were supposed to be watching for highwaymen, but we were playing cards. A horse went by. Faster than most riders go. You didn't see us. You were laughing, a sort of whistling cackle." He rubbed the nape of her neck. "I liked your laugh. Your hair."

Ione was quiet a long time. Elm thought maybe she'd fallen asleep again. Then, "I thought you were beautiful. A beautiful, terrible prick."

A laugh rumbled in his chest.

"When I was a girl, I imagined you belonged in a storybook—no Prince had any right being so handsome unless he lived on a page. But you weren't charming like a Prince in a story. And you made it abundantly clear there was no one besides the Yews worthy of your time." She tugged at his sleeve. "The black clothes didn't exactly make you seem approachable. I didn't know then that Hauth was... hurting you."

Elm swallowed. "Was I rude to you?"

"That would have required you to speak to me."

"I didn't speak much. But I saw you—liked you." He spoke into her skin. "You seemed without burden. So happy and free you were exquisite. I envied you."

"You liked me... out of envy?"

His arm tightened around her. "I'm a rotten thing, Ione. I'm learning as I go."

Another pause. "On Market Day, when Hauth sent those poor people into the mist, you stood up to him. Challenged him, in front of everyone. And I saw the same rage and spite for him that I was beginning to understand." Her voice quieted, her tone confessional. "*I* envied *you*."

She swallowed. "There's so much of myself I haven't shared with you yet. What Hauth did—all the feelings he stole from me. I'm bitterly angry."

"Then be angry, Ione." Elm pressed his mouth to her forehead. "It looks well on you."

She made a small noise of approval, her words to him mirrored back at her. "I say spiteful things when my feelings are hurt. Hold grudges. And the highwaymen—I'm not sorry for what I did to them. Not even a little. It was frightening and awful, and I'd do it again without thinking to keep you from getting hurt." She took a rattling breath. "I think about how easy it would be to do horrible things if I felt I had a good reason."

"So do I."

"I liked that I might be Queen one day. I liked how the Maiden tempered things, how I stopped feeling regret and worry and fear. It felt a lot like power." She tilted her chin up until their lips were almost pressed together. "Maybe you liked me that way, too."

"I like that I can finally read your face, and that you've chosen to show it to me. You can tell me your terrible truths, Ione. I'm not going anywhere."

Elm sat up, awake, hungry. And, for the first time in memory, happy the day was only beginning. "Do you still like to ride?"

They dressed quickly. This time, Elm made sure Ione had shoes and a damn cloak.

Fortified against the mist with their charms, they found Elm's horse in the stable, then a chestnut-brown palfrey for Ione. When Elm handed her into the saddle, he caught himself wondering once more if the Spirit of the Wood did indeed dabble in the lives of men. If she'd pitied him that day he rode with Destriers to Hawthorn House. If she'd sensed all the rot inside him and gifted him, the ruined Prince, this moment with Ione to tide over his darkness.

They rushed out of the bailey and over the drawbridge. Wind blew Ione's hair behind her like a thousand beckoning ribbons, and Elm let out a breath. He always felt washed clean, riding away from Stone.

Autumn was slipping, the frost slow to melt. Soon, it wouldn't melt at all. They kept to the main road for a quarter of a mile, and then, so fast Ione had to jerk her reins, Elm veered his horse west, down an embankment. When they bottomed out, he took the path he'd long since memorized. Then, across a grassy plain, Elm unleashed his horse.

They cantered through the open field, parting the mist with their speed.

Ione spurred her horse—caught him until they rode neck and neck. Her eyes were wide, yellow hair a storm. But just as Elm began to worry the speed was too much, she tilted her head back, deficient of all pageantry—

And laughed.

The sound rolled through her body into Elm, undoing his last brick, his last barb. Ione's face was wide open, not a hint of ice or restraint. Her eyes were creased and her freckled nose wrinkled, the gap between her front teeth visible as she smiled. Elm took in the sight of her—memorized her—praying he could get to his sketchbook before the lines of her smile faded from his memory.

He doubted they ever would.

She must have felt his stare, because when Ione shifted in her saddle and looked at him, her gaze was expectant.

Elm reached over, snagged her reins. It was impossible to kiss on horseback, but he leaned over—brushed his mouth over hers—kissed her just the same.

Ione tugged the reins. When the horses stopped, Elm dismounted and reached up for her waist. She slid from her saddle into his grasp, crashing her mouth down upon his. "Thank you for this, Elm," she whispered into his lips. "For everything."

He'd never get used to how it felt, hearing her say his name. Heady, sweet, wistful.

They made it to a copse of trees before sprawling out in the grass, fumbling with one another's clothes. Salt stung the air. Elm kept his charm woven tightly around his wrist and Ione wore hers on its mended chain around her neck.

They rolled, caged in each other's arms. Elm pinned her to the ground and put a knee between her legs, guiding them open, whispering words of adoration into her mouth, words like *warm* and *divine* and *I can't fucking breathe when you look at me, Ione.*

Ione's hand slid beneath his undershirt and up his back, pressing into the lean muscles along his spine and shoulders—the places he'd taken beatings as a boy. When she freed him from his tunic, her eyes traveled over his bare chest, studying its contours. Fingers wove into his mess of auburn hair. Her voice was hushed, coated in awe. "You're beautiful."

"No. That word is only for you." Elm leaned back and pulled her onto his lap like he had on the throne. Only now, there was no shadow forged of rowan trees looming over them. There was fresh air, mist. Mourning doves cooed. A gossamer breeze came in waves. It draped itself over Elm, pushing the wild hairs along Ione's forehead into his face. Everything was gentle, soft.

Delicate.

Elm found the knot at the end of her bodice. There would be no knife. No tearing of fabric. He took his time, his fingers slow as he loosened her laces.

Ione didn't rush him. She was too busy memorizing his face. Running her fingers over it. Searching, measuring. When her bodice fell, dragging her dress down with it and leaving her bare to the waist, her hazel eyes were still on him.

"The way you're looking at me," he said, cupping her chin, "terrifies me."

"Why?" She ran a hand down his neck, his chest, the line between his abdomen muscles. "Did no one ever love you before, Elm?"

"Not like this." Closer. He needed her closer. "There's never been anything like this."

Elm lay on his back atop his cloak. He dragged Ione's leggings off and she straddled him, light hovering over her yellow hair. He reveled in how warm she was, how perfect the weight of her was against his body, how delicious it felt when she freed him of his pants.

Her eyes went wide. She dropped her hand—measured him anew. "*Elm.*"

He hissed through his teeth and pressed his fingers over her lips. "Careful what you say. You'll spend me too soon with that wicked mouth of yours." He pulled her down, kissed her slowly. "I want this to last, Ione."

She braced herself on his chest, and when they started, it was agonizingly slow. Elm watched her face, looking for pain, ready to stop the moment he saw any. But Ione eased onto him, hips tilting this way and that, finding her comfort, which became Elm's comfort, too. Inch by inch, she descended. And every memory of pleasure Elm had ever carried fractured in his mind, replaced by this. By her.

He held her hips. When he arched up into her, Ione sucked in a breath. He froze. "Did that—Are you—"

"You won't hurt me. There won't be any pain between us."

She dragged her thumb over his bottom lip. Elm nipped it, and she smiled. “Unless we’re in the mood for it.”

“There’ll be time for all manner of sordid things, Miss Hawthorn. For now, just—” His voice quieted. “Just keep looking at me.”

When Elm started moving inside of her, he couldn’t think. Couldn’t focus. Yellow hair was spilling everywhere and Ione’s face was flushed and so vulnerable, hazel eyes searching him, that he felt his chest constrict.

The slowness didn’t last. There was too much need—too much newness—between them. Elm stroked his thumb over her sex, his fingers digging into her bottom and hips as he moved with her, caught between savoring the moment and the insatiable need for more.

He reared up, grasping the back of her neck. “What do you feel, Ione?”

Like a rush of wings, she sighed. “*Everything.*”

Elm thrust harder, dragging his mouth over her jaw, her throat. “I’m yours. Even if you won’t be Queen—I’m yours.”

Ione’s eyelids fluttered, her pace quickening. Elm palmed her breasts, meeting the hummingbird thrum of her heartbeat with his mouth. She fell back onto their clothes, pulling him on top of her, wrapping her legs around his waist. Her breaths came faster, laborious, and then she wasn’t breathing at all, tensing around him.

Elm looked down through a haze. Ione’s brow furrowed, her eyes still on him. She opened her mouth, let out a sharp cry—

Pressure, so much pressure, Elm felt every muscle clench, then powerfully unwind. His head crashed forward onto her breast. He bared his teeth, a curse slipping out—

And saw stars.

Ione folded him in her arms. When they’d stopped panting,

they shared lazy kisses, pleasure-spent. And it was so heart-breakingly perfect, that moment with her, that Elm told her everything.

About his childhood, the death of his mother, the horrors of what happened after. About hating Hauth and his father. About wanting to die until the Yews took him in. He told her about becoming a Destrier. About Emory's infection and his slow degeneration. About Providence Cards, and how the King had planned to spill Emory's blood to unite the Deck.

About Elspeth. Her magic. The voice—the Shepherd King—she carried in her mind.

About the Twin Alders, and how Ravyn and Jespyr had gone to find it. And how Elm, the new heir, would do everything in his power to fight for them when they returned.

All while he talked, Ione stayed silent, her grip on him tightening. When he finished, she put a hand over his heart. "So that's what you've been doing with all your time."

"I'd be a liar if I said I wasn't damn tired from it all."

"Thinking you could collect the entire Deck under the King's nose, including a Card that has been lost five hundred years, is the most arrogant—most *Elm*—thing I've ever heard."

He chuckled, curling a strand of her hair around his finger. "I wasn't the only mastermind."

"What about my mother and brothers? The Spindle girls? I thought you'd know where they'd gone. But when I asked, with the Chalice—"

"It was important I didn't know. That way, not even a Chalice could make me share their whereabouts."

Her eyes widened. "*You* got them out?"

The Scythe was never far. Elm found it in his cloak pocket and moved it between his fingers, flipping it until the edges blurred. "Jespyr warned your mother and brothers, and I compelled the Spindles to flee. I tried to get you out, too. I had no idea you were at Hawthorn House. No idea what Hauth had done."

Twin tears fell from Ione's eyes. "Why?"

Elm sat up, took her face in his hands. "Because I don't believe in it, Ione. Any of it. Five hundred years of Rowan law—it doesn't mean a thing to me. Better we all dropped our charms and let the Spirit consume us than live in a place that punished people for magic not of their own doing. I'd rather Stone burned before I saw a woman and her children killed for hiding an infected niece." He brushed her tears away. "Your family will be safe someday. I'm going to change things. I'm going to be the worst Rowan King in five hundred years." The tips of his lips curled. "I might even enjoy it."

Ione's tears stopped. She was looking at him the same way she had when she'd called him beautiful. She pushed into him, arms wrapping around his neck. "Then let me enjoy it with you," she murmured into his mouth.

The Scythe fluttered to the ground, utterly forgotten.

They decided to announce the marriage contract that night—to put a stake in the heart of pageantry and end the feasts a day early.

It was well after midday when they returned to Stone. Somewhere deep within the castle, a bell was tolling. Ione looked up at the tall, looming towers. "What's that?"

Elm passed the groom the reins and took her hand. "I'm not sure."

Baldwyn wasn't there to ask. Neither was Filick. A string

pulled in Elm's chest. He thought maybe Ravyn had returned early.

Fingers laced with Ione's, Elm took the stairs to the royal corridor and stepped into his chamber. A shadow rose in the corner of the room. It wasn't Ravyn waiting for him.

It was Hauth.

PART III

To Bend

Chapter Thirty-Nine

Elspeth

The Spirit of the Wood's shore was much like the one I'd occupied in the Nightmare's mind. A listless, infinite space. Only this beach was pale. The sky, the rolling waves, the fine sand—all a wan, lifeless gray.

Ravyn sat in the sand, Jespyr in his arms. He could not reach her, not with his Nightmare Card, not with his voice. No matter how he shook her—called out her name—she would not wake.

I don't know how long we sat on that beach, waiting for the Spirit of the Wood. The Nightmare gnawed at a fingernail, watching the Yew siblings from the corner of his eye.

Ravyn's voice was ragged. "How long do we wait?"

"The Spirit keeps her own time."

Dozens of cuts from branches and thorns marred Ravyn's face. He looked so tired. When he pressed a calloused finger to his sister's neck, a pained sound came out of his mouth. "Her pulse is slowing. The fever is killing her."

Do something, I pleaded in my dark chamber. *Don't let him lose hope.*

"Your family is steeped in magic," the Nightmare replied, harsher than he should. "She will live."

Ravyn clamped his eyes shut and said nothing.

"You did not come all this way to yield to despair."

Ravyn didn't answer. But another voice did.

It came from the sea, deep and vast. It filled my dark room, echoing near and far. "The King of Blunder," it called, "come to barter once more."

When the water parted, a creature with claws and pointed ears and silver eyes slipped out of it. And I knew, deep within the inky blackness in my veins, who she was.

The Spirit of the Wood.

"Welcome back, Shepherd King. Welcome, Ravyn and Jespyr Yew." Her unearthly eyes met my window. She smiled. "Welcome, Elspeth Spindle."

Chapter Forty

Elm

A flash of red. "Don't move," came Hauth's voice. "Don't even speak."

Salt stung Elm's senses. His mind skittered to a halt, locking his muscles along with it. He was frozen, one hand in his pocket, the other laced with Ione's.

Hauth stood before them. Tall, menacing, and entirely flawless. The scars—bruises and claw marks—were gone, his skin unblemished. He wore a gold tunic and a deep crimson doublet, his chest wide as he squared off with Elm. A pair of daggers was fastened to his belt.

He looked younger. But that was only because the deeply embedded frown lines in his brow had been smoothed over. Hauth glanced down, his green eyes tracing Elm and Ione's clasped hands. "I shouldn't be surprised," he said, his tone idle. "You've always been a cocky little runt."

The last time Elm had seen his brother, Hauth had been lying in a puddle of his own drool. There was no poultice, no medicine—no magic—in the world that could have healed him so well.

Save one.

Hauth lowered himself to a seat atop Elm's chest of clothes. "I see you thinking, Renelm. Trying to work it all out in that weaselly little mind." His eyes flickered to Ione. "Did she tell you? About that night at Spindle House? About what I did to her?"

Rage coated Elm's throat. He tried to open his mouth, but his jaw was locked.

Hauth's eyes raked over Ione's body. "How different you look, my dear, from the bloody shell of a woman lying beneath my window at Spindle House. When I opened my eyes two nights ago and saw you, so perfectly whole, I knew. Even when I understood nothing else, I knew." The words slid between his teeth. "The Maiden Card healed you, Ione."

Ione's hand was cold in Elm's, slick with sweat.

"When Father tapped the Nightmare Card and entered my mind, I tried to tell him. But the fool was too drunk, too unfocused. He didn't hear me." A touch of satisfaction crossed Hauth's face. "But a night later, Linden did."

The door opened behind him. And then Linden was there. Only now, his face was clear, his skin unblemished—his scars gone.

"Take his Scythe," Hauth said, nodding at Elm.

Brutish hands pushed into Elm's pockets. Linden looked up at him with a sneer. He ripped Elm's Scythe free. Then, for good measure, rammed a fist into his stomach.

Breath rushed out of him and nausea rolled. But he couldn't even double over. The Scythe's leash, holding him in place, was too tight.

The old panic Elm had shoved behind walls was back. It clawed out of his chest, up his throat, into his mouth, begging him to scream. He was a boy again, tethered by his brother's Scythe.

Waiting for pain.

Hauth held out his hand, and Linden dropped Elm's Scythe into it. "When you returned the Nightmare Card last night, Linden used it. He found me. And pieced together what Father couldn't."

"'Maiden,'" Linden said, glowering at Elm, then Ione. "That's what I heard him say into my mind. Over and over. 'Maiden Card.' Then, 'Ione.'"

Linden stood in front of Elm. Looked him up and down with an unmasked leer. "Hauth told me some time ago where he'd made Miss Hawthorn place her Card. But when I went to the throne room, it was not under the hearthstone. I thought maybe she'd recovered it. I went to her room to search. Her door was locked." He reached for his belt. "But yours, Prince Renelm, was not."

There was a clang of iron. Linden pulled a ring of keys—Elm's ring of keys—free and dangled it in front of him. "You should really take your duties more seriously, Prince. It took me less than five minutes to unlock her door and find her Maiden. I tapped it three times, and then—" He ran a hand over his face, where the skin had once been cleaved. "My scars vanished. I was healed."

Elm had to do something. Or else he and Ione might never escape this room. But he couldn't. Fucking. Move.

A smirk graced the corners of Hauth's mouth. "Not so tough without Ravyn, are you, brother?" He stepped forward, took Elm by the throat. "Where are they—Ravyn and Jespyr? Tell me."

Another wave of salt hit Elm's senses. His jaw ached. When he opened it, venom pooled, his brother's Scythe dragging the truth out of his mouth. "Gone for the Twin Alders."

"Where?"

"I don't know."

Hauth ripped the ring of keys out of Linden's hand and hit Elm across the face with it. "When will they be back?"

"I don't know."

Another blow.

Ione made a noise in her throat.

"What's the matter, Renelm?" Another blow. "Nothing clever to say?"

Elm's mouth filled with blood. He spat, painting Hauth's boots red. "You may be healed, but your time is marked, *brother.* I know who it is you woke when you bashed Elspeth Spindle's head into the wall." He looked deep in Hauth's Rowan-green eyes. "And not even a Maiden Card can save you when he returns."

Fear flickered over that perfect brutish face. Hauth's fingers tightened around the ring of keys. Elm sucked in a breath, waiting for another blow.

It didn't come.

Hauth reached into his pocket. "Linden," he said, keeping his gaze locked with Elm's. "Give Ione her Maiden Card back."

Linden's brow knit. But he did as he was told. When he touched the Maiden, releasing Hauth from its magic, the cruel, familiar lines of Elm's brother's face returned.

Linden slipped the pink Card into Ione's hand.

"Tap it," Hauth bade her.

The Scythe wouldn't let him turn—Elm could only see Ione in his periphery. He heard the soft sound of her finger against the Maiden Card. *Tap, tap, tap.*

"Better." Hauth stepped away from Elm, moving with menacing slowness until he stood opposite of Ione.

He pulled a dagger from his belt.

Elm's insides seized. "What are you doing?"

"Conducting an experiment."

He didn't even afford Ione the ability to speak. Hauth merely dipped his head toward her, a mocking bow, and said, "Let's try this once more, betrothed." He raised his dagger.

And plunged it to the hilt into Ione's chest.

Air washed out of her, a long, ragged breath. Ione's hand went slack in Elm's, then she was falling out of his line of sight, out of his grasp.

The world darkened at the edges. The scream welling in Elm ripped free. Linden hit him across the face, but he didn't stop shouting. Lights burst behind his eyes, every last muscle spent fighting the red Card's grasp.

In the end, it was Hauth's brutal hand that turned Elm's head. "Let us see how well the pink Card fares against a fatal blow."

There was so much blood. Red like the rowan berry, like the Scythe. Red in Ione's dress and skin and hair, red all over his bedroom floor.

She'd survived the fall from Spindle House. The Maiden had kept her alive then. She could survive this. *Had to* survive this.

But the blood—it was heart's blood. Dark. Complete. The kind Elm saw on the hunt, when he made sure the stag had a quick, clean death.

The light in those hazel eyes was fading. Ione's mouth parted, tears slipping over her cheeks, fear etched over her face. And Elm understood. This was what it was like when Hauth sent her falling the last time. When she was certain she would die. Only this time, Ione wasn't looking up at the indifferent moon, waiting for the great stillness to claim her.

She was looking up at him.

Her hands were the color of snow, bloodless. They lifted to the dagger in her chest, ghosting over the hilt. Her lips, a sickly gray, moved, but no words came out.

"Let her speak," Elm shouted—pleaded.

Hauth's laugh cut through the room. "I don't think I will."

Ione's gaze stayed on Elm, holding him in those hazel wells. She pulled the dagger out of her chest and dropped it on the floor. Closed her eyes.

And stopped moving.

Twenty seconds.

Forty.

One minute.

Hauth made an indifferent noise in his throat and looked down at the Maiden in Ione's hand. "Seems there are limits to the pink Card after all."

Two minutes, and Ione still did not stir. Elm was shouting so loud his brother flinched. Hauth shoved him to the floor—kicked him—then flinched again.

A bead of blood slid from Hauth's nostril. He pulled his Scythe from his pocket and tapped it. "Stay down," he told Elm. "Or you'll regret it."

When salt finally fled Elm's senses, he didn't hear what Hauth and Linden were saying to one another. He didn't care. He was dragging himself through blood, all of his might spent keeping the last thread of hope he carried within himself from snapping.

He cradled Ione's head in his hands. She was so pale, not a trace of pink anywhere. "Hawthorn?"

Nothing.

He pressed his forehead over hers. "Please, Ione."

When she remained unmoving, Elm shut his eyes—slammed his teeth together. But no effort could restrain the tears burning down his cheeks.

Then, like a rush of wings—

"Elm."

His head shot up.

Ione was moving. Just a finger. Then a hand, which came to rest over the wound on her chest. Then that chest rose with a deep, desperate breath. Her eyelids fluttered, then opened, and Elm looked into her eyes.

Hazel—heat and life.

He wrapped his arms around her and pulled her into his chest. When a sob finally cleaved itself from him, he wondered bitterly if it had been her who'd nearly died, or him.

Like poisonous clouds, Hauth and Linden loomed from above.

"Incredible," Linden mused. "A blade through the heart and still the Maiden lets her live."

Hauth's voice was slow. Awestruck. Ravenous. "Invincibility."

Darkness pooled in Elm. It didn't matter that he was weaponless, naked without his Scythe. He still looked up into his brother's face and said, without an ounce of doubt, "*I'll kill you for this.*"

The door banged open.

Filick Willow stood at the threshold, with his books and his dogs, eyes wide as he took in the room. Hauth and Linden, standing over Elm and Ione. Blood on the floor. His gaze found Elm's face, tracing the budding bruises, the tears in his eyes. "Forgive me, Prince," he said. "I should have knocked louder."

Elm could have kissed the ground. He nodded at Ione in his arms. "Take her," he said, his voice breaking. "Help her."

When Filick stepped into the room, Hauth straightened his spine. "You aren't needed, Physician."

The dogs growled. Filick stayed them with a firm hand. "Prince Hauth. You—you were missing from your chamber. We rang the bell."

"I heard it." Hauth shifted his Scythe Card between blunt fingers. "But, as you see, no one stole me from my bed. I am quite well. You may go."

Filick didn't move. His eyes were on Ione. "She's lost a lot of blood."

"I'm aware."

Footsteps lumbered down the hall. Someone heavy was running, and then the King was there, pushing past Filick, tramping through Ione's blood on his way to Hauth. When he wrapped his arms around his eldest son, his voice came out fractured. "My boy. You're alive."

Elm looked down at Ione's chest. She was still covering her wound. "Let me see," he whispered.

She was reticent, her hand pressed so hard over her chest her fingernails had left crescent indents. Slowly, she took it away.

The wound was shrinking, half the size of the blade that had made it. The Maiden—still clutched in Ione's other hand—was healing her.

Elm raised his eyes to the ceiling and, with every part of himself, thanked the Shepherd King for his horrible, wonderful Maiden Card.

Ione's hand grazed his sleeve. "I thought I'd slipped through the veil. I was riding in the wood, mud on my ankles." A small smile graced her colorless lips. "With you."

Elm buried his face in her neck. "Someday. But first, I want a hundred years with you."

Above them, the King's voice came in waves. "How?" he

asked, his voice hitching as he put a calloused hand to Hauth's cheek.

Hauth's own voice was even. He patted his father's shoulder. "I hear you've been hosting feasts. Host tonight's in my honor, and I'll tell you all about it."

Chapter Forty-One
Ravyn

The last barter waits in a place with no time. A place of great sorrow and bloodshed and crime. No sword there can save you, no mask hide your face. You'll return with the Twin Alders...

But you'll never leave that place.

Ravyn heard the crack of bones. The Spirit of the Wood rolled her jagged shoulders, whipped her tail through the air, dug her claws into sand. Her ears were long and pointed, and when she smiled, short, jagged fang-like teeth peeked out from behind her lips.

She was not human or beast, but something in between, like the monster depicted on the Nightmare Card—only her eyes were silver. She marked Ravyn with them, unblinking. Then she aimed the tips of her claws at her own torso—

And buried them in her stomach.

Silver blood poured down her fur and fell into sand. The sea lapped it up, ravenous.

Ravyn stared, wide-eyed in horror.

The Spirit heaved a sigh and the bleeding stopped. She dug into her own stomach, as if all that blood had dislodged something deep within her. When her hand came back, coated in silver, something was wrapped in her claws. Small, rectangular, with an emerald-green trim.

The twelfth Providence Card. The Twin Alders.

The Spirit's talons unfurled.

"She wants you to use it," the Nightmare said behind Ravyn.

Ravyn set Jespyr, who had not stirred, into the sand and dragged himself to his feet. "What will happen when I tap it?"

"A meeting of minds."

"Like the Nightmare Card?"

"I cannot say. I have never used the Twin Alders."

"And if I use it too long?"

The Nightmare's voice quieted. "You will lose all sense of time."

Ravyn met the Spirit's eyes. Silver, unblinking, and without pupils. He shivered, reaching forward, grasping the velvet edge of the Twin Alders Card. But when he tried to pull it out of her clutch, the Spirit's claws closed in a vise over his hand.

Ravyn cried out. When he met that eerie silver gaze again, he understood. She hadn't been offering it for him to take—only to use.

There was still a final barter to make.

Ravyn relaxed his grip on the velvet edge. "I won't steal it."

Her claws retracted, Ravyn's skin scored red. When he reached into her hand a second time, it was with only a single, trembling finger. It hovered over the Providence Card five hundred years lost. He closed his eyes, took in a breath of salt, and tapped the Twin Alders.

Once.

Twice.

"Measure your words carefully with her," the Nightmare warned. "They may be your last."

Thrice.

Wind ripped over the sea's salted lip. It blew into Ravyn's face, blinding him. The Spirit spoke once more in her vast, stormy voice. "I watched you in the mist, Ravyn Yew. Tasted your blood. Stripped away your stony armor." Her gaze shifted between him and the Nightmare. "You have traveled to the heart of my wood at the edge of the Shepherd King's crook, like a lamb to slaughter."

Ravyn's jaw set. "I'm not a lamb."

Her silver eyes traced him—knew him. "Yet you are determined to die like one, come Solstice."

Behind them, the Nightmare let out a sharp hiss. "What does she mean?"

When Ravyn looked back into the Nightmare's yellow eyes, he knew, somehow, he was looking into Elspeth's as well. "You must know," he said, "that I was never going to allow the King to spill her blood to unite the Deck."

The Nightmare was still a long while. Then, so quiet it might have been waves upon the shore, he said, "You would bleed in Elspeth's place? In *my* place?"

Ravyn straightened his shoulders and spoke with enough conviction to reach every one of the Nightmare's five hundred years. "Yes."

He turned to the Spirit of the Wood. "Blood is the price to unite the Deck. To lift the mist and heal the infection. *Your* price. And I will gladly pay it. Gladly die. I've been dying piece by piece since Emory grew sick." His throat constricted. "I have died tenfold since Elspeth disappeared. And now your mist has claimed my sister. So do not speak to me of cost, Spirit." His eyes fell to the Twin Alders in her claw. "I am leaving here with that Card. Or I am not leaving at all."

Her lips peeled over jagged teeth. She breathed in, and the sound of water upon the shore disappeared, as if sucked into her mouth.

All was silent.

The Spirit held Ravyn in her unblinking silver gaze, then lunged forward, her claw catching his hand. With incredible strength, she pulled him off the shore into the frigid sea. Ravyn was afforded only a brief glance back at the Nightmare and Jespyr before the Spirit plunged him beneath water, the salty tide slipping over his head.

When Ravyn opened his eyes, he wasn't underwater—he wasn't even wet. He was standing in a field of snow. Jespyr and the Nightmare were gone. It was just him, alone, with the Spirit of the Wood.

Birds called overhead. Not the caw of ravens or crows, but songbirds. The sweet tune of larks. Wings fluttered above a meadow coated in snow. When Ravyn looked up, his breath caught.

It was clearly winter. But he'd never seen the sky so blue, the light so strong—entirely unencumbered by mist. It stole the breath from him, the beauty of it.

"Where are we?"

"Eight hundred years in the past," came the Spirit's dissonant reply.

"Why?"

She let go of his hand and stalked through the snow. "Magic has little use for time. I walk through centuries like they were my own garden." Her eyes fixed on Ravyn over her shoulder. "Human life is short. You are not as a tree, stoic and unyielding, but a butterfly. Delicate, fleeting. Inconsequential."

Ravyn shook his head. Lamb, butterfly. The Shepherd King had described the Spirit of the Wood in *The Old Book of Alders* as neither kin, foe, nor friend. He might have saved ink and called her what she truly was. A proper asshole.

Her tail flicked, as if she knew his thoughts. She opened her claws. Beside the Twin Alders, eleven other Providence Cards appeared in her palm. They floated in front of Ravyn, suspended in air, turning with the slow flourishes of the Spirit's finger. "The Cards. The mist. The blood," she said. "They are all woven together, their balance delicate, like a silken web."

"Which makes you the spider."

She smiled at that. "The Shepherd King was clever, imaginative. No ordinary soul could have made such a varying, intricate Deck. He knew neither virtue, nor love, greater than his want for these Cards." She snapped her fingers, and the Cards came rushing back into her claws. "Are you the same, Ravyn Yew?"

Measure your words carefully with her. They may be your last.

Ravyn took a deep breath. "I'm a thief. A liar. Most would find my virtue lacking."

"And your love?"

Ravyn's chest tightened. If he were to close his eyes, he knew what he would see. His parents' faces, bent as they read books in silence by the library fire. Elm and Jespyr and Emory, riding on horseback down the forest road. Elspeth, sitting across from him at Castle Yew's table, pink in her cheeks as she smiled at him from behind a teacup. "I have something of love in me."

With another snap of the Spirit's fingers, the Deck was gone, leaving only the Twin Alders in her claws. "Then I will make you an offer. Leave this Card with me, and I will save the people you love. Your siblings shall be free of the infection. Elspeth Spindle will be released from the Shepherd King, body and mind." She drew a claw through snow. "And the Rowan Prince shall be saved from his almost certain, ruinous fate."

Birds were still chirping—the sun still on Ravyn's face. But he was cold all over, the only sound to reach him the thrum of his unsteady pulse. "What fate should Elm need saving from?"

The Spirit did nothing but watch him through unblinking silver eyes.

"I should know what I'm agreeing to."

Silence was her only reply.

The ever-present tremor in Ravyn's hands quickened. When he spoke, his words clung to the back of his neck. "Then I have no choice but to save them myself come Solstice. *With* the Twin Alders Card."

Dark fur and wide, unyielding eyes made it difficult to discern emotion upon the Spirit of the Wood's face. But by the momentary twitch of her ears—the flick of her tail—Ravyn was certain she was displeased with his answer.

"You spoke of me, once," she murmured. "You were walking through the Black Forest on your way to steal Wayland Pine's Iron Gate Card. You led the party, but your gaze was cast back. To Elspeth Spindle."

Ravyn pressed his lips together. "I remember."

"You said to her, 'Magic sways, like salt water on a tide. I believe the Spirit is the moon, commanding the tide. She pulls us in, but also sets us free. She is neither good nor evil. She is magic—balance. Eternal.' "

The wind in the meadow picked up. The Spirit's voice grew louder. "I would have all of Blunder believe the same. And so, Ravyn Yew, my second offer to you is the throne."

When Ravyn did not speak, a snarl touched the edge of her voice. "You have the makings of a great King. Measured, careful. Wary of balance. You need not go back to Stone and bow before your uncle—no more lying or stealing or pretending. Find your own virtue, keep your own rules." She nodded at the

Card in her claws. "Leave the Twin Alders Card with me, and I shall make you Blunder's King in Quercus Rowan's stead."

"You do not have the power to do that."

She was paces away, then suddenly—too close. Her silver eyes filled Ravyn's vision, her claws pressing into his chest.

"You stand here, hundreds of years in the past, and speak to me of power?" The smell of salt was everywhere. "The Shepherd King was born with the fever because *I* deemed it so. His children were gifted magic by *me.* Brutus Rowan took the throne because *I* did not intervene. Kings and monsters can be made, and butterflies can be crushed. All that you know, I have created. I am Blunder—her infection, her trees, her mist. I am *brimming* with magic."

"And yet you barter with a liar and thief, just to remain so." Ravyn leaned forward, letting the tips of her claws press harder against his chest. "You are eternal. And you are magic. But I know as well as you that magic is the oldest paradox. The more power it gives you, the weaker you become. The Shepherd King taught me that."

A low, scraping sound resonated in her throat. She pulled back. "You are determined, then, to overlook my generosity and take back the Twin Alders Card?"

"I have no ambition for the throne."

Her voice held an edge. "Perhaps you should."

Ravyn bit down. "Time is precious to me, Spirit. Name your price for the Twin Alders. I would like to go home."

Her silver eyes narrowed, her dark tongue dragging over the tips of her teeth. "Then answer me this." She drew in a rasping breath. "The dark bird has three heads. Highwayman, Destrier, and another. One of age, of birthright. Tell me, Ravyn Yew, after your long walk in my wood—do you finally know your name?"

A memory tugged at Ravyn. He'd heard those words before. Emory had whispered them back at Stone.

"That is my price," the Spirit continued, a smile snaking over her lips. "My barter—my cost. If you answer correctly, I shall grant you the final Providence Card. If you cannot, it remains with me." Her claw tightened around the Twin Alders. "Your name, Ravyn Yew. Tell me your name."

The riddle cantered forward in Ravyn's mind, leaving behind a sense of dread. He felt like he was sitting down to a game of chess with Elm. That, by simply being there, he had already been utterly outmaneuvered.

"You offered me two things," he said slowly. "I denied them both. For my restraint—and for the sake of balance—I ask for two clues."

"I'll tell you what I told the Shepherd King when he visited long ago." The wind picked up, and her voice grew louder. "The twelve call for each other when the shadows grow long—when the days are cut short and the Spirit is strong. They call for the Deck, and the Deck calls them back. Unite us, they say, and we'll cast out the black. At the King's namesake tree, with the black blood of salt. All twelve shall, together, bring sickness to halt. They'll lighten the mist from mountain to sea. New beginnings—new ends…"

"But nothing comes free," Ravyn finished.

"Upon Solstice," the Spirit said, her silver gaze unrelenting, "the Deck of Cards will unite under the King's namesake tree. That tree is not a rowan. *That* is your first clue."

Her words played in Ravyn's ears, unharmonious. He tapped his fingers along the ivory hilt on his belt. "And the second?"

"That, I will not tell you." Her smile was all teeth. "I will show you."

The world tilted. When it righted, they were still in the

meadow—snow all around them. Only now, they stood under the shadow of yew trees.

At the meadow's cusp was a stone chamber, fixed with one dark window.

Ravyn whirled, searching the tree line for Castle Yew's towers. They were not there. A different castle loomed ahead of him.

One he had only ever seen in ruins.

"How far in the past are we now?"

"Five hundred years. We shall be neither seen, nor heard." The Spirit of the Wood gestured a gnarled claw toward the castle. "Shall we go inside?"

The castle was bustling. Musicians tightened the strings of their instruments. Servants hurried down corridors and up stairs with silver trays stacked with food, children with dark hair weaving between them, snagging pieces of sweet bread and spiced fruits. Holly and mistletoe garnished every door. Red and green and yellow velvet cords were strung between the iron arms of chandeliers.

Solstice, Ravyn realized.

Five long tables parceled the great hall, their benches full of courtiers, laughing and drinking. There was no dais at the end of the hall, but there was a throne. Wooden, fashioned of thick, interlocked branches.

Upon it sat a man.

He was not caught up in the revelry around him. He spoke to no one, his face downturned over a book splayed open in his lap. *The Old Book of Alders.*

There were lines in his copper skin, his face angular—mouth drawn. He had a long, hooked nose. When he lifted his gaze, Ravyn caught a glimpse of his eyes.

Yellow.

"Is that—"

"The Shepherd King, in the flesh," the Spirit whispered.

A crown rested upon his head, tangling in his dark, wavy hair. A gilt circle of gnarled, twisting branches and greenery.

Ravyn had seen that crown before. It waited in the stone chamber at the edge of the meadow, five hundred years in the future.

He kept his eyes on the Shepherd King. It seemed like a dream, seeing the face behind the voice. The slippery whispers, the grating snarls and hisses. Those were the embellishments of a monster. But this—this was undoubtably a man.

There was something strangely familiar about his face. But before Ravyn could put his finger on what it was—

Smoke filled the air.

It came from every doorway, dark and oppressive. Courtiers bolted from their seats, cries filling the great hall as they trampled over one another to get out. Castle guards peeled themselves off walls, guiding frantic men and women and children out of the castle. *The Old Book of Alders* fell from the Shepherd King's lap. He stood—

But a gloved hand held him back.

A man came from behind the throne. His body was broad and his face sharp with angles, frown lines carved deep into his brow. In his other hand, he held two Providence Cards. The Black Horse, and the Scythe.

There was blood on his upper lip, dripping slowly from his left nostril. But Ravyn was focused only on his eyes. Green, like his uncle's. Like Hauth's and Elm's.

Brutus Rowan.

He put his Cards into his pocket, leaned over the throne, and spoke words Ravyn could not hear to his King. He reached for his belt, withdrew a dagger—

And drove it in the Shepherd King's ribs.

Men in black cloaks stepped into the smoke, their eyes unfocused, fixed on Brutus Rowan. "Find his daughter," he commanded them. "Don't let her heal him. Then bring me the other children."

The Shepherd King reared. The back of his head collided with Brutus's jaw, and loud, ugly shouts filled the room.

Ravyn coughed for the smoke—rubbed his eyes. When he opened them, the Shepherd King and Brutus Rowan were gone.

"Come," the Spirit of the Wood said, taking his hand in her claws. "It's almost finished."

She led him outside. It was night now. The sky was black, the crescent moon masked by smoke. Orange flames licked up the castle towers, the last of the screaming courtiers fleeing into the night.

Ravyn's entire body tensed as the Spirit of the Wood brought him through the meadow. He knew where they were going. He'd walked these steps a thousand times. The Shepherd King's chamber.

And his grave.

"I don't know if I can stomach this."

Her tail flicked through smoky air. "Would you like it to stop?"

Figures darted past them, hurrying through the snow. The Shepherd King—followed by four boys. Tilly was in his arms. Ravyn could tell by the way her neck and limbs flopped—her eyes open and unseeing—that she was dead.

They left a trail of blood in the snow as they ran toward the stone chamber.

Ravyn's hands shook. "They're all going to die, aren't they?"

The Spirit of the Wood's voice held no love, no hate—no pity. "Yes."

When the Shepherd King and his children reached the stone chamber, disappearing into its window, the Spirit urged Ravyn forward. "Go inside."

The chamber was dark. But the flames from the burning castle flickered in through the window, revealing a shape in the corner of the room. A man.

Brutus Rowan. Waiting.

He'd donned a cloak. Gold, with the rowan insignia embroidered upon it. With a swift, brutal blow, he knocked the Shepherd King's sword from his grasp—kicked it away.

"The trees can't help you now."

The Shepherd King set Tilly down and planted himself between Brutus and the children. "I didn't know the Spirit would take Ayris. I didn't mean for her to die."

"I don't believe you. You are a liar, my old friend. Magic has made a soulless wretch of you—twisted you beyond all recognition." He pointed his sword at the Shepherd King's chest. "You are no longer fit to rule."

"So you would take my throne? Kill my children?"

Brutus's jaw set. "It will pain me. Losing your friendship pained me. Losing Ayris *pained* me. But what was it you once said to me?" His grip tightened upon his hilt. "To command the Scythe is to command pain. What is commanding a kingdom to that?"

Men spilled into the chamber. Eleven of them—each gripping a Black Horse.

"Tell me where to find the Twin Alders Card," Brutus said, his voice louder now with the men at his back. "I will do what you could not and lift this vile mist."

The Shepherd King put his hand to where he'd been stabbed. When he pulled it back, it was covered in blood. He swayed, a laugh slithering out of his mouth. "No."

Like a hunter, Brutus stalked forward. When the Shepherd King did not acquiesce, Brutus took him by the throat—slammed him upon the stone.

And buried his sword in his chest.

The children cried out, but the Shepherd King made not a sound, save a long, low hiss. He fell from the stone to the earth beneath it, his crown slipping from his head. He held out a bloodied hand to his children.

"I will find you on the other side of the veil," he murmured. His gaze turned back to Brutus. Yellow, wicked—

Infinite.

"For even dead, I will not die. I am the shepherd of shadow. The phantom of the fright. The demon in the daydream. The nightmare in the night."

He lay upon soil at the foot of the stone. Bled his life's blood. Did not stir.

Brutus looked down upon him, teeth bared, tears dropping from his eyes. When he wiped them away, his gaze was cold. He tapped his Scythe three times. "Kill them," he said to the men at his back.

Ravyn lunged at him. Fell right through him.

"Wait," came the Spirit's stormy voice. "Watch."

When the screams filled the air, Brutus threw himself out of the chamber. The burning castle was set before him, an inferno of orange and black.

A boy stood in the meadow, framed by fire and smoke.

He looked like his father. Dark hair, tall, angular. A distinct, beak-like nose. The only difference was his eyes. They were not yellow—

They were gray.

"Traitor," came his snarling voice. He pulled a sword from his belt. "I'll kill you for what you've done."

"You won't," Brutus said, holding the red Card out between them. "You're going to walk toward me, Bennett. And, just like your father, you're going to feel my blade in your gut."

The boy paled. But he did not move.

Brutus's voice grew louder. "Come here."

Bennett tilted his head to the side. His eyes fell to the Scythe. "No."

Brutus began to shout. He came closer. They parried, and in three blows, the much larger man knocked the sword from the boy's hand. He lifted his blade for a final strike.

Bennett closed the distance between them and ripped the Scythe from Brutus's hand. Then, as if it were truly no more than paper and velvet, he took the indomitable red Card, smiled up at Brutus—

And tore the Scythe in half.

Brutus's eyes went wide. He took a faltering step back, then lifted his sword once more. But before the blade could find Bennett, the boy reached into his pocket. Extracted a Mirror Card—

Disappeared.

The world shifted.

Ravyn and the Spirit were on a dirty street in town. They watched Bennett, hood up, begging for food. Watched him on the forest road band together with a party of highwaymen to rob a caravan. Watched as Destriers hunted the streets, posters with crude portraits of Bennett's face decorating hitching posts throughout Blunder.

Bennett, now a man of middle age, wrapped his arms around a woman with wavy black hair and brown eyes. Stood with her under tall, twisting trees. Said marriage vows.

The vision ended where it began—in the meadow.

The yew trees surrounding the Shepherd King's stone chamber

were tall. They, along with the chamber they guarded, were the only things left unscathed by the fire. Bennett walked, now stooped with age, through the ruins. He climbed into the chamber—bled into the stone.

The chasm opened up, and he dropped his Nightmare and Mirror Cards into it. "Be wary, Father," he whispered. "Be clever. Be good."

Then he was gone.

Ravyn and the Spirit of the Wood were alone in the meadow once more, snow at their feet.

For the first time since the Shepherd King had taken command of Elspeth's body, Ravyn's hands did not shake. He stood perfectly still, five hundred years washing over him.

"That boy," he murmured. "Bennett. The Scythe. He destroyed it?"

"Four Scythe Cards were made," the Spirit replied. "Yet no one has seen the Rowans use more than three."

"But Providence Cards are ageless. Their magic does not fade. They do not decay with time. They *cannot* be destroyed. The Shepherd King declared it so."

"And he, like you, is certainly a liar." The wind whispered through branches. "Your time is up, Ravyn Yew," the Spirit said. "I will have your answer now. Tell me—what is your name?"

His throat tightened. His eyes rushed over the meadow, the tips of trees. Trees he and Jespyr and Emory had swung from as children.

Just like Tilly did, waiting for her father.

Breath bloomed out of Ravyn's mouth in the cool air. So often was he fixed on going forward—always forward—that he hadn't let himself look back. But the past had been shown to him. Written out for him. Laid bare at his feet.

The branches carved into the Shepherd King's crown—his

hilt. The blade, swinging through the air, rearranging the wood. A name, whispered against a yew's gnarled trunk.

An old name. For an old, twisted tree.

The Shepherd King's face. His son Bennett's gray eyes.

The Scythe had not worked on Bennett. Just as it did not work on Ravyn.

I'm nothing like you.

But you are. More than you know.

Ravyn met the Spirit of the Wood's silver gaze. When he finally said the words, he knew, with every piece of himself, that they were true. "Taxus. My name is Taxus."

Chapter Forty-Two

Elm

Of all the people in the great hall, the monster was the most pleasing to look at.

Hauth sat in his rightful chair in a gold doublet trimmed with white fox fur. He played with the horsehair charm on his wrist and didn't smile, but his laughter echoed as he accepted compliments from courtiers. He didn't mention the Maiden Card he'd taken back from Ione—didn't attribute his sudden recovery to anything but himself. But he was undeniably using it. His face was too perfect—his features too steady.

He held his goblet up for the fifth time, a false toast to Rowan stamina and health, and drank.

All the while, he kept Elm tight under his Scythe's leash.

Shoved into the corner of the dais, no one paid Elm any mind. Now that Hauth was back, he was of little interest to Blunder's court, the fresh bruises on his face just another reason for them not to look at him.

Hauth sat next to the red-eyed King, Ione in her customary chair on his other side. Linden hovered nearby, arms clasped behind his back, satisfaction in the newly unblemished lines of his face.

Elm's pulse pounded in his head. He could not hear what Hauth told the King in a low voice. But by the way the King's eyes widened, it was clear he was riveted. Tales of the pink Card's unforetold magic, perhaps.

Elm didn't look at them long. His eyes belonged to Ione. She was in one of those horrid gray dresses again. This time, it had been Hauth who'd compelled her to wear it. He hadn't given her time to fully wash away the blood from the wound he'd dealt her, and the gown's collar was the only one high enough to conceal the red stain upon her skin.

Ione sat rigid in her chair, her hazel eyes clouded by whatever command Hauth had bade her with his Scythe. To sit still and keep silent, most likely. No one asked after her, or why she was so pale—why some of the yellow hair knotted at the nape of her neck had blood in it. Like Elm, Ione received few looks at all.

When the line of well-wishers along the dais eased, Hauth took his goblet and stood. Baldwyn's voice boomed. "His Second Royalty, Hauth Rowan, High Prince, Heir to Blunder, Destrier, and Keeper of Laws."

The echo of scraping chairs filled the hall, and then the court was on its feet, eyes trained on their perfect Rowan Prince.

Hauth's smile did not touch his eyes. "As your High Prince and Destrier, my days are parceled by duty. I am proud to say I protect Blunder well from the infection. I uphold my father's laws, his commands." He put a hand on the back of Ione's chair. "I even agreed to marry, so that my father could add the elusive Nightmare Card to his collection. That he, one day, might be the Rowan King to finally collect the Deck and lift the mist."

Hauth drew a finger along the back of Ione's neck. It looked like a gesture of affection, but Elm saw it for what it was.

A threat.

"But I was injured," Hauth continued. "Gravely. I didn't know how full my life was until I'd nearly lost it." He turned to the King, who was watching his son with captivated focus. "And now that I am healed, there are things besides duty and honor I no longer wish to take for granted." He put a hand on his father's shoulder. "The bonds of family, for one."

An appreciative murmur sounded in the hall.

"It makes me glad," Hauth said, something darker hiding in the low notes of his voice, "to hear how well you accepted my brother in my absence." His eyes jutted to Elm. When blood hinted beneath his nostril, he wiped it away before anyone could see. "Come join us, Renelm. Refill our goblets. Drink with us."

Salt stung Elm anew. Linden came beside him, thrusting a cup and a flagon of wine into his hands. Elm tried to look at Ione, but the Scythe kept him rigid, compelling him forward, marching him onto the center of the dais.

Hauth pulled his own goblet close and looked down at the King's empty one. "Fill it."

Elm tipped the flagon, and wine flowed into his father's cup. Hauth's mouth quirked. "To family," he called, raising his goblet.

The great hall answered in kind. "To family."

Elm didn't drink, helpless to do anything but stand still and breathe. When the King drained his cup, the smile teasing Hauth's mouth widened. He turned his back to the hall, facing Elm and the King. "On the subject of family," he said in a low voice only they could hear, "I understand Ravyn and his party will return shortly. Along with the woman who attacked me." His eyes lowered to the King. "A woman who should be dead. Or rotting in a cell."

King Rowan straightened in his chair, a flush coloring his neck. "Elspeth Spindle has old knowledge. I need her to find the Twin Alders."

"Old knowledge indeed," Hauth murmured into the rim of his cup. "You're a brute and a drunk, Father. But I never took you for a fool."

The King's flush crawled into his face. His voice was a growl—a warning. "Hauth."

He kept going, quiet as he leaned forward. "All your life, you've fretted over the Twin Alders Card, lifting the mist, healing the infection. When in truth, it is the mist—the infection—that feeds the throne. People *fear* the mist. They fear the Physicians and Destriers who come to their doors to root out the infection. No one has challenged a Rowan in five hundred years because of *fear*. And now you've gone and given Ravyn Yew a way to undo all of that. What's more, your beloved, infected Captain is coming back with more than the Twin Alders Card." Hauth's mouth drew into a tight line. "He's coming back with the goddamn Shepherd King."

The King's cough was a loud, barking strangle.

"And it will be you, *brother*," Elm said through his teeth, "who will have to face them when they return."

"That's why you're here, Renelm. You and Ione Hawthorn. I never wanted either of you—but you'll make fine bargaining chips all the same." Hauth laughed to himself. "Let's hope the fire of your budding romance doesn't snuff out in the dungeon."

The King's tumbler crashed onto the dais. He made a choking noise, his thick, brutish fingers clawing at his own throat. His face had gone red, mottled. Blood spiked over his eyes. He grasped for Hauth's sleeve, his words wet and garbled. "H-help—"

"What's wrong?" Elm regarded the flagon Linden had

shoved into his hands, then the King's empty goblet—drained of the wine *he'd* poured. His gaze shot to Hauth. "What have you done?"

Heads turned. A few courtiers stood from their seats, while others remained arrested in stillness, their attention fixed upon the dais.

Hauth inhaled deeply. "Ignore the King," he said beneath his breath.

King Rowan hacked. His eyes were bulging now, the spit on his purple lips turning to froth. No one moved to help him. Not his servants or Destriers—not Baldwyn or the lords and ladies of Blunder who'd hurried to Stone to partake in his feasts. Their opinion of him, of his Rowan legacy, had made him into the King that he was. And now that he was choking, dying before them—

They would not even look at him. All of them, compelled by Hauth's Scythe to deny him their notice.

Hauth watched his father struggle to breathe with cold indifference, his nostrils laden with blood.

Elm was shouting. "Don't do this!"

"It was not I," Hauth said, nodding at the flagon in Elm's hand, "who poisoned the King."

Elm looked down at his father, that unfeeling, ungiving man—and felt a terrible, wrenching pity. The King's mouth dripped blood, the great bear of a man passing through the veil.

But even with the death hounds stalking him, the bear had teeth. The King lunged forward, knocking Hauth to the ground. With blunt fingers, he tore at Hauth's gold tunic, ripping free his Scythe Card—throwing it to the floor.

Salt fled Elm's senses. He dropped the flagon.

Hauth flailed beneath the King's weight, shoving and

kicking him—trying to free himself. Quercus Rowan looked up one last time. His swollen hand fumbled along his own clothes now. He pulled something free from his doublet. Red as the rowan berry—as poisoned wine. The King's Scythe Card.

He thrust it at Elm. "Take it." His eyes rolled back and he dragged in a final, halting breath, then went still. His gilded crown of twisted rowan branches slipped from his brow.

The King of Blunder was dead.

Everyone moved at once. Screams filled the room, a surge of noise. Free of Hauth's Scythe, half the courtiers tripped over one another to get out of the great hall while the other half pressed forward for a better look. Destriers lunged from shadow, caught in the tumult as they hurried toward the dais.

Hauth shouted above the bedlam, struggling yet to get out from beneath his father's weight. "Arrest Prince Renelm—he's used his Scythe on us—he's poisoned the King!"

More screams. Fearful gazes turned on Elm.

Footsteps thundered behind him. Fingers shaking, Elm tapped his father's Scythe three times and shut his eyes. The statuary of ice was waiting in the darkness. He pushed it out on a salt tide, just as he had in the throne room. Ice. Stone. Stillness. Silence. "Be still," he said, homing in on everyone in the great hall—castle guards, courtiers, Destriers—everyone. *Be still.*

When he opened his eyes, the great hall was unmoving. Hundreds of people, frozen in place.

Needle-thin, a pain began in the corner of his mind.

He found Linden—ripped his stolen Scythe from the Destrier's pocket—and shoved him on the floor. Ione was still at the table, frozen, half out of her chair. Elm rushed to her, pressed his forehead into her shoulder, breathed her. "Come with me."

The bailey was empty. Even the stable boys, the guards in the tower, were frozen. Elm found his horse. "Can you ride without a saddle?"

Ione nodded. She reached up under his nose. When she pulled her hand back, his blood was on it.

They cantered into the night. And with every clack of hooves upon the road, the Scythe dragged a knife across Elm's mind. His vision blurred, his hands shaking on his horse's mane. "We're far enough," Ione said. "Let go of the Scythe, Elm."

"The Destriers will catch up. We need to get you farther." But a high-pitched whining sounded somewhere in his head, pain drilling into him until he couldn't see.

He sucked in a breath, slumped, and fell off the horse.

Gravel flew, flashing past Elm's face as he lay in the road. His horse whickered, and then Ione was there, kneeling next to him.

Elm reached for her neck, checking she still had her charm. "Don't take the main roads," he managed. "Find the others. Ravyn. Jespyr. The Shepherd King. If you cannot, keep to the mist—out of sight." He kept his hand caged around his father's Scythe. But the other—his own he'd reclaimed from Linden—he held out to her. "If anyone so much as looks at you wrong, use this."

Ione didn't move. "You're not coming with me?"

With every breath, pain, like glass, cut deeper into Elm's mind. "Hauth needs someone to barter with when Ravyn returns. And I cannot let it be you." His voice hardened. "I'm not going to run away from him this time."

He laced his fingers in Ione's, pushing his Scythe into her hand. "I wish we could have had those hundred years, Hawthorn. I wish you could have been Queen."

"I don't care about being Queen." She pulled him close—pressed quivering lips to his mouth. "You are not Hauth, and you are not the boy he tormented. It would be terribly unclever to die, just to prove it. Please, Elm. Come with me."

Her kiss tasted like tears. Elm was lost to it. He pulled back. "Get on the horse and ride away, Ione."

When her hazel eyes went blurry under his Scythe's command, it took all of Elm not to look away. Ione got on his horse, spurred it, her hair catching moonlight, a dreamy yellow ribbon in the wind. She cried out, calling his name, ripping the last whole piece of his rotted-out heart to tatters.

Go, he commanded. *Don't look back.*

She fought it. Damn her, she fought to look back. Tears burned Elm's eyes. "See you in the woods," he murmured. "Mud on my ankles."

Blood slid from his nostrils, dripping into his mouth. He sat down on the road and bore the pain like he always had. Twenty minutes later, he finally tapped his father's Scythe.

When the Destriers found him, Elm was looking up at the moon, bright and indifferent, worrying its way across the sky.

Chapter Forty-Three

Elspeth

The Nightmare stood in silence upon the shore. Ravyn had not returned. And Jespyr—the darkness nestled in her veins had stemmed. But her eyes remained closed, and her breathing was slow. Labored.

The Nightmare peered down at her. Then, hunching over himself, he slowly curled into the sand and pulled Jespyr into his arms like she were a child. He looked into her face, his whisper no louder than the waves upon the shore. "When I look at her, I do not know if she reminds me more of Ayris or Tilly."

Like the gilded crown he'd once worn atop his head, time was a circle. Ravyn, Jespyr—Taxus, Ayris. Five hundred years was nothing, there on that pale, listless shore.

I already knew the answer. Still, I asked. *Did your sister die in the alderwood?*

Yes. His voice was low, soaked in regret. *I tried to carry her body home. I made it halfway, but I was so tired. I wanted to preserve my strength—to remember everything the Spirit and trees had told me about how to unite the Deck and make a charm. I—*

He said nothing for a long time. *I set Ayris down in a quiet glen. Walked away.*

What did Brutus Rowan do when you returned and his wife was gone?

Broke my nose. Waited three months.

Then killed you and your children.

Yes.

I didn't know what to say to him, now that all of his secrets had finally bled into me. He had always been the keeper of great magic—of knowledge—and I his destitute ward, greedy for any crumbs he might share with me.

But the tide always turns, and the truth always outs. He'd said as much himself, once. I had no way to hold him. But I pressed my consciousness against the wall of our shared mind. Whispered to him. *No more riddles, my friend. What is it you truly want?*

To keep on rewriting things, he said. *Eleven years I took from you, Elspeth Spindle. When I go, I aim to leave you a better Blunder than the one I forged as King.*

I turned my name over in my mouth. *Elspeth Spindle. I'm not sure who that is without you.*

You will learn. You'll meet yourself—without me—soon enough.

I didn't know why, after so many years of wishing him gone, his words struck sadness in me. *When?*

After the Deck is united, come Solstice.

It will not unite with Ravyn's blood, I said. *He will not die, bleeding over your Cards. I will not allow that, Nightmare.*

Nor will I.

Then whose blood will unite the Deck?

I have a plan.

I probed into the darkness of his mind—and found nothing. Just images, and all of them blurry. Ravyn's face. Elm's as well. Then, clearer than them both, Brutus Rowan's.

Well? I demanded. *Care to enlighten me?*

His teeth clicked together in a familiar lullaby rhythm. *I find it strangely comforting, even with our minds threaded together, that I must endlessly explain things to you, Elspeth.*

Perhaps if you didn't speak in half-truths and intimations, I might not PESTER you so.

You would pester me no matter what I said or thought.

I sighed. *I dislike you greatly.*

But do you trust me?

Do I have a choice?

He said the same thing he'd said to me in my chamber at Spindle House—just before he took over my mind. *My darling, you've always had a choice.*

Silence crept over the beach.

The Nightmare noticed it and put a protective hand over Jespyr. The wind strengthened, and the tide withdrew.

When a tall, cresting wave heaved, Ravyn was in it. He broke the water's surface and pushed to the shore, his chest rising and falling with swelling breaths.

The sea was heavy upon him, his clothes waterlogged. When he pushed wet hair off of his brow and stepped onto the beach, his gray eyes were bright. He seemed taller than before he'd left. Less tired. Wherever he had gone, whatever he had seen, it had fortified him.

The Nightmare met him at the water's edge. "Well?"

Ravyn towered over him, shoulders broad. "Is Jespyr—"

"Alive. The Twin Alders Card?"

Ravyn held out his hand. A brilliant green light appeared, emanating between his calloused fingers.

I let out a gasp. *He's done it.*

The Nightmare's voice went low. "Your barter?"

"All it cost me was my name."

"Your name?"

"You know it already." Ravyn looked deep into the Nightmare's eyes. "It's yours, after all."

The dark chamber I occupied went utterly soundless.

Ravyn cleared his throat, his voice quieter, as if he was taking pains to soften it. "You might have told me the Mirror and Nightmare Cards I keep in my pocket belonged to your son, *Taxus*."

It seemed there were some secrets that had not bled out of him after all. *Nightmare*, I said, a vicious whisper. *What does he mean?*

His voice thinned, like smoke up a flue. Gaze narrow, he peered up at Ravyn. "Seems you're less stupid than I thought."

"And you're just as horrible as ever."

The Nightmare let out a humming laugh. "Yes, well, it took me longer than it should have to recognize you. I imagine it was Bennett who revised our family name. But magic, and degeneration, runs in bloodlines. Your inability to use the Cards—*that*, I did recognize." Warmth stole over his mind. "Along with your nose."

The past and present marked themselves over my eyes. There had always been something so terribly familiar about Bennett, lost in the inky darkness of the Shepherd King's memories. Bennett—who'd peered at me through gray eyes, not yellow. Bennett, who'd stood in his father's library, birdlike the way he tilted his head, the same Cards Ravyn held in his pocket twirling between his fingers. I saw it now—the truth grasping me around the throat.

Bennett. He looked like Emory—like Ravyn.

Blunder families have always taken the names of the trees, I whispered. *But I have never heard of a tree called Taxus.*

That's because it is an old name, came his oily reply. *For an old, twisted tree.*

Like the last line of a poem, the truth fell into place. *A yew tree.*

Ravyn searched the Nightmare's eyes. "Does Elspeth know?"

"Only just."

"Why didn't you tell us?"

"Would you have believed me, monster and liar that I am?"

Ravyn's pause was answer enough. "The Spirit showed me your death." He heaved a sigh. "I can guess what it is you want from me, Taxus. But I am not the dark bird of your revenge. I will not be another Captain who steals the throne. I will unite the Deck—but I will never be King of Blunder."

I watched Ravyn, weighing words that he—a man who uttered so few—had offered.

"Our walk in the wood," the Nightmare replied, "was about more than the Twin Alders Card, Ravyn Yew. There was five hundred years of truth to unravel. And now that you and Elspeth know it—" His sharp laugh echoed over the water. "You still do not understand. My revenge is not merely a sword. It is a scale. It is *balance.* I will take the throne of Blunder back. But not for you." He straightened his spine, fixing Ravyn in his unflinching gaze. "For Elm."

Ravyn's eyes tightened at his cousin's name, emotion settling over them like glass.

"The Scythe I created has been used for unspeakable crimes. Infected children have been hunted—killed. Physicians have turned to murderers. *The Old Book of Alders* has been defiled by Rowans to justify their every whim. *Pain* is Blunder's legacy. It has perforated the kingdom for centuries, and would continue to do so if your family—my rightful heirs—were to forcibly take it back. There would be terrible unrest. You and I are Blunder's reckoning, Ravyn Yew. Not its peace."

His voice softened, as if he were easing a child to rest with a story. "I had five hundred years to imagine my revenge. Hauth Rowan tasted it, that night at Spindle House. But poetry is as judicious as violence. And wouldn't it be poetic to undo the Rowans from within? To take that legacy of pain, and watch one of their own grind it under his heel? To carve the way for a Prince who never used the Scythe for violence? Your cousin Elm has done more than Brutus Rowan or I ever could. He has looked pain in the eye—and refused to let it make a monster of him."

The air thinned. Before Ravyn or I could speak, thunder rolled.

The sky went an inky black, and the Spirit of the Wood returned. She walked upon the water to the shore, her lips peeled back in a sneer. "You are clever, Shepherd King." Her silver gaze turned on Ravyn. "As are you. But if you wish to rewrite history and unite the Deck—to strip Blunder of my fever, my *mist*—you must be quick about it." When her eyes dropped to the Twin Alders Card in Ravyn's hand, her sneer curled into a smile. "You've been using that Providence Card for a long time."

The corners of my dark room seized. Ravyn's face drained of color. He fumbled—tapped the Twin Alders.

The world tugged at the seams, the pale shore quaking, then leaching away to darkness. The Nightmare lunged for Jespyr, caught her in his arms.

Then he was falling.

His head hit something hard. When the world came back into focus, I looked up through the Nightmare's gaze, the branches of two trees tangling above him. One pale, the other dark.

We were back in the alderwood. Only now—

There was snow on the ground.

Chapter Forty-Four
Ravyn

The knobs of Ravyn's spine collided with tree roots. He wheezed and spat out a curse, his vision blurring. When it focused, the twin alders loomed above him. He turned on bruised ribs, scanning the hilltop for Jespyr.

She lay several feet away, caged in the Nightmare's arms.

"Are you all right?"

The Nightmare didn't reply. He was dragging the tip of his boot over the ground—over a fresh layer of white, powdery snow. Only then did Ravyn note how cold it was. Far colder than it had been when they'd entered the alderwood.

The Nightmare set Jespyr on the ground—drew his sword. He slid his palm over the edge of the blade. When the cut bled, he swiped it over both alder trees. "What day is it?"

The day of the long night, came their horrid, dissonant reply.

The Nightmare's yellow gaze crashed into Ravyn. "How long were you using the Twin Alders Card?"

"I don't know." Ravyn looked up at the sky, snowflakes brushing his face. It was night. But the hour, he could not tell. He rose to his feet, panic thinning his voice. "It's not—it *can't* be Solstice."

More than it has ever been, said the pale alder.

Less with every passing moment, said the other.

Ravyn felt sick. "How long were we on that shore?"

Twenty-four turns of the sun. Hurry back to your chamber, Taxus, said the dark alder. *You have until midnight to unite the Deck.*

The Nightmare gnashed his teeth. On a crashing rumble, he reached for Jespyr—flung her over his shoulder—and fled the hill.

Ravyn tore after them.

His descent was reckless. Twice he tripped on the rocky hillside and caught himself with bruising effort. When he got to the bottom and the valley that waited, the mist bloomed with bones and corpses.

Forward, always forward.

Out of the rotting valley, into the ravenous wood. Trees swung at them and thorns hungered for a bite, the song of the wood a discordant call of wind, screeching through branches. Animals stalked and lunged. They clambered over roots—swung their swords at beasts of prey. The Nightmare kept Jespyr in his arms and Ravyn shielded them, taking the brunt of the branches that managed to land their blows.

Ravyn had not eaten for what felt like an age, but he was not hungry. He'd been afforded centuries—walked with the Spirit of the Wood through time. And now that he was back, he knew only one urge.

To outrun the clock.

The wood hunted them through the night. Then, like a candle in the darkest room, a pale light shone ahead. The Nightmare saw it, too, and his pace quickened. The light came from a small gap in the trees. It beckoned Ravyn just as strongly as the mist had beckoned Jespyr into the alderwood.

Dawn.

Nothing is free, the trees called after them. *Nothing is safe. Magic is love, but also it's hate. It comes at a cost. You're found and you're lost. Magic is love, but also—*

"For mercy's sake." The Nightmare spat phlegm onto roots. "Shut the fuck up."

They shot out of the alderwood into pale gray light. When Ravyn looked back, the gap in the trees had closed. He took in a full breath, the air bereft of rot. It washed down his lungs, so pure it made him cough. They stood in the aspen grove they'd slept in last night. Only, it hadn't been last night. It had been nearly a *month* ago.

Then Ravyn remembered Petyr.

His gaze darted left, then right. He called his friend's name. "Petyr. Petyr!"

"He wouldn't have waited this long." The Nightmare panted, his arms still wrapped firmly around Jespyr. "A clever man—which is giving him a deal too much credit—would have returned to Castle Yew." He hurried west. "As must we. And fast."

Ravyn's stomach plummeted into his boots. "The Cards," he gasped. "Even if we get to Castle Yew before midnight, we can't unite the Deck. I—I don't have all the Cards."

The Nightmare stopped so abruptly Jespyr fell from his shoulder. He caught her before her head could hit soil. She groaned, eyelids flickering.

Ravyn staggered forward, put his hand on his sister's overwarm forehead. "Jes?"

Bleary brown eyes opened. Jespyr reached for Ravyn, her fingers grazing over his face, his swollen nose. "What happened?"

It hurt, the place her fingers trailed. A sharp, consuming pain touched Ravyn's face. He drew back. "I'll explain everything soon. But we've got to get home."

"Home," Jespyr said, eyelids dropping once more. She rested her head against the Nightmare's chest. "Tell the Shepherd King... he needs a bath."

She slipped unconscious, and the Nightmare pressed her over his shoulder once more. When he glanced back at Ravyn's face, his yellow eyes widened.

By instinct, Ravyn touched where the Nightmare was looking. His nose.

"What do you mean you don't have all the Cards?" the Nightmare demanded.

Ravyn kept running his hand over his face, looking for injury. He felt nothing—no swelling, no pain, just a lingering tingle where Jespyr's fingers had grazed his skin. "The Deck is divided between the Cards hidden in the stone in your chamber and those I have in my pocket. We have all but the Scythe, which is with—"

"The Princeling." Sounding of a serpent's hiss, the Nightmare's breath came fast. "Then we must find him. This is the only chance we have. Emory will not live to see another Solstice."

"I know that well enough." Ravyn reached for Jespyr. "Here, let me—"

"*No*," he snarled. "I will carry her."

Crows cawed overhead. Ravyn and the Nightmare continued west. They found a small stream and drank deeply, only for Ravyn to spit most of the water back up on a sprint through a glen.

The Nightmare held tight to Jespyr. Even when he spoke to the trees, asking for the way, he never set her down. Never let her go.

Dawn slipped into day, then dusk. The path wasn't easy. At times, there was no path at all, just rocks and thorns and dense underbrush.

Ravyn tripped, panting. "Need—to stop."

The Nightmare kept going, pulling in rasping breaths. "Elspeth says if you do not get up, she'll never kiss you again."

"That's—not—what she—said."

"Get up, Ravyn." The Nightmare's oily voice echoed through the wood. "*Get up.*"

Ravyn dragged himself off his knees and followed. He'd never pushed this hard, not in a decade of training. Not even when his opponents were fitted with Black Horses and he had only his strength to rely upon. He'd never needed so badly to keep—going—forward.

The underbrush was gone, and suddenly his boots were clogging with mud. Ravyn looked up.

The lake.

Night had fallen, darkness pressing down onto the water's eerily still surface. The last time they'd crossed, the lake had been a pale silver. Now, it bore the color of the blackest of inks.

Ravyn stood next to the Nightmare on the shore's muddy lip and put a hand into his pocket. His fingers brushed the velvet of five Providence Cards—Black Horse, Maiden, Mirror, Nightmare, Twin Alders. If he drowned, the Cards would be lost at the bottom of the lake.

"Will there be more monsters in the water?"

"No. That barter was already paid." The Nightmare tightened his grip on Jespyr. He waded up to his knees into the lake. "Hurry."

Water filled Ravyn's boots. But before either of them could dive—

Salt filled his nose, only to retreat a moment later. Ravyn knew that feeling. Someone had tried to use a Providence Card he was immune to against him.

His hand fell to his dagger. A moment later he heard it: the thunderous sound of a cantering horse.

It came from the path behind them, bearing two riders. The horse, white with gray speckles, Ravyn recognized at once. It was Elm's horse.

The first rider dismounted with a booming curse before the animal could reach a full stop. "Where the *bloody hell* have you lot been?"

Petyr ran full speed at Ravyn. "I've never been so happy to see your ugly face."

Wind soared from his lungs, his friend's arms a vise around his chest. "Likewise," Ravyn managed. He looked over Petyr's shoulder, eyes widening.

Ione Hawthorn wore a tattered gray dress and stood next to Elm's horse. Her chest heaved, eyes darting between Ravyn to Jespyr to the Nightmare—lingering upon the latter. "Elspeth?"

"She's with me." The Nightmare rolled his eyes. "And she is very loud in her enthusiasm to see you, yellow girl."

Petyr pulled back. "What the hell happened—is Jes all right?" He tripped over himself, getting to the Nightmare. He reached for Jespyr.

"*I'm* carrying her—"

"Shove off, you ancient windbag." In one impressive maneuver, Jespyr was in Petyr's arms. "You still with us, princess? Want to hold my lucky coin?"

She stirred in his arms. Grimaced. Her brown eyes opened a sliver. "You smell worse than he did."

Petyr barked a laugh. "I haven't wanted to go near strange bodies of water for some reason." He glanced up at Ravyn. "You've been gone an age." He nodded at Ione, lines drawing across his weathered face. "Much has happened."

Ravyn's eyes were still on the horse. For every breath he took, dread twisted his stomach. "Where's Elm?"

Ione's face crumpled. Ravyn forgot his exhaustion. "*Where is he?*"

Ione opened her hand. Nestled in the folds of her palm was a Scythe Card. "He's at Stone." Her hazel eyes rose to Ravyn's face, laden with fury. "With Hauth."

It had happened weeks ago.

Hauth, healed by the Maiden Card.

The King, murdered.

Elm, framed and presumably kept alive so Hauth might trade him for the Twin Alders. But as to the condition he was kept in—

Ravyn could only guess.

Fingers wrapped into fists, his mind went somewhere so dark and terrible he had to look away as Ione explained to them what had happened. All he really heard was *Elm. Elm was alone, at Stone.*

With Hauth.

Ione's skin was red all over, tears and rage marking her face. She told them how Elm had compelled her to flee and remained behind to confront his brother. She'd ridden to Castle Yew, pounded upon the door at midnight—begged to know where Ravyn and Jespyr and the Shepherd King had gone.

Fenir had readied himself to go with her into the wood, but Ione hadn't waited for him. "I shot into the wood behind Castle Yew like an arrow—and was immediately lost," she said, looking out over the lake. "All night and into the morning I rode, calling out. No one was there. But then, I found a path. It was as if the trees—" Her brow knit. "As if the trees had moved. I know that sounds strange."

"It doesn't," Ravyn said, urging her on.

"I rode to the lake, then crossed. The horse was frightened and hurried through the water, like he was afraid of it. We reached the other side, but I had no idea where to go. I got lost again. Only this time, it cost me days." A faint smile touched her mouth. "When the crows found me, I thought they were going to eat me. Or that I might try to eat them, I was so hungry. But not an hour later women wearing masks of bone came out of the trees." Her eyes went glassy. "My mother and brothers were with them."

"She found me two days later," Petyr finished. "I'd gone back to—" His voice clogged. "To bury Wik. I was wandering, waiting for you all to come out of that wood. And now that you have—" He swallowed. "Do you know what day it is?"

"Solstice." The Nightmare cocked his head to the side, his eyes dropping to the Scythe in Ione's hand. "I am very pleased you're here, yellow girl. For now we have all twelve Cards."

"Not yet," Ravyn reminded him. "Six await in the chamber. We need to get back before midnight—then we can unite the Deck." He set his jaw, and did not say the words haunting his tongue. *With my blood.*

The Nightmare's knowing gaze swept over his face. They looked at each other, two liars struggling with the truth. "Regarding that, and the Princeling—I have a plan. But time—"

"Is short." Ravyn looked out over the lake. "We'll speak on your plan. But first, we swim."

They put Jespyr on Elm's horse and waded into the water. It was so much colder than when they swam last. The Nightmare pushed ahead, and Ione held the horse's face—spoke into its ear—and led it through the water, breath pluming out of her mouth. Petyr was pale as death, muttering to himself about never leaving home again.

Ravyn swam last. Not even his burning fury for what had happened to Elm could keep him warm against the water's bite.

No lake monster came to claim him. The only things that fought Ravyn now were his own straining muscles. Somewhere near the middle of the lake, his left leg cramped. He compensated with his right and kept going. But just as he neared the shore, his right leg seized as well. Ravyn dipped into darkness, a path of bubbles fleeing his mouth.

No. He'd gone to hell and back. Found a Providence Card five hundred years lost. Destroyed parts of himself to get it. He wasn't going to drown on Solstice, mere miles from home.

He'd pretended so long to be strong—but he wasn't pretending now. On powerful arms, Ravyn breached the water's surface and sucked in a breath. His legs met slippery mud and he hauled himself onto the shore, heaving heavy breaths until the war drum in his chest quieted to a rhythmic march.

It was night. There was no light to see their way home. But Ravyn had entered the wood a Destrier, a highwayman. He was used to traveling in the dark. On trembling foot, he stepped with the others into the forest.

The wood was just as the Nightmare had left it—cleaved. The path was open to them, swaddled by mist.

When moonlight cut through the edge of the wood, Ravyn let out a shaky breath. It wasn't trees on the horizon, but Castle Yew's towers.

Home.

He pushed ahead of the others, stepped out from the wood into the meadow—

And smelled smoke.

The Nightmare wrenched him back, clasping a hand over Ravyn's mouth. He put a finger in the air, gesturing for the others to halt.

Ahead, just on the other side of the trees, voices sounded in the meadow. One was louder than the others, echoing with harsh clarity, both brutish and cold. Ravyn's skin went clammy, then fiery hot. He knew that voice.

It belonged to his cousin Hauth.

A smile haunted the Nightmare's silken timbre. "How poetic. I couldn't have asked for a better Solstice." He put his mouth to Ravyn's ear. "Now, stupid bird, will you listen to my plan?"

Chapter Forty-Five

Elm

Elm wasn't alone in Stone's frozen underbelly. Erik Spindle and Tyrn Hawthorn were there with him. Separated by iron bars, they were the only three prisoners in their row.

The torches outside their cells had been neglected—or forgotten. It was so dark Elm's mind played tricks on him. Disembodied shapes danced before his eyes and voices rang in his ears. They sounded like children, crying. Like himself as a boy, crying.

Every bit of skin, every hair follicle, felt like a rotten tooth—a raw nerve exposed. He was cold in ways that felt physically impossible.

No one came for days. Not Hauth, not a Destrier or a guard save the one with water and rotten bread, and even he arrived with such errant consistency Elm had no accurate way to measure time.

He thought Hauth would come, that there would be some kind of reckoning between them. That they would stand—green eye to green eye—and only one would walk away.

But the night the King had died, Elm had been so tattered, so desperate to save Ione from Stone, that he had used the

Scythe too long. He'd lost himself to agony, the pain doing something it never had before.

Make a fool of him.

He should have gone with her, should have fled. He was supposed to be clever. Clever men didn't freeze to death for pride, thinking they could right old wrongs. They certainly didn't die believing their older brother—who had been nothing but a brute—would suddenly fight fairly.

Clever men died on their own terms. And if they were wary, clever, *and* good, they perhaps died in peace.

He, apparently, was none of the three.

A tonic and blanket passed between the bars. "Hold strong," Filick Willow whispered. "Ravyn will come for you."

Elm danced at the edge of consciousness. "Not this time."

On the ninth—tenth, perhaps—day of captivity, echoes sounded down the corridor. Erik cocked his head to the side, his voice rusty with disuse. "They're coming, Prince. Do not falter."

The Destriers were not gentle. When the beating finished, someone shoved a crude cup into Elm's hands. The wine was bitter, settling in all the dry places in his mouth.

Linden stood in front of him—tapped the Chalice Card. "Where did Ravyn and Jespyr go to retrieve the Twin Alders?"

Elm had no answer. "I don't know."

Hours later, after the beating was done, Linden returned with more wine, and tapped the Chalice thrice more. "Where is Ione Hawthorn?"

Elm shut his eyes. "I don't know."

Another Card had joined the Chalice. Elm immediately recognized the feel of a Scythe. A cold hand cupped his jaw. Elm looked into green eyes.

Hauth's face, carved by the Maiden's magic, was beautifully unholy. "You had your chance to flee with her, yet you didn't. Why?"

Elm's head rolled. Blood dripped out his mouth onto the dungeon floor. "You never cared for her. If you wish to barter with Ravyn, I am hostage enough." He laughed, then coughed. "And I wanted to stay and kill you."

Any other time, his brother would have answered with his own laugh, then a fist. But Hauth was inexpressive, fringing on disinterested, the Maiden's ill effects masking him in chill. "You are right," he said. "I never cared for her. Still, I will hunt her. Take back the Scythe she holds. This time, there will be no Maiden to save her. All you've done is buy her time—and made even more of a traitor of yourself."

Elm spat blood on the floor. "I've been betraying you for years," he ground out. "I was there on the forest road the day your face was cleaved. I was a highwayman, there to steal Wayland Pine's Iron Gate. I helped collect the Deck right under your nose." He took in a slow, rasping breath. "I'd do it all again, just to watch you flinch."

Hauth's hand tightened over Elm's throat. "I'm not flinching now. And as for killing me, brother—" His green eyes were cold. "You cannot. *Nothing* can."

He dropped Elm to the floor and quit the cell, Destriers on his heels.

Darkness took Elm away.

"You were on the forest road when Wayland Pine's Iron Gate was stolen?"

Elm jumped. He didn't recall dozing off—or how long he'd slept. There were food trays upon his floor. Three of them, untouched.

Erik Spindle watched him through the bars between their cells.

"I—" Elm winced. It hurt even to speak. "I was there. You nearly ran me through, actually." He traced a finger over the split in his bottom lip. "Your daughter was there, too."

Steam plumed in his periphery. Erik Spindle's voice was ragged. "Elspeth? Why?"

"She was helping us collect the Deck. She wanted to heal Emory's degeneration—her own as well. She saved me from your sword." He let out a weak breath. "And I returned her favor with distrust and contempt."

Someone coughed in the adjacent cell. A weak, trembling sound. Tyrn. "M-my Ione. She escaped? She's safe?"

"I don't know." Elm put his face in his hands. "Pray she forgives you for trading that Nightmare Card for a marriage to Hauth. Because I never will."

Wakeless, Elm dreamed in yellow.

Summer grass and a muslin dress caught between his fingers. Hair swept over his face, a sigh, like a rush of wings, in his ear. There was no mist, no salt, no Rowan red. Everything was slow, soft. Delicate.

But he couldn't escape the cold. He woke to the sound of his own teeth chattering, shivers racking his body raw.

"You shouldn't sleep so long," came Erik's voice. "Get up. Move your limbs."

A crazed half laugh crawled out of Elm. He looked down at his frostbitten fingers, which had all gone black. Some to the knuckle. “Sorry, Captain—I don’t think I’m up for a training session.”

Erik crouched on his side of their shared bars, finally close enough to be more than a vague outline. His face was pale—his skin ragged with frostbite and mottled with old bruising. His beard had grown long and his clothes were tattered, bloodstained. When he spoke, his voice was solemn.

“Elspeth’s mother was infected,” he said. “She tried to hide it from me. She degenerated, suffered terribly, in silence. All because I was the Captain of the Destriers. Iris knew if a Chalice was levied against me, her secret would be my death. So she said nothing. And I”—he ran his hand over his face—“I did nothing. She died. And when Elspeth caught the infection as well—”

The great tree of a man splintered, his steadfast expression finally giving way to sorrow. “I began to hate myself. To hate my Destriers and the laws we upheld. In my heart, I was a traitor.” He sucked in a quivering breath. “When the Yew boy took my place and I was free of my charge, I thought my hatred might dissipate. It didn’t. And Ravyn Yew—he was just as strong as me. Just as cold and unrelenting as I’d been. I knew, so long as men like he and I were Captain, Blunder would never change.”

His voice softened. “But then I saw him on Market Day. Holding my daughter. Wrapping her in his arms the way I’d once held Iris in mine. He was not the same man who’d taken my place as Captain.” Erik shook his head. “Because that Captain of the Destriers is not a man, only a mask. A show of Rowan might. And there will always be stronger things in this world than Rowan might.”

Elm shut his eyes. "Why are you telling me this?"

"I've never said any of it out loud. I wanted to see what it tasted like, being honest."

"And?"

"Bitter."

The corner of Elm's bruised mouth lifted. "Don't worry, Captain. I'll take your confessions to my grave soon enough."

The sound of coughing came from the next cell. "I can't stomach this rot they feed us," Tyrn Hawthorn wailed.

Erik paced, kicking his boots together every so often to keep his toes alive. "So starve."

Tyrn's platter of food ricocheted off the bars, an ugly knell that echoed through the dungeon. "You think I'm weak."

"I know you are," Erik answered.

"Would it surprise you that I've killed a man?"

Elm raised his brows. He'd tried to pace as well, but after an hour, he'd gotten sleepy. "A little."

Tyrn's voice went thin. "He was a highwayman. It was by chance that he and I traveled the forest road at the same time. When I saw the Nightmare Card's burgundy velvet, peeking out from his sleeve, I didn't think—I just ran him through and stole it."

He rasped another cough. "I thought of him while I plotted a way for the Card to earn my family favor. But even when it did and Ione was engaged to the High Prince, I felt no joy, only fear of losing everything I'd gained. I betrayed Elspeth, because I was afraid that—" His voice began to wobble. "That if Ione didn't become Queen, I'd be a murderer for nothing."

Erik stopped pacing.

"So you're right," Tyrn said. "I am weak. My wife and children know it. Everyone knows it. I'm weak, and entirely bloodstained."

Elm was drifting, near and far. "Welcome to the club."

The clanging of a sword against the cell bars ripped Elm's dream away. The cell door wrenched open. His hands were tied behind his back, and he was dragged along with Erik Spindle and Tyrn Hawthorn out of the dungeon up the long, winding stairs in a sea of black cloaks. He vaguely recognized the men whose fingers dug into his skin. Destriers. Not only the ones he'd trained with, but older ones, too.

The way their fists slammed into Erik's stomach confirmed it. "Traitor," they spat at him.

Erik said nothing. Unmoved, unwavering. Even Tyrn had the decency not to cry out when a Destrier shoved his face into the castle door.

Gray morning light made Elm wince, his eyes slow to focus. When they did, he saw that there was snow upon the ground.

Destriers, old and new, sat upon their mounts in the bailey, waiting.

At their lead, tall and broad and beautiful, Hauth wore their father's crown and a deep blue doublet with a gold rowan tree embroidered across its chest. He spun his Scythe between his fingers and surveyed the prisoners down his nose. When his green eyes landed on Elm, he nodded. "Your misery is almost at an end, brother. The highwayman meets the hangman. But first—how about a ride into town?"

They strapped him to a horse like a newly slaughtered deer.

Elm could see only the ground—the path directly beneath the animal's legs.

Nearly all of it was covered in snow.

He felt every break, every bruise upon his skin expand on the journey into town. When the dirt road ended and the clacking knell of hooves against cobblestone met his ears, he knew they were on Market Street.

He strained against his tethers—tried to look up. There were red and gold ribbons, strewn over doorframes and lantern posts. "What day is it?"

Linden rode next to him. He reached down—hit Elm over the back of his head with a club. His voice was a sneer. "Solstice."

Elm's vision tunneled, a sticky warmth sliding through his hair.

When he came to, the horses had stopped. Rough hands untied him—yanked him out of the saddle and set him on weak legs and screaming, frostbitten feet.

Castle Yew's reaching towers loomed over him.

The castle door was open—not latched how Jon Thistle usually kept it. When the Destriers dragged Elm and Erik and Tyrn inside, the air was cold. Stale.

The knot in Elm's stomach shot up into his throat. Something was horribly wrong.

Castle Yew was abandoned—its hearths left untended, the estate empty of laypeople, doors and windows left open despite the chill air.

"Take one last look, Renelm," Hauth said. "At midnight, this creepy old place will make a proper Solstice pyre."

They passed through the house and out the eastern doors into the gardens, stomping over shrubs and brambles until they were in the meadow near the ruins.

There were Destriers—six more of them, waiting. Morette

and Fenir and Jon Thistle were with them. So was Emory. When they saw Elm, their chests heaved, tears turning Morette's green eyes glassy.

Elm's relief to see them lasted only as long as it took to take in their appearances. They were bruised, pale—shivering. They wore no cloaks against the chill. Emory was swaying on his feet, held up by his mother and father's arms.

There was a cut in his left hand. Long—deep, dripping red into the snow.

Elm choked on his breath. "What have you done?"

Hauth walked down the line of Destriers. "Our aunt and uncle—with a little persuasion from my men, my Scythe, and a Chalice, of course—have informed me that this is where Ravyn and Jespyr and their friend Elspeth Spindle entered the wood in search of the Twin Alders Card." An unfeeling smile touched his mouth. "They told me a fascinating story about a stone, hidden in a chamber behind the castle."

He reached into his pocket—pulled out six Providence Cards. A Prophet. A Well. An Iron Gate. A Golden Egg. A White Eagle. A Chalice.

Elm's gaze shot back to the cut in Emory's palm.

Hauth sucked his teeth. "I told you, Renelm. I have no desire to unite the Deck. The mist, the infection, keeps Blunder small. Terrified. And terrified people are easy to control. Ravyn's little collection—all his lying and thieving—was merely to adorn the vaults at Stone with more Providence Cards."

Erik Spindle cursed, spitting blood into the snow.

Hauth ignored him. His eyes were on the tree line, fixed near the stone chamber. "He's taken his time, Ravyn. My men have been watching these woods for weeks. Still, he may yet come. He has until midnight to make that Twin Alders Card count for anything."

Elm had wondered, down in the frosted dungeon, why his brother hadn't come for him or Erik or Tyrn yet. Now, he knew. "We're your bait." He was shaking. He'd spent a month being cold. But now—there was an inferno in his chest, clawing up into his throat. "You'd trade us for the Twin Alders?"

"Of course not. You're all traitors. You'll *all* die tonight." Hauth picked under his fingernail, his tone bored. "But Ravyn won't know that, will he?"

Daylight bled away into night.

Elm counted fifteen Destriers in total, including Hauth—which meant not all of them carried Black Horses. He watched their movements, noting the ones who had been conscripted during his stint in the dungeon. They moved on silent step through the snow, collecting shrubbery and bramble and wood, spreading it into four pyres around the meadow.

When it was fully dark, they lit the pyres, the snow reflecting yellow and orange flames. No one said anything, all of their gazes tight on the tree line, watching for Ravyn.

Then, quiet as a bird, Emory's voice broke the stillness. "You won't win."

Hauth stopped pacing. He came to stand in front of Morette and Fenir, who were trying to shield Emory behind their backs. "What's that?" Hauth put a mocking hand to his ear. "I couldn't hear you under the grating sound of your dying breaths, Emory."

Elm yanked against his restraints—tasted blood on his tongue.

Emory swayed. Then, quicker than a dying boy should, he lunged forward. Grasped Hauth's wrist. His eyes rolled back in his head, and when he spoke, his voice was strange, smooth—as if slick with oil. "You won't win," he said again. "For nothing is safe, and nothing is free. Debt follows all men, no matter their plea. When the Shepherd returns, a new day shall ring. Death to the Rowans." His gray eyes focused, homing in on Elm. "Long live the King."

Hauth ripped himself out of Emory's grip. Expressionless though it was, his face had gone the color of paper. He raised a hand—hit Emory across the face with a closed fist.

The boy fell into snow and did not get up.

Morette screamed. Fenir reached for his son, but the Destrier on his left twisted his arm behind his back. Elm surged against his restraints, only to feel the ropes cut tighter into his wrists. "Hauth," he said, half curse—half plea. "Don't do this. He's just a boy."

Hauth looked down at Emory. There was nothing in his green eyes.

"Movement, Highness," a Destrier called, pointing his sword to trees on the other side of the meadow. "There—just ahead."

Hauth's gaze wrenched forward. The line went still, prisoners and Destriers alike all holding their breaths as they watched the wood.

There was nothing at first, just the whisper of wind. Then, so silent and ethereal she might have been the Spirit of the Wood herself—

Ione Hawthorn stepped into the meadow.

She wore the same gray dress she'd worn when she'd fled Stone, only now it was filthy, wet. Her face was red from the cold, her hair roped into a thick braid down her back. Elm drank in the sight of her, elation spoiling to dread as his gaze dropped to Ione's hand.

Three Providence Cards lay in her open palm. The Maiden,

the Scythe, and a third. It was forest green, depicting two trees—one pale, one dark—interwoven at their branches and roots.

The Twin Alders Card.

Ione's hazel eyes shifted over the crowd—over Hauth and his horde of Destriers, then the Yew household and her uncle and father. When her gaze collided with Elm's, her chest heaved, her brow going soft.

Then she took in his face. The damage they'd done to it. Ione stiffened, the red in her cheeks going wan. When her gaze returned to Hauth, those hazel eyes burned.

Hauth stepped into the meadow and offered her a curt, mocking bow. "You've always had a knack for unpleasantly surprising me, Ione." He nodded to the Twin Alders in her hand. "Where did you get that? Did Ravyn give it to you?"

She said nothing.

Hauth took another step. "Where is he?"

Elm needed her to look at him. Needed her to know that it couldn't end like this. "Ione," he said, his voice in tatters. "Go. Please—go."

She didn't budge an inch, save to plant her feet deeper into the snow.

Hauth kept stalking forward, eyeing her like she were an injured animal in the wood. "Are you going to use that Scythe on me, betrothed? On *all* my men?" He sucked his teeth. "Go ahead. But be warned—you better be skilled enough to compel all of us at once. Because if you're not, well. You remember what happened in my brother's chamber."

Behind Elm, Linden laughed.

"If you tell me where Ravyn is, I'll make it painless. But if you fight me—" Hauth took his own Scythe from his pocket. "Then I will take my time killing you. So by all means, Ione, fight me. You've always tried to."

Tyrn Hawthorn heaved a terrible sob. "Go, Ione!"

She didn't listen. She was staring down the man she might have married, her face an open book of loathing. "You want to watch me die, Hauth?"

He raised a finger over his Scythe. "It'd be the only enjoyment you could offer me."

Ione's finger was faster. She tapped the Maiden once—twice—thrice. "Then kill me. If you can."

A knife sang through the air.

Hauth doubled over, cursing. Blood dripped from his hand, the knife buried in his palm. His Scythe slid out of his grasp, catching the wind and fluttering onto snow.

Elm tasted salt. Not the sweat or tears or blood that had slipped down his face into his mouth, but a different sort of brine. An older sort.

Then he heard it. The thing he'd waited for around every corner, listened for in every pause.

Ravyn's voice.

Elm.

He appeared out of nothingness and stood in front of Ione, a dark, vengeful bird of prey. Hauth's eyes went wide and he took a step back, the only man he'd ever feared standing in front of him—marking him.

And Ravyn Yew, the stony Captain of the Destriers, grinned. He drew his sword, his eyes moving from Hauth to Elm. *You look terrible.*

It hurt too much to smile back. *I'm still better looking than you.* Elm's breath shook. *Hauth took the Cards from the chamber. They're in his pocket.*

I'm going to get them back. Ravyn lifted his sword, pointing it down the line of Destriers. "I am your Captain no longer," he said. "My business is with your new King, and the Deck of Cards. If you wish to live, leave this place. Now."

Hauth stood straighter. Ripped the knife out of his palm. Wherever he kept the Maiden Card he was using, it was already healing him. "A bold claim from one man—and a whore—against the King's guard." He jerked his head, scanning the tree line. "I assume you killed Gorse. Where are the highwaymen and Jespyr and that *thing* you left with?"

"Close," Ravyn replied. "Very close. They're waiting. Watching."

"Traitor," a Destrier called.

"Infected bastard," another spat.

With a clamor, they drew their swords—pointed them at Ravyn.

Hauth looked down the line, arrogance lighting his words. "Seems they've made their choice. Surrender the Twin Alders to me, cousin. Or watch your family die."

Ravyn looked at his parents—at Emory in the snow—muscles bunching in his jaw.

Don't yield, Elm shouted into his mind. *Don't. Fucking. Yield.*

Ravyn's gray eyes found him. *Follow Ione into the wood,* he said. *Get to her—then meet me in the stone chamber. We're going to end this, Elm. All of it.*

Salt fled Elm's senses. Ravyn touched Ione's shoulder, then rushed forward, went invisible.

Ione turned on her heel and ran back into the wood.

"Kill the prisoners," Hauth commanded the Destriers. He lunged into the snow, searching for his fallen Scythe. "And bring me the Twin Alders."

Blades lowered over the Yew family's necks. Elm felt a knife near his jaw, its bite just below his ear. He shut his eyes. There was a deep, wrenching groan—

And the earth began to roll.

Snow shook from treetops, the world a flurry of white. The terrible groan was coming from the wood. *Something* was coming from the wood.

The trees, Elm realized. The trees were moving.

Roots tore from the earth, boughs whipping through the air. Twisting, the yew trees rushed into the meadow from all sides, swiping—grasping—at the Destriers.

The first tree that made contact burst through the ruins, knocking ancient sandstone pillars to the ground. It caught two Destriers in its branches—wrenched them back from Emory and his parents. With a sickening snap, the yew ground the men beneath its roots.

When the earth rolled again, Elm lost his footing. He crashed into Erik and Tyrn, the three of them a tangle of limbs. When he looked up, the meadow was a chaos of trees and snow, lit by the menacing light of the pyres. The Destriers were a whir of darkness, several of them running through the bedlam.

Running after Ione.

Chapter Forty-Six

Ravyn

Ravyn and Jespyr were practiced. Twisted and intrepid, like the branches of their namesake tree, they'd learned by now how to keep steady when the Shepherd King commanded the wood.

When the earth began to roll and the Destriers near their parents stumbled, Jespyr lunged from the shadows. She was still too weak to use her sword, even with Petyr and a Black Horse for aid. But her knives—she was strong enough for those. Two Destriers fell at the edge of her blades. When a third got to his feet and lunged at her, she dodged him, his sword grazing just beneath her chin.

Petyr tore from the shadows, knocking her assailant off his feet. The Destrier fell into snow, and then a yew tree was upon him, wrenching him away with a sickening snap.

The last Destrier who had not run after Ione was Allyn Moss. He'd been standing with his sword drawn behind Jon Thistle. But when the rumbling trees knocked him from his feet, Moss stayed down, fear washing over his eyes.

Ravyn appeared out of thin air and knelt over him—put a hand to Moss's throat. "I don't want to kill you." Gorse's face flashed before his eyes. "But I will if I must."

The Destrier trembled. He took his Black Horse from his pocket—threw it onto the snow in surrender.

Ravyn pulled back, a familiar tremor in his hand. "Go."

Moss fled into the night. When Ravyn glanced back over the meadow, it was just in time to see Ione disappear into the trees behind the stone chamber. Destriers—he counted eight of them—chased her. Elm and Erik Spindle and Tyrn Hawthorn were hobbling behind.

All was going to plan.

Hauth was still in the heart of the meadow, kept busy by three yew trees. They circled him—whipped at him. Hauth felled several branches with his sword, dodged and tried to slip between trunks, but the trees kept twisting, bending. Guided by the Nightmare's sword, they would keep him at bay, distracting him from picking up his Scythe—

Until Ravyn was ready to deal with him.

But first, his family. Ravyn ran to them, drawing a knife through the ropes restraining Thistle and his parents. Jespyr was in the snow, wrapping Emory in her arms. She let out a shaking exhale. "He's still breathing."

"Take him back into the castle." Ravyn handed Moss's Black Horse to Petyr, then pressed his palm against his mother's cheek. "Keep him safe."

"We can help," Thistle said, picking up a fallen Destrier sword.

"Everything is under control. Go inside."

Fenir found a second blade in the snow. "You'll want another pair of hands—"

Ravyn's nostrils flared. "If you do not get your asses into the castle, I'm going to tell the Shepherd King, and then the bloody trees will *drag* you away. Jespyr needs rest." He looked down at Emory. "So does he. We started this for him, and it's almost over. So, please—pretend I didn't inherit a lifetime of stubbornness from you, and get. Inside. The castle."

They stared at him, jaws slack. "I've never heard you talk so much," Morette muttered.

"Best do what he says before he keeps blathering," Jespyr said with a wink. But her face was drawn, her shoulders rounding with exhaustion. She wobbled, and Thistle caught her.

Fenir gave Ravyn a narrow glance. "See you soon?"

"See you soon."

They carried Emory between them. Petyr stepped forward. "I'll escort them, then I'm coming back." He offered a crooked smile. "Or are you gonna yell at me, too?"

"Likely."

They clasped hands, then Petyr hurried after Ravyn's family and Thistle, slipping through the mist, snow flurrying in his wake.

Ravyn turned and scanned the meadow. It was darker now. Several of the yew trees had dragged their roots through the pyres, scattering the flames—smothering the light. But Ravyn could still see everything he needed to.

Hauth, caged in the heart of the meadow by the yew trees.

He stepped forward, looking out into the wood. He could not see him, but he knew the Nightmare was there, guiding the trees with his sword. Waiting. Watching.

Ravyn reached into his pocket—tapped his burgundy Card. *Elspeth?*

She answered right away. *Ravyn. Is your family safe?*

Yes. Ione and the Destriers are headed your way.

Good, came the Nightmare's oily timbre. *The Princeling?*

Right behind them. What time is it?

The trees declare we've thirty minutes until midnight.

Elspeth returned. She made a noise in her throat. *Ravyn?*

Even now, taut with strain, her voice eased him, like a warm cloth pressed over his eyes. *Yes, Elspeth?*

Don't die.

I won't.

Because if you do, and we never get the time we're owed, I'll hate you, Ravyn Yew. I'll love you and hate you forever.

The corner of his lip quirked. *This will all be over at midnight, Elspeth. After that, you can love me as thoroughly as you like.*

The Nightmare made a retching noise. *Not to cut this tender moment short, but time is somewhat of the essence. You sure you don't want the trees to help you, stupid bird?*

I can handle Hauth.

Good. Bring him, and the Cards he carries, to my chamber. His laugh was heady as smoke. *By whatever means.*

Ravyn's hands dropped to the ivory hilt of his dagger. *I will.*

The three yew trees caging Hauth went still. Hauth stepped away from them—his face unreadable, save the angry veins that protruded from his neck and brow. His eyes were cast downward, combing the snow for the Scythe he'd not yet recovered.

Have at him, the Nightmare murmured.

Ravyn drew in a breath. And because he'd never said it when he first felt it, and never after she'd disappeared into the Shepherd King, he spoke one last time into Elspeth Spindle's mind. *I love you, too, Elspeth.*

And then he was running.

He crashed into Hauth just as his cousin's fingers closed around his Scythe. They rolled in the snow like snapping dogs. When Hauth found his feet, he shoved the red Card into his pocket and sliced a dagger through the air. Ravyn reared back, but not fast enough. There was a tearing sound, the blade ripping through leather, drawing a fine line of blood across Ravyn's torso.

Hauth let out a triumphant bark. "The untouchable Ravyn Yew, finally made to bleed."

Ravyn pivoted, moving on the balls of his feet. He reached into his pocket—tapped his Mirror Card. Disappeared.

Hauth gnashed his teeth. "Coward!"

If you imagined I'd fight fairly after everything you've done, Ravyn said into his cousin's mind, *you're a fool.*

Hauth blanched and replaced his dagger with his sword. "A Nightmare Card? Did you steal it upon the forest road as well, highwayman?"

Ravyn laughed, his steps light. *Not this time. This Card, I inherited.*

He reappeared in front of Hauth and slammed his fist into his cousin's jaw. Hauth hit the ground with a thud and rolled, dodging Ravyn's boot. He was fast—using a Black Horse, his motions a blur.

Fast, but predictable. Hauth slashed his blade through the air. Before he could level another strike, Ravyn closed the distance between them. He caught Hauth's swinging arm and bent it back.

Hauth grunted and dropped his sword.

Ravyn poised his dagger to his cousin's neck. "This ends tonight. You, me, and the Deck."

Cold green eyes grew ever colder. "Or what? Any damage you tender me will be undone by the Maiden. I plunged my knife into Ione Hawthorn's heart, watched her bleed out—and still, she lived. I've hidden my Maiden Card deep within the vaults at Stone, Ravyn. You cannot kill me."

Hauth pushed forward, his neck pressing over Ravyn's dagger until it split his skin. Blood wept from the wound, but Hauth didn't even flinch—he barreled into Ravyn with the force of a charging horse.

Ravyn's feet dragged backward through snow, and Hauth landed punches into his sides, again and again, fueled by the unflagging strength of the Black Horse. Ravyn's ribs absorbed the blows. They bent, bent—

Broke.

He groaned, took Hauth by the throat, and slammed him onto snow. Pinning his cousin to the ground, Ravyn leveled him with a decade of malice. He'd saved it, praying a day would come when he could unleash it. Hit after hit he paid Hauth with a closed fist. One for killing the King. Two for telling Orithe Willow that Ravyn was infected as a boy. Three for doing the same when Emory got sick. Four for the Rowan bloodline and the heinous violence Brutus Rowan had commanded. Ten for Elm.

And for what Hauth had done to Elspeth, Ravyn took his ivory-hilted dagger and shoved it into his cousin's gut.

Hauth coughed, his face marked only briefly by pain. He was a mess of blood and spit, but his eyes were cold.

"You're coming with me to the chamber," Ravyn snarled. "Whole, or in pieces."

"Says the man who can't even wield a Scythe." Hauth spat in his face. "You want to bring me to heel, Ravyn? *Make me.*"

Knuckles screaming, broken and bruising, Ravyn reached his hands into his cousin's doublet. He felt velvet and wrenched it free.

All the Cards Hauth had stolen from the chamber scattered, falling upon snow. Golden Egg. Prophet. White Eagle. Iron Gate. Well. Chalice.

Ravyn ignored them. He was reaching only for Hauth's Scythe. Blood red, he held it between his hands.

But Providence Cards are ageless, he'd said to the Spirit of the Wood. *Their magic does not fade. They do not decay with time. They cannot be destroyed. The Shepherd King said so himself.*

And he, like you, is certainly a liar.

"I may not be able to use the Scythe," Ravyn said. "But I can undo it." He hauled in a breath, clenched his jaw—

And tore the indomitable red Card in half.

Hauth's mouth fell open, twin pieces of red fluttering above him. The Scythe fell to the ground, reduced to nothing more than paper and velvet.

A smile bloomed over Ravyn's face. He laughed, triumph rearing in his veins.

Pain sank into his side.

Ravyn's laugh fell away. When he looked down, a ceremonial dagger was lodged between his ribs. It struck him as strange, how easily the blade had slipped to the hilt into his skin. As if he, like the Scythe, were no more than paper—frail as the wings of a butterfly.

Stranger still that the wound should be in the same place Brutus Rowan had stabbed the Shepherd King, five hundred years ago.

Blood seeped into snow. Ravyn flinched. Fell.

Hauth shoved him aside and rose to his feet. The places he'd been injured were already healing. He leaned over, his fingers probing at Ravyn's pockets. He withdrew Ravyn's Cards—his Nightmare and Mirror. The corners of Hauth's lips twitched, and he collected the rest of the Providence Cards, splayed out like pieces of stained glass upon the snow.

"Pity the Maiden will not work on you, cousin." When Hauth stood over Ravyn, he was without blemish once again. Brutal, perfect. A true Rowan King. "I'd always hoped I'd be the one to kill you." He tapped Ravyn's Mirror Card three times.

And disappeared.

Chapter Forty-Seven
Elspeth

I could not yet see Ione—but her Cards were brilliant in the darkness of the wood. Pink and red and forest-green lights emanated, and I knew my cousin was out of the meadow and into the trees, retrieving Elm's horse where she'd left it. Mounting. Riding this way—just as the Nightmare had planned.

He hunched low to the ground and cocked his head to both sides, cracking the joints in his neck. Grip lax around his sword, he'd stopped moving the trees after we'd spoken to Ravyn. His self-imposed task was one he'd honed for centuries.

He waited.

He'd waited, while Ione and Ravyn confronted Hauth. Waited, as Jespyr and Petyr crept through shadow undetected. Even as he'd guided the trees into the meadow, he'd been waiting. Waiting.

For the Destriers to come.

But I was not so practiced in the art of stillness. My mind ticked on a steady rhythm, not a chime, but a chant. *Midnight. Midnight. Midnight.*

Hush, the Nightmare admonished. *I can feel your worry in my teeth.*

It can't be helped. I let out a long breath, which did nothing to ease me. *You have so little time.*

I heard them then. Footsteps. Several pairs, all of them running.

Ione rode loudly, weaving through the wood. The Destriers behind her were far quieter—difficult to home in on. But not impossible.

The Nightmare tightened his grip on his sword and tapped it upon the earth, his namesake tree slithering out of his mouth like a hiss. "Taxus."

Shepherd King, came the chorus of their reply.

"How many Destriers are in the wood?"

The Black Horses arrive, eight in their rank. They verge near the Maiden—to chase and to flank. Mind all your circles, guide the wood as you please. To hunt the King's guard—cut them down at the knees.

The Nightmare stood to full height. Veins dark with magic, he swept his sword into the air. The wood trembled, then began once more to move. Dirt and mist and snow shrouded his eyes, so he shut them, content to listen to the noises of the wood.

I listened with him. I heard the groaning of trees—the rumbling of roots as they ripped toward the Destriers. I could hear the beats of Ione's horse. Then, above it, men's voices echoed.

The Destriers were shouting. Screaming.

The Nightmare opened his eyes, and Ione cantered past. The horse whickered, dodging through shifting trees. Ione kept her seat, turning the animal in wide circles through the wood. For each pass, she drew more Destriers from shadow, and the Nightmare, with swings of his blade, cut them down with the trees.

When four Destriers were left, Ione turned the horse,

hurtling once more toward the Nightmare. One Destrier was so close behind her the tip of his blade cut several strands of hair from the horse's tail. He pulled a knife, flinging it at Ione. But with one swipe of his sword, the Nightmare bade the trees to knock it from the air—and the Destrier from his feet.

Ione rode until she was next to him, dismounting in a flurry. She dropped her hand into her pocket and seized the red light therein. "Be still," she said, panting. "Be still, Destriers."

Louder, Ione, I called in the dark.

"Louder," the Nightmare echoed.

Ione clamped her eyes shut. When she commanded the Scythe a third time, her voice shifted to a thunder greater than the whickering horse or the rush of incoming Destriers—greater than the wood itself. *"Be still!"*

Salt touched everything. Even me, though the Scythe had no sway over the Nightmare. When I looked through my window, three Destriers stood paces away—arrested in utter stillness.

Darkness emanated from their Black Horse Cards. Unmoving, the Destriers looked upon my cousin, unmistakable disgust flashing over their eyes.

Ione came to stand next to the Nightmare. She measured the Destriers, taking in their frozen statures and hateful gazes. With the Scythe, and her thunderous command, she'd bent them to her will.

But it took only a needle-thin whisper to break them. Ione turned to the Nightmare, dropping her hazel eyes to his sword. "Go on, then."

His mirth coated our shared darkness. When the Nightmare's sword sang through the air, the yew trees answered its call. With an impact so great I heard nothing but a terrible *snap*, the Destriers were knocked from their feet, ground by roots into snow—into nothingness.

I let out a shaking breath, and Ione winced. A drop of blood fell from her nose. She reached into her pocket—released the Scythe. "Is that all of them?"

The Nightmare closed his eyes, listening to the wood.

"Is Bess—Did she see all of that? That must have been terrible to watch."

The Nightmare ignored her, clearing his throat to speak once more to the trees.

"Will you tell her I'm sorry about Equinox?" Ione scrubbed a hand over her face. "I feel sick, thinking we fought over Hauth bloody Rowan—"

"You know, yellow girl, I've always liked you best. But if you do not be quiet and let me *listen*, I'm going to tell the trees to press their branches over your mouth."

Ione balked, and I swatted at darkness. *Would it kill you to be civil?*

I'm already dead. But yes. Decidedly. He opened his eyes a sliver. Peeked at Ione. "Elspeth is lecturing me."

Hesitant at first, then blossoming, a smile spread over my cousin's mouth. She could not see it, but I answered with my own. *Oh, give her a hug.*

Don't be grotesque.

A moment later the Nightmare's spine straightened. He put a finger to his mouth, warning Ione to remain silent. There were voices in the wood again. Men, shouting.

"For fuck's sake, Tyrn," a booming voice called. "Stop cowering. They're only trees."

I jolted forward in the Nightmare's mind. *That's my father's voice.*

A second answered, pointed and snide. "Only trees? When was the last time that wiry shrub in your courtyard ripped itself free and wrapped branches around your neck, Spindle?"

My smile widened. Elm.

The third voice was my uncle's. "At least the wood doesn't seem angry with us, that's someth—oh, Spirit, another one." Wet coughs echoed through the trees. "I can't look at another dead Destrier."

"Huh," Elm said. "I don't feel that way at all."

The Nightmare rolled his eyes. He tapped his sword upon the ground. The wood went still, dirt and snow settling.

Three figures stumbled into view, like ships upon stormy seas. Wrecked ships, by the look of them. Their shoulders were slumped—their hands tied behind their backs. Their skin was bleeding and bruised and blackened with frostbite. None of them walked without a limp.

Ione's breath caught. She ran forward.

Don't be shy, I chided. *Go say hello.*

When Elm and my father and uncle saw the Nightmare and Ione coming, their mouths fell open.

Tyrn stumbled forward first. With his hands tied, he could do little besides push his broad chest at Ione and the Nightmare. He smelled of sweat—grime and filth. "Ione," he sobbed. "Elspeth. I'm so sorry."

The Nightmare hissed and wrenched away. "Get away from me, you traitorous scab."

At least untie him.

Grumbling, he passed Ione his sword, discontentment sliding over his mind. *I might stab him if I do it.*

Ione cut her father's restraints, then my father's. Erik Spindle had more poise than Tyrn—he didn't try to hug the Nightmare. But he stared into his yellow eyes. "What's happened to you, Elspeth?"

"I'll explain later," Elm said, breathless as Ione cut his binds. When his hands were free, he shook them at his sides and looked down at my cousin, a flush sliding over his marred skin. "Hey, Hawthorn."

The Nightmare took his sword back and snapped a finger in Elm's face. "Focus, Princeling. Time is running out. Heal yourself with the Maiden—then we must get to the stone chamber. How many fallen Destriers did you count in the wood?"

Elm dragged his gaze from Ione. "What?"

The Nightmare ground his molars. "How many—"

"Four," my father said. "We passed four dead Destriers."

Ione met the Nightmare's eyes, her face stricken. I knew what she was thinking. Eight Destriers had chased her from the meadow into the wood. Four were dead on the forest floor, three crushed by the trees behind us. Seven. Seven had fallen.

Which meant the eighth—

There! I shouted.

He was paces away, walking on silent step, fitted with a shortbow. Even behind the darkness emanating from his Black Horse, I recognized him. He was the same Destrier who'd chased me through the mist on Market Day—the one whose face the Nightmare had cleaved. Royce Linden.

The Nightmare slammed his sword back against soil. But before he could command the trees, Linden's arrow flew. It grazed Elm's arm, then lodged itself into the muscle of Ione's shoulder.

She faltered back a step.

The Nightmare sprang forward at the same time as Elm. Linden pivoted—let loose a second arrow. The Nightmare cut it from the air and kept running. Linden threw down his bow and drew two knives. But the Nightmare's gait was so fast, so trained and full of fury, that when he reached Linden—limbs and blades colliding—the unflinching force of him knocked the Destrier onto his back.

Linden's skull collided with roots. He looked up, awash with loathing. The Nightmare drew in a breath, lifted his blade once more—

"Give me that," Elm said, ripping the sword out of his hands. Auburn hair in his eyes, he placed the blade over Linden's chest and spoke through his teeth. "You know how this goes, asshole. Be wary. Be clever. Be good."

I shut my eyes. When I opened them, a fatal blow had been dealt through Linden's heart. Blood wept from it onto the forest floor. The Destrier shut his eyes, gasping only a moment before the great, final sleep called him through the veil.

Elm stared down at him a second longer, then turned away. He handed the Nightmare back his sword and had the good sense to look contrite. "I was keeping a promise."

By the time he and the Nightmare got back to Ione, the arrow from her shoulder was on the ground—her wound already healed. She held her Maiden Card in her hand and tapped her foot, hazel eyes narrowing over Elm. "That was excessive."

He let out a broken laugh, then surged forward. Catching Ione's face between his palms, Elm leaned over, crashed his mouth against hers, kissed her feverishly. "I'm sorry. I should have gone with you. I'm not clever at all. I'm sorry—I'm sorry."

The Nightmare and I stared. *We seem to have missed something rather important,* I said.

Small mercies.

My uncle and father turned away, scarlet. When Ione managed to pull herself from Elm, slightly dazed, she passed him the Maiden Card. Elm tapped it, letting out a sigh of relief when his wounds—his cuts and bruises and blackened bits of frostbitten flesh—healed until he was without blemish.

My father and uncle did the same. I felt my own relief, seeing them restored. But the chant in my mind returned, louder than before. *Midnight. Midnight. Midnight.* I cleared my throat and spoke to the Nightmare. *Thank you. They are alive because of you. And now—*

We must take the Cards and meet Ravyn in the chamber. But just as he said the words, the line of his shoulders went rigid. The Nightmare looked out into the wood, and I saw what he sensed. Light, flickering in our shared vision. A flurry of color.

There were Providence Cards in the wood. Only, they weren't headed in the direction of the stone chamber, but the opposite. And fast.

I called out into nothingness. *Ravyn?*

No answer.

My heart bottomed out. *Something's wrong.*

The Nightmare clasped his hand over Ione's shoulder. "Bring the Maiden and Scythe and Twin Alders to the stone chamber." His gaze found Elm. "I have plans for you yet."

He ran. Not after the lights, but toward Castle Yew. *Faster,* I called over the drumming of his heart. *Run faster.*

He ripped through the tree line and faced the meadow. Snow decorated every blade of grass, but it was not pale.

It was red.

Ravyn was on his back, a hand pressed against his side, his copper skin the color of ash. His eyes were open, glassy, his breath coming in quick, halting breaths.

Blood. In the snow, in his clothes, upon his face and hands. So much blood.

The Nightmare let out an inhuman snarl. And I saw what he was focused on. The hilt of a dagger—lodged between Ravyn's ribs.

I screamed.

The Nightmare dropped to his knees at Ravyn's side. "*No,*"

he said, stilling Ravyn's trembling hand. "Do not pull the blade out. It stanches the blood."

Ravyn blinked and looked up with unfocused eyes. He said my name, a whisper, just between us. "Elspeth."

I thrashed against darkness—against nothingness—trying to get to him. My consciousness rattled so greatly the Nightmare began to shake. "Hauth Rowan?" came his venomous question.

Ravyn managed a nod. "My Mirror, the Cards—he—"

"I will find him."

Ravyn winced—tried to focus. "Elspeth," he said again. "Tell Elspeth not to hate me."

Something fractured in the dark room I inhabited.

The Nightmare's hands shook on his sword. Unflinching, five hundred years old, he looked down at Ravyn, his lost descendant, and trembled. "I wanted a better Blunder for her. If you perish, that Blunder will never exist."

"It cannot exist unless the Deck is united," Ravyn growled, blood on his lips. "Only you can see my Cards. Find Hauth. End it the way you wanted to, Taxus. I'll be fine."

The sound of snapping—teeth and bones—filled my dark room. And I realized that the thing that was fracturing—breaking in a thousand razor-edged pieces—was me. *It can't end like this.*

The Nightmare clenched his jaw. "I'll come back," he said, to me, to Ravyn, to himself. "How long can you last?"

"I was ten minutes late to Spindle House." An invisible thread pulled the corner of Ravyn's lips before pain stole it away. "I'll be ten minutes late through the veil."

I wouldn't let him go. I could not. *No, no, no—*

But the Nightmare was already running. Faster than I'd ever felt him go. His sword sang as it cut through the cold Solstice air. He ripped through the meadow, flinging us back into the wood.

It didn't take long to find Hauth. He was bright with color—nearly the entire Deck tucked in his pocket. He released himself from the Mirror Card—no longer invisible. I could see his broad back, his pumping arms.

The Nightmare stopped running and lowered to a crouch, holding his sword above the earth. He tapped it three times on hardened soil, *click, click, click.* His eyes rolled back, darkness eclipsing our shared vision. The space around me widened, as if the Nightmare and I were expanding. I could not see him, but I knew the Shepherd King with golden armor was with us. For he was the Nightmare, and the Nightmare was the King, and I was both of them.

Magic burned up our arms, powerful, vengeful, and full of fury.

We looked out onto the wood, marking Hauth Rowan, and spoke the name of our flock. "Taxus," we said in a long, scraping call.

The earth answered on a thunderous boom, the yew trees awake once more—and moving. Their roots ripped from the ground, cleaving the wood as they hurtled toward Hauth.

He looked back, eyes wide. With another clamorous roll of earth, Hauth shouted and fell. The yew trees encircled him. We guided our sword in intricate arcs through the air, casting nets, moving branches and roots to cut him off at every turn.

The trees caught Hauth at his middle. He shouted, swore, swinging his sword. But the branches tightened their hold, knotting around his ankles and wrists until, pressed with his back against a gnarled trunk, Hauth could no longer move.

We raised ourselves to full height, Shepherd King—Nightmare—I. When we stepped forward, the forest stood still for us.

"You should have known better than to flee into my wood, Hauth Rowan," the Nightmare seethed. "Your Destriers met their end here. So, too, shall you."

Hauth's green eyes narrowed with recognition. He spat my name like a curse. "Spindle. Or do you go by a different title now?" The thin line of his mouth twitched. "How's Ravyn?"

The Nightmare's hand found Hauth's throat, just as it had at Spindle House. Only now it was not just he who was ravenous for blood, but I as well.

I screamed into the dark. The Nightmare opened his mouth, and my scream became his, a horrid sound of despair and hate and rage so complete it shook the trees, dousing the arrogance in Hauth's face and painting dread upon him.

And suddenly it was not Hauth that we were looking at—but another man with cunning green eyes. Brutus Rowan.

The Nightmare—Taxus—I spoke in a low, menacing whisper. "There was a time, once," we said, "when rowan and yew trees grew together in the wood. They spoke in delicate rhymes—whispered tales of balance, of the Spirit of the Wood. Of magic. But time is as corrosive as salt. As rot. And now the rowan's roots are bloodstained, and the yew tree twisted beyond all recognition. We are monsters, the pair of us."

Brutus Rowan's brow lowered. When I blinked, it was Hauth's face once more. "That is what it takes," came his acidic reply, "to be King of Blunder."

The Nightmare let go of his throat. With a swing of his sword, the trees holding Hauth began to move. They dragged him through the wood, following the pull of the Nightmare's sword as he walked ahead.

The trees reached the edge of the wood. Loomed over the stone chamber the Shepherd King had built for the Spirit of the Wood. They dangled Hauth a moment over the rotted-out ceiling—

Then dropped him.

He crashed into the chamber. When his back collided with the stone below, Hauth let out an ugly groan and thrashed, draped over the stone like an offering.

The Nightmare entered the chamber through its window. *Midnight?* he asked the yew trees.

Minutes away.

Salt coated the air and mist slipped over us, a cool, silver wave—a turning tide. Hauth struggled to his feet, nine Providence Cards slipping from his pocket onto the chamber floor, a mural of vivid color in the darkened room. Nightmare. Mirror. Iron Gate. Well. Chalice. White Eagle. Prophet. Golden Egg. Black Horse.

Hauth backed against the far wall of the chamber. His crown had fallen. He picked it up and placed it back on his head, his foot knocking against another crown upon the earthen floor. One with twisting yew branches instead of rowan.

The Shepherd King's crown.

The Nightmare picked it up—placed it on the stone where he had forged his Cards, where his children had died—the place that had become his grave. There was no time, no time at all. Still, guarding the window to the chamber, trapping Hauth inside, he waited.

Midnight, I urged him. *Ravyn!*

And yet, he waited.

Waited.

Waited.

Then, like spider silk, his voice strung itself around the chamber. "You are the final Rowan," he said. "The last of your kind. Know that, before the Spirit takes you to rot."

"You are wrong," Hauth answered, his voice dripping disdain. The trees had stripped him of weapons, but his hands knotted to fists at his sides. "You may have an easy enough time killing my brother—but you'll find *this* Rowan difficult to dispatch, Shepherd King."

The Nightmare laughed, wicked and infinite. "Fool. I'm not going to kill your brother." He opened his arms, a beckoning—and a promise. "I'm going to crown him."

He looked over his shoulder, waiting once more. "Neither Rowan nor Yew, but somewhere between. A pale tree in winter, neither red, gold, nor green. Black hides the bloodstain, but washes the realm. First of his name—King of the Elms."

I saw them then. Out of darkness, three lights shone. Red, pink, and forest green. The Nightmare stepped aside, and the lights drew closer.

Elm and Ione climbed into the chamber, the final Cards of the Deck—Scythe, Maiden, and Twin Alders—cradled in Ione's hand. Neither of them wielded the Maiden. But to me, they seemed so beautiful they were terrifying. Elm glanced between Hauth and the Nightmare, his green eyes narrowing.

"You know what you must do?" the Nightmare asked him.

Elm nodded.

The Nightmare caught Elm's hand and pressed the hilt of his sword into it. "Then it's yours. All of it."

Elm took the sword. Searched the Nightmare's eyes. "You won't stay?"

"I've got to get back." He glanced one last time at the glowing lights of the Providence Cards he had lived—bled—died for. "They're waiting for me."

He turned out of the chamber.

Chapter Forty-Eight

Elm

Ione had told him, the two of them sprinting to the stone chamber, what must come next. Elm stood opposite Hauth, the two of them leveled. One the hunter, and the other the fox who had grown so tired of being hunted, he'd forged his own snare.

The Shepherd King's blade fit perfectly in Elm's hand, the engraved hilt stamping itself into the grooves of his palm. It was forged for a tall man, its reach longer than Elm's Destrier blade. He held it out—the tip hovering over the stone that stood between him and his brother. "He's a clever man, the Shepherd King," he murmured. "Strange, but clever. Far more than I." His gaze narrowed over Hauth. "And certainly more than you."

Hauth said nothing, unreadable, untouchable.

Elm took a step forward. Rolled his shoulders. "I wasn't ready before," he said. "I'm ready now."

"For what?"

"To be King of Blunder."

"To change things," Ione said at his side.

Eyes the color of emeralds measured Elm and Ione. Hauth glanced at the Providence Cards in Ione's hand, then the rest, spread upon the chamber floor. A low, unfeeling laugh bubbled from his throat. "You think you can unite the Deck? It'll be midnight in moments—if it hasn't already passed. For someone so clever, the Shepherd King missed one rather important detail. No one in this room is *infected.*"

Ione bent, picking up the fallen Providence Cards. Elm stood over her, keeping his sword pointed at his brother's throat. One by one, Ione placed the Cards on the stone in the heart of the chamber near the gold crown that rested there. "Yet."

When she placed the Scythe upon the Deck, the muscles in her jaw tightened. "You used this Card for many terrible things, Hauth. And not just for me or Elm." She lay a finger over it. "The first time I truly understood who you were was when you used your Scythe to send people into the mist without their charms."

Hauth sneered. "Whatever plot that monster has fed you—he was wrong." He touched the crown atop his head. "I will die before I give this up. And I will not, brother, for I have the Maiden. *I cannot die.*"

He lunged toward Elm. Caught the Shepherd King's sword by its blade. Blood seeped through Hauth's fingers as he held the sword still. With his other hand, he reached—reached—until his fingers wrapped around Elm's throat.

Elm felt the familiar strength of his brother's brutish hand. It was the first time in his life he did not tense against it. He held the sword still with one hand and caught Hauth's wrist with the other, feeling for the horsehair bracelet he knew was there. Elm looked into his brother's green eyes. Smiled.

And ripped his charm loose.

Hauth's gaze went wide. He opened his mouth to swear—to scream—

Mist rushed into him.

So strong it burned, the salt in the chamber quickened, cloistering around Hauth. He shook himself, running his hands over his face—his nose and mouth—as if he could drag the mist out of him. He was still beautiful—the mist had done nothing to erase the Maiden's hold over his body—

But his mind, the Spirit laid claim to. Sank her teeth into. Hauth's eyes went glassy, then bloodshot. He fell over himself, hunching upon the stone in the heart of the chamber, twisting and wailing and pinning his ears with his hands, as if he didn't wish to listen to something wretched only he could hear.

When he reached for his arms—tore at his sleeves—his veins were the color of ink. The infection crept into him on a salt tide, unbidden. Dark, magical, and final.

Elm backed away. When his spine hit Ione's chest, she wrapped her arms around his middle. Elm watched his brother writhe in the mist. His stylus would never forge this image. But he wanted to watch. Needed to remember.

"Help me," he whispered to Ione.

She put her hand over his, the two of them bearing the weight of the Shepherd King's sword. They pulled in a breath at the same time. Then, over the Deck of Cards, they held the tip of the sword against Hauth's chest—the same place he'd stabbed Ione.

And pressed.

He hardly seemed to notice when the blade pierced his heart. The mist, the Maiden—and an education in pain—had stolen something vital from Hauth Rowan. When his blood spilled, first slow, then in earnest upon the Deck of Providence Cards, saturating the ancient velvet trims, Elm clamped his teeth. Held his breath.

For a terrible moment, nothing happened. Then, one by one, the Providence Cards disappeared.

Hauth kept on thrashing. The Maiden was beginning to heal him, his flesh closing around the blade in his chest. But he was still lost. "No!" he shouted. "No, I will not go!"

Ione began to shake. But her grip on the sword—on Elm—held firm.

On a wretched gasp, Hauth went eerily still, his eyes rolling until they were not green any longer but white, parceled by angry red veins.

When the mist began to pull out of the chamber, it dragged Hauth with it. He ripped his body off the sword and stumbled past Elm and Ione—flung himself out the chamber window. Without a sound, without a final word, the King of Blunder was gone, disappeared—the last casualty to the mist and the Spirit of the Wood's ravenous snare.

All that was left of him was the crown he'd dropped, a gilded ring of twisted rowan branches, fallen upon the Shepherd King's grave.

When Elm and Ione looked back at the blood-soaked stone in the heart of the chamber, the Deck of Cards was gone. A chasm had opened in its place. In it, a single, unfamiliar Providence Card remained.

Ione's voice broke, tears falling down her face. "We did it."

Moonlight filled the chamber through the rotted-out ceiling. Elm looked up. Felt his heart expand. The night winter sky, bereft of mist, was a color he didn't know the name of. Moon, stars—all of them so bright it stole the breath from him, the world around them without tarnish.

Ione held tight to him—tilted her head skyward. "It's beautiful."

Elm pulled her hand to his mouth. He was sure the Spirit of the Wood didn't attend to the meager lives of men. But in that moment, when, after five hundred years, the mist did finally lift and he became King of Blunder, Elm looked up into the night sky. Held Ione Hawthorn close. He knew, in all the rotten, broken pieces of himself, that everything in his life had led to that moment, as if written in the lines of the trees. A crooked, wonderful circle, with his name in the heart of it.

He picked up the Card resting in the center of the stone. Placed it in his pocket—climbed with Ione out of the chamber. When they stepped into the meadow, the pyres had all burned out. Everything was quiet, the world around them gentle and unmarred.

All but for a trail of crimson blood, leading back toward the castle.

Chapter Forty-Nine

Ravyn

Wherever Ravyn was, it was far too loud to be the other side of the veil. Death was supposed to be peaceful, like slipping off to sleep. And this—

This was agony.

He'd dragged himself through snow toward Castle Yew, trailing blood. The pain in his side went white-hot, and for a moment his vision winked and he lost consciousness. When his eyes opened, there were hands on him, harsh voices calling somewhere above his head.

He was lifted—carried.

"Trees, you're fuckin' heavy."

Ravyn's neck flopped, his head dragging on snow, then stone floor. Hands caught it—yanked it up. Ravyn blinked, shadows dancing across his vision.

Petyr held him below his shoulders and walked backward, leading the others—Jon Thistle and Fenir and Morette—through the castle. "Don't die on us," he warned.

Hauth's dagger was still in Ravyn's side, jutting out of him like a dead, venomous branch. His hand trembled over the hilt.

"Leave it," Morette snapped, carrying the weight of his legs.

Ravyn tried to speak, but his jaw was an iron cage, his teeth gritted against pain. His words came out a muffled groan.

"Put him on the table," Fenir said, heaving breaths.

Ravyn looked up at a ceiling. Vaulted, with stubborn spiderwebs in the corners. Castle Yew's great hall.

All he could think was that he was bleeding on the table where his parents ate breakfast.

"Where does Filick keep his medical supplies?" Morette called.

"I'll get them." Jon Thistle knocked over chairs as he tumbled out of the great hall.

Ravyn's siblings appeared at his side. Jespyr gasped when her eyes fell to his wound, her face losing whatever color it still held. "Oh no."

Emory took a seat at the table—lay his head on Ravyn's chest. "Not yet, Ravyn." His breaths were slow, uneven. "Not yet."

Ravyn closed his eyes, tears slipping out the corners.

Thistle returned, his booming voice echoing through the hall. "I've got linens and sutures and balms and—trees know what kind of tincture this is, it smells ripe." He dropped the supplies on the table, the reverberation sending a shock of pain into Ravyn's side.

Jespyr swore, her hands trembling as she unwrapped the linen. "What—what do we do? If we pull the knife—"

"He'll bleed out in moments," Morette answered, her voice hard.

They argued over how to save him. And while their voices grew louder, more panic-tipped, Ravyn weaved in and out of consciousness. He wanted to ask one of them to light the hearth. He was so terribly cold. But it hurt too much to speak—to breathe—to even blink. He kept his gaze fixed on the ceiling, and with each passing second, the great hall grew colder. Darker.

Shadows closed in around him, calling him by name.

Ravyn Yew.

Ravyn Yew.

"Ravyn Yew!"

Everyone went still. Again, the voice called, louder this time. *"Ravyn Yew!"*

The door to the great hall crashed open with enough violence to rip the wood off the top hinge. For a moment, Ravyn couldn't see anything but a dark, menacing shape. The shape stepped forward—pushed Fenir aside—and bent over Ravyn.

Yellow eyes.

"Taxus," Ravyn managed.

The Nightmare heaved a breath, nostrils flaring. "Still alive, then."

"Just," came Morette's thinning voice.

"He's lost too much blood," Petyr whispered.

"He's cold." The Nightmare's gaze flashed across the room. "Light a fire."

Jespyr put a hand on Ravyn's chest. "What are you going to do?"

The Nightmare ignored her. He was carrying on a separate conversation—with himself. "I'm aware, Elspeth. Shouting at me won't help." His eyes returned to Jespyr. "Did you lose your wits in the alderwood, Jespyr Yew? *Light a fire.*"

Jespyr dove for the hearth.

"You," the Nightmare said, snapping his fingers at Jon Thistle. "Cut away his tunic." He rolled up his sleeves. "I'm going to need the rest of you to help me hold him down."

"What supplies do you need?"

"The only thing that can save him now is magic."

Morette and Fenir exchanged a glance. "Ravyn can't use most Providence Cards."

"I'm very aware of that."

"What magic, then?"

The Nightmare slammed his hands on the table, making Ravyn wince. "It's hardly my fault, Elspeth," he muttered under his breath, "that I am constantly surrounded by idiots." He turned to Morette and Fenir. "Magic moves in families. You have two other children with the infection, do you not?"

Their gazes shot to Jespyr at the hearth.

"I don't—" she stuttered, "I don't know what magic I got in the alderwood."

"You're about to find out," the Nightmare said.

A light chased away some of the shadows in the room. There was crackling wood, warmth. All the while, Thistle did his best not to touch Ravyn's wound as he cut away the clothes above his waist.

Somehow, Ravyn's hand found the Nightmare's wrist. He looked up, firelight catching those eerie yellow eyes. "The Deck?"

The Nightmare's face was unreadable. "We'll know soon enough."

"The fire is going," Jespyr called from the hearth. "Now what?"

"Warm your hands. Then come stand by me."

Jespyr hurried to the side of the table a moment later. "He's so pale."

"I'm going to wrench the knife out of him. And you, Tilly—" The Nightmare bit the inside of his cheek. "Jespyr. Put your hands on his open wound. The rest of you, hold him down. If a petty thing like a broken nose can make him thrash, this certainly will."

Jespyr tensed at Ravyn's side. "You want me to…put my hands on his wound?"

The shadows around Ravyn were deepening, despite the fire. He was cold again, shivering. More tired than he had ever felt.

"I can hear his heart stumbling," Emory whispered, voice breaking. "He's going."

Ravyn made a low groan and flinched, sending a new wave of agony up his body. "I'm all right."

"Trees, you stupid pretender." The Nightmare gripped Jespyr's wrists—brought her hands near the dagger in Ravyn's side. His father and Thistle gripped Ravyn's legs, and his mother and Petyr moved to his shoulders. "Ready," Morette said.

"Ready," Fenir and Thistle echoed.

The Nightmare's gaze collided with Ravyn's. "Elspeth says she's utterly sick of you."

His voice was weak. "She didn't say that."

"No. She didn't." The words slipped out of the Nightmare's mouth on a fine thread. "Time to be strong, Ravyn Yew. Your ten minutes are up."

He ripped the dagger out of Ravyn's side, and Jespyr pressed her hands into his wound. A pain such as Ravyn had never known swept into him.

The world went black.

When Ravyn woke, he was no longer in the great hall but in his bedroom, sweating beneath several layers of quilted blankets. He tried to sit up, but a firm hand on his chest kept him down.

Ravyn raised his gaze and caught his breath, a lump rising in his throat. "Elm."

His cousin looked down at him, auburn hair a tousled mess,

a smile teasing the corners of his mouth. "Now who's the one who looks terrible?"

Ravyn started to laugh, but pain shot up his body, cutting it short. He put a hand to his side. He was shirtless, his entire abdomen wrapped in thickly padded linen.

He sat up too fast. "How long have I been asleep?"

"Two days."

"Is the Deck—Has the mist—"

Elm's smile widened. He moved to Ravyn's bedroom window. Drew back the curtains. "See for yourself."

Blue sky met the smudged glass. Ravyn's breath caught, sunlight pouring into his room. He'd never seen the world in that color before. Yellow. Full of warmth. Of promise.

"Beautiful, isn't it?"

Ravyn felt dizzy—hollowed out. "Elm."

His cousin raised his gaze.

"I'm sorry."

Elm's smile dropped. "What for?"

"I should never have left you at Stone." Ravyn swallowed the lump in his throat. "I knew how much you hated it there, and I left you."

Elm had barely opened his mouth to answer before the door burst open. Jespyr squealed, then hurtled toward Ravyn's bedside. "Oh, thank the bloody trees, I thought I'd killed you." She put her hand on his forehead—grabbed at his bandages. "Filick's been to check on you. He said it was a miracle you didn't bleed to death—"

"You're elbowing his windpipe, nitwit," Elm said, dragging her off. "Imagine how humiliated you'd be to kill him after bragging to everyone under the sun about saving his life."

"That's rich, seeing as you've been twirling that new Providence Card in everyone's face for two days straight."

They bickered—an old, familiar song. Ravyn hardly heard it. His eyes were on another figure in the doorway. One who stood straight, with light in his gray eyes and warmth kissing his skin. Ravyn held out a hand. "Come here, Emory."

A crooked smile slid over the boy's mouth. He lunged for the bed—landing on Ravyn so hard it tossed the wind from his lungs. He groaned, mussing his brother's dark hair. "You're better."

"I am. Three taps of that new Card, and look"—Emory reached out, pressing his bare palm against Ravyn's cheek—"I can touch people. No visions. No magic. Blissful nothingness. Fit as a fucking fiddle."

Jespyr feigned a gasp. "Emory. You can't talk that way in front of the *King*."

Emory jumped from Ravyn's bed. Curtsied with an invisible skirt and bowed before Elm. "Apologies, Your Holiness."

"It's *Highness*, you little—"

Elm stopped short. Ione Hawthorn was passing the doorway, yellow hair tied over her shoulder in a white ribbon. She caught the doorframe—lingered at the threshold. "I'm happy you're doing better, Ravyn." Her eyes moved over Jespyr and Emory and Elm. "Don't mind their teasing. They've been moping incessantly, waiting for you to wake."

Elm slouched against the wall next to Ione, curling a finger in her hair. "Moping," he said, "is a firm exaggeration."

She smacked his hand away and continued down the corridor, but not before she tendered Elm a lingering glance that, even half-dead, Ravyn knew the meaning of.

He waited for her to go before shooting his cousin a grin. "Well, then."

Elm's teeth tugged at his bottom lip. "Shut up."

Emory and Jespyr snickered behind their hands, cackling

as Elm shoved them out of the room. He closed the door. "As much as I enjoy your brooding, guilty conscience, Ravyn, it's wasted on me. I was meant to stay at Stone. With Ione." He stood straighter, pulled something out of his pocket. "This is the proof."

Ravyn stared down at it—a Providence Card he'd never seen before. It was not one color, but twelve, iridescent as stained glass. Depicted upon it was a man—with brilliant yellow eyes and a gold crown of twisting yew branches resting upon his head. Above him were two words.

The Shepherd.

Ravyn's eyes stung. "Where is he?"

"Retrieving something at Stone. He'll be back soon." Elm closed his fingers around the Shepherd Card. "He asked that you not use this to heal your infection until after you've spoken with him."

Ravyn nodded. His eyelids began to droop. It hurt to stay awake. "You're going to be a great King, Elm. We all think so. Even Taxus."

"Who?"

Ravyn shut his eyes.

When he opened them again, it was night.

Moonlight streamed through his bedroom window. The pain where Jespyr had healed him was gone, but he was stiff all over. Ravyn sat up slowly, ran a hand over his face, and coughed, his mouth dry.

"Here," said a voice in the corner of his room.

Ravyn's hand flew to his belt—which he was not wearing. "Trees. You might have said something sooner."

The Nightmare handed him a cup of water. Ravyn drained it in three gulps. "What are you doing here?"

"Waiting for you to wake. There is something I must show you."

"What is it?"

The Nightmare paused, the only noise between them the clenching and unclenching of his jaw. Then, slowly, his hand slid out from behind his back. In it, limned with burgundy velvet, was a Nightmare Card.

Ravyn sat up.

The Nightmare bent his neck, observing the Card in his hand. "The twelve Cards that united the Deck disappeared. The rest, scattered through Blunder, remain. This is the only Nightmare Card left. It was hidden away at Stone, just as it had been in Tyrn Hawthorn's library." He ran a curled finger over the velvet—heaved a sigh. "It's been a long time since I've touched a Providence Card."

He closed his fingers around it and turned to the door, lingering at the threshold. "Will you follow me into the wood one last time, Ravyn Yew?"

It wasn't far. Ravyn could have walked the path blindfolded. When they got to the meadow behind Castle Yew, the Shepherd King's chamber was bathed in moonlight. Breeze caught yew tree branches—made them sway. Ravyn wondered if Tilly and the other children were there, just on the other side of the veil, watching for their father. Waiting, as they'd always done.

Ravyn needed help into the chamber's window. He hissed out a breath, and the Nightmare lent him his strength, pulling him up by the arm.

They stood in darkness together, near the stone. Upon it rested the ancient adornments of Aemmory Percyval Taxus and Brutus Rowan. Gilded, bloodstained. Two twisted crowns.

The Nightmare cast his gaze upward to the rotted-out ceiling and the yew tree above it. "Will you tell your family who they really are? Who they are descendants of?"

"I don't know."

"Perhaps you worry they will see themselves differently."

"Perhaps."

The Nightmare's laugh was a hum. A minor tune. "That is what Elspeth thought. That no one would care for her if they saw her for who—what—she truly was."

"I do," Ravyn said without pause. "I care for her."

"I know," the Nightmare murmured. He rolled his jaw, as if it cost him something dear, telling Ravyn the truth. "I thought I was the father she deserved. That I could carry her through this terrible, violent world. I hadn't done it well with my own children, and when I woke in her young mind, the first thing I felt, after five hundred years of fury"—his voice softened—"was wonder. Quiet and gentle. I remembered what it was to care for someone."

"She gave me that, too."

The Nightmare lowered his head, his spine hunching. "Elspeth will not heal if she touches the Shepherd Card."

Ravyn froze. "She has to."

"The thirteenth Card will heal anyone who wishes to be healed of the infection—permanently, just as the Maiden heals permanently. It will not be limited to one user at a time, nor will there be any ill effects for using it too long." His jaw went hard, his words slipping through his lips. "But Elspeth's magic is... strange. If she touches the Shepherd Card, she will absorb it. Every last barter—every payment I made. All twelve Providence Cards." He shook his head. "She will not be healed."

His words ripped into Ravyn. He bent, his breaths growing shallow.

A cold hand slid over his shoulder. Ravyn was too tired to shake it away. "Please. Have I not paid? Have I not lost pieces of myself, following you into the wood? It was for *her*." He looked up into those ancient yellow eyes, tears threatening his own. "Tell me the truth. Is there a way Elspeth and I will meet again on this side of the veil?"

The answer was a cold, deafening silence.

Ravyn squeezed his eyes shut and bit down so hard his jaw seized. He felt like he was back in the meadow, a knife in his side, bleeding out.

Then, soft as a shifting breeze through yew branches, the Nightmare answered. "Only one."

Ravyn opened his eyes. The Nightmare stood before him like he had in his bedroom. Hand extended, palm open.

And the Nightmare Card therein.

"Destroy it," he whispered. "With the final Nightmare Card gone, my soul will disappear. Her degeneration will have nothing to cling to. She will return. And I..." His voice faded. "I will finally rest."

Ravyn reached for the Nightmare Card, hands shaking. "Destroy this, and Elspeth returns?"

"Yes."

Something hot touched Ravyn's relief. "You're telling me I've had the means to free her all this time?"

The Nightmare grinned. "Yes."

"You didn't—Why—" He pinched his nose, swallowing fury. "You make it so hard not to hate you."

"I had my Deck to collect. History to revisit—and rewrite. A path to draw for you and the Princeling, both of you Kings in your own right." The Nightmare clung only a moment longer to his namesake Card, then released it into Ravyn's hand. "And I was not yet ready to bid Elspeth goodbye."

Ravyn watched the monster closely. He didn't pretend to understand their connection—Elspeth and the Shepherd King. He knew it was deeply forged. Ancient, terrifying magic. "But you're ready now?"

The Nightmare nodded. "She's clawed through hell with me." His voice grew colder. "It's time to let her out."

Ravyn didn't move.

The Nightmare turned, his mouth a hard line. "Do it now."

"Don't you want to say goodbye?"

"To you, stupid bird?"

Ravyn crossed his arms over his chest. "To her, parasite."

Those yellow eyes flared, wicked, infinite. Ravyn held the Nightmare Card in a vise and quit the chamber, wincing over the windowsill. "Goodbye, Taxus. Be wary. Be clever. Be good."

He waited ten minutes in the meadow.

Then tore the Nightmare Card in two.

Chapter Fifty

Elspeth

Memories cloistered around me. Lullabies, riddles, rhymes. *I know what I know, my secrets are deep, but long have I kept them, and long will they keep.*

What creature is he, with mask made of stone? Captain? Highwayman? Or beast yet unknown?

Yellow girl, plain—unseen...

The berry of rowans is red, always red...

You are young and not so bold. I am unflinching—five hundred years old.

The Nightmare sat on the stone in the chamber, looking up through the rotted-out ceiling. The same place where Aemmory Percyval Taxus had once lived, bled, died. *Here we are, my darling girl,* he whispered to me. *The end of all things. The last page of our story.*

I tried to reach out for him like I used to, but it was me, not him, trapped in the darkness. This time, he reached for me. *Just know that I am sorry, Elspeth.* His presence was a hand against my cheek. *I was too long in the dark. And I am sorry for that, too. For I dragged you in with me.*

It was well worth it, I said. *To unite the Deck and lift the mist. To watch you right old wrongs. I'd do it all again, just to know you a little better, Taxus.*

He said nothing to that, reticent to accept, even now, that he was anything more than a monster. *I don't know what it will be like to finally slip through the veil,* he whispered. *I hope it is as it was, eleven years ago, when you freed me from the Nightmare Card, Elspeth Spindle. Quiet. Gentle. Full of wonder.*

It will be. It will be just like that.

He unclenched his jaw and hauled in a breath.

I'll tell you a story, I whispered. *It always helped me sleep as a child.*

He nodded, folding his hands over his lap, and closed his eyes.

There once was a girl, clever and good, who tarried in shadow in the depths of the wood. There also was a King, a shepherd by his crook, who reigned over magic and wrote the old book. The two were together, so the two—

I couldn't go on.

Elspeth.

No. I'm not ready. Not yet.

Finish the story, dear one.

My voice shook. *The two were together—*

Together.

So the two were the same.

The girl, he whispered, honey and oil and silk.

The King…

We said the final words together, our voices echoing, listless, through the dark. A final note. An eternal farewell. *And the monster they became.*

Epilogue

I have submitted to the Chalice, the truth heralded for all of Blunder to hear. Hauth Rowan committed regicide, thus ending the reign of our King, Quercus Rowan, who was buried beneath his namesake tree at Stone. Upon Solstice, when the mist did finally lift, Blunder began a new day. Our borders are open, the kingdoms and queendoms beyond the mist welcome to our home.

To all infected who desire a cure, seek the Shepherd Card at Castle Yew. To any displaced, Stone is no longer a fortress, but a refuge. To those who wish to remain as they are, christened by the fever, gifted with old magic, you are safe.

Let us not hold The Old Book of Alders as our steadfast law. Rather, let us cherish it for what it is—Blunder's twisted tale. A book of time, written by a man who knew magic like his own name, and bent to its sway.

But remember, though the mist is gone, the Spirit of the Wood remains, watching, measuring. To my kingdom, my Blunder, my land—be wary. Be clever. Be good.

—The King of Elms

Castle Yew's bells chimed on spring Equinox morning. A peal of jubilation.

The houses of Blunder answered, and the ringing of bells echoed down the street deep into town. The clamor rose, the chimes high and low, near and far. They sounded so much louder now that the mist did not confine their noise.

I wore my mother's red dress and tarried through the ruins behind the castle gardens. The meadow was beautiful, quilted in grass. I waited under a yew tree, for though I could no longer see the purple light from his Mirror Card, I knew Ravyn was near.

He appeared next to me a moment later. "They're there," he said, tucking the Mirror Card Elm had gifted him from Stone's vault into his pocket. "All of them. Even Ayris this time. Even Bennett. All of them, with him."

I nodded, and a tear fell down my cheek. Ravyn's calloused thumb brushed it away. He wrapped me back in a hug he'd been reluctant to break since the night he'd destroyed the Nightmare Card. "Time to go," he whispered into my hair. "He'll kill us if we're late."

We gathered outside Hawthorn House's aged door. My aunt hugged me and danced on her toes, tears in her eyes. My half sisters, Dimia and Nya, ran through the shrubs, followed by my young cousins, Lyn and Aldrich. My stepmother hissed at them to behave, but her voice was drowned out by Jon Thistle's booming laugh. My stern, severe father had told him a joke. When I caught his eye, he reached behind his back and offered me a blooming stem of yarrow.

I put it in my hair.

"You're meant to throw those *after* the ceremony," Ravyn said to Jespyr, who was busy with her own flowers, strewing them first along Petyr's, then Emory's collar.

"Just dressing them up a bit," she replied, pinching her brother's cheek. "Handsome devils."

Petyr puffed his chest proudly and Emory swatted Jespyr away, muttering something about abject humiliation as he handed Filick Willow a handkerchief from his pocket. "Trees, Filick, it hasn't even begun yet and you're already blubbering."

Ione wore a white dress and no shoes. Elm, the King, bore no crown upon his head—no adorned robes—just a plain black tunic. I could not prove it, but I was certain it was the same one he'd worn guised as a highwayman. Only now, the Shepherd King's sword christened his belt.

When the ceremony began, Ravyn stood at Elm's side and I at Ione's. Ravyn's hands were clasped in front of him, unshaking. When he glanced my way, the corner of his mouth lifted as it often did. Only this time, he let his smile bloom until it took over his entire face.

Thistle cried. My aunt cried. Morette and Fenir and even my uncle, who had been relegated to the back of the room, away from those of us who had not yet forgiven him for what had happened to me at Spindle House, shed tears.

When Filick handed them their gold bands, Elm looked into Ione's eyes. "A hundred years," he said to her, as if she were the only one in the room. "I'll love you for a hundred years—and an eternity after."

Ione didn't wait for him to slip the ring over her finger. She threw her arms around him, kissed him unabashedly, earning a jubilant shout from Emory and many more tears from the rest of us.

When they stepped out of Hawthorn House arm in arm,

King and Queen of Blunder, we threw yellow irises in the air. Irises, for my mother. And yellow because... well, Elm had been particular about that.

Ione caught my arm—hugged me tightly. Over her shoulder, Elm put his hand on the Shepherd King's hilt. Winked at me.

"None of this might have happened without you, Elspeth," Ione whispered. "And isn't that such a beautiful thing."

We walked the forest road together.

It seemed strangely poetic that I had once thought the world would end should my cousin Ione marry the heir to Blunder's throne. There was so much balance in everything that had happened since the last Equinox. It was as if all of our lives, drawn in long, separate lines, had curved together. Curved so much that all of us had become interlocking circles. As if we had been destined together. Shepherded together.

All the trees were in bloom. The forest filled with our voices as we walked into town. It was the same stretch of road I had, months ago, walked with Ione on my nameday. The same place I'd met Ravyn and Elm for the first time. They'd been highwaymen then. And I—

I'd changed since then, too.

Laughter echoed through the trees, and sunlight caught the blooming wood, plants and thorns so much larger now that they were no longer guarded by mist. Someone would have to hack them back soon, lest the road be overrun by greenery.

I hoped it did become overrun. I liked the wild parts of Blunder best. I felt at home in the untamed wood.

A twig snapped to my left, and my gaze shot to the trees. And I must have been slow to understand, after a lifetime of gray mist, just how brilliant the sunlight was. Because for a moment—a fleeting, wonderful moment—I thought I saw him. Yellow eyes, peering at me through the trees.

But it was only the sun, shining through a rotted-out log.

Ravyn waited for me at the bend in the road.

"Thinking about the last time we were here?" he said, offering me his hand. "When you pummeled me to the ground?"

I pulled him close, stood on my toes, whispered into his lips. "One of my fondest memories."

He kissed me, fingers weaving into my hair. "Mine too, Miss Spindle."

Ravyn had not tapped the Shepherd Card. He did not cure himself with Emory and Jespyr and the others that came to Castle Yew. He'd used his magic to destroy the final Scythe Card. And though he had said it to me only in the quiet of our room, he did not wish to be cured. He, in his own small way, was still holding on to what had happened in the alderwood. To his magic, his secret legacy. To Taxus.

Which was why, when I looked back up the forest road, clenching and unclenching my jaw—*click, click, click*—Ravyn didn't shy away from me. He knew as well as I did that the Nightmare was gone. But Aemmory Percyval Taxus had bled into me for so long that, somewhere in the dark, listless shore of my mind, he remained with me. For it was we who had drawn the circles. We, who had shepherded the others toward their destinies. We, who had rearranged the kingdom like trees in our very own wood.

And though it had taken slow, painful time, I knew who I was without him. I was more than the girl, the King, and the monster of Blunder's dark, twisted tale.

I was its author.

Acknowledgments

It's true what they say. Second books are fickle. Even a little monstrous. The hardship of writing my own didn't spring forth in an all-out attack. It crept up slowly. I knew what I wanted for *Two Twisted Crowns*, and I knew how I wanted to get there. But the inevitably of saying goodbye to this duology, these characters, after so many years of carrying them with me, made writing devastating at times. This book had no regard for my marshmallow-soft heart. It did, however, help me grow in mindfulness and in skill. It taught me to get up and keep going. I will always cherish it for that. And, of course, I didn't get through it alone.

To John and Owen. I love you and our quiet little life. Sometimes I can hardly believe it's real, or how I got so unbelievably lucky.

To my family and friends. Thank you for all your love and support and for letting me just sit and stare at the wall when my brain was soup over this book.

To Whitney Ross, my amazing agent. Thank you for your wisdom and for keeping my chaos tempered with your unflagging consistency and support. I still think about that email four years ago when you asked if I had time to "hop on a call" and my soul careered out of my body. I couldn't have asked for a better teammate and friend along this journey.

To the team at Orbit. As a publisher—as a group of individuals—your consistent hard work and integrity blow me away. I look at my bookshelves, laden with Orbit titles, and feel such overwhelming pride. It's been an honor and a dream to work with you on this duology.

To Brit Hvide, my editor—my Team Elm conspirator. I absolutely loved every moment of our collaboration. Your clever insight and encouragement made this book what it is today.

To my friend Kalie Cassidy. Our chats mean the world to me. It's been so freaking nice to have someone to squeal (and wail into the void) with.

To Sarah Garcia. I know you're proud of me because you display *One Dark Window* on top of those important medical books in your office. Thank you—I'm still cackling about it.

Lastly (but never least), to the readers and reviewers and artists who have cheered this duology on. You have knocked me over with your adoration. I get all misty-eyed thinking about it. Thank you. Thank you. Thank you. I have so much in store for you yet.

extras

meet the author

Rachel Gillig

Rachel Gillig was born and raised on the California coast. She is a writer, with a BA in literary theory and criticism from UC Davis. If she is not ensconced in blankets dreaming up her next novel, Rachel is in her garden or walking with her husband, son, and their poodle, Wally.

Find out more about Rachel Gillig and other Orbit authors by registering for the free monthly newsletter at orbitbooks.net.

if you enjoyed
TWO TWISTED CROWNS
look out for
HALF A SOUL
Regency Faerie Tales: Book One
by
Olivia Atwater

It's difficult to find a husband in Regency England when you're a young lady with only half a soul.

Ever since she was cursed by a faerie, Theodora Ettings has had no sense of fear or embarrassment—an unfortunate condition that leaves her prone to accidental scandal. Dora hopes to be a quiet, sensible wallflower during the London Season—but when Elias Wilder, the handsome, peculiar, and utterly ill-mannered Lord Sorcier, discovers her condition, she is instead drawn into dangerous faerie affairs.

If her reputation can survive both her curse and her sudden connection with the least liked man in all high society, then she and her family may yet reclaim their normal place in the world. But the longer Dora spends with Elias, the more she begins to suspect that one may indeed fall in love even with only half a soul.

Chapter One

Sir Albus Balfour was nattering on about his family's horses again.

Now, to be clear, Dora *liked* horses. She didn't mind the occasional discussion on the subject of equine family trees. But Sir Albus had the most singular way of draining all normal sustenance from a conversation with his monotonous voice and his insistence on drawing out the first syllable in the word *pure*bred. By Dora's admittedly distracted count, in fact, Sir Albus had used the word *pure*bred nearly a hundred times since she and Vanessa had first arrived at Lady Walcote's dratted garden party.

Poor Vanessa. She had finally come out into society at eighteen years old – and already she found herself surrounded by suitors of the worst sort. Her luscious golden hair, her fair, unfreckled complexion and her utterly sweet demeanour had so far attracted every scoundrel, gambler and toothless old man within the county. Surely Dora's lovely cousin would be equally attractive to far better suitors…but Dora greatly suspected that such men were out in London, if they were to be found anywhere at all.

At nineteen – very nearly pushing twenty! – Dora was on the verge of being considered a spinster, though she had supposedly entered society alongside her cousin. In reality, Dora knew that Vanessa had only put off her own debut for so long in order to keep her company. No one in the family was under any illusions as to Dora's attractiveness to potential suitors, with her one strange eye and her bizarre demeanour.

"Have you ever wondered what might happen if we bred a horse with a dolphin, Sir Albus?" Dora interrupted distantly.

"I— What?" The older fellow blinked, caught off his stride by the unexpected question. His salt-and-pepper moustache twitched, and the wrinkles at the corners of his eyes deepened, perplexed. "No, I cannot say that I have, Miss Ettings. The two simply do not mix." He seemed at a loss that he even had to explain the second part. Sir Albus turned his attention instantly back towards Vanessa. "Now, as I was saying, the mare was *pure*bred, but she wasn't to be of any use unless we could find an equally impressive stud—"

Vanessa winced imperceptibly at the repetition of the word *pure*bred. Aha. So she *had* noticed the awful pattern.

Dora interrupted again.

"—but do you think such a union would produce a dolphin's head and a horse's end, or do you think it would be the other way around?" she asked Sir Albus in a bemused tone.

Sir Albus shot Dora a venomous look. "Now see here," he began.

"Oh, what a fun thought!" Vanessa said, with desperate cheer. "You do always come up with the most wonderful games, Dora!" Vanessa looped her arm through Dora's, squeezing at her elbow a bit more firmly than was necessary, then turned her eyes back towards Sir Albus. "Might we inquire as to your expert opinion, sir?" she asked. "Which would it be, do you think?"

Sir Albus flailed at this, flustered out of his rhythm. He had only one script, Dora observed idly, and absolutely no imagination with which to deviate from it. "I... I could not possibly answer such an absurd question!" he managed. "The very idea! It's impossible!"

"Oh, but I'm sure that the Lord Sorcier would know," Dora observed to Vanessa. Her thoughts meandered slowly away from the subject, and on to other matters. "I hear the new court magician is quite talented. He defeated Napoleon's Lord Sorcier at Vitoria, you know. He does at least three impossible things before breakfast, the way I hear it told. Certainly, *he* could tell us which end would be which."

Vanessa blinked at that for some reason, as though Dora had revealed a great secret to her instead of a bit of idle gossip. "Well," Vanessa said slowly, "the Lord Sorcier is almost certainly in London, far away from here. And I wonder if he would lower himself to answering such a question, even if it *were* the sort of impossible thing he could accomplish." Vanessa cleared her throat and turned her eyes to the rest of the garden party. "But perhaps there are some here with a less *impossible* grasp of magic who might offer their expert opinion instead?"

Sir Albus's moustache was all but vibrating now, as he failed to suppress his outrage at the conversation's turn away from him and his prized horses. "Young lady!" he sputtered towards Dora. "That is *quite* enough! If you wish to discuss flights of fancy, then please do so somewhere far afield from us. We are having a serious, adult conversation!"

The man's vehemence was such that a drop of spittle hit Dora along the cheek. She blinked at him slowly. Sir Albus was red-faced and shaking with upset, leaning towards her in a vaguely threatening manner. Dimly, Dora knew she *ought* to be afraid of him – any other lady might have cringed back from such a violent outpouring of passion. But whatever impulse normally made ladies wither and faint in the face of frightening things had been lost on its way to her conscious mind for years on end now.

"Sir!" Vanessa managed in a shocked, trembling voice. "You must not address my cousin in such a way. Such behaviour is absolutely beyond the pale!"

Dora glanced towards her cousin, considering the way that her lip trembled and her hands clutched together. Quietly, she tried to mirror the gestures. Her aunt had begged her to act *normal* at this party, after all.

For a moment, as Dora turned her trembling lip back towards Sir Albus, a chastised look crossed his eyes. "I...I do apologise," he said stiffly. But Dora noticed that he addressed the apology to Vanessa, and not to her.

"Apologise for what?" Dora murmured absently. "For impacting your chances with my cousin, or for acting the boor?"

Sir Albus widened his eyes in shocked fury.

Oh, Dora thought with a sigh. *That was not the sort of thing that normal, frightened women say, I suppose.*

"Your apology is accepted!" Vanessa blurted out quickly. She pushed to her feet as she spoke, dragging Dora firmly away by the arm. "But I...I'm afraid I must go and regain my composure, sir. We shall have to discuss this further at another time."

Vanessa charged for the house with as much ladylike delicacy as she could muster while hauling her older cousin behind her.

"I've fumbled things again, haven't I?" Dora asked her softly. A distant pang of distress clenched at her heart. Acute problems rarely seemed to trouble Dora the way that they should, but emotions born of longer, wearier issues still hung upon her like a shroud. *Vanessa should be married by now*, Dora thought. *She would be married if not for me.* It was an old idea by now, and it never failed to sadden her.

"Oh no, you haven't at all!" Vanessa reassured her cousin as they slipped inside the house. "You've saved me again, Dora. Perhaps you were a bit pert, but I don't know if I could have stood to listen to him say that word even one more time!"

"What, *pure*bred?" Dora asked, with a faint curve of her lips.

Vanessa shuddered. "Oh, please don't," she said. "It's just awful. I'll never be able to listen to anyone talk about horses again without hearing it that way."

Dora smiled gently back at her. Though Dora's soul was numb and distant, her cousin's presence remained a warm and steady light beside her. Vanessa was like a glowing lantern in the dark, or a comforting fire in the hearth. Dora had no joy of her own – though she knew the sense of contentment, or a kind of pleasant peace. But when Vanessa was happy, Dora sometimes swore she could feel it rubbing off on her, seeping into the holes where her own happiness had once been torn away and lighting a little lantern of her own.

"I don't think you would have enjoyed marrying him anyway," Dora told Vanessa. "Though I'll be sad if I've scared away some other man you would have liked more."

Vanessa sighed heavily. "I don't intend to marry and leave you all alone, Dora," she said quietly. "I really worry that Mother might turn you out entirely if I wasn't there to insist otherwise." Her lips turned down into a troubled frown that was still somehow prettier than any smile had ever looked on Dora's face. "But if I *must* marry, I should hope that it would be a man who didn't mind you coming to live with me."

"That is a very difficult thing to ask," Dora chided Vanessa, though the words touched gently at that warm, ember glow within her. "Few men will wish to share their new wife with some mad cousin who wears embroidery scissors around her neck."

Vanessa's eyes glanced towards the top of Dora's dress. They both knew of the little leather sheath that pressed against her breast, still carrying those iron scissors. It had been Vanessa's idea. *Lord Hollowvale fears those scissors*, she had said, *so you should have them on you always, in case he comes for you and I am not around to stab him in his other leg.*

Vanessa pursed her lips. "Well!" she said. "I suppose I shall have to be difficult, then. For the only way I shall ever be parted from you, Dora, is if you become mad with love and desert me for some wonderful husband of your own." Her eyes brightened at the thought. "Wouldn't it be wonderful if we fell in love at the same time? I could go to your wedding, then, and you could come to mine!"

Dora smiled placidly at her cousin. *No one is ever going to marry me*, she thought. But she didn't say it aloud. The thought was barely a nuisance – rather like that fly in the corner – but Vanessa was always so horrified when Dora said common sense things like that. Dora didn't like upsetting Vanessa, so she kept the thought to herself. "That would be very nice," she said instead.

Vanessa chewed at her lower lip, and Dora wondered whether her cousin had somehow guessed her thoughts.

"... either way," Vanessa said finally, "neither of us shall find a proper husband in the country, I think. Mother has been bothering me to go to London for the Season, you know. I believe I want to go, Dora – but only if you swear you will come with me."

Dora blinked at her cousin slowly. *Auntie Frances will not like that at all*, she thought. But Vanessa, for all of her lovely grace and charm and good behaviour, always did seem to get her way with her stern-eyed mother.

On the one hand, Dora thought, she was quite certain that she would be just as much a hindrance to Vanessa's marriage prospects in London as she was here in the country. But on the other hand, there were bound to be any number of Sir Albuses hunting about London's ballrooms as well, just waiting to pounce on her poor, good-natured cousin. And as much of a terror as Vanessa was to faerie gentry, she really was as meek as a mouse when it came to normal human beings.

"I suppose I must come with you, then," Dora agreed. "If only so you needn't talk of horses ever again."

Vanessa smiled winsomely at her. "You are my hero, Dora," she said.

That lantern light within Dora glowed a tiny bit brighter at the words. "But you were mine first," she replied. "So I must certainly repay the debt."

Vanessa took her by the arm again – and soon Dora's thoughts had wandered well away from London, and far afield from things like purebred horses and impossible court magicians.

Auntie Frances was *not* pleased at the idea of Dora accompanying her cousin to London. "She'll require dresses!" was the woman's very first protest, as they discussed the matter over tea. "It will be far too expensive to dress two of you! I am sure that Lord Lockheed will not approve the money."

"She can wear my old dresses," Vanessa replied cheerfully, as though she'd already thought this through. "You always did like the pink muslin, didn't you, Dora?" Dora, for her part, merely nodded along obligingly and sipped at her teacup.

"She'll drive away your suitors!" Auntie Frances sputtered next. "What with her *strangeness*—"

"Mother!" Vanessa protested, with a glance at Dora. "Must you speak so awfully? And right in front of her as well!"

Auntie Frances frowned darkly. "She doesn't *care*, Vanessa," she said shortly. "Look at her. Getting that girl to feel anything at all is an exercise in futility. She may as well be a doll you carry around with you for comfort."

Dora sipped at her tea again, unfazed. The words failed to prick at her in the way that they should have. She wasn't upset or offended or tempted to weep. There was a small part of her, however – very deep down – that added the comment to a longstanding pile of other, similar comments. That pile gave her a faint sinking feeling which she never could quite shake. Sometimes, she would find herself taking it out and examining it in the middle of the night, for no particular reason she could discern.

Vanessa, however, was quite visibly crushed. Her eyes filled up with tears. "You can't mean that, Mother," she said. "Oh, *please* take it back! I shan't be able to forgive you if you won't!"

Auntie Frances stiffened her posture at her daughter's obvious misery. A weary resignation flickered across her features. "Yes, *fine*," she sighed, though she didn't look at Dora as she said it. "That comment was somewhat over the line." She pulled out her lace handkerchief and handed it over to her daughter. "Do you really wish to go to London, Dora?" she asked. It was clear from her tone that she expected to hear some vague, noncommittal answer.

"I do," Dora told her serenely. Auntie Frances frowned sharply at that and glanced towards her.

Because Vanessa wants me there, Dora thought. *And I don't want to leave her.* But she thought that this elaboration might complicate the point, and so she kept it to herself.

Auntie Frances said that she would think on the matter. Dora suspected that this was her way of delaying the conversation and hoping that Vanessa would change her mind.

But Vanessa Ettings always did get her way eventually.

Thus it was that they soon took off for London, all three of them. Lord Lockheed, always distant and more consumed with his affairs than with his daughter, did not deign to accompany them – but Auntie Frances had pulled strings through her sister's husband to secure them a place to stay with the Countess of Hayworth, who was possessed of a residence within London and only too pleased to have guests. Since Vanessa had declared her interest so belatedly, they had to wait for the roads to clear of mud – by the time they left Lockheed for London, it was already late March, with only a month or two left in the Season.

After so much fuss, the carriage into London was not at all how Dora might have imagined it. Even in her usual detached state, she couldn't help but notice the stench as they entered the city proper. It was a rude mixture of sweat, urine and other things, all packed together in too close a space. Auntie Frances and Vanessa reacted much more visibly; Auntie Frances pulled out her handkerchief and pressed it over her mouth, while Vanessa knit her brow and craned her head to look outside the carriage. Dora followed Vanessa's lead, glancing over her cousin's shoulder to see out the window.

There were so very *many* people. It was one thing to be told that London was well-populated, and another thing entirely to see it with one's own eyes. All those people running back and forth in the street got into each other's way, and they all seemed somewhat cross with one another. Often, their driver had to yell at someone crossing in front of their carriage, shaking his fist and threatening to run them down.

The noise would have been startling, if Dora were capable of being startled. It settled into her bones more readily than anything else had ever done, however – the biggest fly yet in the corner of the room. Dora found herself frowning at the chaos.

Thankfully, both the hubbub and the awful scents died down as their carriage crossed further into the city, onto wider, calmer avenues. The jumble of buildings that passed them slowly became more elegant and refined, and the suffocating press of people thinned out. Eventually, their carriage driver stopped them in front of a tall, terraced townhouse and stepped down to open the doors for them.

The front door of the townhouse opened just as Dora was stepping down after her cousin and her aunt. A maid and a footman both exited, followed by a thin, steel-haired woman in a dignified rose and beige gown. The two servants swept past, already helping to unload their things, while the older woman stepped out with a smile and took Auntie Frances's hands in hers.

"My dear Lady Lockheed!" the older woman declared. "What a pleasure it is to host you and your daughter. It has been an age since my last daughter was married off, you know, and I've had little excuse to make the rounds since then. I cannot wait to show you all around London!"

Auntie Frances smiled back with unexpected warmth,

though there was a hint of nervousness behind the expression. "The pleasure is all ours, of course, Lady Hayworth," she said. "It's ever so gracious of you to allow us your time and attention." Auntie Frances turned back towards Vanessa, who had already dropped into a polite curtsy – this, despite the fact that they were all certainly stiff and miserable from the journey. "This is my daughter, Vanessa."

"It's so delightful to meet you, Lady Hayworth," Vanessa said, with the utmost sincerity in her tone. It was one of Vanessa's charms, Dora thought, that she was always able to find *something* to be truly delighted about.

"Oh, how lovely you are, my dear!" the countess cried. "You remind me already of my youngest. You can be sure we shall be fighting off more suitors than we can handle in no time!" Lady Hayworth's eyes swept briefly over Dora, but then continued past her. Dora was wearing a dark, sturdy dress which must have made her appear as a very fine lady's maid, rather than as a member of the family. Lady Hayworth turned back towards the townhouse, beckoning them forward. "You must be awfully tired from the road," she said. "Please come inside, and we shall set a table—"

"This is my cousin, Theodora!" Vanessa blurted out. She reached out to grab Dora's arm, as though to make sure no one could mistake the subject of her introduction. The countess turned with a slight frown. Her gaze settled back upon Dora – and then upon her eyes. Lady Hayworth's warm manner cooled to a faint wariness as she took in the mismatched colours there.

"I see," the countess said. "My apologies. Lady Lockheed did mention that you might be bringing another cousin, but I fear that I quite forgot."

Dora suspected that Auntie Frances might have downplayed

the possibility, in the hopes that Vanessa might change her mind before they left. But Lady Hayworth was quick to adjust, even if she didn't quite pause to finish the formal introduction.

Still, Lady Hayworth led them into a comfortable sitting room, where a maid brought them biscuits and hot tea while they waited for supper to finish being prepared. The countess and Auntie Frances talked for quite some time, gossiping about upcoming parties and the eligible bachelors who were known to be attending them. Dora found herself distracted by the sight of a tiny ladybird crawling across the knee of her gown. She was just thinking that she ought to sneak it outside before one of the maids noticed it, when Vanessa spoke and broke her out of her musings.

"And which parties will the Lord Sorcier be attending?" Dora's cousin asked the countess.

Lady Hayworth blinked, caught off-guard by the inquiry. "The Lord Sorcier?" she asked, as though she wasn't certain she'd heard Vanessa correctly. When Vanessa nodded emphatically, the countess frowned. "I admit, I do not know offhand," she said. "But whatever romantic notions you may have taken up about him, I fear that he will not be a suitable match for you, my dear."

"Why ever not?" Vanessa asked innocently over her tea. "He's quite young for the position of court magician, I hear, and very handsome as well. And is he not a hero of the war?" Dora heard a subtle, misleading note in her cousin's voice, however, and she studied Vanessa's face carefully, trying to pick apart what she was up to.

"That much is true," Lady Hayworth admitted. "But Lord Elias Wilder is really *barely* a lord. The Prince Regent insisted on giving him the French courtesy title, of course, with all those silly privileges that the French give their own court magicians. Technically, the Lord Sorcier may even sit in on the House of Lords. But his blood is common, and his manners are exceptionally uncouth. I have had the misfortune of encountering him on several occasions now. He has the face of an angel, and the tongue of some foul... *dockworker*."

Dora found it amusing that the countess apparently considered dockworkers to be an appropriate foil for angels. She was briefly distracted by the notion that hell might be full of legions and legions of dockworkers, rather than devils.

"He does sound terribly unsuitable," Vanessa said reluctantly, regaining Dora's attention. "But please, if you don't mind – I would love to meet the Lord Sorcier at least once. I've heard such stories about him, and I would be crushed to leave London without even seeing him."

The countess tutted mildly. "I suppose we shall see," she said. "But for the very first thing, I have a wish to see you at Lady Carroway's ball. She has *many* fine and suitable sons, and you could do worse than entering London society at one of her parties..."

The subject meandered once again, until they were brought into dinner. They met Lord Hayworth that evening in passing, though he seemed quite busy with his own affairs, and less than interested in his wife's social doings. Once or twice, Dora thought to ask Vanessa about her interest in the Lord Sorcier, but her cousin kept demurring and changing the subject of conversation, and she eventually decided it was best to drop the matter while within current company.

Dora next thought that she would wait to ask until they were off to bed... but directly after dinner, she was swept away by a maid and given a hot bath, then bundled into a very lovely feather-down bed a few rooms down from her cousin.

Tomorrow, Dora thought distantly, while she stared at the foreign ceiling with interest. *I am sure we'll speak tomorrow.*

Quietly, she pulled the iron scissors from the sheath around her neck and tucked them beneath her pillow. As she drifted off to sleep, she dreamed of angels on the London docks, filing up and down the pier and hustling crates of tea onto ships.

if you enjoyed
TWO TWISTED CROWNS
look out for
TONIGHT, I BURN
by
Katharine J. Adams

Thorns, Tides, Embers, Storms, and Ores. All five covens are bound in servitude to the tyrant High Warden of Halstett.

Penny Albright is a daughter of the Thorn Coven, forced to patrol the veil between the realms of Life and Death, keeping it safe and whole. Each night, one thorn witch—and only one—must cross the veil by burning at the stake. Each morning, that witch returns with the help of their magical lifeline. Failure to follow the rules of Death risks them all.

But one morning, Penny's favorite sister, Ella, doesn't return. And that night, determined to find her, Penny breaks the rules. She burns in secret.

What she finds in Death is a manor that shouldn't exist, home to the devastating Lord Malin, who shouldn't be there. Malin offers Penny a dangerous deal: Ella's freedom in exchange for information about the High Warden.

But all isn't as it seems in Life or Death. Penny's bargain leads her to Alice, a mysterious captive prophet... and to a rebellion brewing in the shadows of their city. And as Penny's world splits between her growing love for the ethereal Alice in Life and her attraction to the seductive Malin in Death, she'll face a devastating choice.

Because it's not just her sister's life that hangs in the balance. It's the fate of all magic.

All it takes is one witch—and one spark—to set the world ablaze.

Chapter One

A witch will burn today.

This time it isn't me.

This time I'm lighting the match.

A coven of witches should have a more efficient way to start a fire; with magic at our fingertips, sparks should fly with a wave of our hands. Regrettably, we don't. My coven and our thorn magic is bound entirely to Death. And the ember witches don't like to share. Not with us.

The first strike of the match-head against the box fails. Sparks fly and wink out as they fall. The second strike catches and gutters down to a tiny orb of flame before flaring, pale wood curling black as fire consumes the matchstick.

My sister catches my eye. She's the one who should be trembling; she's the one about to be burned alive on the Warden's orders. But Mila's been walking in Death for years. She's the oldest of the three of us, the Thorn Queen's heir. She gives me a superior smile, the kind of smile she'd accompany with a flounce of her hair if her hands weren't manacled to the iron stake behind her. "Penny, you're going to burn yourself if you're not careful."

A low chuckle ripples around the coven. Twelve of us laugh.

I don't. It isn't funny.

I drop the match, right into a little pile of straw set at the base of the pyre. It catches without hesitation, and *that* is courtesy of the embers.

I wish there was an easier way—a way that didn't feel so needlessly brutal. But leaving a body behind rather complicates the whole thing. I'm not sure it's even possible. Spell books state that burning is the most effective method of crossing the veil if we want to return, but then again, the spell books we're allowed to access are all preapproved by the Warden or his council of sadistic old men. At best, they're watered-down versions of the truth. And I know everything in Halstett is a lie.

Mila's smile wavers, falters a little. Reforms.

Pain is coming. She knows it. She's done this before. But tonight is my first time lighting the pyre, and my oldest sister is the first witch I burn.

Smoke wisps around the straw, wraith-like fingers rising to clutch at her ankles.

Her bare toes press into the platform in a tiny movement of unease. We all feel it, linked as we are. Ella slips her hand in mine, a sisterly gesture, a squeeze of solidarity. "Breathe, Pen," she murmurs. "It's going to be fine."

Then, the chanting starts, ancient words that open the veil between Life and the cold plains of Death. The low hum of magic builds in my ears, and I join my voice to theirs—words I learned as a child, words I wished I'd never have to say. Yet I've repeated them each night since we were brought to Halstett thirteen years ago.

I didn't want to be a death-walker. But I am. And as Grandmother says, we can't fight the truth of who we are, only choose what we do with it. Not that we have a lot of choice. Imprisoned within the Colligerate walls, those with our particular power have two paths: serve the High Warden as a death-walker or become one of his soulless Gilded army. There's no in between.

Grandmother reaches for my hand, her eyes flashing with a glint of the queen I haven't seen since the Gilded tore us from our village. She was respected once—an ageless beauty who fearlessly guarded Death from those who sought to defy it. Now, her gnarled fingers ensnare mine and the circle around the pyre closes. Warmth prickles at the soles of my feet, though the flagstones beneath them are cold as winter ice. The scent of singed cotton clogs my nose and throat. Mila begins to burn, her feet blistering, smoke rising from charring skin, and searing heat claws at my own.

Still, we whisper; still, we chant.

I watch my sister die and it's eerily like watching myself. With our colouring so similar and only a few years between us, Mila and Ella and I used to be mistaken for one another. Until they began to walk and the light began to fade from their eyes, their skin grew dull and paler, their bodies somehow diminished. Auburn hair flickers with fire, and I lose the line where Mila ends and the flames begin. Her silver eyes squeeze shut. Her fingers dig into the post she's bound to.

As my sister burns, we burn with her in spirit. We're stronger together. Every moment is shared, divided by thirteen. I wonder how bad this would be alone, without a coven to ease the passing.

Mila doesn't scream. No one does. Death for us must be quiet and emotionless. Screaming wakes the dead; fear summons fog-wraiths hungry for destruction.

Pain lets us pass.

With a soft sigh, Mila is gone.

My sister is dead. But it's a routine patrol, a walk along the borders between Life and Death. She won't go deep. Thorn witches rarely go far from the veil. She'll be back by morning. Then, tomorrow night, we'll do it all over again. It's a vicious life, a brutal one, slowly stealing a part of our soul each time we walk. Still, it's better than being Gilded. Anything is better than that.

In two days, it is my twenty-first birthday. And I will be ordered to burn for the very first time.

The ritual demands that the witch who strikes the match stays to undo the empty manacles and ensure the veil closes behind the witch who burned. Not having come of age, I don't sense the veil yet, so Ella takes on that role tonight. A light frown creases her brow as she nods, confirming Mila has passed without incident, and I gingerly release the manacles. They clatter against the stake accusingly, and I wish I'd been more careful. Ella's still frowning while I place the key neatly on the low wooden workbench in the corner and wipe the ash coating my fingertips against my shift skirts.

The chamber allocated to our burning is deep beneath the Colligerate wing we are told is our home. Vents draw in the cool autumn night—and filter the smell of burning flesh from the smoke when it rises up the chimney and into the sky, ensuring our regular demise does not disturb the Warden's evening stroll.

Ella wrinkles her nose, freckles twitching. "You've got Mila's ash on your ankle."

I snatch a checked cloth from the bench and scrub. I long for a bath, a small consolation—a piece of privacy and quiet. I can slide under the water, close my eyes, and pretend I am anywhere but here. I wonder if that sense of comfort will fade, once I walk. When I step into Death for the first time, which fragment of my soul will I leave behind?

Ella pulls the cloth from my hand and there's an odd glint in her eye that I don't like at all. "Pen, I need a favour."

"What kind of favour?"

She rubs her elbow, pressing a thumb into the crook of it, thinking her way around a problem like she used to when Mother set us potion tests. Then her frown clears to a calculated satisfaction that sharpens her eyes. "Remember how we used to sneak out?"

My heart sinks as my hope of a bath floats away. "You mean, when we were little and the worst punishment we faced if we were caught was a rap on the knuckles. Yeah, I remember. Why?"

"I left something in the library." Ella bunches up the cloth and shoves it back on the bench.

"We can't get into the library," I protest as she pushes me out the door.

"We can." She hurries a bit faster up the stairs and down the passageway, past the doors to the baths.

"What's so important it can't wait until tomorrow?"

"A book."

I huff with frustration. "Fine, be like that."

Ella halts so suddenly, I barrel into her back. "I'm not lying."

She most definitely is. "Just being economical with the truth?"

We're by the entrance to the Thorn Coven's wing, an arched door made of grey, polished wood. Gold studs mark a pattern of diamonds that reflect flickering lamplight, and there's a keyhole to which our coven has never seen a key. I'm not sure it's ever been locked. Beyond it lies the Colligerate hallways.

Ella's silver eyes sparkle, bright with challenge, and she's the sister she was before she first walked, when we used to sneak out all the time. "Scared, Pen?"

"No." My answer is reflexive, not a well-thought-out response. Going to the library after the curfew bell rings is a terrible idea.

"So you're in?" Ella's tone, the way she raises an eyebrow daring me to back out, makes it feel bigger than a trip to the library.

I shrug. "Someone probably needs to keep an eye on you. Who knows what trouble you'll get into on your own."

Ella grins, flashing white teeth and dimpling her cheeks. "Stay close. Once the curfew warning rings, we have precisely ten minutes before the next round of the guard."

Before I can ask how she knows, Ella slips out, leaving me no choice but to go after her.

The bell sounds as the door clicks shut behind me. The hallway lamps dim in response to the warning, ember magic burning low in glass-scalloped sconces set high up the walls. Night hangs outside the windows, creeping over the sills as the chime reverberates through flagstones and drifts up to ceilings the lamplight can't reach. When the next bell rings, anyone in a corridor without permission will be at the mercy of the Gilded, and the Gilded and mercy don't mix.

The buildings that make up the Colligerate compound are perched high on the peak of a hill right in the centre of Halstett's fortified city walls. A second wall circles the foot of the hill, and a third rings the Colligerate itself. I think it was a sanctuary once, a place of knowledge and learning before the Warden criminalised the truth and bent history to flatter his image. The library tower is in the very middle, seven corridors spread out from it like the spokes of a spiderweb. Each coven has its own spindle, five wings with a tower at the end.

The sixth corridor is wider, more extravagant, a gold-carpeted path to the Warden's luxurious palace where he keeps his consort wife and his pet prophet locked away. It's heated in the winter and cooled in the summer, that corridor. The three of us sisters, Mila and Ella and I, used to hide behind the tapestries when the cold of our own wing turned our fingers numb. Aunt Shara caught us one day, wrapped in fabric and giggling. She taught us a lesson, one we didn't forget in a hurry: She took us to watch the next trials, showing us precisely what the Gilded's punishment would be if we were found out. I still remember the sound of blood dripping to the courtyard flagstones, the shock in the woman's eyes when she saw her finger on the ground.

Yet, here we are again, out of bounds. Holy Dark Mother, Ella should know better than this. So should I.

She slows and holds out a hand behind her, twitching a finger to send me closer into the wall. We're at the circular juncture where the spokes of the Colligerate meet. If we're caught anywhere, it's most likely to be here, close to the seventh corridor, which leads to the courtyard outside the Gilded Barracks and the amphitheatre that houses the eternal fires.

I hate those fires and so does every other witch I know. Halstett is built where the veil is thinner, and where the fires burn is the thinnest place of all. Magic creeps from Death into Life there. It scratches our skin and crawls down our lifelines like carrion beetles scuttling into a corpse.

Hidden in the shadows between lamps, we listen. It is utterly silent, amplifying the quiet thud of my own heart in my ears, the movement of cotton against my ribs as I inhale, the soft wheeze we all get after a burning as I breathe out. Ella squeezes my hand once. A signal to wait, stay still—don't breathe.

Boots sound in the distance, along with a male laugh and a deep-voiced reply. I imagine the palace guard are spiders creeping along spidersilk, hunting their prey. I hope it's the guard and not the Gilded.

As we huddle close, I can smell the smoke clinging to us. If the Gilded catch that scent on the dry Colligerate air, their attention will swivel in our direction, and once they begin a hunt, their quarry never escapes. The Gilded can manipulate lifelines and control consciousness, holding prisoners aware as they punish at the Warden's command. In their hands, death is a distant hope. An impossible dream.

The boots turn a corner and fade into the quiet of the night, and we run the rest of the way to the library.

Ella has had some bad ideas over the years, but this is one of the worst. In the shelter of the library entrance, I hiss in her ear, "What now, genius?"

"We go in." Ella pulls a ribbon out of her pocket, black velvet tied with a bow to a key the length of my pinkie finger.

My eyes widen. "Where did you get—"

"Don't ask, and I won't lie." She's so sure of herself, so determined, and it's infuriating. I hate getting half a story, and she knows it.

Her tone softens as she sees my scowl. "I'll tell you a secret?"

A secret? She's reaching if she thinks a promised secret will convince me. If she's reaching so far, she needs me more than she's letting on. "It'd better be a good one."

"It is." She pauses. "Please, Pen?"

Reluctantly, I nod, and she unlocks the door.

We step together into the hushed library quiet. I close my eyes, savouring the smell of books. Even the air is respectful here, a gentle reverence that would not be out of place in a church or temple. It's also the only place in the whole Colligerate where the Warden and his Gilded do not step foot. Here we are safe, free of the Warden's demands. For a while, anyway.

Ella slips a hand into mine and takes a lantern from the hook by the door. With a snap of her fingers, she activates the ember spell in her lantern, and light pools around us, illuminating the library reception desk, an island of warm-polished cherrywood in a sea of black-and-white checked marble floor.

The library belongs to us all.

And some of us belong to the library. Reading is a faith requiring suspension of belief in a shrine of knowledge and imagination. Stories feed my soul and words are sharper than knives if you know how to wield them—and how to listen.

Here, magic cooperates even if the witches who wield it do not. The covens hate one another, Grandmother says, and I've never seen evidence to suggest she's wrong. Our villages were divided by forest and water and vast expanses of wilderness. We only came together once each season for the coven leaders to sit in council and to barter magic in times of peace. I don't know how it was in times of war. The only war I ever knew, we lost. History has a nasty habit of erasing lost people from its pages.

But the covens refuse to be erased. Ore magic is woven into the stones of the library tower, shimmering in the moonlight and making the impossible spiral of stairs and landings a magnificent reality. Ember magic glows softly in the dormant lamps that circle each landing. Storm magic shines in the glass windows, filtering the light of the moon, and tide magic hums quietly in the air vents, pulling the moisture from the air to preserve the ancient tomes. Only thorn magic is missing. Not even the library welcomes Death.

The stairs alternate black and white as they curve up the

circular library tower. Nine floors of books rise into the darkness above. We listen and pray we are not listened to by whatever shuffles books about on the shelves in the night. When we hear nothing, Ella gives me a little nod, and quietly we climb the stairs to the first floor where spell primers live and small witches cluster when their lessons are done. We tread carefully, light footsteps barely making a sound on the semicircle landing that takes us to the next flight of stairs.

On the second floor, the shelves are lined with fairy tales, so many it might hold all the fairy stories ever written in all the world. Each spine is a dark rainbow shade and it's the closest we get to full colour. I wonder if they know, the Warden and his council, that the library defies their colour restrictions. Maroon and bottle-green and midnight-blue leather all embossed with silver and gold take on a brightness they never had before the laws came into force. If the leather bindings are precious, the pictures inside are priceless. I used to wish I lived in a fairy story. Now I wish I had a little more time before I walk in Death and lose fairy stories for good.

Follow us:

/orbitbooksUS

/orbitbooks

/orbitbooks

Join our mailing list
to receive alerts on our
latest releases and deals.

orbitbooks.net

Enter our monthly
giveaway for the chance
to win some epic prizes.

orbitloot.com